The Best Collectibles of Larry L. King

WARNING:
Writer at Work

The Best Collectibles of
Larry L. King

With a Foreword by Edwin Shrake
Drawings by Paul Rigby

Texas Christian University Press
Fort Worth

Selections in this book have previously appeared in the following
publications: *Harper's*, the Washington *Post, Texas Monthly, Parade .
Magazine, Life, The Atlantic Monthly, Reader's Digest,* and *Today's
Health*, and in books by Larry L. King published by NAL-World, Viking
Press and the Encino Press. "Redneck Blues," "Playing Cowboy," and
"Body Politics" are reprinted by permission of Viking Penguin Inc., the
publisher of the author's latest collection, *Of Outlaws, Con Men,
Whores, Politicians and Other Artists.*

Library of Congress Cataloging in Publication Data

King, Larry L.
Warning, writer at work.
I. Title.
PS3561.I48W3   1984   976.4'062   84-24013
ISBN 0-87565-004-X
ISBN 0-87565-016-3 (pbk.)

Designed by Whitehead & Whitehead

Contents

Also by Larry L. King

Non-Fiction

Novel

Plays

For Children

This book is for two old friends
who were there when it counted
and who willingly offered their
helping hands:
Aubra R. Nooncaster
and
Willie Morris

Foreword

IT IS A VERY GOOD THING for the memory of Texas that just as the peculiar and fascinating qualities of the place—the colors, the sweet air, the loyalty, the room enough to caper—began abruptly vanishing from the earth, Larry L. King elected to become the poet of their passing.

I thought the Texas of Dobie, Bedicheck and Webb was pretty remote from my own, but it was still recognizable. Matched against the Texas of today, that trio of deities read as if they are writing about the Pharoahs. Today's Texas is where Southern California collides with Georgia on a vast sheet of concrete. It remains for some future mutant to try to explain where the trees and water and space went. But for us fortunate ones who knew Texas during its most bountiful years—the three decades following World War Two—it is only a matter of picking up this collection of essays by Larry L. King to cue a parade of memories that is warm and wonderful, painful and touching and at the same time comic.

Old myths of Texas—wildcatters who discover Spindletop, cowboys who drive herds to the railhead through storms and stampedes, the belief that bigger is better and there's plenty for everybody willing to work to get it—have crashed against today's overcrowded reality and are sinking with all hands on board. So it is a comfort to find in the world of Larry L. King the reassurance that "perhaps out on those few old frontiers where there is still elbow room we can rediscover charms, virtues and vitalities that speak well of our roots and suggest options for our futures."

King's examinations of our recent past are bathed not in honey but in truth. Racial bias, poverty, brutally hard work, oppression—he tells us of these things with a wisdom forged in experience and tempered with humor. Like so many other Texans of his age, King was awakened to the possibilities of life beyond the tool rig by a stint in the Army which is movingly described in "Confessions of a White Racist," one of the first pieces of work that attracted a large audience for this most unlikely of creatures—a genuine writer from Texas.

More and more I believe there are certain people who were born to be writers. How else explain Lawrence Leo King emerging from the oil patch untarnished by serious formal education and marching into the Ivy League as Nieman Fellow at Harvard and teacher of writing at Princeton? From digging post holes in the hard rock ground of West Texas (a fact of life he was unable to explain to a fatuous Hollywood director, as you will learn in these pages) to jostling elbows with literary folks in New York City is a journey that can't be made on the back of a mule, nor judged by mileage. It is a trip of the mind that requires inspired navigation.

Listening to King talk—which you will invariably find yourself doing in his joyful company—you immediately know he is either a preacher or a writer. Many writers are shy and quiet mumblers, struck dumb for dinner conversation. But King delivers opinions spontaneously and copiously with natural, forceful eloquence, and shares a headful of juicy anecdotes and reminiscences without prodding. Hearing him, you realize he is in fact a natural. He talks like he writes.

Back in the days when Austin was still a pleasantly eccentric college and political town—an oasis in the true sense of being a fertile place in the midst of a desert—instead of a landlocked imitation of Anaheim, King used to hold forth frequently on his dream of retiring to a front porch about an hour away from the Capitol, watching the cars go by and knowing he was home again at last from his expatriate lodgings. Home is where the heart is, of course, and the next best thing to being there is reading or writing about it. Like his made-in-Texas peers (Dan Jenkins, Gary Cartwright, Larry McMurtry, A. C. Greene, Willie Morris and the late Bill Brammer come to mind), no matter where King is when he rolls a sheet of paper into his trusty Smith-Corona, the words that result will most likely have a vital connection to his native earth.

In the fifth grade I rode a spotted pony eleven miles roundtrip to a two-room schoolhouse near Handley. It was indeed, as King writes of his own youth, a way of life that was passing without our knowing it. At Rice University these days they teach a course on how to live in Texas as a foreign country. For the millions of fresh immigrants to Caltexorgia, this collection by Larry L. King should be required reading. While these hordes of newcomers are surveying with bewilderment the traffic jams and monstrous garbage heaps that remain from our once grand republic, and wondering why in hell they ever decided to move to the land of the tornado and the fire ant in the first place, they can console themselves with King's prose about a place that unlike Camelot actually did exist not very long ago.

Edwin Shrake
Austin, 1985

Introduction

FOR A LONG TIME I bristled when described as "a Texas writer." The appellation seemed to imply limitations or handicaps. One so designated seemed forever ineligible to be considered for membership in the brotherhood of first-class talents; rather, he always would be doomed to judgment among such fellow curiosities as dancing bears and talking dogs. The miracle was that the bear could dance or the dog talk or the Texan write at all—never mind how badly they performed their unnatural acts.

Some who called me "a Texas writer" no doubt meant to be disparaging. There are those serious pucker-brows in the groves of academe, or editing their dry little "literary" magazines, who automatically curl their lips on sighting the offerings of mere "story tellers" from the hinterlands who—without permission or official anointings—presume to practice the craft of Shakespeare and Shaw. We are especially deserving of being reviled should we insist on writing of life at the crossroads or along the creekbanks without offering forests of footnotes, thickets of symbolism, acres of the latest jargon currently growing in psychoanalysis hothouses or the behavioral science labs. It naturally follows that we are barefoot bumpkins . . . talking dogs and dancing bears.

And yet, the reader should join me in suspecting that much of my old anguish was self-inflicted because I—not some humorless, pretentious literary tutti-frutti with a Harvard accent—had a difficult time coming to grips with the notion that anything approaching literature might be made of my roots, my native place, my people.

As a young West Texas newspaper reporter witnessing the rituals and rain dances of my time and place—brutal murders, courtroom dramas, political knife fights, backstreet love affairs, runaway boosterism, overt racism, an aggressive new wealth superimposing itself on the old fading horse culture—I cried out to friends and associates that nothing in my life or observations provided material for the books I was determined to one day write. Where was material to be found among the aimless cavortings of drunk oilfield roughnecks, the occasional tornado or flash flood, the constant wind and grit and baking sun of an isolated desert culture suddenly pretending to skyscraperdom and imported civic symphony orchestras?

Though I aspired to write almost from the moment I could read, there grew the firm conviction that I must escape Texas to do it. Yes, I must seek those teeming centers of civilization in the ill-defined, if vital, mystic east—New York, Washington, Tokyo, London, Moscow—where things *happened*, where "material" grew on trees, where "stories" clumped up out of subway caverns or burst out of the concrete canyons to nip at one's heels or lick one's face until one took notice and dutifully wrote them down.

In 1946, at age seventeen, I joined the army in search of story material more than out of any patriotic reflex to help keep the uncertain, emerging Cold War peace. I was delighted to be stationed in Queens, then but a nickle subway ride away from the clamorous glamour of Manhattan across the river. Somehow, though, Manhattan failed to turn me into the new Scott Fitzgerald or Thomas Wolfe. A few years later I rode the shoulders of a newly-elected Congressman out of West Texas, and away from my newspaper job, to seek the holy grail of literature in the nation's capitol.

I blush to recall that my first short stories and novels—each quickly rejected, recycled, rejected again—were played out in Korea (!), Washington, New York, Paris and other sites I thought of as "exotic" and knew absolutely nothing about. I now realize my acquaintance with New York and Washington then was only a nodding one; I would not get to Paris for another thirty years; to this good day I have never visited Korea or had any twitch to.

Call it a failure of the imagination if you wish, but there came a day when it dawned in my foggy brain that perhaps the old adage "Write what you know" was not bad advice. And so I began to remember and record the Texas where I had been born and grew to young manhood, treating events, customs and stories that in an earlier time I had walked by seemingly blind. That the old scenes and dialogue and human comedies came rushing back, complete with smells and moods and faces, absolutely astonished me. Sometimes we learn without knowing it.

My early Texas pieces were bought and published in *Harper's* by Willie Morris, bless him. Regular exposure in that magazine (under Morris then the most literate and remarked of American periodicals) prompted other editors to beckon—especially if they had requirements for a Texas-based story. I was dispatched home by *Life, Holiday, Atlantic Monthly, Playboy*, any number of Yankee journals.

That being the case, I suppose I might have logically anticipated being labeled "a Texas writer." But when it happened I was hurt and angry, never mind that I sometimes took dubious "Texas angle" assignments and produced dubious stories because, simply, I needed the money and had learned that it sometimes is better to be a busy writer than a proud one. For fifteen years I seethed because although I constantly crisscrossed the nation for *Harper's* and other periodicals, writing of politics and music and sports and what-have-you from Washington to New York to Iowa to California to the halls of Harvard to the North Carolina outback, I was in the eyes of many a mere "Texas writer."

At one point I became so sensitive to the regional label I determined to write a novel set wholly in Manhattan; my protagonist would be a man with no roots, no discernible past beyond the moment he lived in; nowhere in that book, I vowed, would the word "Texas" appear. Lo and behold, halfway through the manuscript I suddenly found my man flying to Austin to deal with the problems of his young daughter at the University of Texas! I silently packed the manuscript in a trunk—where it still reposes, unfinished—sighed and muttered to myself, "Ok, dammit, I guess you *are* a Texas writer." Not long afterward came *The Best Little Whorehouse in Texas* and from that moment my long, peculiar fight against the truth was forever lost.

I have not written much of modern-day, urbanized Texas; it is a strange territory, no longer my special turf. This fact seems to somehow anger a handful of critics who complain that the Texas I write of is old, vanished, no more. I plead guilty, though finding the charge a curious one. My writing has been about, and was *meant* to be about, the Texas of my time there. I felt it my job to define and record the Texas culture as I best knew it before (and perhaps in the beginning of) transitions toward what it has become, to leave signposts saying to those coming along later, *This is how it was then.* Indeed, I have the vanity to fancy myself a minor historian of a limited period in Texas history; an eyewitness reporter if you will. Those who have grown up, or who are now growing up in modern, urbanized Texas are better qualified to write about it than am I. It is their turn to establish signposts.

When Keith Gregory and Judy Alter of Texas Christian University Press proposed this collection in the summer of 1984, their guideline being to gather in one book my best previously-published work, we soon agreed that a high percentage of that work was about Texas. And so we have lumped eleven such articles together in the first section, calling them "Echoes of Texas." They have been arranged so as to constitute a loose autobiography—with one eye on chronology—though they deal with varied specific subjects: going home again to view with an adult's eye what a child once saw, racism, redneckery, movie myths and frontier myths, change and transition, fathers and sons. I have never had much luck keeping myself out of my work.

The second, shorter section—containing five "non-Texas" pieces—we have named "Other Echoes" to distinguish it from the down-home stuff. I am not entirely satisfied with that section; it showcases none of the many political pieces published over two decades and therefore is not wholly representative of what I've been up to as a working writer. But political issues and political faces rapidly change; political articles, therefore, are endowed with such built-in impermanences they become perishable in a short span.

I wanted to offer in this collection pieces that perhaps will last awhile, pieces—may I be forgiven the self-flattery?—I hope have at least an outside chance of standing the test of time.

Larry L. King
Washington, D.C., 1984

PART I

Echoes of Texas

Requiem for a West Texas Town

All the stores were dark and shuttered,
No scarlet ribbons in our town . . .

IT WAS A VERY SPECIAL PLACE, and those of us lucky enough to live there felt somehow set apart. Many signs ratified our suspicions.

Didn't visiting politicians confess that reaching our town was the high point of their peregrinations? Of all the towns on the Texas & Pacific railroad, wasn't ours the only one through which the westbound Sunshine Special clattered at exactly 4:14 p.m.? The Stamps Quartet, Somebody-or-other's Circus, Toby's Medicine Show—none dared pass us by. We had the word of our preachers that the Devil himself placed the highest premium on earthbound souls whose mail came addressed to Putnam, Texas.

Life had its absolutes: the world domino championship was settled behind Loren Everett's icehouse each Saturday afternoon. An aged citizen of ours had perfected the telegraph only twenty-four hours behind Thomas Edison. On evidence collected from all quarters of the town, no rational resident could doubt that in the tomb of the Unknown Soldier there slept in honored glory a Putnam boy.

If Notre Dame had its Four Horsemen, the Putnam Panthers had Jiggs Shackelford, Turkey Triplett, Tuffy Armstrong, and Hooter Allen. Where Bernard Baruch advised Presidents from Washington park benches, Ole Man Bob Head, perched on the ledge of sidewalk-level windows in the Farmer's State Bank, warned of hogs expiring of cholera and of our delivery to the Soviets in gunnysacks before FDR had completed the mischief of his first term. Even in our recreations we proved superior. Summer visitors were almost always treated to a "snipe hunt"; many an outlander, given the honor of holding the sack while other hunters fanned out to flush the "snipe" and drive it to him, figured out the game in strange

pastures at dawn. More than one boy, taken by a carload of Putnam contemporaries to pick up his blind date—a bucolic beauty
named Betsy, whose loose charms had been carefully advertised
in advance—bolted for the woods in panic when Betsy's angry
"father" fired a stream of oaths and a double-barreled shotgun into
the night air.

Putnam was on Highway 80. Cisco was a dozen miles to the
east, Dallas 159 miles in the same direction; New York was
rumored just a little beyond that. To the west, Highway 80 curved
around Utility Hill before winding eleven miles through wooded
rangeland offering protection from our natural enemies in Baird,
running thence to a mysterious land called California where Tom
Mix, Tarzan, and my Aunt Dewey lived. Nothing much was to the
immediate south or north of Putnam, though Mississippi presumably occupied acreage somewhere over Harper's Hill, and if you
struck out toward the water tower you'd eventually stumble onto
the North Pole.

It was here I had discovered the magic little Ulysses Macauley
knew in Saroyan's *The Human Comedy*, when upon finding a hen
egg he presented it to his mother, "by which he meant what no
man can guess and no child can remember to tell." Here I had
known the pains and pamperings attendant to that universal dis-
temper, whooping cough; shivered at my first funeral; and roamed
rocky foothills in search of Indian arrowheads and in honest fear
of God.

I was born in Putnam on New Year's Day, 1929. The oil boom
had peaked out a few months earlier, yet the familiar sound of

hammer-on-anvil could still be heard in my father's blacksmith shop. Roadwise drummers in straw boaters and polka-dot bow ties still brought their sample cases into our two hotels to stay the night. The cotton gin ran in season a dozen hours a day, during which a good gin hand could make three dollars. On Saturday nights, when the feedstore turned into a magic palace by the mere hanging of a bed sheet, addicts of the silent flicks came with their dimes. Though Ole Doc Britton had owned the town's only automobile in 1910, dozens of Tin Lizzies were backfiring in the streets by the time of my bones. For some five thousand salts-of-the-earth Putnam would still be standing when Rome had only a general store and an old stadium.

2.

That was almost forty years ago as the life flies. Now the faded sign pointing vaguely north of Interstate Twenty proclaims: *Putnam. Pop. 203*. But even this is a gentle fiction. "You might dredge up that many," old-timer Ellison Pruett says, "by countin' chickens, dawgs, and Republicans." Probably no more than a hundred survivors could be mustered for all-day singing with free dinner on the grounds.

The new slab that is Interstate Twenty, down which traffic thunders at terrible speeds, rises thirty feet above what once was the familiar town square with its pick-up baseball games, mineral-water wells, and ancient hitching posts. I had always assumed a stone monument would one day be raised there to commemorate my triumph as All-Pro Quarterback, America's Most Decorated Marine, Famous *Arthur*, and Richest Man in the World. But the square is gone, along with those dreams, and so for that matter is most of Putnam. The skeleton that is the business district—a dozen sad, sagging buildings, half of them wearing padlocks—faces bare dirt walls serving to underpin the overpass forty yards away.

Putnam had been sick for more than twenty years, but it took Congress to kill it. The Federal Highway Act did it in. Supposedly the Interstate System prevents congestion in our towns and cities, speeds commerce, and strengthens national defense. Perhaps more money will be made faster, and bigger bombs hauled over better roads, with Putnam out of the way. But I have wind of darker plots involving jealousy in high places, and possibly Castro's land reforms.

Whatever the motive, some invisible bureaucrat with an operable slide rule (but with no operable heart) decided an imposing overpass, or viaduct, would look good at a given point on proposed Interstate Twenty. He laughed madly, no doubt, as he made his fatal mark on the map. Four-fifths of my birthplace rested on the mark he made.

One day two years ago the growling machines came. An iron ball swung its fist, and bulldozers with metal jaws took bites from the earth. The barbershop, that exciting Istanbul of spicy tonics, racy stories, and old shaving mugs—where my Uncle Claude cheerfully and for two bits skinned young heads before drenching them in Red Rose Hair Oil—fell under the assault. So did the offices of the weekly Putnam *News*, where my first literary work appeared— a bit of doggerel called "The Indian Squaw," sufficient to crown me undisputed poet laureate of the third grade and to inspire several fistfights seeking to prove the scientific fact that all poets are born sissies. The wonder that had been, in turn, the Hotel Carter-Holland, the Mission Hotel, and finally the Hotel Guyton was reduced to rubble along with its splendid sunken rose garden. De-Shazo's Variety Store, famed for its square deals on pocket knives, Halloween masks, and sacks of shiny marbles, came down. Pierce Shackelford's Farm Implements, the corner "filling station" where you could pump up your bicycle tires with free air or flag the Greyhound, my father's blacksmith shop, the telephone exchange where my Aunt Flora was the friendly Central who answered when you cranked out one long ring—all are no more. When the bulldozers were gone so was the town square and everything to the east, west, and south of it. All for an overpass.

Alton White, suspecting his hometown held little future for grocers, moved twenty-two miles down the highway to Eastland. When progress wiped out Charlie Davis' service station, he moved to Cross Plains. Mrs. Bess Herring went 225 miles west to live with her widowed sister. The Sandlin Brothers sold their farm and used the money to buy another two counties away. You can't boss a ranch or tend cattle by long distance, so it became R. D. Williams' lot to suffer the greatest indignity. He moved to Baird.

The government man sent to pacify the survivors told them the town was lucky to have held losses to a minimum. This is roughly comparable to congratulating Whitey Ford should he lose only three fingers on his pitching hand. Local citizens were gratified when they learned the government man wasn't one of our leading diplomats, Averell Harriman, perhaps, or Henry Cabot Lodge, but a representative from the Bureau of Public Roads.

3.

I. G. Mobley thinks Putnam is coming back. Richard Nixon may come back, Krushchev conceivably could, and some say Jesus Christ surely will. But Judge Crater is not coming back, nor Benito Mussolini, and neither is Putnam.

Sitting in I. G. Mobley's air-conditioned living room on a modern farm near Putnam a few months ago, I could not tell him that. His roots go deep in home. He pays his debts, lives by his labor, and keeps his barn painted. He has served his neighbors as county commissioner and member of the school board.

Mobley sat on the edge of a rocking chair, tensely unfolding his slender hands and long legs. "I tell 'em," he said, "that it's up to the people of Putnam whether we have a town here or not. We're the only town *on* Interstate Twenty from Fort Worth to Cahoma and—why, that must be over three hundred miles! Other little towns are *off* the highway by a right smart. Folks are gonna need gasoline, food, rest rooms. Maybe they'll want to mail a letter." I thought of how, earlier in the day, I had clocked traffic speeding along Interstate Twenty at an average of 72 miles per hour, and of the small sign warning of Putnam's decaying carcass down there beneath the slab.

I. G. Mobley took no note of these facts. Miracles were like buses: if you missed one, you simply caught the next. "The gloom merchants have prayed over Putnam's remains before," he said. "When I was a small kid things were slow as winter molasses. Then the mineral-water boom hit."

That was in 1908. People swarmed in to bathe their tortures—lumbago, gout, arthritis, rheumatism. The Carter-Holland Hotel was built: a mission-style palace of forty-six rooms, and a polished ballroom for dancing if you weren't bedeviled by lumbago or Fundamentalist parsons. For three dollars a day you could bathe in Putnam's miracle waters, have meals in your room, and take treatment from the well-known "rubbing doctor," Doc Milling. By 1912 completion of three red-brick buildings of two stories each—a bank, Yancy Orr's drugstore, the new school with its imposing bell tower—gave the town a slight case of skyline fever. An Opera House was opened over the protests of the preachers, and traveling shows took away dollars Heaven had earlier designated for the collection plates. When, almost without warning and for no obvious reason, the mineral-water craze ended in 1916, nobody had to ask why. The preachers told them.

For the next few years Putnam was in the doldrums, though crops were generally fair. Then came the drought of 1917–18. Creeks, tanks, and cisterns dried up. Water was hauled twelve miles from Cisco by wagons and teams. But May of 1919 brought a new miracle. "It rained frogs and fishes," I. G. Mobley recalls. Wheat made fifty bushels to the acre that year and each bushel sold for $2.75. The following season Putnam's two gins handled 5,000 bales of cotton. On top of the agricultural prosperity came the oil boom of 1922. Wildcatters fogged in to drill shallow wells, and the rocky foothills around Putnam seemed loaded. Once again the hotels were filled. Tom Davis operated a flourishing wagon yard; in my father's blacksmith shop fires were seldom banked. Yancy Orr got competition from the new Black's Drugs, and the Putnam Supply Company was founded.

I. G. Mobley had put himself through Draughton's Business College in Abilene by clerking part-time in one of the hotels, before a few producing wells blessed his acres. "Everybody was drilling for oil and swinging big deals," he recalls. "We had more paper millionaires than Carter had little liver pills."

The boom had almost everything associated with booms—inflated prices, muddy streets, the tents and shacks of nomadic "boom hands." Everything, in fact, but open saloons. Saloons weren't really needed; drugstore counters did a booming business in a patent medicine of high alcoholic content said to cure nagging coughs, chest colds, and other convenient ailments. Old heads recall that one of the parsons who fought so fiercely against the Opera House developed the most persistent cough in town.

In 1928, with no more warning than might be given by the rattlesnakes on Harper's Hill, the boom went bust, and the Depression followed. Oil dropped to thirty cents a barrel, a lease pumper was grateful to keep his job at $30 per month, and fly-by-night oil operators left town by the dozens even if their unpaid bills didn't. My father could only sigh and write off the $10,000 due him for services rendered. Putnam Supply Company and Black's Drugs folded, and the movie house cut its schedule to Saturday Nights Only. Men who had swarmed to town for good-salaried jobs, or to wheel-and-deal in oil speculation, went back to farms long lying fallow where they could at least grow food for their families. Some left for good, riding the rails in search of jobs or dreams, or joining the westward migration of jitneys laden with household goods in the manner of Steinbeck's Joad family.

Putnam had one more opportunity to snap back. About 1932, as New Deal pump-priming measures brought faint signs but great hopes of relieving the misery, a stranger came to town from "across the waters"—though no one seems to have pinpointed his sources better than that. The foreigner charmed Putnam's ladies with deep bows, pretty speeches, and hand-kisses. Within a few months he promoted money from hard-pressed Main Street merchants to finance what he envisioned as "the largest automobile dealership in Texas." The daughter of a prominent citizen consented to be the go-getter's wife. She sold her diamond rings and persuaded her father to add $5,000 to her fiancé's venture. After hot excitement and speeches at the depot, the promoter left by train to arrange for the first shipment of cars. He was slightly delayed to the extent that he has not been heard from again. Even I. G. Mobley gave up hopes of his coming back about three years ago.

Not all Putnam natives share I. G. Mobley's optimism for the future. "She's about dried up and blowed away," grocer Charley Odom says of the town. Some worry about losing their churches. On a typical Sunday there had been eight, nine, and eleven worshipers at the Campbellite, Methodist, and Baptist Churches, respectively. One recent collection plate at the Methodist Church brought in $3.48. You can't keep a preacher on that.

Miss LaVerne Rutherford has worked in the post office almost since graduating from high school in 1943. She was appointed Postmaster by John F. Kennedy, and she now worries over the possibility of the office being closed. She would be transferred to a larger office, reduced to clerk, forced to live away from Putnam for the first time. Hopefully she says, "These people have to get their mail *somewhere!*"

The title of chief optimist of Putnam, and maybe of the world, must go to Jim Meador, a newcomer. He opened J. E.'s Steak House, at a reported $5,000 investment, *after* the bulldozers had done Putnam dirt. The J. E. Steak House sign is new, orange and green, made of a glittering substance which dazzles the eyeballs in the sun. It cannot, however, be seen from Interstate Twenty.

4.

Putnam cannot fairly lay all its troubles at the feet of Washington. Its alternating cycles of boom and bust are common to many of the nation's small towns. Census figures show the startling migration from rural to metropolitan areas. In 1940, some 43.5 per cent of Americans lived on farms or in rural hamlets. By 1960, only 30.1 per cent did.

Rural America is full of towns dead or dying. In Texas alone there are examples without end. Take Thurber, for instance. In 1887, after the discovery of a rich bituminous coal vein, it grew into a city of 10,000. For several years it supplied all the coal or building bricks used in the state. Thurber grew its own Nob Hill of haughty homes, a spacious Opera House, a man-made lake stocked with fish or suitable for boating. The local Poohbah of commerce and industry tooled about in his own plush railway car and hand-picked his mayor. When the coal supply and brick orders ran out, so did Colonel Pooh-bah and everyone else.

The death blow fell in 1933. General offices of the Texas & Pacific Coal and Oil Company were ordered to Fort Worth. Stocks were sold from store shelves; buildings were wrecked and moved away; wires and poles came down; water and gas mains were removed. Where in 1930 Thurber had almost 6,000 people, it was virtually gone by 1935. The population in 1960 was eighty. Today it is exactly zero. All that is left is the remnant of an old smoke-stack bearing a bronze marker saying in twenty-five words or less that Thurber once knew glory.

Shafter and Terlingua, in the Big Bend Country, were booming mining towns as recently as the mid-1940s. Now they are ghost towns, too. Wink, in the western sands of what has been called "the Texas Sahara," was born with the oil strike of 1926. Little more than two years later it was a shack-and-tent Baghdad of 7,000 people, mud-bog streets, and open saloons serving up red-eye whiskey and sudden death. It knew a decade of stability, during which its Wink Wildcat football teams earned the reputation of being meaner than your ex-wife. But oil production petered out. By 1960 the federal government decided to restore Wink as a model city in the new urban-renewal program. At a cost of only two million of your tax dollars, planning geniuses replaced rusty tin pool halls and dilapidated sandwich shops with modern, sani-tized miracles of glass, brick, and fluorescent lights. The scheme didn't work. Too many of Wink's 1,863 remaining citizens used profits from condemnation proceedings to hightail it to where the action is.

Ranger, in Eastland County, reached 16,205 in 1920. Old-timers swear its oil boom of that era pushed it 5,000 higher than that. Drinking water fetched ten cents a glass in restaurants, and special policemen who dealt in mayhem were hired to handle street rowdies. Long on the wane, Ranger today claims only 3,113 residents.

Even home bogs of Great Men and their ladies have declined. Only one member of Lyndon Johnson's 1926 high-school graduat-ing class chose to build a future in Johnson City. The President has said, "I go back to my hometown and I find difficulty locating anyone under twenty-one years of age that has finished high school. They have moved on."

Jefferson, a bustling seaport of 38,000, was Texas' second-largest city from 1867 to 1873. Then Jay Gould, the genius of the T & P, incensed when he had trouble getting right-of-way through the town, ran his railroad tracks *around* it. Jefferson started to wither.

Soon the natural dam that backed the water up and made Big Cypress Bayou and the lakes navigable was removed. Jefferson is now a sedentary village of 3,000. The biggest attraction is the birthplace of a local girl everyone remembers as Claudia Taylor, now Ladybird Johnson.

Putnam, too, knows the loss of its young. In the words of one old nester, "Every kid with good sense and the price of a bus ticket leaves." Figures back him up. Where Putnam High School graduated twenty-six seniors in 1941, it conferred degrees on only eleven a decade later, and the Class of '64 consisted of Doris Lee Donaway, Charlie Ivie, and Farrell Thorp.

The bottom dropped out of Putnam for good about 1942. The peak population of 5,000—reached during the oil boom of the 1920s—shrank to less than half that figure by 1936. In 1940, the census counted only 1,403 people. When World War II came, Putnam had no munitions factory to brighten the times and nobody looked after it when military bases were passed around in Washington. Following Pearl Harbor Putnam boys answered the call to arms; fat paychecks lured their elders to shipyards and factories. Seventy-five houses moved away in the single year 1942, and a dozen more were shuttered. A dozen cousins of mine joined the military that year, Uncle George Gaskins sold his grocery store and moved to California, and my father took a job with a New Mexico oil company. The exodus was on.

5.

It was a broiling-hot day when I went home again last summer.* My head was full of memories and my car full of kinfolk. The air conditioner was on full volume, while on the car radio T. Texas Tyler sang "When I Look up My God Looks down on Me."

We flashed by Baird (Pop. 1633) at a high speed, and it seemed but a couple of minutes before my father said dourly, "You better slow this thing down to about a thousand. It's right down yonder."

But we had gone past the sign pointing north to *Putnam. Pop. 203.* Seeking a spot on Interstate Twenty to turn around, I noted Harper's Hill with shock. In my youth it had towered over the countryside, and probably no man had scaled it, even if Lem

* 1965

Harper did grow peaches and apples up there. I recalled when a committee of jelly-smeared faces had solemnly judged it three million feet high. But now. . . .

"Look at Harper's Hill," I said. "Somebody's sawed the top off."

My father chuckled. "Naw, it never was anything but a little ole mound of dirt."

Where the depot had been was only the wooden platform on which it had rested. The platform seemed no bigger than a life raft. I complained that not only was the depot gone, but part of the platform as well. My father enjoyed another laugh. No, the depot had been that exact size. I didn't dispute him, though I clearly recalled when dozens of us—Benny Ross Everett, Bobby Gene Maynard, Kenneth Gaskins, Humph Weeks, Buck Yarborough, a barefoot army—had stood on that platform with acres of wooden boards running in all directions, and the yellow depot looming grandly behind us like Convention Hall in Atlantic City.

As I U-turned on Interstate Twenty, my mother fretted how this was the exact spot where so-and-so got killed turning *his* car around in March of 1926. There was little point in reminding her this particular highway had not existed then, for my mother is blessed with an infallible memory for tragedy. Nobody got killed this time, much to her surprise and, perhaps, slight disappointment. I followed the highway signs as we tooled under the viaduct and drove by sixteen strange white pillars supporting it like sentinels of an enemy army.

That couldn't be Putnam there! Not that collection of frayed little buildings, bare and huddled against the sun, where once had been a proud line of stores grandly sending forth all the world's good smells. There were skips between buildings: vacant lots overgrown with weeds and Johnson grass. Grass poked up through the sidewalks, cracking and crumbling them. A patch had burst through almost at the exact spot Ole Man Bob Head had angrily scuffled his feet while warning that grass would grow in the streets should FDR be much longer tolerated. In the silence my father said, "It was a purty good town, once."

On this hot Saturday afternoon only two cars, one ancient pickup truck, and absolutely no human beings were visible on the single, one-block business street. In Putnam's salad days the sidewalks would have been crowded with round-eyed urchins, women sampling cloth bolts in Norred's Dry Goods, farmers hustling to sell their butter and eggs in time to sweat the domino matches. While my father conducted a door-to-door search for friendly natives, I explored the short stretch of sidewalks in pursuit of memories.

Orr's Drugs was padlocked. Peering through the glass I could see, under layers of dust, the marble soda fountain with its brass-headed spigots, three marble-topped tables with wire wicker chairs, the cumbersome upright scales that for a penny had given your weight and the bonus of a small trinket. Long, narrow shelves held ancient concoctions Putnam mothers had sworn by: Dr. Caldwell's Syrup-of-Pepsin, a bitter brew called Al-Da-Eureka (once assumed more vital to health than sunshine or surgery), and I wondered if in the clutter there remained that miracle cure for coughs, Jamaica Ginger.

I walked over to the lonely site of Uncle George's grocery store, where the Candy Bandits of 1936 did their work. Cousin Kenneth would enter a rear storeroom, banging among crates and boxes, whooping like an Apache until his father rushed back to deal with the menace. With the candy case unguarded, I would scoop up jawbreakers, peanut brittle, chocolate bars, and peppermint sticks in quantities that would have foundered all the inhabitants of Boy's Town. We divvied up in a jungle of back-alley weeds after each successful foray. But the community's leading busybody entered the store one day to buy some baking powder and caught the bag man of the duo. The flogging administered by the village black-smith to his youngest son was painful, though less so than Cousin Kenneth's bawled denials that the conspiracy involved him. The final indignity came when my blood cousin publicly forgave me for swiping from his daddy's store, then led the First Baptist Church Sunbeams in loud, pious prayer for my long-range rehabilitation. This act of charity was enough to win for Kenneth the Jesus' Little Helper Award. I was delighted when his prize proved to be nothing more interesting than a New Testament.

6.

My father's return interrupted this reverie. He complained over having recognized three people who had not recognized him. Nor had he found any of his old cronies. Morosely we ambled toward Tood Cunningham's service station. As a battered pickup truck rattled down the street my father bellowed in a bass key that was stunning for lungs pushing eighty years' service: "*Ellison!*" The truck faltered, zigzagged, and stopped. The driver gazed out suspiciously.

"Don't set there with egg on your face," Dad called. "Get down outta there."

The old man didn't budge from the truck. "Says who?" he demanded.

"By durn, says *I*."

That seemed to settle something. Ellison Pruett climbed stiffly down, a large, raw-boned, red-faced man who probably tended his own fractures with cow-chip poultice. He wore a Western-cut shirt, khaki pants, scuffed boots, and the cattleman's coiled hat.

"You know me?" my father demanded.

Ellison Pruett studied my father's face. He probably recognized that it had known hard work and the outdoors, but that was all. "Naw." Then his shotgun-eyes moved over and got the drop on me. He jerked a thumb like Randolph Scott uses in warning bad-hat gunslingers to hit the road. "Don't know the feller with hair on his face, neither."

"That's my son." The beard needed some justification. "He's a writer."

"*Hell* he is." Ellison Pruett examined me down to the skin pores. He nodded, slowly and with stern sympathy. He watered the dusty earth with a golden stream of tobacco juice. "He uses a name when he writes?"

"Yeah," said my old man. "Same one I do. Leastwise, the *last* name." He chortled in delight, slapping his knee. Ellison Pruett grinned, shoving his hat to the back of his head. Knowing when he'd met his match he said, "Thunder, I give up. I couldn't name you if I was a-gonna be hung."

"Well, I worked for you once upon a time."

Light dawned in Ellison Pruett's old eyes. "You ain't Clyde *King*?"

"I reckon I am. What's left of me."

"Naw. *You* ain't Clyde King!" This time it wasn't open to question. "Why, Clyde King weighed over two hundred pounds and was stout as a mule. He wasn't no little ole dried up nobody like you!"

They gurgled in delight, embracing in the street. "Clyde King!" Ellison Pruett repeated. "By *damn*!" He slapped his old comrade on the back, then whirled on me. "Boy, I seen this man lift a whole barrel fulla water from the ground and set it *flat-dab* in the bed of a wagon without straining hisself."

My father grinned. "Can't do much anymore. I'm kinda like Putnam. Too old and wore out."

"Why," Ellison Pruett said, "this burg never amounted to much, anyways." Then his eyes walked slowly along the solitary main street, as if he'd noted its diminution for the first time. "Things change," he said. "I don't care for some the changes, neither. Do you, Clyde?"

"No," my father said. "I'll betcha there's one thing hasn't changed, though."

"What's that?"

"I'll bet you still can't play dominoes!"

"Why, I'm *teachin'* dominoes. Got a beginner's class you might be able to get in." They whooped and hoo-hawed, and when the mirth died down Pruett said, "We been playin' all afternoon up in the old Odd Fellows hall."

My father was chagrined. "Why, durn it! Who all played?"

"Same ole bunch. Me and Lee White. Elmer McIntosh, Walter Caldwell. Feller named Truman Blaylock, from over at Scranton."

"I sure wish I'd knew it," Dad said. "It wouldn't of taken much to clean *that* bunch's plow."

They talked then. Of crops and the Bible and men a long time dead. When Ellison Pruett took his leave my father watched the dust of his pickup as far as the eye could see.

7.

Though the school house was locked for the summer, an official yielded to my attack of nostalgia and provided a key. "Look around," he said. "Likely there's not much in there you'd have."

Yet the place held many treasures. In a glass display case was the silver-plated trophy won by the Bi-District football champions of 1937. Misshapen and deflated but awesomely majestic was the historic football Oliver Davis had romped with for the 65-yard touchdown that had brought Putnam its championship—and, far more important, a 13 to 6 victory over the loathsome Baird Bears. Had I not feared the grip of superintendent R. F. Webb reaching from out of the past, I might have copped it.

The grandfather's clock in the principal's office had ticked off doom while I once awaited judgment for having talked in assembly. President Johnson's portrait was next to the one of Franklin D. Roosevelt, hung when Federal Emergency Administration of Public Works Project No. 1295, more commonly known as Putnam High School, had been dedicated. We had been proud when we moved into the shining new palace of cream-colored bricks in 1937. It was a showplace. Even ill-at-ease farmers had shuffled in to view the Central Sound System (*i.e.*, a public-address hookup to every room) dedicated at a cost of $200 by the Class of '37 to give "our Beloved School access to the diffusion of knowledge that will aid pupil advancement." Some of the charm wore off when school authorities failed to pipe Jack Armstrong or Amos 'n' Andy into the classrooms.

It wasn't a showplace anymore. Cracks ran through its bricks in several places, the summer grounds were a jumble of grass and weeds, a disreputable car with three flat tires sat near the flagpole. The auditorium, where I had played Grumpy in a very swinging one-night production of *Snow White* to the applause of several thousand people, now seats only a couple of hundred and doesn't need half that. They have lowered the drinking fountains three feet each. The walls of my old classroom have been moved in by several feet, and the wall lockers are scaled for midgets.

Nor were outside objects in their rightful places. The pine-board lunch stand, where I had violated home training by first buying on credit, is no longer there as a temptation to hungry schoolboys. The football field—where I played two heart-bursting minutes in my first "real" game as the Putnam Grammar School Pussycats routed Scranton, 28 to nothing—is grown over with alfalfa. Missing, too, was the clump of trees where ranch boys had tied their horses and fed them bundled roughage during the noon hour. My father counted the absence of nineteen houses he recalled near the school. In a growth of mesquite bushes stood the concrete steps which once led to the house where I was born.

8.

Was Putnam just another of man's experiments gone bad, no better than those tens of thousands of isolated villages where people had dandruff and gas pains and warts on the nose?

What we had produced in the way of native sons and daughters would not cause the earth to move. Statesmen? Billie Mack Jobe had served two terms in the Texas legislature and called the Governor by his first name, but his name appears in no histories I have read. Athletes? Stanley Williams played pro football with Dallas and Baltimore, but his name became a household word only in Putnam. The arts? Lewis Nordyke published a couple of books and several articles in *Saturday Evening Post*, not quite enough to rank with Sartre or Faulkner. Most ex-Putnamites were safe in the anonymity of our society, working for a weekly wage in undistinguished jobs, watching "Bonanza" on television, and fretting over income-tax forms. This knowledge was painful for me, and altogether new.

Our town had not been a complete one—not even an "average" one by national standards. No Negroes lived in Putnam within the range of my memory, nor Jews, and the only Catholics had been Mexicans who lived in converted railroad boxcars for a few weeks each year when their work as itinerant section-gang hands brought them briefly our way. We were, I could now acknowledge, a bigoted town. I remembered the despair of local people when Joe

Louis knocked out Jimmy Braddock to win the world heavyweight championship in 1937. I had learned of this the morning following the fight, when a gentle Putnam lady remarked to a companion in the post office, "Well, the ole nigger is champion." And the other woman answered, "I guess they'll be pushing white folks off the streets and into the gutters now." In November of 1937, when the Japanese seized an American vessel, tore down our flag, and tossed it in the Hwang Pu River, many of our natives said the U.S. could "whip those little brown monkeys in ninety days"; Japan wasn't even as big as Texas. We were narrow in politics: you were a Democrat because Daddy was, and his father had been before him. Our theology fell just short of teaching a flat earth, and in some cases it did teach that eternal damnation followed infant baptism. Sin had meant the strict idea of the word: drinking spirits, dancing to music, or wearing lip rouge. The more destructive sins—gossip, bigotry, indifference to injustice, oppression of free thought—were cheered in the streets.

Man being the weak creature he is, no doubt Putnam had known its share of commerce in Prohibition dew, its backstair romances, small larcenies or other transgressions that I had always assumed to be the property of New York, Washington City, or Baird. We were not rampant with wrongdoing, but for the first time I questioned whether we had been creatures of Utopia.

We left in the late afternoon. I stopped by the only business house open, J. E.'s Steak House, for cigarettes. Four men in work clothes sipped coffee while on the jukebox a cowboy singer urged us to "Cross the Brazos at Waco." I wondered how long it might take Jim Meador to get his $5,000 investment back at ten cents a cup.

As I drove away into the sun, the loss of the town saddened me beyond the telling of it; it may not have been anything unusual, but it had been home. Suddenly I was angry—at Congress, the Bureau of Public Roads, the Depression-makers on Wall Street, the greedy oil speculators, the foreigner who had failed to open the biggest automobile dealership in Texas. How could a place be allowed to die?

But the anger passed, for I knew I would not find the answer—not this side of whatever Heaven there is that has rewarded all Putnamites who lived by the code. And even then the answer would probably lie on the farther slope of the last holy hill, guarded by a mean old dog.

1966

The Christmas Santa
Robbed Our Bank

MY WIFE claims I always act a little goofier than usual around Christmas time.

Well, maybe so. I grew up hearing how Santa Claus himself robbed my hometown bank only two Christmases before I was born. A tale like that, documented by his own father and yellowing newspaper clippings, may make a boy flinch when he hears folks singing that Santa Claus is coming to town.

"Santa" was a hometown boy, Marshall Ratliff, though no one knew it at the time. Marshall was 24 when he took a notion to rob the First National Bank of Cisco, Tex.—in the Yule season of 1927—and already had served a three-year stretch in the state lockup at Huntsville for a backfired bank caper in another Texas town.

He returned home with the idea that much profit might accrue should he rob the Cisco bank after local merchants had stuffed it with their Christmas deposits.

The problem was, Marshall's face—as well as his reputation—was known to just about everybody in the little town of 8,000 folks. One night while he brooded on the problem, he chanced upon a woman friend sewing a Santa Claus suit. Tiny little wheels commenced turning faster than usual in Marshall Ratliff's head.

Marshall approached three of his best pals—Bob Hill, 20; Lou Davis, 28; Henry Helms, 32. All were a little down on their luck, being ex-convicts. Marshall told 'em this neat idea he had to dress up like Santa Claus and hit the Cisco bank. Who would give Santa a second glance, or suspect him of felonious intent, during the cheery Yuletide? The three country boys accepted Marshall's bid to become Santa's helpers so quickly you might have thought it an invitation to eggnog. Marshall Ratliff drew diagrams of the bank, mapped getaway routes and assigned his helpers their roles.

The planning failed to take into account several matters that later would assume great importance. Marshall decreed that the getaway car would be parked in a wide alley behind the bank for quick egress. Sounds about half-smart until you know that the Cisco Police Station fronted on the same alley and the cops used it for a parking lot. The decision to hit the bank at high noon, on the theory that a lot of folks would then be out to lunch, smacks of bad research. Even a minor casing job might have shown that the Cisco bank, like just about any bank in the world, does it rush business during the noon hour. This might be expected to be doubly true, in a time before credit cards, when folks needed ready cash for Christmas shopping. Marshall and his boys forgot a couple of other vital matters, as they soon were to learn.

The Santa Claus Gang went off to Wichita Falls, a couple hundred miles away, and stole a big, blue Buick for their escapade. On the way to the robbery they drank a bit of whiskey and sang songs. When they approached Cisco, Marshall Ratliff—already in his Santa suit—lay down on the floorboards. Santa was dropped off near the railroad tracks, a few blocks from the First National Bank; his helpers parked the car in the alley the cops used for a parking lot and strolled casually around to what everybody called "Main Street"—officially Avenue D—to take up their positions in front of the bank and await their leader.

It was a long wait. Marshall Ratliff had failed to consider that Santa Claus in uniform might attract a large crowd of kiddies. As he humped and bumped up the sidewalk, his padded belly and Santa blouse hiding a sawed-off shotgun, half the kids in Cisco seemed to be trailing along beseeching him to bring them cap guns and little red wagons and rubber dollies. A bold few tried to pull his beard. Santa attracted attention to himself by cursing them and was admonished by an adult passer-by. By the time he had managed to beat and thresh his way through the kiddies, he was in a sweat and off schedule. Santa entered the bank with his helpers shoving in on his heels. There they found a milling crowd almost as big as a football squad. A prudent man might have issued a few Ho-Ho-Hos and backed off with the excuse he had to go feed his reindeer.

A 6-year-old girl, Frances Blasengame, saw Santa enter the bank. She tugged her mama across the street to instruct Santa what to leave in her stocking. They arrived just as Santa exposed his concealed shotgun and sang out, "This here's a holdup!" Santa's helpers also pulled their guns.

The little girl, thinking the old, mean men intended to shoot Santa Claus, began screaming. Her mama screamed too and ran for the back door opening onto the alley, dragging the hysterical child. Jolly old St. Nick shouted to his henchmen to shoot that damn woman. They all gaped dumbly while she broke through the door and clattered into the police station. Mrs. Blasengame screamed "They're robbing the bank! A big gang is robbing the bank!"

It took some doing to convince Chief G. E. (Bit) Bedford that Mrs. Blasengame was sounding a serious alarm. He suspected some sort of prank. Finally he grabbed his pump-action shotgun and he and two other officers charged out the door into the alley.

The chief suddenly pulled up short, as if lame. It had occurred to him he might use a little more help. He began to form a ragtag posse of sidewalk gawkers and local merchants. The owner of a hardware store handed out rifles and shotguns from his inventory. Within moments about 40 armed citizens had surrounded the bank. It may be—since wide publicity had been given to an offer from the Texas Bankers Association to pay "$5,000 for any dead bank robber and not one cent for a live one"—that sugarplum visions of reward money danced in some heads.

Meanwhile, back in the bank, Santa and his helpers acted as if the screaming Mrs. Blasengame and her yowling daughter, once out of sight, were out of mind. They stood haggling with bank officials over whether one of the bank's two vaults was truly time-locked or the bankers were trying to fool them. Santa lost the argument. He entered the one vault that was open, ripped out his belly padding—a large gunnysack advertising potatoes—and ordered it stuffed with big bills. One of his helpers earned a tongue-lashing for wasting time gathering up rolls of nickels.

Santa was quite surprised to see a number of faces peering over firearms into the bank's windows. He fired a "warning shot" through the glass and somebody fired back. Deciding those fools out there needed a little more warning, he and his helpers blasted the ceiling four times. Everybody with a gun began firing into the bank, breaking windows and chipping marble and causing folks inside to scream, faint and scramble for cover.

"Break for the car!" Santa yelled. "Bring some them hostages!"

He didn't know about the reception committee waiting out back. Postmaster J. W. Triplett, armed with a government-issue service revolver he never had fired, had organized a dozen men to ambush the robbers should they flee out the back. What he didn't know was that he was using the robbers' getaway car for cover.

The robbers burst out the back door, pushing hostages ahead of them, firing as they came. The posse fired back and adroitly hit a male hostage in the jaw. Santa, propelling a young woman hostage forward while firing over her shoulder, gained the Buick and tossed the bank loot in the back seat. He, his hostage and Lou Davis and his hostage tumbled in after the money. Davis was hit badly and lost consciousness. Santa bracketed himself between two women hostages, as if they were bookends, and bellowed that Bob Hill should haul ass. Police Chief Bit Bedford ran at the car firing his shotgun. Someone—whether Santa, a helper, or the wild-firing posse—shot the chief in the chest; a second policeman collapsed when hit in the head. People ran along the sidewalks and streets pumping lead at the Buick as it lurched out of the alley and, with one flat tire, careened onto Avenue D. Wheelman Bob Hill caught a slug in one arm.

Santa knocked a hole in the back window and fired back. Henry Helms tossed out roofing nails to puncture the tires of any rolling pursuit. A half-dozen cars joined the chase. Santa took a grazing hit in the chin and bled all over his costume. Behind the getaway car, the pursuing vehicles broke down with flat tires and collided with each other.

"We got to git another car," driver Bob Hill yelled.

Santa cursed and allowed as how they'd have to wait until they had more time.

"I mean right now!" Hill insisted. "We ain't got any gas. This one's damn near empty!"

Apparently, what with passing around the jug and singing songs on the 200-mile ride down from Wichita Falls, the robbers had neglected to check their gas gauge.

By now the bandits had reached the south city limits of Cisco. Santa, spying a farm family coming into town to shop, jumped from the Buick and waved them down. The farmers stopped their new Oldsmobile, grinning, thinking themselves lucky participants in some fun Christmas stunt. Until Santa waved a gun in their faces and demanded their car. One Mrs. Jake Harris began screaming; Santa told her if she didn't hush that infernal racket he would shoot her. Mrs. Harris stopped, looked at him and said, "I can't. You'll just have to shoot me." And went on screaming.

Santa ordered Mrs. Harris and her 80-year-old mother, Mrs. Sarah Graves, out of the car. The women sat tight, one screaming and the other disdainfully staring straight ahead. Santa tugged them from the car and poked a gun in the face of 14-year-old Woodrow Harris, the driver. "I'll take over," he said. The boy politely said "Yessir," and—while the excited Santa screamed at his helpers to git theirselves and them damn hostages in this here Olds—he quietly locked the ignition, put the key in his pocket, slid out of the car and walked away.

Santa and his helpers, unmindful of this development, moved their wounded comrade and their hostages to the new car. The gunnysack full of bank money was tossed inside. Bob Hill got behind the wheel.

"Gimme the keys," he said to Santa.

"Ain't they in the ignition?" Santa asked.

"Hail no."

"Well, jump the wires!" Santa barked.

"Can't. This sumbitch has a lock on the gearshift. I gotta have a key."

"Jesus God!" Santa bellowed—which, considering the way things were going, exhibited a certain admirable restraint. Santa looked wildly for the Harris kid, but Woodrow had run off and hid hisself.

By now the posse had cleared the road of its own wreckage and was bearing down again. Santa slowed them with gunshots while Hill and Helms yanked the terrified hostages out of the Olds and restuffed them back into the near-gasless Buick.

"What about Lou?" one of the robbers yelled of their wounded and unconscious comrade.

"Leave him!" ordered jolly old St. Nick. "He's about dead anyway."

They lurched away in the bullet-riddled Buick, still firing while their hostages screamed anew. Helms threw out more retarding nails. They cursed and bickered about who was at fault with respect to the gasoline shortage. Maybe a mile down the road Santa yelled, "Whur's 'at damn money sack at?"

The bleeding Bob Hill jerked the battered car to a shuddering stop. The robbers stared at each other. They had left the bank loot back in the Olds with their deserted companion. No one had the heart to suggest going back for it.

Only days later, after their capture, would members of the Santa Claus Gang learn they had abandoned $162,200 in cash and securities.

Ho-Ho-Ho!

The Santa Claus caper had inflicted gunshot wounds on two police officers, two hostages, four posse members, two bystanders and three robbers. Police Chief Bedford and the abandoned robber, Lou Davis, would not live out the night; a second wounded policeman, George Carmichael, would last only a few days more. It wasn't a very merry Christmas in Cisco that year.

The robbers released their two women hostages upon abandoning their gasless Buick. Carrying foodstuffs they'd brought along for just such an eventuality, they tromped off into the woods—but not before one of the hostages recognized Marshall Ratliff when he thoughtlessly removed his Santa whiskers to attend his bleeding chin. She was smart enough not to reveal her knowledge until safely home. Within hours the Cisco authorities had guessed the identities of Santa's remaining helpers.

For several days, though hampered by a lack of radio communications or other modern equipment, police officers and citizens' posses beat the bushes and established roadblocks.

Santa and his helpers hid in a clump of woods a few miles from town—cold, running fevers from their wounds and generally miserable. Santa discovered he'd also been hit in the leg as well as the chin and soon developed trouble walking. Christmas night, under cover of darkness, Hill sneaked back to Cisco and stole another car. The road-blocks made the gang fearful of movement, however, so they concealed the car in the woods and sat around lamenting not having reached into the bank loot for a handfull of bills. "We ain't even got gas money," Santa grumbled. Once a posse came within 200 yards of their hiding place. The posses, meanwhile, were having troubles. A deputy sheriff somehow blew off his left thumb, and an old county judge lost a leg while trying to unload his shotgun after returning home from a roadblock.

On the night of Dec. 28, attempting to flee the Cisco area, the robbers were ambushed at a river crossing near the town of South Bend. A deputy felled Marshall Ratliff with a shotgun blast and captured him, though Hill and Helms escaped on foot into the river bottom and again disappeared. A couple of days later they were captured by an armed posse as they skulked through the alleys of Graham, Tex., looking to steal a car.

Marshall Ratliff, sentenced to 99 years because it couldn't be proved he had personally killed anybody, cracked, "That's no hill for a high-stepper like me." Bob Hill, the wheelman, also got 99 years. Henry Helms, described by the prosecutor as "the most savage" of the gunmen, was sentenced to death.

"Santa" Ratliff, awaiting removal from the Eastland County Jail to the state penitentiary, overpowered and shot an aging guard in an escape attempt. Captured within moments, he was hanged by an angry mob from a light pole near the courthouse square, though the rope broke the first time and Ratliff had to be hauled up for a second hanging. This gave me the distinction of growing up near a place that, for a long while, bore the label "The Town That Lynched Santa Claus."

Merry Christmas. And be careful of strangers coming down your chimney.

1983

Grateful acknowledgment is made to my friend A. C. Greene for use of materials from his book, *The Santa Claus Bank Robbery.*

Confessions of a
White Racist

SHE WAS A BIG, DARK, SORROWFUL WOMAN, my Aunt Clara's
domestic in the dusty little West Texas town of Rotan—the first
black person to register on my young mind. The New Deal was
perhaps a year old, and I was five: a curious and excited farm boy
reveling in his first extended town visit with its indoor plumbing,
daily comic strips, and creamy fresh doughnuts brought home
warm each night from my Uncle John's bakery.

I kept a safe distance in spying on the strange black creature
while she dusted, made beds, swept, and mopped. Though my attentions were constant, we passed no words. I was introverted and
shy; she seemed private, withdrawn, impervious to my stubborn
scrutiny.

"Mama," I asked, "why is the ole nigger woman so sad?" My
mother recoiled. "Oh, honey! Don't call her *that*! They want to be
called colored folks. They get mad when you call 'em niggers."

How typical that the white child would be conditioned to brand
the first black person of his experience with the meanest of racist
terms. And would be rebuked only in self-serving whispers.

The town where I was born discouraged Negro residents. I was
fifteen before moving to where the black man was even statistically
visible. The citizens of our little town willingly fed most Depression hoboes who hopped off freights on the Texas & Pacific to beg
food at our back doors. When an infrequent black hobo appeared,
however, he was driven away with outraged oaths and threats to
call the constable.

I would sit on my father's knee while he sang "The Nigger
Preacher and the Bear." The black preacher is shot through with
cowardice, malapropisms, and so deserted by the presumably white
God to whom he frantically prays that the bear is eventually permitted to squeeze the life from him. One of our family's private
jokes, never told in the presence of company, concerned the hor-
rifying moment when my older brother was discovered in the act

of taking alternate bites off an apple with a Negro boy whose family paused briefly in Putnam. I remembered the scandalized whispers when an eight-year-old cousin was caught playing bridegroom to a little black bride in a backyard mock wedding.

In the middle of World War II we moved to Midland in the oil-rich Permian Basin of Texas. Midland looked both east and west for its influences, 300 miles in each direction. Dallas, to the east, provided an example in its pretentious homes, aggressive boosterism, and select ruling oligarchy. We shared with El Paso an arid landscape not much different from the moon as lately we have come to know it, along with that general unrest indigenous to a people beset over the years by Spanish *conquistadores*, marauding Indians, and those eternal gritty sands shifting and blowing in oven temperatures. Though Midland claimed a disproportionate share of wealth for an isolated village of 12,000 (satisfying fortunes had been established in cattle and cotton before soil erosion, oil strikes, and mini-skyscrapers then reaching twelve stories high had transformed the lonesome territory from agrarian to industrial), my father signed on as an oil-company night watchman for little more than a dollar an hour.

Midland had its "old" pioneer aristocracy. A secondary social formation was comprised of the cream of the awakening oil industry. The perceptive, however, must have discerned that genealogy was prized far beyond the accidents of geology—especially if the genealogy contained an affluent mix. While the district manager of an oil company, even though recently removed from New Jersey or Tulsa, might soon become a power among Rotarians or at the country club, he should never assume his sons would automatically be welcomed everywhere.

The son of the night watchman, the railway clerk, or the town cop (if unusually handsome, exceptionally gifted at athletics, or of stunning scholastic prominence) might be invited to a few parties by the new money. He might even be asked on special occasions (graduation night, for example, or when one of our first-family belles announced her engagement to his fellow co-captain of the basketball squad) to visit some of the old homes. He would also have ample opportunity, however, to ponder why he had been overlooked when invitations went out to other celebrations on Country Club Circle or West Missouri Street.

The son of a certain night watchman did not then suspect half as much as he now understands of inherited limitations, and so he hopefully drove himself to performances beyond his normal athletic capacities as well as to the district debate championship, class offices, roles in amateur theatricals, and work on the school newspaper and yearbook. Such "accomplishments" primarily signify the youth's pathetic thirst for some vague assimilation or acceptance. Just such a mindless, burning lust would eventually prompt him to the most overt racist act of his life.

2.

Because domestic jobs as cooks, maids, butlers, and gardeners were always available in the affluent homes of Midland, the little city's black population was larger and more visible, in the daylight hours anyway, than I had known before. At sundown black women waited in the alleys behind their places of employment for their husbands or sons to fetch them in one quaking old smoke-belching car or another. Then they would rattle off down East 80 past our central business district, the rodeo arena, tin-topped garages advertising mechanics on duty, a Mexican restaurant or two, and on by the Blue Goose Tavern before going south across the railroad track to their shacks or tents, barbecue stands, storefront prayer halls, and beer joints in their lowlands ghetto known as "The Flats." Our town policemen diligently discouraged whites from "being down here after dark." A single carload of white teen-agers in search of beer or general mischief was certain to be stopped by cops warning that "these niggers don't bother us at night and we ain't gonna bother them. You boys go home some night with the clap or get rolled down here, and we never will hear the last of it from your mamas and daddies."

We Midland High School Bulldogs played our well-attended football games on Friday nights; the George Washington Carver Hornets played on what we considered "our field" on Thursday or Saturday nights when it was available. We sometimes visited Carver games, swaggering in our purple and gold letter-jackets, sure of our superiority as men and athletes. We laughed at the high-stepping antics of the Carver band ("They move in jig time," we cracked) and selected the strutting drum majorette most likely to assist in "changing our luck." We were disappointed when the stands failed to erupt into multiple razor fights, as we had every confidence they would.

After one Carver victory we were leaving the stadium, loud and boisterous in the exhilarations of youth, when we passed the Carver football bus loading for its return to The Flats. A big Carver lineman called from the bus, "Hey, Bulldogs, yawl think yawl can play football?" We stood rooted, amazed at his black audacity. "Bet we can beat you," he said. "Yawl get all the newspaper headlines, but we got the team. *Everybody* know a Hornet can sting a ole Bulldog." The Carver lads laughed and hooted. "Ask your coach to scrimmage against us sometimes," another voice called from inside the bus. "Unless yawl are fraidy-cats."

We stood mute as the bus pulled away, though Burton, a wild and wiry little wingback, recovered sufficiently to shout, "Piss on you, you boog fuckers"—for which withering witticism we young gentlemen roundly congratulated him. Over cherry Cokes and hamburgers at the Minute Inn we boasted of how we would stomp those black bastards 60 to 0 if only our authorities would permit.

One might have thought we had proposed naked dancing girls serving free beer in study hall. No sir, a school official said (his mouth puckering as if he had just sampled an alum milkshake), it just wouldn't be done! One of our coaches barked, "We got our hands full playing Abilene and San Angelo back-to-back. I hear any more about this Carver crap, and there'll be enough extra wind-sprints to keep air and ideas off your brains."

Word somehow got around that I had originated the idea of "playing the niggers." Aldrich, the school's self-appointed social arbiter, accommodated me in a fistfight behind the gym by way of straightening out my role. The young lady who most consistently cavorted through my sexual fantasies refused to go out with me again.

3.

When I was sixteen I worked out of the Midland post office as a mailman. My route that summer went to many of our leading homes, some few of which I had violated socially. Frequently a carload of my more privileged contemporaries zipped by on wisps of gasoline, perfume, or beer, the occupants calling back greetings lost on the wind as they headed for a dip in the country-club pool or to the Turners' tennis courts or to the Cowdens' for a patio cookout. The night watchman's son plodded along under the fiery desert sun and the burden of a mailbag, cursing his birthright while indulging in brain-movies about his return to Midland in later years to receive the town's congratulations on the books he had written, the medals he had won at war, and the Hollywood hearts he had broken for mischief and whimsy.

One afternoon in the post office I found my fellow carriers in a private huddle. Slim, a big-boned redneck in his thirties, spoke for the older carriers to the three of us working as the summer-vacation help. "The postmaster is hirin' a nigger," he said. "He says one of us got to take the nigger around our route and train him. Well, *I* ain't gonna. And Red ain't and Don ain't and Cecil ain't. They'll probably try to push the jig off on one of you kids. If you let 'em get away with it, we won't have nothing but nigger carriers in six months." A few minutes later I was called to the postmaster's office.

Postmaster Noel G. Oates was a friendly, easy man who handled his job in a low key, a former mailman who knew about dog-bite and thirst. On that summer afternoon so long ago, however, I would learn that he contained a certain hardness. He began by telling of his difficulty because of the wartime manpower shortage, then said he had hired a young Negro just returned from the military. "I've decided you would be the best man to train him," he said.

"No," I said. "I can't do it."

The postmaster sat a bit straighter in his chair. "Why?"

"Well, none of us wants to do it. We've been talking about it."

"Give me your reasons for not wanting to."

"Well, hell . . . he's a *nigger*. And all the other guys will be mad if I do it. And I don't want everybody from school seeing me work with him."

"We're not gonna debate it," Mr. Oates said. "I've got my job to do, and if you can't do yours you can turn in your time. Anybody else who can't follow orders can turn in their time. You've got until eight o'clock tomorrow morning to make up your mind."

I consulted my father, who said it was the kind of decision each man must make for himself. He sat on a carpenter's sawhorse in the backyard, whittling with his pocket knife, his lower lip bulging with Garrett's Snuff: he understood how I felt; on the other hand, I did need the job. So work it out in my own mind. Pray on it.

The following morning, as I sorted the mail for delivery, Postmaster Oates appeared with Tim—a dark young man in his early twenties, neat and tense. We shook hands (the first time I had shaken hands with a black man); after a few joshing words meant to ease the strain, the postmaster left us. I explained the mail-sorting process to Tim, painfully aware of the malevolent glances the sullen Slim cast, and of the snickers and whispers of Red and Don. (Cecil had turned in his time, on the theory that his own turn at "nursemaiding niggers" was then being planned in secret councils, to become a rack boy in a pool hall—where, ironically, he worked side by side with two black rack boys.) When the rest of us adjourned to Agnes' Café for lunch, Tim ate from a brown bag under a tree at the rear of the post office.

Tim shared my route for two weeks. Though we were carefully polite, we had no conversations beyond the job at hand or routine agreements on the weather. Several times I was embarrassed when we encountered my classmates while walking in affluent neighborhoods. The day Tim was assigned his own route was a happy one for me.

4.

The summer of 1946 began in the oil fields (where, incidentally, I never saw a single black man employed). We lowly roustabouts pissanted heavy joints of pipe, and dug pits and ditches. One stifling July afternoon I emerged from cleaning an oil-storage tank, sweaty and reeking oil, when it occurred to me that no law in the world said I ever had to clean another. I was completing my third or fourth hitch in the oil patch (having lied about my age shortly before my fourteenth birthday to secure a job in a clean-up crew) and such romance as had attended working around hard-drinking, hard-swearing older men had long since faded. Within an hour I had drawn my time.

This impulsive act forced an agonized decision: whether to remain in school or join the Army. I was to have graduated in May, but had permitted coaches, school officials, and the businessmen active in the Bulldog Booster Club to persuade me that I should deliberately fall one credit short of my diploma so I could again serve Midland High on the football field. They made flattering predictions: "Why, a big ole tough boy like you could make All-State. Then all the big Southwest Conference colleges would line up to offer you scholarships."

I came to regret the scheme shortly after agreeing to it: another year of high-school tedium suddenly loomed as pointless, overpoweringly unbearable; I was anxious to seek a larger world. Drake and I had, indeed, sought out the local Navy recruiter just as school ended (selecting the Navy over other military units because it was said to admit few blacks) but I failed the physical because of faulty depth perception. On the basis of a preliminary eye test, an Army recruiter had virtually guaranteed my acceptance and promised I could attain my lacking credit for graduation by passing a high-school equivalency test. On quitting the oil patch I persuaded my parents to sign consenting papers and was given thirty days in which to close out my civilian affairs.

I first hitchhiked to Amarillo, arriving in the back of a pickup truck on top of coops of squawking chickens, where I blew half my $180 bankroll buying bootleg whiskey for two aging prostitutes who delighted my room between the appointments to which they were summoned by a black bellhop. A drunk Indian in an Oklahoma City beer joint guzzled and conned his way through much of my remaining resources on some blowzy promise to introduce a beautiful tribal princess, whom he gave the qualities of Hedy

Lamarr in heat and loincloth. One purposeless morning while touring for fifty cents an old house said to have been the hideout of the outlaw Dalton Brothers near Dodge City, Kansas, I impulsively opted to return to Putnam, Texas, the little town of my birth, for what I dramatically assumed would be my last inspection. A couple of days later, a bit road-grimy, I arrived in the Texas village of Albany with only seven dollars. Two of these were invested in a decrepit hotel room.

The bellhop was a fat, middle-aged Negro with drooping eyelids; though I had only a small canvas bag he insisted on taking it to my room. He opened the steamy room's single window, drew a pitcher of tepid tap water, and made other busy-work motions. "Young mister," he said, "you like to buy a little pussy?"

Well, maybe. How much was it?

"You work that out with the girl. You ever changed your luck?"

Though I knew full-well what he meant I blurted, "What?"

"Colored nookie. You ever had you any colored nookie?"

Well, no.

"You got anything against it?"

Well. No. Not really.

"She be here in a half-hour," he promised, then extracted one of my remaining dollars as his service charge.

I think I began the transaction as a lark; certainly I was mindful of my destitute condition more than 200 miles from home, though by the time I heard the lady's knock my enthusiasm was genuine. Possibly this was because I had convinced myself she would be a ringer for Lena Horne, down to her very light, bare skin. I was startled when she proved bony, darker than bittersweet chocolate, and wildly frizzy-haired. She was perhaps seven years my senior, perhaps ten; she wore a sagging skirt and a thin blouse denying even the promise of breasts.

"Well," I said. "How much?"

"Ten dollar straight and fifteen dollar for French," she mumbled.

"Well, I'll give you three for a straight date."

"Shit! Eight, or we can't do no business."

"I ain't got that much."

"How much you got?"

"Four," I admitted. "And maybe a little change."

"Goddamn you," she flared. "And here I went and dressed and owe a man a goddamn taxi-fare! You white asses come over here from Breckenridge and Abilene and Cisco looking to get your jassam free. I got two little babies to feed."

"Oh," I said, inanely, "I didn't know you were married."

"Kiss my dead ass," the disgusted young woman said, slamming the door.

5.

At Fort Sam Houston the authorities shoved a half-dozen of us on the train for shipment to our basic-training tortures in New Jersey. We were all Texans, all white, none as old as nineteen. We arrived at the Trenton station wrung-out, pale, wrinkled, and shorn of our earlier confidence.

Awaiting transportation to Fort Dix, we went into a lunchroom. Two black men entered. One sat on a stool to my immediate right. Manning of San Angelo and Edwards of Sweetwater lifted their eyebrows, watching carefully to see what I would do.

Fifteen years later, visiting home, I was piously lecturing my relatives on the insanities of racial exclusions when my mother laughed and said, "Lawrence, do you remember when some niggers set down by you the first day you got up to New Jersey? And what a fuss you made?"

Whatever do you mean?

Mother returned from her rummagings in an old trunk, bringing a letter I barely recognized to be in my own hand:

> *Dear Folks. Got here Thursday on the train from Ft. Sam. We no more than set down in the depot to eat than some niggers plopped down next to us and I can tell you they didn't stay long. We told them we were from Texas and we didn't go for that stuff, and believe-you-me they cleared out in a hurry. . . .*

It is interesting to speculate on why this fiction was composed, for we had actually eaten our hamburgers in a choked and humble silence.

6.

President Truman had not yet issued his order desegregating the military. Black troops at Fort Dix were fed and quartered apart from us, served by their own PXs and service clubs. Except when we encountered them as they marched out to a rifle range while we marched in from the field, we had no contact. I did not think this peculiar: who recalls seeing John Wayne or Humphrey Bogart assisted in their heroics by black troops as they tamed the Japs or routed Nazis? Had I not known that during World War II black troops had rebelled against segregationist practices at Midland Army Air Field by refusing to come out of their barracks one morning (they were sprayed with pressurized fire hoses) I would not have suspected that Negro GIs even marginally helped defeat Hitler.

The Army sent me to Fort Monmouth to flunk out of cryptography school, radio operator's school, and radio repair school. Fort Monmouth did, however, introduce me to racial integration, though only our "service" troops (cooks, bakers, supply-room toilers) were black. Here, too, I came face-to-face with my first black officer and felt a moment of panic while old attitudes struggled with newly acquired military disciplines: then I snapped him a proper salute.

The only black man among the service troops I came to know more than slightly was Brewster, a cook from Alabama. Where most of us had less than a year's military service, Brewster had ten; he had served in France, and had several times reached the rank of sergeant only to be restored to lower stations after certain picky military regulations had been strictly interpreted. "I been busted for drinkin' and I been busted for thinkin,'" he liked to say, "and thinkin' get you in *boo-coo* more trouble."

"Yawl goddamn privates shut your faces and let us private first classes get our rest," he might sing out from cooks' quarters shortly after lights-out. The white troops would laugh and say ole Brewster was something else, a real card, a good goddamn nigger.

On weekends I became a regular visitor, sitting on Brewster's footlocker while we drank vodka from paper cups, chasing it with tins of GI fruit juices he had liberated from the mess hall. Brewster was full of outrageous tales of the women he had loved from Mobile to Pigalle, the officers he had outwitted, the big deals he had temporarily enjoyed before they turned to clabber. He also confessed, in the same high glee, to his own victimizations and defeats; I now know he had a marvelous sense of the absurd and cunning instincts for survival. I realized that Brewster was brighter than most people I had known, more complex, full of hidden secrets and silent victories. Though this worried me as being against the Lord's intent, I continued to sit at his feet.

One night the vodka passed back and forth enough that some few old inhibitions flew away; I found myself drinking from the same bottle with the black man, not bothering to wipe the neck off, and feeling a little noble and extremely daring. I blurted out a question: "What's it really like to be a . . . a Knee-Grow in a white outfit?"

Brewster paused with the vodka bottle near his mouth and stared into my eyes. "It's all right," he said, slowly. "If you ain't got no pride."

After a few throbbing seconds of silence he burst into laughter. I was vastly relieved, because then I could laugh too.

7.

The Army suspended its segregated customs in stockades where prisoners served time for breaches of military etiquette, perhaps to demonstrate to what low estate troublemakers might sink.

One day I drew detail as a prisoner chaser. My duty was to trail three stockade baddies with an M-1 rifle while they emptied garbage cans and ash cans into a truck for disposal in the post incinerators. Rumor had it that if one permitted a prisoner to escape, he must serve the balance of the escapee's time. I drew three long-termers: a tall, round-shouldered black man, and two white men. I somehow assumed that the black man was the potential jail-breaker; through the morning I kept my M-1 so nervously at the ready that had he sneezed unannounced it might have cost him his liver.

We had started to the incinerators when our driver suddenly applied the brakes to avoid running a stop sign. I catapulted across the truck bed, bouncing off my charges, my rifle sailing away. One horrible thought occurred to me: *I'll be killed now or court-martialed later.* Frantically I struggled up, shedding ashes, egg shells, and old orange peels, to find myself staring into the barrel of my M-1—and the tall black man behind it. "Bang!" my prisoner said, softly, before handing my weapon back. "Hey, driver," he called out, laughing fit to break a stitch. "Be careful up there—you goddamn near killed my guard, and it would of went on my record."

In the spring of 1947, I was threatened with shipment to the Army of Occupation in Germany where, a stern major promised, I might anticipate frequent KP, the "honor" of guard duty as a routine, and the permanent rank of private. Pentagon Gods were slightly kinder: I was ordered to the Signal Corps Photo Center in Astoria, Long Island, and I soon discovered the sophistications of Times Square, a Brooklyn telephone operator, and any number of friendly taverns.

The arrival of black troops at the Photo Center coincided with my own. They were to be methodically assimilated: to sit with us at table, sleep alongside us, and be assigned jobs without regard to color. Lt. Ken Thomas, a slim and erect young North Carolinian, was company commander; I was, in effect, his administrative aide. "Washington orders us to make this thing work," he said of our integrated unit. "They've assigned me a Negro first sergeant. The white troops may resent him. I won't tolerate any unmilitary displays. I hear any racial slurs around here, I'll be mighty hard to live with."

First Sergeant Percy, a native of rural Georgia, had more than a decade in the Army. Though he carried himself with careful dignity, I would soon learn his private fears. "When a man is colored he can't do everything he like to do," Sergeant Percy confided. "I never served with white troops before. They've never served with my kind. Everybody got to step real easy. We can't let the troops know we're walking on eggshells, though. I wear a Top's stripes and draw a Top's pay, and I'm gonna *act* like a Top."

Perhaps not fully appreciating the problem, I said, "You've got the rank. Use it."

Sergeant Percy's smile was a bit cynical. "Someday," he said, "some white GI gonna bow his ass up at what I got to tell him. Then I'll need a little white rank in here to back me up. I'm recommending Lieutenant Thomas make you corporal immediately, and a sergeant sixty days later—if you work out. You don't work out, you can go soldier for somebody that need you."

My relationship with Sergeant Percy was proper and generally easy—though not until years later would I realize we had not been the close friends I once presumed. We listened to baseball on his radio (bantering over whether to tune in "his" racially integrated Dodgers or "my" then-segregated Giants) and occasionally each went to see his favorite—but we never went to a game together. Though we shared a table in the mess hall and talked over drinks in my private squadroom after retreat formation, he never invited me to his apartment, nor do I recall asking him to an evening on the town. I gave him a piece of china for his wedding but was not invited (nor did I consider that I might be) to the ceremony.

A frequent embarrassment was old Sergeant Smitty, a thirty-year man, serving his final hitch before retirement, whom we loosely utilized as company runner. By noon, Sergeant Smitty had paid several duty calls on the nearby Studio Bar, where he was known for his partiality to rotgut bourbon chased by draft beer. By mid-afternoon his old face was fire-red, his shirt flapped out over his bloated belly and he literally drooled tobacco juices while spinning as many yarns about the glories of The Old Army as his slurred speech permitted.

Sergeant Smitty invariably committed the same racial indiscretion. Halfway through some tale of his triumphs as a youthful muleskinner in Panama, or while relating a particularly satisfying old debauchery in the Orient's sin palaces, he would refer to one or another "nigger." Then he would realize that he had done something wrong or out-of-joint. His besotted old brain would grapple with the mystery as he wheezed and tottered in confusion, blinking at Sergeant Percy until he could recognize him as black. "I'm sorry, Sarjint," he invariably said—and never without a certain shy shame—"I plumb forgot you're colored." Sergeant Percy routinely responded, "That's all right, Sergeant. Sometimes I forget it myself."

Young Lieutenant Porterfield was Officer of the Day when two drunken GIs engaged in a bloody fistfight. One was white and the other black, but no racial slurs were delivered. Neither did the racially mixed spectators jump into the fight—which had originated over who owned how much liquor remaining in a common jug. Lieutenant Porterfield, however, became flustered; he spoke loudly enough to the Charge of Quarters that all could hear: "We're sitting on a powder keg. All we need to kick off a bloody race riot is one incident like this. I tell you, it won't work."

Sergeant Percy was icily furious in protesting to Lieutenant Thomas: "Sergeant Smith's just old and ignorant and don't know no better. But that Lieutenant Porterfield, he *supposed* to be an officer and a gentleman." Privately he railed, "Race riot, shit! The only way we gonna have a race riot is if peckerwoods like that Porterfield talk us into one."

The day came when I received my own come-uppance. A cute black chick employed at the Photo Center began to find excuses to visit the Orderly Room, determinedly flirting with Sergeant Percy. One day he grumbled that he wished the lady would cease her attentions because he wasn't "available."

"*I* am," I said. "Why don't you fix me up?"

"Sure I will," he said, coolly. "Then maybe you'll take me to Texas on furlough and fix me up with one of your friends." For the next few days we were excessively cordial.

8.

In August, on a weekend outing to Jones Beach, I slept for hours under the sun and had to go to the post hospital with severe burns. Then followed recuperation in my squadroom. Twice each day, by holding to supporting objects, I managed to anoint the seared flesh with lotions and salves. Since a trip to the mess hall was impossible, Sergeant Percy saw that KPs brought trays to my quarters.

One day a young black man from Philadelphia looked in. Twice a day for two weeks Private First Class Robinson called to sweep and mop my room, change the linens, carry out laundry; sometimes he brought snacks or magazines. We talked about sports, Robinson's foul luck in not having been selected for Officer's Candidate School, and my own wish to quit the military.

I was suspicious of Robinson's attentions. Why would a black man devote so much labor to a white man he hardly knew? Perhaps he wanted favors I might bestow as company clerk: KP with less frequency than normal, an occasional three-day pass, a cushy job. I even considered the possibility that Robinson's attentions might be sexual. As time passed and he asked no favors, however, my suspicions changed to curiosity. One night I stammered thanks. "Don't mention it," he said. "This is part of my life's work." I thought this over while Robinson pushed the mop back and forth. "What were you in civilian life?" I asked. "A porter?"

Robinson gave me a strange, unbelieving look. "No, Sergeant," he said. "I was a student in a seminary, studying to become a minister. I've had three years of college." He never came back.

9.

Several times I hinted to black soldiers with whom a certain rapport was assumed of my willingness to accompany them on one of their sojourns to Harlem. These generous offers were met with vague references to some unspecified future.

Harlem was a foreign port in the mind, a paradise where Clark Gable, conveniently shipwrecked, cavorted with dusky dancing belles while some fat, jolly chieftain urged on him feasts of suckling pig and ritual honors.

One adventurous evening I determined to explore New York's dark interior in the absence of a native guide. Three other white crackers (from Georgia, West Virginia, and Texas) accompanied me. We ordered a reluctant white cabbie to deliver us to "the heart of Harlem." "It's no skin off my ass," the cabbie said, "but I won't be surprised when the Army comes up four soldiers short tomorrow. Them damn niggers will rob you blind and leave you dead in a alley."

Harlem was not the kind of street carnival I had imagined. There were the old eyesores and dangers one would later come to expect in other black ghettos: sorry old tenement buildings, peeling and rotting in dull reds and grays; pawnshops with their pitiful treasures locked behind iron grills; hole-in-the-wall liquor stores with gaudy displays of half-pints; storefront missions smelling of sweat and disinfectants; poor restaurants specializing in chicken wings or cheap barbecue plates; crowded, noisy bars wailing soul music above the human babble; clots of gutter trash and street debris.

We had not advanced a block before a comely young hooker accosted us. While we stood making uneasy conversation a sharply dressed Negro man approached us. "You got more sense than to hustle them here," he scolded the streetwalker. "You trying to get somebody hurt? Go on over to Chunky's to hustle your ass." And to us: "Get on out from here. This a bad-ass street and it won't do nothing for you."

We fled rapidly down the sidewalk, fending off happy drunks who invited us to buy them drinks and sullen ones demanding money. A grossly fat woman in a silk print dress dashed from a door to damn us in a raging, profane gibberish. Cool-eyed dudes in padded-shoulder sport coats, tapered trousers, and porkpie hats offered to provide certain recreations for slight profits. Street urchins howled and danced with their hands out, berating us when our conciliatory contributions proved miserly beyond their expectations. A drunk in tattered clothing sipped the last dregs from a wine bottle. He offered his hand, and as one of our number reached to take it the drunk laughed and broke the wine bottle under our feet, showering us with glass particles and wine droplets.

We ducked into a bar where a dozen men and women laughed and talked above the throbbing juke box. All sounds except the music seemed to stop as we entered, doubtless looking a bit panicky and trying to cover up by affecting a blustering chatter. "The Marines have landed," somebody hooted. My companion from West Virginia didn't help by responding, "Marines, my ass, Mac! We're soldiers."

The bartender hesitated when we ordered beers, though he finally produced them. He kept a close watch, however, and came quickly when a slight, reed-thin man the color of lightly creamed coffee, imagining we were staring too openly at his lady friend, cursed us as "goddamn mother-fuckin' white hunters"—white men on the prowl for black women.

The bartender, aided by the aroused citizen's lady friend, persuaded him to move to a table where he might find us less offensive. Then he leaned across the bar: a burly, middle-aged, slick-bald man. "What you boys lost in Harlem?" he demanded. Not waiting for an answer he said, "Some places in Harlem you can go and everything be just dandy. This not one of 'em. All you gonna find here is trouble—hot weather like this, shit it just *breed* meanness. People get all hot and sticky and about half out of their heads." He snapped and crackled a bar rag, scowling. "You boys got money for a taxi?" We nodded. "I'll phone you a taxi and you ride on out of here."

Safely back in midtown Manhattan, we speculated on the reasons for our hostile reception. West Virginia saw no riddle: niggers were niggers and could be expected to act like niggers. Georgia, who had done a hitch in Army counterintelligence, was mindful of the Communistic influences pervading Harlem. My Texas friend, of a genteel and moneyed old family, felt that much of what we had seen and heard could be attributed to a lack of proper breeding. I thought that possibly all three of my companions were a little bit correct.

10.

Staff Sergeant Hutchinson, a black man from Louisiana, had more than ten years' exemplary service when family problems turned him into an habitual AWOL. He explained why he needed emergency leave: "My wife, she pretty young and I been away in the Army so much and now trouble has come. I think a leave straighten her out. We can talk, it might get her thinkin' on our babies again."

Lieutenant Thomas granted the emergency leave and several subsequent ones. Sergeant Hutchinson's allotted leave time expired; his domestic torment did not. Higher brass refused any more leaves, so Hutchinson went over the hill. He was let off with company punishment. For subsequent offenses, however, he was reduced to private and sent to the military stockade on Governors Island. Within a week after completing each sentence, Hutchinson would disappear. The fourth time he was apprehended, I was sent to a stockade near Shreveport to return him to New York under guard.

Master Sergeant Bad ran his stockade much as I imagine Hitler commanded the Third Reich. He was broad, florid-faced, a ham-handed son of Ohio, and a former deputy sheriff. He received me while relaxing among his private collection of handcuffs, zip guns, switch-blade knives, and rubber stanchions artistically mounted on beaver board behind his desk. He was drinking coffee served by an obsequious prisoner who bowed out of the room as if departing the odor of royalty. "Prisoners are shit!" Master Sergeant Bad thundered at the bowing lackey. "Sound off!" "Prisoners are shit!" the lackey obediently bawled.

Reading my orders Master Sergeant Bad said, "That's a smart-ass nigger you've come after, Sarjint." Well, I said, Hutchinson had been a good soldier before his family torments. "He tried that sob-sister shit on me," he said. "I told him if his old lady was humpin' outside the home he wasn't no worse off than half the white men I know and all the niggers."

He entertained me with stories of all the heads he had been privileged to knock. Criminal types could never be rehabilitated beyond their lower instincts: "They just like a bad buckin' broncho or a mean dawg. You got to clobber the puredee shit out of 'em often enough they'll remember who's boss." Niggers, he said, were more troublesome than whites: they didn't feel as much pain, and they had shorter memories.

Master Sergeant Bad led me through three locks and by a cadre of guards. As we approached the bullpen cell where Hutchinson and other transient offenders bunked, he bellowed, "Prisoners, Up!" There was a wild stampede of nervous sweaty flesh; the prisoners sprinted into a single long rank facing the door and perhaps six feet from the bars. "You're drag-assin', you're drag-assin'," the sergeant accused. "Come again! Fall out!" The prisoners rushed back to their assigned bunks, straining and grunting. Some had not yet reached their proper places when their master thundered, "Prisoners, Up!"—again inspiring the frantic forward scramble. Bad ran the prisoners through the exhausting exercise again and again.

When the prisoners had lined up to his satisfaction, Master Sergeant Bad spat, "Prisoner Six . . . toe the line!" Hutchinson leaped from the ranks as if kicked, his toes exactly touching a thin red line extending the length of the cell and ending no more than a foot from the bars. "They fuck up and step on that line," Bad said, "and I treat 'em to a little practice with some ass-paddlin' on the side. We call it a Piss party." He raised his voice: "Prisoners, do I give good parties? Sound off!"

"Yessir!" the prisoners shouted.

"Had one old jug-butted boy never did learn to toe the line without steppin' on it," the Sergeant said. "Dumb goddamn nigger! He come here weighing two hunnert pounds and left with a skinny ass didn't have nothing on it but calluses and blood."

Hutchinson had unfortunately relaxed his West Point brace; just as he cut his eyes ever-so-slightly toward us, Master Sergeant Bad screamed, "What you wallin' them maroon eyes at, you burr-headed bastard? Goddamn your black hide, you're in my custody till I sign your release slip. I tell you to eat shit you *eat it*, right? Sound off!"

"Yessir," Hutchinson barked.

"You're a smart-ass runaway nigger, ain't you? Sound off!"

"Yessir!"

"You got shit for brains and piss in your blood. Sound off!"

"Yessir!"

Hutchinson was forced to affirm every insult Master Sergeant Bad was capable of delivering. Nothing was out of bounds: Hutchinson's race, sex habits, wife, and mother. Marching the prisoner to the office, his tormentor prodded him in the ribs with a nightstick. While he signed papers to transfer the prisoner, he warned Hutchinson what might happen to his black ass should it ever again know that particular stockade.

Hutchinson remained discreetly silent while a driver delivered us to the Shreveport train station. When we were alone he said, "Man, I'm gladder to see you than Christmas. That Sergeant Bad, he the meanest mutha in uniform. Especially if you colored." Had he actually hit Hutchinson? "Name me a day he didn't," the black man said. Later, when I delivered Hutchinson to Governors Island, and he was being stripped for processing, a ferret-faced white corporal grinned at welts and bumps on his back and shoulders. "I guess you got those falling in the shower, didn't you?"

"Yessir!" Hutchinson said.

II.

Down in Louisiana, handcuffed to my prisoner as regulations prescribed, I boarded the train; we took seats near the rear of a coach car. A conductor approached, apprehensively eyeing my side-arm. "You gonna have to take him to the colored section," he said, pointing at Hutchinson. No, my prisoner would go where I went—and I was not going to any colored section.

There was a delay while the Shreveport station sent reinforcements. A civilian with a public-relations smile and a squishy handshake was full of soft Southern assurances that he knew I could understand and sympathize with the railroad's position in honoring local customs. No, I did not, and would remain in place with my prisoner. The baffled railroaders, faced with conflicting authority, decided in favor of the man with the gun: "But really, suh, the dining car *must* be off-limits. Any violation will unfortunately require the police."

Hutchinson slept or feigned sleep, arousing only to share the gummy sandwiches and tepid soft drinks purchased from an aisle barker, or to visit the washroom with his guard closely trailing. After each trip a porter, called by the alert conductor, entered the washroom for purposes of fumigation. "Hello, Brother," he said in a whisper to Hutchinson on each occasion. A skinny white man in a short-sleeved sport shirt, with the seedy look of a failed road drummer, grew talkative as he siphoned off bourbon in the seat behind us. He leaned forward to cool our faces with whiskey breezes while telling how the white man had busted a gut to help the Nigra but the Nigra wouldn't help himself: refused work, stayed drunk or in jail, stole with more talent than Gypsies. "Don't you know that boy's closer to Heaven right now than most niggers ever get? Riding with white folks, havin' em look after him." When I replied that Hutchinson's care was provided at gunpoint, and therefore might not be fully appreciated, he looked at me with suspicion. Soon he began whispering around the car: why was that damned black nigger outlaw allowed to ride in the same coach with patriotic, God-fearing white people? A conductor moved the troublemaker to another car when I explained that should he further disturb me or my prisoner it would be both my sworn duty and my personal pleasure to shoot him.

At Washington the train became racially integrated. Hutchinson was relieved: "Man, I'm glad to be rid of them peckerwoods. All that shit about me being in Heaven . . ."

I apologized for the peckerwood's remarks, noting that I had silenced him and had him moved. You're back among friends, I said, so relax.

"You didn't do me no favors bringing me up on that white car, Sarjint," Hutchinson said. "I would rather have rode with my own people." Such a possibility had not occurred to me.

12.

When I left the Army in mid-1949, the Photo Center had suffered no major incidents; I considered our "experiment" a success. In retrospect, I see it as more of a compromise or accommodation. For all his bold talk of "acting like a Top" and treating everyone uniformly, I now know that Sergeant Percy gave more severe tongue-lashings or punishments to erring black soldiers than to whites. On the other hand, I spoke softly to black soldiers in need of company disciplines, while leaning heavily on whites who I feared might give Sergeant Percy difficulty. We had no such reverse-racist policy as a matter of understanding: it merely evolved out of caution born of our unspoken fears.

It was never suggested that our Enlisted Men's Club be host to a dance or other social affair which might mingle drinking with social integration between two races and two sexes. And while, theoretically, we could bring out dates or spouses to the EM Club three nights in the week, few white GIs did so; I don't recall ever seeing a black woman there. On base, the troops themselves intermingled freely. We played poker and drank together, exchanged the rough, friendly insults traditional between soldiers. We played as equals on the post football, basketball, and baseball teams. On outings when the Army provided transportation to beaches, boxing matches, or other diversions, I recall no particular groupings or division by color. When a half-dozen white civilian toughs beat and put the boots to two black soldiers in a Queens bar, two dozen of us—black and white—marched on the bar to clean it of Irish influences. When we left the Photo Center to seek our private amusements, however, one rarely saw racially mixed groups troop out the front gate. I can now recall the names of only a half-dozen blacks with whom I soldiered—and am amazed to realize how little of their personal lives I learned. We simply didn't know each other.

The night following my discharge a captain from upstate New York invited me to the Officers' Club. I had always considered the captain a good man, and gave him credit for his contributions to our integrated post; he seemed friendly to the black troops and had assigned them jobs and promotions in his office without apparent bias. For several hours we reveled, other officers joining our table to toast my new civilian status and to wish me luck "on the outside." (No black officers were present; indeed, despite the integration of enlisted troops only two or three black officers were among the several dozen assigned to the Photo Center.)

Late in the evening my host expressed regrets that I had accepted my discharge: he felt I was career material. Well, I said, I wanted to attend college and thought perhaps I had it in me to write.

The captain lowered his voice: "I really don't blame you. I might resign my commission if I were younger and didn't have so much time in. There's no future in the Army if they continue to mix the races."

13.

Perhaps the Army's brand of racial integration had its limitations or dirty little secrets, but when I returned to my native Southwest I would again encounter a society totally segregated.

Among the six thousand students then at Texas Tech, in Lubbock, was not a single black face. Lubbock was one of those growing, sprawling, newly prosperous cities the South and Southwest seemed to spew in the postwar boom—cities rising out of the desert, or from the pine thickets, multiplying themselves for reasons not often apparent.

A young, toothy minister full of prattle of his love for Jesus and Jesus' love for all, singled me out at a meeting in the Baptist Student Union (to which I had been attracted in the courtship of a particularly well-stacked young child of God) and asked, "What might we, as Christians, do to better serve the Lord in our daily contacts with others?" I answered something like, "End our hypocrisy in treating the black man like a slave or an animal, while claiming fidelity to Christian brotherhood." The young minister's Jesus-loving face caved in, his eyes glazed over; he stuttered aimlessly until someone else suggested that we might visit civic clubs to urge Christian principles on businessmen—which the minister gratefully endorsed.

On New Year's Day, 1952, I drew a seat in the Sun Bowl at El Paso near three former Texas Tech football players on hand to watch their old school try College of the Pacific. The California school's star was Eddie Macon, a lithe and speedy black man named to several All-America teams. The ex-Red Raiders could hardly contain themselves while waiting for "Ole Gerald and Ole Red to lay that jitterbuggin' jig out," as one of the less subtle old grads promised everyone within earshot. Indeed, when Macon carried the ball on the initial play, he was laid low behind the scrimmage line. Great approving roars and whoops stirred Tech partisans: normal enough. What was perhaps less normal was the number of persons who cried, "Kill that black ape," and other racist exhortations.

Late in the game, with Texas Tech two touchdowns ahead and obviously in control, the same fans cheered Eddie Macon for his fine play, which had included a long touchdown run. My thought was one I wouldn't have had a few years earlier: that all their cheers could not erase the original ugliness. For the first time I was thinking about our segregated society, observing it for what it was. Though my experiences in the Army and in the East were never as assimilating as I then presumed, the exposure to black men at least had taught me that they had minds, dreams, and hurts like the rest of us, and in no way deserved their automatic exclusions. It wasn't so much seeing the black citizen without social or economic opportunity, or confined to his slums and inferior schools—though, God knows, these were major causes of our terrible social impasse. No, it was the million mindless "little" humiliations that stirred my tardy rage and soon caused me to be looked on as a little crazy and unreliable.

Working on the sports desk of a West Texas newspaper, I ordered photographs of the local Negro high-school basketball team—only to be instructed that the paper's policy precluded publication of "nigger art." (And, it developed, wedding or engagement announcements, or almost anything the black citizen involved himself in except crime or violent death.) For years the newspaper ignored the black community's plea that "Negro" be capitalized in print.

The President of the Negro Chamber of Commerce appeared to be reasonably bright and articulate, but held a janitor's job for a white concern prone to brag about its civic contributions. A Cuban-born baseball player for the local Longhorn League entry, dark enough to invite speculation, might be cheered for pitching a two-hitter, but an hour later he might be refused service at a restaurant. When I accompanied policemen in their patrol cars in my role as police reporter, I was almost certain to see some Negro hailed as "Hey, Boy!" and forced to stand respectfully with a flashlight in his eyes while explaining where he was going on the public street. Though oil-field workers and ranch hands might brawl with beer bottles or knives in their hillbilly-music emporiums, police responded only when carnage prompted the worried owners to call for assistance. In black clubs, however, police were always present: circling the dance floor, hard-eyeing the customers, checking for liquor violations or concealed weapons. On slow nights when traffic patrol or station-house duty failed to excite, it was routine to hear officers say, "Let's go bust us a few jigs."

Any black man called for jury duty was excused from service on one grounds or another—once the lawyers, and possibly the judge, had properly enjoyed him: "You the same Willie Johnson who beats his wife and works as a bellhop over at the ho-tel selling bootleg liquor?" Condescending chuckles would sweep the courtroom while the poor black man struggled with the question.

I went to my editor with a suggestion that we run a series on double standards in our courts, police operations, and other public institutions. He tried to laugh the subject away, but said he would speak to the publisher. Weeks passed. When I brought up the topic again, the editor told me to write a sample of what I had in mind. I turned in a well-documented story, and heard no more. One night when we shared more drink than was good for secrets, I raised the sore subject again. "Look," he said. "Stop spinning your wheels.

The publisher hit the ceiling when I mentioned your goddamn nigger series. If I turned in that story you wrote he'd probably fire us both."

Dammit, I said, the obligation of a newspaper was to publish the facts.

My editor, who had already served on a half-dozen newspapers without being hurt in any big crusades, grinned cynically. "The duty of *this* newspaper," he said, "is to make money and boost the town and confine our muckraking to bitching about taxes. I understood that when I took my job."

14.

An old friend had become addicted to a fundamentalist brand of religion. Each beer I drank, each weak oath I muttered, each awkward cowboy waltz my legs attempted at roadside honky-tonks, brought dire predictions of the temperatures my soul would know through eternity's long and parching night. One day he invited me to attend a black Sunday School class he taught on alternate Sundays: he had headed a drive of his sect to establish a church of The Faith among Negroes. Well, I thought, perhaps some good has come from his crazed commitments. Maybe he would get to know the black person as an individual, not merely as somebody to mow his lawn or do his chores.

How long had he been teaching the black class?

Oh, for almost a year.

And how did he approach the task?

He sprang to a small blackboard in his study and began to draw crude pictures to illustrate creation as reported in Genesis: the sun to represent light, stick figures representing Adam and Eve, and so on. His art was accompanied by Dick-and-Jane prattle to explain the language of the Bible.

"Do you think all that primitive art is necessary?" I asked.

"Oh, sure," he laughed. "Those niggers eat it up. You got to put on a show to keep their attention. They're just like a bunch of little children, or monkeys."

My father was working on a construction job; one night he told me how much fun the crew had out of "Nigger James."

"He's a purty good ole nigger," Dad said of the black man hired to step-and-fetch for carpenters, plumbers, and other craftsmen. "He don't hardly ever get mad, though we guy and hoo-raw him a right smart." He told how one of the white carpenters had asked, "Why all you black boys have such terrible smells." James had finally agreed, under duress, that perhaps black people were not as inherently sanitary as whites. "If you don't take more baths," the white bully instructed, "we're gonna give you a GI bath on pay-day." James reportedly laughed, perhaps nervously, in promising to mind his sanitation. On payday, the fastidious carpenter filled a barrel with cold water, provided brushes and strong soaps, and invited his companions to help scrub James down.

Though my father had not participated in the scrubbing, he was almost helpless with laughter in recounting the scene. "You ought to a-seen that nigger fight and squawl. Lord God, you would a-thought they was tryin' to electrocute him. They throwed him in that barrel clothes and all, and scrubbed him awhile and then let him go. He taken it so well they made up a little collection and give him five dollars."

"Well, Jesus Christ!" I exploded. "How the hell else could he take it, without you peckerwoods hanging him?"

My father's face froze; he picked up his newspaper, crackling it angrily. When he had regained control he said, "They were just havin' a little fun. Nobody was tryin' to hurt him. You don't seem to know the difference."

15.

When I came to Washington in 1954 as assistant to a Texas Congressman, I assumed our nation's capital to be a showplace of racial equalities and opportunities.

It soon became apparent on Capitol Hill that Negroes were only a small part of democracy's daily operations. Some few atypical Senators and Congressmen had a showcase black or two on their staffs; one rarely saw the Negro among the several thousand Hill employees, however, except in his role as waiter, mailman, elevator operator, custodian, truck driver, or lower-echelon committee clerk. With few exceptions, only Negro Congressmen such as

Adam Clayton Powell or Chicago's William Dawson trusted their black employees with anything more than minor tasks.

The District of Columbia was then on its way to becoming our first major city with a black majority. Yet the District was ruled by Congressional Committees heavily weighted with powerful old Dixiecrats to whom "integration" had become the foulest word in the language. Their contributions to District schools ended with harassing a superintendent whom they blamed for excess enthusiasm in trying to make integrated classrooms work. Laws enacted by Congress permitted loan sharks, wig sellers, used-car tycoons, or other dollar-oriented types to prey on the black poor virtually without regulation. While adequate public housing was never raised, bus fares often were. Slums were knocked down not to provide decent low-cost housing, but to reclaim preferred lands where private developers were thriving through their expensive high-rises and town houses; displaced blacks were forced into other crowded ghettos. While officially Congress refused Home Rule to Washington because "Our forefathers intended this to be a Federal City," more than one statesman privately expressed his real fear: the election of "a nigger mayor," whom it would not do to have greeting Queen Elizabeth or Khruschev should they visit. A liaison man to Capitol Hill from the metropolitan police department understood why funds for the Police Boys Club were increasingly difficult to raise: nobody wanted to donate to "a bunch of little pickaninnies."

The Texas State Society, composed of several hundred Texans in Washington including Senator Lyndon B. Johnson and Speaker Sam Rayburn, then maintained segregation by requiring that multiple members in good standing sponsor all proposed new members; a select panel screened applicants. When word got around in mid-1955 that several Young Turks might sponsor a black candidate, we received suggestions from congressional offices, well-connected lobbyists, old biddies known for their social pretentions, and others in the hierarchy that we ran the risk of embarrassing our bosses should we persist.

Our West Texas Congressional District was inflamed by the 1957 civil-rights bill, mail running hundreds to one (or maybe a thousand to nothing) against. Not all the fearful mail came from sour-dough cowhands or oil-field rednecks: bankers' wives, news-paper reporters, ministers, oil-company bigwigs, old school chums, and Chamber of Commerce types wrote of Communistic influences at work in Washington. The mayor of a thriving city told my Congressman, "I feel like posting machine gunners on the outskirts of town, and mowing down every federal son-of-a-bitch who comes down Highway 80." A bank president voiced his disillusion: "You young men want to change the rules. Well, I like the old rules. If I could find somebody seventy-five years old running for Congress, I'd vote for him without asking if he was Prohibitionist or Vegetarian. I'd figure him to have his racial pride."

There was a limited mingling among the races on a social basis in Washington in the 1950s and early 1960s. Friendships did exist with blacks who were among the few Hill employees, executive agency middle ranks, a smattering of newsmen, lawyers, doctors, military officers, or embassy attachés.

These were from the Negro elite; few of these even discussed race except with reluctance. They had struggled out of their own private ghettos; now they wanted to forget them: one soon discovered that not only the night watchman's son desired social assimilation more than was good for his character. They might have served as bridges of understanding to a small but influential segment of the white world.

Possibly I do them a disservice: perhaps many had experienced so many rejections they had despaired. "A white man ought to assume that if the Negro before him is twenty-five years old, he has had twenty, if not twenty-five, years of insults and rebuffs, and that that Negro may have had quite enough," John A. Williams has written. "A white man ought to assume that, and if he had any sense he would."

I have had an honest, easy rapport with only one black man. Moe and I were thick in the early 1960s, when some racial progress—however reluctant—seemed in the air. He was then in his forties, and worked on Capitol Hill under the patronage of a California Senator. Moe had originally come from the Denver slums, was a long-time Los Angeles resident, an Army veteran, and had pieced together three years of college by attending nights and in short stretches as his pocketbook permitted. Though he was a minor functionary in the U.S. Senate Post Office, Moe was hip to what was happening to a degree that continues to escape many of our public officials.

Moe warned four or five years before Watts that a Watts was destined to happen—though he predicted that ghetto outbursts would first occur in the great cities of the East, which he considered much more segregationist than the American West. Over many a drink and until numerous dawns he reviewed the rots and ruins of his black world, the white man's indifferences, his own personal humiliations. What made this so effective was the cool, matter-of-fact manner in which Moe recited.

"Driving across country," he said, "black people key their kidneys to their gasoline tanks. We know there are more mean bastards than not; we don't assume anything good. So we pull up to the gas tanks when we get nature's urge, but before we ask the man to fill 'er up we inquire if his rest room is open. If we get turned down, we drive on to the next station." He told how blacks pass the word among travelers: this is "a good town," that one's "a shit town"; here you can safely rent a motel room, there they might lynch you for trying. "Even with all the tips you can pick up," he said, "you stay tense and nervous. When you see a black man stagger into his motel after a day on the road, he's tired for reasons other than the highway and the traffic. If you'll notice, black people drive within the speed limits more than whites—because cops are quicker to bust 'em. If a black man has car trouble it will be ten times more difficult to get anybody to stop and help him, and when he gets to a garage they'll stick him for all they can. . . .

"How'd you like to explain to your son why you couldn't buy him an ice-cream cone in a white drugstore on a hot day, or take him in a hotel lobby to piss when his little bladder's bursting?" he asked one night, coolly enraged, when a white Hill secretary suggested that perhaps blacks were "pushing too fast."

One evening when liquor had worked on Moe while we sat in his small efficiency, from which he had a great view of the spotlighted Capitol dome if not the darkened slums directly behind it, he said, "I'm not talking shit, and I'm not crying on your ofay shoulder. For a black man, I've got it made. At least I don't have a survival problem. I lay the truth on a few whites I think capable of understanding and, more than that, caring—otherwise, why bother? And I'm not telling it like it is because I love the white man so goddamn much. Nobody much is telling Whitey what the black dude is feeling, or how full he is in his craw. And Mr. Charley isn't straining anything to find out. The goddamn thing's gonna blow up in his face one day, and then he's gonna wonder how he got something nasty in his hair."

Sometimes Moe sounded militant, sometimes tame. When he heard, through the gossip of children, that one of my neighbors in a solidly white middle-class Washington residential section had complained of interracial parties in my home, he seemed more amused than angry or embarrassed. Yet, when I retaliated on the crotchety neighbor (by urging free beer on a four-man crew of blacks working with me in my yard one Saturday, to the extent their more uninhibited street expressions violated the suburban air) he was not only not amused, Moe was outraged. "You're not helping anybody by showboating," he complained. "You're just agitating tensions. Hell, *I* wouldn't want those 14th Street cats drunk, cussing, and cutting up in my neighborhood. You've made black people look bad by trying to get revenge on some miserable ofay prick not worth your trouble."

One night in 1963 my friend knocked on my door at midnight. "I'm all packed," Moe said. "Going home to California." His sponsoring Senator had failed to provide a promised better job, George Washington University had reneged on accepting credits to be transferred from USC, and he could no longer tolerate the depressing influences of the East. "This is shitbird country," he said over our final drink. "Not much better than your dear ole Dixie. Sometimes I think the Confederacy won the fucking war."

He telephoned from Los Angeles the night of John F. Kennedy's assassination, and we cried together; I telephoned him some months later at 5:00 A.M. to discover him as inebriated, gloomy, and incoherent as I was. We have had no contact since.

16.

Except as handy straw men for demagogues to flay, black people were not a political factor in our West Texas Congressional district. Few enough lived there; a minority of these troubled to vote. When I placed a Negro school official on the list to receive my Congressman's weekly newsletter (a distinction held by a mere 20,000 people plus all possible newspaper, radio, and TV outlets) he troubled to thank my Congressman for "the nicest thing a politician ever did for me." Perhaps twice in eight years my Congressman addressed black audiences: for one thing, he wasn't invited, and for another his time simply might be better spent. We always carried our black precincts, however, for the opposition was generally so wrong-headed and reactionary that we looked better than our stains.

In 1962 (when a Republican troglodyte would defeat my Conservative Democrat), worried and fearing democracy's verdict, I discovered while checking polling places in Odessa in midafternoon that blacks simply were not voting. I sought out the local black baron on whom we relied for whatever political influence we had among Negroes. "Sam," I said, "your people aren't voting. Let's get them to the polls."

"I been trying to get the cats out all day," Sam said. "They don't have much appetite for it."

I was angry: "Goddamnit, have they forgotten the votes for civil-rights bills? And votes for minimum-wage bills, public housing, a dozen other things that Republican bastard would die before he'd vote for?"

"Maybe they have," Sam said, looking out from the rickety two-chair barbershop across the waste and shanties of the local Flats. "Them things don't seem to have made much difference around here, now, do they, laddie?"

Perhaps "them things" didn't make much difference in Odessa, Watts, Newark, or Mississippi. There was a time when I believed they had: believed that the lunch-counter sit-ins had made a difference, the Freedom Rides through Dixie, the bus boycott in Montgomery, the march on Selma Bridge.

I believed it strongest on a sun-dappled day in August 1963, when Martin Luther King had his dream in the shadow of the Lincoln Memorial. We thrilled to that dream and to the fantastically huge, orderly, singing, loving crowd of all shades and hues, backgrounds and heritages, opportunities and privations.

America seemed ready to deliver its ancient promises: we had made laughingstocks of panicky Congressmen who had predicted blood in Washington's streets, had closed their offices and sent their secretaries home to lock themselves in against gang-bang rapes.

My friend Richard Gallagher, a writer with whom I attended the Freedom March activities, sent me a note on returning to New York:

Coming down on the charter train that fresh Freedom morning, it was a love feast. Brotherhood. Forgiveness. Unity. Songs. Let-my-people-go. Please, won't you take my seat and how about sharing my coffee cake, and, Brother, have you met my wife? Going back on the train that night, after Dr. King's big dream, everybody was their usual bitchy griping selfish suspicious selves, growling how you should get your fucking feet out of the goddamn aisle, and what mother-raper had stolen their sack lunch? I hope it ain't an omen.

17.

After Watts and other insurrections, I heard many whites reassure themselves in Washington or its nervous suburbs that "it can't happen here." With the President and Congress in residence, provisions had been made to protect the Capitol; a single Molotov cocktail would bring thousands of riot-trained policemen and paratroopers. Washington Negroes had decent government jobs and therefore wouldn't fall prey to outside agitators or professional militants.

These graveyard whistlings ignored several near-misses: the sacking of Glen Echo Amusement Park (segregated for years after many Washington institutions bowed to the inevitable), a mini-riot at D.C. Stadium during a game for the city football championship, countless skirmishes between ghetto blacks and their police tormentors, dozens of instances where black toughs had attacked whites driving through the rowdier sections of Anacostia, Southeast, or Northeast Washington. Washingtonians read these reports, and refused to believe. I was never able to convince anyone that we lived in a fool's paradise.

For I had become (for the first time since my invasion of hostile Harlem almost twenty years before) sorely afraid of the black man. I had seen his growing hostility, not only in the more miserable slums where I had occasionally gone to perform a bleeding-heart good deed or two (helping to keep slum playgrounds open when Congress threatened to close them, or other such stopgap gestures), but in the whole of the city. Within a stone's throw of Hubert Humphrey's plush high-rise with its stunning view of the Potomac and green Virginia fields, I had incurred the wrath of a black street gang by unwisely attempting to rescue a small black boy in the process of being robbed of pocket change—and had paid for my rashness by having to steer my wife through the bawled invitations to inventive fornications.

I had been the handy object of rock-throwing bands of small Negro boys, none surely above the age of ten, who chose me as the target of their unspoken frustrations near our neighborhood shopping center. When I drove a black woman to her home in a scabby section at the end of her workday as our weekly domestic, carrying a box of clothing she had gratefully received as a gift, up several flights of foul-smelling stairs, her young daughter had fixed me with a glare of pure hate and the lip-curling thanks of "Shit!" Following Louis Armstrong on a writing assignment, my wife and I made a tour of Negro nightclubs with Armstrong's trombonist, the merry and talented Tyree Glenn, and Mrs. Glenn. Tyree and I more or less alternately were picking up the series of bar tabs; in one joint, about three o'clock in the morning, we struggled over a check until a black man on a neighboring stool clearly and with passion instructed Glenn, "Man, let Whitey pay. *Always* let Whitey pay. The cocksucker can pay till Christmas and he *still* owe us."

Time after time in Washington stores I had seen young blacks rude, threatening, obscene, or violent to white customers and clerks. I understood why such things happened, but where once I walked the streets in confidence, I came to look ahead like a soldier advancing into enemy territory, alert for unfriendly blacks or side-street dangers, vulnerable, tense, and marked. Meanwhile, at cocktail parties in segregated living rooms, I would hear the many reasons why "it can't happen here."

18.

On a warm, rain-threatened evening in April of 1968, an old friend with whom I had served Capitol Hill time telephoned my Washington home: "Have you heard what happened to Martin Luther King?"

I knew as surely as an eyewitness: "Oh, goddamn! Somebody shot the poor son-of-a-bitch!"

"The lid will blow now," I said. "Especially if he dies. They'll burn it all down." Within a short time King's death was confirmed. I called my friend back, noting his excellent White House connections while I currently was in bad odor there: he should contact a mutual friend on LBJ's staff and beg that all possible conciliatory gestures be made—a shutdown of business operations, all manner of pledges to employ unlimited federal power in bringing the assassin to justice, the President's promise to attend the funeral service or a promise to transport the body to wherever Mrs. King might choose.

My friend called back within the hour: "They're reserving Sunday as the official day of mourning. Businesses will be closed, and everything." Was that all? "Yes."

"Well, fuck that! It's not enough. Most businesses are closed on

Sunday, anyway. Dammit, they've got to do something meaningful. Otherwise, it will be construed as an insult."

"They seem to think they know what they're doing over there," my friend said. "The President's going on TV here in a little bit and tell everybody to simmer down." Though we did not know it then, the first plate-glass windows were being kicked in around 14th and U Streets.

Through most of a sleepless night I listened to the radio, picking up reports of violence and random burnings. Near dawn I fell into a drugged sleep, awaking in midmorning when my brother telephoned from Texas to see if we were safe. "Sure," I said, groggy and puzzled. "Why?"

"You'd better wake up," he said. "Your town is on fire. I'm watching it on television."

From my yard I could see puffy clouds of smoke in Washington's betrayed and hopeless sections. I tuned in a talk show on a suburban radio station: whites, imitating the fiddling Nero, bitched because government flags would be flown at half mast for the fallen black leader ("After all, he wasn't a government official") or accused Senator Robert Kennedy of grandstanding for political gain in having ordered his private plane to fly the body back to Atlanta for burial. More than one hundred American cities were burning; machine guns protected Capitol Hill; nightly curfews were announced.

Late Saturday night, someone knocked on my door. Through the peephole I saw two well-dressed black men. Though ashamed of myself, I decided for safety's sake not to answer. As they turned away, one laughed and spoke to the other about Whitey being afraid to come out of his hole.

Near midnight there were sirens in the neighborhood, and the sound of gunshots. I keep no firearms, but that night Whitey, the son of the night watchman, slept with a billy club fashioned from a broomstick and a wicked butcher knife next to his bed.

1970

That Terrible Night Santa Got Lost in the Woods

MOST OF MY CHILDHOOD Yule seasons were conventional ones for the time and place: Texas, in the 1930s. They were old-fashioned country Christmases, highlighted by the obligatory big feasts cooked by a mother determined to shower upon her out-at-elbows brood all it was within her power to give.

Certainly Neiman-Marcus gifts were beyond her dreams or comprehensions; perhaps she could do nothing to discourage Santa Claus from leaving more and better toys under the trees of my cousins in Cisco or Putnam or Rotan. No King in Texas, however—or in England for that matter—would sit down to a more complete, groaning table for Christmas dinner.

I loved the preparations of those dinners almost as much as their consumption: the fine odors of bubbling pots on the castiron wood-burning stove and companion pans baking in the oven; the strong, sweet smell of the smokehouse as my father removed a home-cured country ham suggesting essence of brown sugar and sage; the digging of sweet potatoes from the underground bin where they had been stored against the mischief of Jack Frost; the opening of summer peaches my mother had canned in fruit jars and stored in the rude dirt cellar against the good promise of winter cobblers; the warm and joyous bustle as I performed small, presumably helpful chores to the music of mother's hymns celebrating her personal understanding with Jesus.

Everything my mother prepared, everything we ate in that good and rare season—excepting a few condiments—had been raised in our family garden, orchard, or animal lots. That each family member had contributed to the feeding and currying or to the planting, cultivation and harvesting of these foodstuffs somehow made our feasts taste the better.

Mother was not content to serve a single meat dish at Christmas—oh, no! Likely, feet belonging to her adult children and their spouses, a grandchild, and any number of uncles, aunts or cousins would be placed under her table. And so her meal must rival anything the Romans had thought of at the height of their gluttonous debaucheries.

She would serve ham both baked and fried. Chicken fried and chicken with spicy cornbread dressing and chicken floating in giblet gravy. A pot roast. All home grown. Occasionally I attempted to feel pity or sorrow for the beef calves, hogs and chickens I had come to know before their slaughter for our table, though I had small luck at it.

Indeed, the first real rise of Christmas giddiness—the first clear evidence that the long-awaited day was, indeed, not only inevitable but *imminent*—began when I saw my father go to the chicken house to select three or more fat candidates for my mother's hungry pot. As the headless unfortunates flopped, staggered and bled their lives away, making dizzy dark wet trails across the grass, I found myself jumping and bounding and carooming in crazy patterns equal to their own.

Then would come quick visions of other delicacies to follow, dishes to make a dirt farmer's boy almost forget he was rag-tag poor: plum and banana puddings, chocolate and coconut cakes, chess and pecan and mincemeat pies; steaming side servings of sweet corn, green beans, candied yams, fried okra, rich gravies, deviled eggs, and all the piping-hot biscuits that visiting relatives— or probably a thresher crew—could reasonably eat. Through it all my mother clucked and passed dishes and urged everyone to eat to the bursting point. The Romans had nothing on her, save perhaps a few jiggers of sinful spirits.

That magnificent feast would be consumed at high noon on Christmas Day. But festivities began as much as a week earlier when, feeling grand and self-important and perhaps happily feverish, I accompanied my father to the woods to select and cut the family Christmas tree. We loaded the honored tree in a flatbed wagon pulled by horses I loved, Prince and Dutch, and hauled it home to be trimmed with slivers of silvery tinsel, colorful glass or metal balls carefully stored for reuse each year, and strings of dyed popcorn with more colors than the rainbow.

On Christmas Eve night my little niece, Lois, joined me in singing off-key Christmas carols to tolerant grown-ups: *Silent Night, Away in a Manger, O Little Town of Bethlehem, God Rest Ye Merry Gentlemen,* and always—as the capper—*Santa Claus Is Coming to Town.* The lyrics warned youngsters against crying and pouting and assured them Santa knew when they were waking and when they were asleep. My conduct and personality had a way of dramatically improving at each Yule season, if but briefly.

It was our family's tradition, after the songfest, to open the modest packages earlier wrapped and beribboned and positioned beneath the Christmas tree. Lois and I acted as Santa's helpers in distributing the limited gifts—handkerchiefs, socks, toilet water kits, shaving soaps, house shoes, tobacco, shirts and blouses, a pair of shoes, a rare new dress or "Sunday" pants. In time, one knew to accurately predict the contents even before a ribbon had been disturbed.

No toys lurked under the tree at that point. Not yet. No, toys would be magically placed in the dead still dark of night by a benevolent Santa who somehow served every child in the whole wide world without waking a single one, and who took time from his busy duties to eat the plate of cookies and drink the glass of milk I had left for him as a tree-side gift that perhaps smacked, more than a little, of overtones of gentle bribery.

I never paused to wonder why on Christmas Eve my father always chose to sleep in my bed, rather than my mother's. Nor did I question why he never was beside me when I woke in hot, holiday excitement the following morning. I do, however, perfectly recall the difficulty he had persuading me to sleep on the threshold of the year's biggest event. Rigid with anticipation I would prattle in the dark of Santa and his wonderous offerings until my sleepy father in vexation would say, "Consarn it, Son! Santa won't *never* come if you don't go to sleep!" Drowsing close to dreamland I would hear my father stealthily attempt to leave my bed. Like a shot, my small form bolted upright to loudly whisper, "Daddy, you reckon ol' Santa Claus has come yet?" With something between an oath and a sigh he would reluctantly settle back in the bed and say, "Now hush! He won't come 'till little boys is sound asleep and he's *sure* of it!"

Eventually, against all odds, I would sleep—only to bound up and race to the Christmas tree long before the sun had thought of its appearance, and often before first light.

Those Christmases were as alike as peas in a pod, as uniform and indistinguishable as starched soldiers marching on parade. These years later, it is difficult to sort one from another.

Except one. And it is that special Christmas this story is about.

CHRISTMAS 1933

Franklin D. Roosevelt had been in the White House less than a year, and I was only four, when Christmas rolled around in 1933. That Yule season would become a colorful part of our family lore. I heard about it so many times, in such detail, that my memory attempts to trick me by claiming to recall more of it than could have been possible.

We lived on a hard-scrabble dirt farm in Eastland County in a time when much more than one-third of the nation was "ill-housed, ill-clad, ill-nourished" as our President later would calculate. In that bottoming-out year of The Great Depression the King family owned no automobile, no telephone, no radio, no electric lights, no indoor plumbing, no running water and no cash.

The only heat in our farmhouse was provided by a crude stone fireplace in the living room and a wood-burning stove in the kitchen. On bitter nights—and it does get very cold in certain parts of Texas, Sun Belt myths to the contrary—my mother wrapped hot irons or hot bricks in layers of cloth as foot-warmers. On frozen mornings, my parents broke the ice in a large kitchen bucket to wash the sleep from their eyes and to brew bracing coffee. Later, when the kitchen had warmed, but still before sunup and sometimes in the early dark, I would crawl from my chilled bed and dash to the fire in anticipation of hot biscuits, gravy and—after hog-killing time—that marvelous home-cured sausage, ham or bacon.

At four years of age I knew nothing of unemployment, depressed farm prices, instant hobos riding the rails in search of work, the daily economic woes and fears of my parents. That would come soon enough, but in December of 1933 I innocently assumed the visit of a Santa Claus of generous spirit and limitless gifts.

"Your Momma had ordered your Santa Claus doo-dads from a mail-order house that year like she always done," my father would many times recall, "but for some blame reason it never come. She met the mailman ever day for a week, fussing and fuming at him, but it never done no good.

"When your Christmas hadn't come by Christmas Eve day, Cora rung the dinner bell on the porch to call me in from work. I recollect I was chopping wood and stacking it to haul to Cisco to sell for three dollars a cord. Well, I put my ax down and went to the house. Cora met me on the porch so you wouldn't hear her."

"Clyde," my mother said, "if that boy's gonna have any Santa Claus you're gonna have to go to town and buy it."

The Old Man (I think of him that way though he was short of his 46th birthday, six years younger than I am now) asked a direct and simple question: "What with?"

"You can ask Will Gaddis for credit."

Her husband shook his head and mumbled; he thought credit buying unwise, unmanly and probably unforgivable in Heaven. There was a shame attached to a man's not being able to make his own way on a cash-and-carry basis. When he said nothing more, she issued an edict: "Clyde, there's not any choice. We can't disappoint that boy. Christmas is for children." He knew the truth when he heard it.

"It was God-awful cold," my father would recall, "and getting colder. I could tell the clouds had snow in 'em. It was about six miles over to the little town of Scranton—had two stores there, a couple churches and a post office—and I didn't waste no time trying to hunt down a horse in the pasture to saddle. Figured I'd strike out walking and maybe somebody would come along and pick me up. At the least, I figured to run into somebody in town I could bum a ride from coming back home.

"I wrapped up in my heaviest old work jumper, put on heavy

socks, long johns, and struck out afoot. Didn't cut through the fields and pastures, which would of saved me more'n a mile and a half, on account of I had hopes of a car coming along. Well, I'll just be plagued—none did.

"Before I'd went a mile the snow was falling so thick and fast I couldn't see but a few steps ahead of myself. The wind was blowing so hard I had to lean into it, which made mighty tough walking. Time I got to Scranton, I was snow head to toe and half-froze."

Not much was doing in the little crossroads Texas settlement on a Christmas Eve afternoon. The country folks were at home: trimming trees they'd likely cut off their own land or a neighbor's, making popcorn balls, wrapping such few presents as their pocketbooks could afford, cooking the Christmas feasts that were so much a part of the holiday tradition. Perhaps the poorest of the poor would make do with fried catfish, winter potatoes and wild onions, but you could count on them trotting out their best.

One old couple was in Gaddis Brothers General Mercantile, which sold everything from axle grease to large sacks of flour to horsecollars to patent medicines. In season, the Gaddis boys stocked a few toys and special items for Christmas even though most people depended on Montgomery Ward or Sears & Roebuck.

"Me and Will Gaddis had been boys together, but I hated to ask him for credit worse than sin. And I sure didn't want them other people hearing me. So I warmed my backside by the stove there in the store. When Will asked what he could do for me, I said, 'Let me thaw out first, Will.' Well, consarn that old couple, they asseled around in there it must of been a good hour, buying their little dab.

"Soon's they left I said, 'Will, my woman sent a money order to a mail-order house up in Chicago to buy my boy his Christmas, but it never come. I need to buy him a few things, but I flat don't have any money. It's all in Chicago." I went on to tell Will I'd pay him cash when I could. Or, if he'd druther, I'd work it out around his store or on a farm him and his brothers owned.

"Will said, 'Aw, Clyde, don't worry none about that. I know you good for it. You go on ahead and take whatever you want.' I appreciated that. Still and all, I couldn't help but feel little."

My father selected a half-dozen oranges, an equal number of

apples, nuts, hard candy, a small pocketknife and a child's little red rocking chair.

"I don't know if you recollect that chair," he said in later years, "but you was plumb foolish about it. You used to set down in it and play like you was some big boss"—he laughed an old man's cackle— "and the rest of us would have to come ask you for our wages. And you'd make us tell what we'd did to deserve our pay before you'd give it to us—or play like you did."

THE ROAD NOT TAKEN

"Anyhow," he said, "I'd carried a gunnysack to town with me. I put that red rocker and other Christmas things in it, told Will I was much obliged, and started to leave the store."

"Lord God, Clyde," the store keeper said, "you don't want to go out in that danged blizzard! Somebody's bound to come along in a car directly."

The snow was getting thicker, the wind was howling fiercely; my father decided his old friend was right. Probably he secretly delighted in the rare opportunity to escape his daily labors: he loved to talk, to tell stories, to crack dry jokes. The two men sat by the pot-bellied stove, Dad smoking roll-your-own cigarettes and Gaddis chewing tobacco, through much of the afternoon. I am sure they talked of crops and hard times and the Bible and men a long time dead.

"Wellsir, it got later and later and still nobody come to town. And the way that snow was swirlin' and bankin' up, I figured wadn't nobody likely to. The old roads was all dirt in them days, wadn't paved, and I guess folks figured they'd be mean to travel. So along about dusk I told Will Gaddis I'd just as well move on."

"Clyde, you better let me drive you over to your place," Gaddis said. "You can't walk six or seven miles in this mess."

But my father refused. Will Gaddis lived but a few hundred yards from his store, and such a wayward trip might be an imposition. "No, Will," he said, "you already done enough for me as it is."

My old man hoisted his gunnysack full of Santa Claus goodies on a broad shoulder and started the long trudge home through the storm. For a mile or so he stayed on the road, still hoping for the luck to hitch a ride.

"Then I thought, 'Thunder, ain't nobody in his right mind gonna come out in this blizzard.' So I cut through a plowed field, which crossed into some woods over about the old Biggerstaff place.

"Wellsir, outside of voting for Herbert Hoover that was about the biggest damnfool thing I ever done. Ten minutes after I got in them woods it was pitch dark. I hadn't thought to bring a lantern, it being the middle of the day when I'd left home. Snow had covered up any markers I might of recognized, you see, and there I was bumping around in them blamed woods getting myself or that gunnysack tangled up.

"Didn't bother me much at first. I figured I knowed which way I was heading and I'd come out on the road again, up by Ernest Weed's old place, if I walked true. And from there it wadn't but a mile, a mile and a quarter maybe, on home.

"But I walked and walked in that storm, until I finally knowed within reason I'd overshot Ernest Weed's place. So I started back-tracking. But in the dark and that blowin' snow, all that done was get me turned around and twisted. I didn't have no notion of where I was at. You couldn't read the stars—it was overcast and the moon was blotted out. And that snow was falling so thick it was hard to breathe.

"Well, I admit to it, I commenced feeling scared. It was cold enough that night a man could get frostbite or worse. I hadn't never seen a blizzard like that, and never seen another 'un—just my luck. I knowed if I lost my head I'd be worse off than I was. Tried to follow my old tracks back to the road, but in the dark and with new snow falling I couldn't track myself. I tell you, I was between a rock and a hard place."

THE LONG WAIT

My mother usually picked up the story at that point.

"When it got good dark and after, I was worried sick. It just wasn't like Clyde to lay out that way. He didn't drink; he was always particular to be on time and not worry me."

Mother and my nineteen-year-old sister, Estelle, walked the floor of that old unpainted farmhouse, "wringing our hands and wondering." I was darting about underfoot, too excited by the prospect of Christmas and the proximity of Santa Claus, to think of sleep. Not wanting to alarm me, my mother cautioned Estelle against emotional outbursts or tears. They acted out a charade, reading to me and attempting to appear natural.

"I thought it would be better if we had something to occupy our minds," my mother recalled. "We all went in the kitchen and popped popcorn and roasted a big pan of peanuts. You had a good time eating, rattling on about Santa and asking a hundred questions about when he'd be there and what he fed his reindeer and such. I tried to act normal, but I just knew something was terrible wrong. I felt like I had to *do* something. So I told Estelle to stay with you, sing little songs or play little games to keep you occupied."

Telling me she was going to the barn to gather eggs for our Christmas breakfast, my mother bundled warmly and collected three lanterns we kept for pre-dawn farm chores.

"It was the only thing I knew to do," she said. "The nearest neighbors was a mile away. I was afraid to try to go there in the storm—and they had a yard full of big dogs I was afraid of.

"I set out walking to the main road, about a quarter mile from our old house, to set out lanterns. If your daddy was lost in the storm, as I suspicioned, I thought he might see their lights. All I could imagine, if somebody hadn't knocked him in the head or he hadn't been run over by a car, was that he'd got lost in that storm."

As grim as that prospect might be, she clung to it because it seemed marginally better than the alternatives. A young rowdy of the community was freshly home from a second trip to the state penitentiary—once for bootlegging, once for car theft—and my mother, a chronic worrywart by nature, had several times voiced her fears that the ex-convict might somehow do us harm. Suppose he had chanced upon my father bearing gifts, and suspected him of carrying a few dollars. . . .? Or what if my father had been attacked by one of several packs of wild, hungry dogs that often roamed the countryside as scavengers?

"It was all I could do," she said, "to get up our lane to that main road and back—I later heard it snowed way over a foot. And there was drifts that was waist-deep. I know, because I fell in two or three. But I kept on until I got those lanterns lit and set out. I placed 'em in a row right in front of our gate.

"When I got back to the house you'd gone to sleep in Estelle's arms. When we tucked you in bed, you woke up mumbling about Santa Claus. But I sung you back to sleep. Then I said, 'Estelle, I can't think of but one other thing we can do.' So we dropped down on our knees and prayed."

THE COLD WALK

"I don't have no notion how long I stumbled around in them woods," my father said. "Had to be hours and hours. I was wore out, hungry, cold to the bone—but I knowed if I stopped to rest I might go to sleep in spite of all I could do, and then I'd freeze to death. I'd heard of it happenin'.

"After awhile I got mad. I'd been raised on that same farm we lived on then. I'd hunted in that country all my life, walked them woods with dogs, worked the fields all over that part of the country. And it made me want to bump myself that I was lost and couldn't find no landmarks. I might as well a-been in China. But gettin' mad and gettin' to where I wanted to go was two different things."

He found himself thinking that if he could stumble onto a cow he could grab the animal, throw it to the ground and trace its brand with his fingers in the dark. This desperate measure, at least, might tell him whose farm he was on. Surely, then, he would be able to chart a homeward course.

"I knowed cattle clumped up in deep woods and turned their backsides to the wind during a storm," he said. "Ever little bit I'd stop walking and listen for cattle milling around, mooing and such. But all I could hear was the wind. 'Course, now, if I *had* found cattle I'd probably of spooked 'em and they'd scattered in the dark. But I couldn't afford to let myself think about that."

He knew he should have crossed one—possibly two—small creeks that meandered through the countryside, and was puzzled as to why he had not. He didn't think they would have frozen so solid that he might have walked across them without knowing it. No, likely he would have been plunged into a sudden icy bath. Somehow it had not happened. "I studied on it and decided I'd never come to them creeks because I'd probably been wanderin' around in one big dang circle all night. I reckon that was when my spirits dropped just about as low as they could go."

By then he was scratched, bruised and bleeding. Tree limbs, heavily weighted by snow, had lashed his face; he had stumbled face or head first into a number of trees; he had fallen when surprised by snowdrifts or by tangling his feet in small bushes, none of which could be seen in the country dark.

City slickers have no idea how dark is country dark on a blind and moonless night. They are no lights reflecting from traffic or highways or towns, not even helpful glows from *aurora borealis*, the northern lights, on such a night as had victimized my father; one literally cannot see one's hand before one's face. In those conditions, Clyde King most feared breaking a leg or an ankle. "I knowed if that happened I was a gone goose. I'd flat freeze layin' out there in the woods." Occasionally he stopped, cupped his hands and shouted "*Ha-low! Ha-low!* . . ." But there was only the answering wind, and it might have been easy to imagine that it mocked him.

My old man's feet became so cold and wet they were but two dully aching lumps. He decided he must warm them. "My notion was to build a fire if I could scrabble up enough dead wood in all that snow that wadn't too wet to burn. Wellsir, I dug around and found a few pieces wadn't much more than twigs. Figured if I could get 'em lit, I might find more dead wood by the light of the fire. Wadn't no use in thinking of stripping limbs off a tree unless it was a dead one. Green wood won't hardly burn even if it ain't wet."

When he searched himself for matches he found only three— kitchen matches, long and slender, the kind with which he had fired many a fireplace, campfire, kitchen stove, cigarette. One his numb hands dropped in the snow and was lost, despite his searches and curses. A second he foolishly attempted to strike on his wet shoe sole; the sulfurous matter crumbled. The third he managed to strike by popping the match head with his thumb. But when he tried to light the skimpy pile of wet twigs the flame fizzled and went out. "If I had been a woman," he said, "I would of cried right then."

He propped against a tree trunk, took off his heavy denim jumper, and after removing his shoes and wet socks he wrapped his feet in the rough garment. "After a little bit my feet commenced to sting, so I knowed I wadn't dead yet. I cussed myself for not rolling a cigarette before I struck my last match. I swear it, I'd of give a ten-dollar bill for a smoke."

He opened the gunnysack, ate one of the apples he had bought for me—"It was hard and cold, but juicy"—and popped open a few walnuts. These made him thirsty again, so he ate snow.

"I knowed I had to move on, because I was gettin' drowsy." He briefly considered trying to burrow into the snow, building something of a rough igloo, but decided that "Not bein' no Eskimo I didn't know enough about it. It might cave in on me."

Shivering without his jumper, he squeezed out his wet socks— which had stiffened from direct exposure to the cold air—and painfully got back into his high-topped, soaked work shoes. Then he wrapped himself in the jumper again, and resumed his lonely, aimless walk.

THE FENCE

"Maybe it was a hour later I blundered into a barbed-wire fence. Hadn't seen it until I hit it. Wellsir, I knowed a fence had to lead

some place and was likely to be decently close to a house or a road. I naturally decided to follow it.

"Only thing, I didn't know which direction to go: by then I barely knowed up from down. Sure's I followed that fence one way, the right way would prove to be the other 'un. By then I was just hopin' to stay on my feet 'till daylight. I knowed blamed good and well I'd be all right when mornin' come.

"When I tried to start off again—I'd kinda sagged against that fence to rest a spell—my durned jumper had got caught on them barbs and I couldn't pull loose. Had to fish for my pocketknife and cut myself a-loose with my hands half-froze. Seemed like it took a week and a day.

"I followed that fence by feel: carried the gunnysack in my left hand and slid my right one along the wire. Them barbs cut that

hand up somethin' awful. Maybe it was twenty to thirty minutes later, I dunno, I broke out into a open field.

"It was still pitch dark and the wind was blowin' worse than in them woods, but it felt good to be out in the open even if I didn't know where I was at."

He stood perfectly still, listening. He heard creaking sounds, metal blowing against something in the wind. Carefully he made his way toward the rasping sound, stopping periodically to make certain he wouldn't lose it.

"It was a old cabin, hadn't nobody lived in it for years and years. What I'd heard was a piece of the old tin roof blowin' against what was left of the chimney.

"When I got up to it, I recognized it as a cabin Joe Lee Brown had lived in when he first married maybe thirty years before. Wellsir, it looked better to me than a palace. I knowed exactly where I was. I meant to say 'Thank you Lord, for answerin' my prayers,' but the words that come out of my mouth was 'It's about goddamn *time!*'"

Though still two miles from home, so great was his relief at knowing the spot of ground he occupied in God's dark and boundless universe that he celebrated by eating another apple and yelling *Yahoo!* several times.

"I et that second apple in the shelter of that old cabin, stompin' my feet to get circulation goin'. Didn't stay long, though, knowin' your Momma would be standin' on her head worryin' about me.

"I set out from that cabin towards the way I knowed the road was, walkin' as true a line as I could. When I found that ol' road I wanted to kiss it. I turned left and started stepping it off a mile a minute, feelin' like I wanted to sing."

A couple of hundred yards from the gate leading down to our farmhouse, he saw through the slackening snowfall a grouping of lights. At first he thought he was hallucinating, that the mental strain and physical drain of the long dark night of cold and fear had caused his senses to betray themselves.

"Then I thought, 'Thunderation, that's a blamed search party lookin' for me.' Wellsir, the notion of gettin' lost on my home grounds made me so ashamed of myself I went back in the woods again—just the edge, now, you can bank on that—and squatted down. Figured I'd let whoever it was go on by, then I'd sneak on home. I just couldn't stand to think of people guyin' and hoorawin' me about gettin' lost like some damn tenderfoot.

"But them lights, after a while, hadn't come no closer. I got back on the road and walked down there, where I found them lanterns Cora had set out. Well, goddurn, be damn if I didn't hull down and cry." And telling it, in later years, his eyes always puddled up when he reached that point in the tale. Then he would chase the tears away with an abrupt laugh and say, "Them durn lanterns, they

looked better to me than a fried-chicken dinner. I blowed two of
'em out and put 'em under the culvert there by our gate. Then I
hung the other one on my arm and stumbled on towards the
house."

THE HOMECOMING

It was a bit after four o'clock in the morning. My mother, sleepless and sitting in front of the fireplace with a patchwork quilt
thrown over her legs, saw a tiny blob of light moving raggedly
down the lane toward the house. At first she thought she, too, was
seeing things. "Then I realized it was Clyde, that he'd found the
lanterns." Now it was her turn to cry.

"I had already decided your daddy was dead or bad hurt. At first
light, I planned to walk to Tal and Ola Horn's place and get help to
start looking for Clyde. But in my heart I'd come to believe we'd
find him in a bad way. I was sitting there wondering how to prepare
you kids for it when I looked up and seen that lantern bobbing in
the lane."

Dad was, she remembered, "an awful sight"—covered with
frozen snow from crown to toe. Her hand flew to her mouth when
she saw his swollen, bloody face and the hand so cruelly ripped by
barbed wire.

My father grinned at her and said, "Breakfast ready yet?"

And somehow that made my mother mad. Perhaps she had anticipated something more dramatic, for she was not without drama
in her own nature. Or maybe it was a reaction against having sat
home, helpless and unknowing, while her man knew an adventure
she could neither share, imagine nor describe. Perhaps, more prac-
tically, in her lonely solitude she had permitted herself a fearful
glimpse of what might be her future, with children and only a
sixth-grade education, left to make her way in what then was very
much a man's world. At any rate, she gritted her teeth at her man
and said, "*Clyde King, where in the world have you been?*"

"I ain't got any idea," he said. "But I sure ain't going back without no breakfast."

She embraced him then, helped him out of his wet, stiff clothing and wrapped him in a blanket before attending his cuts, lumps and scrapes. He dozed by the fire while she hurried to brew coffee, and he later remembered that as he fitfully slept—awakening with sudden jerks and starts before dozing again—he was aware of her singing hymns of praise to Jesus.

While Dad drank the coffee and ate hot buttered biscuits, I rolled out of bed—full of a tingling, four-year-old awareness of a Christmas that, as usual, had taken forever to arrive—and romped into the living room to see what surprises Santa had left under the Christmas tree. Even in his weary state, my father had removed my rocking chair from the soaked, frozen gunnysack and placed it under the tree; he also had patiently stuffed my hanging stocking with the oranges, apples, nuts, hard candy and small pocketknife.

I fancy to recall that scene dimly, though probably I do not. Certainly I don't recall my contribution to what came to be known as The Christmas Daddy Got Lost In The Woods, though it was the part of the story my old man most enjoyed telling.

"There I set feelin' half dead," he chuckled, "and you runnin' around all hot about your Christmas presents and squealin'. But after a few minutes you looked over at me—after all I'd been through to be sure ol' Santa Claus come to see you—and you said, "Dingbust it! Old Santa never brought me no stickhorse and cowboy suit like I asked him for. I ain't ever writin' to that old fool again!"

And the old man would laugh and laugh and laugh until tears came into his eyes and, later, as he aged and as I matured, into my eyes as well.

1980

Redneck Blues

THE MADDEST I REMEMBER BEING at my late wife (a Yankee lady, of Greek extraction and mercurial moods) was when she shouted, during a quarrel the origins of which are long lost, that I was "a dumb Redneck." My heart dangerously palpitated; my eyes bugged; I ran in tight circles and howled inarticulate general profanities until, yes . . . my neck turned red. Literally. I felt the betraying hot flush as real as a cornfield tan. My wife collapsed in a mirthful heap, little knowing how truly close I felt to righteous killing.

Being called dumb wasn't what had excited me. No, for I judged myself ignorant only to the extent that mankind is and knew I was no special klutz. But being called a Redneck, now, especially when you know in your genes and in the dirty back roads of your mind that you *are* one—despite having spent years trying not to be— well, when that happens, all fair has gone out of the fight. I do not cherish Rednecks, which means I dislike certain persistent old parts of myself.

Of late the Redneck has been wildly romanticized; somehow he threatens to become a cultural hero. Perhaps this is because heroes are in short supply—we seem to burn them up faster nowadays— or maybe it's a manifestation of our urge to return to simpler times: to be free of computers, pollution, the urban tangle, shortages of energy or materials or elbowroom. Even George Wallace is "respectable" now, having been semimartyred by gunfire and defanged by defeat. Since 'Necks have long been identified with overt racism, we may be embracing them because we long ago tired of bad niggers who spooked and threatened us; perhaps the revival is a backlash against hairy hippies, peaceniks, weirdos of all stripes. Or the recent worship of Redneckism may be no more than the clever manipulations of music and movie czars, ever on the lookout for profitable new crazes. Anyway, a lot of foolishness disguised as noble folklore is going down as the 'Neck is praised in song and story.

There are "good" people, yes, who might properly answer to the appellation "Redneck": people who operate mom-and-pop stores or their lathes, dutifully pay their taxes, lend a helping hand to neighbors, love their country and their God and their dogs. But even among a high percentage of these salts-of-the-earth lives a terrible reluctance toward even modest passes at social justice, a suspicious regard of the mind as an instrument of worth, a view of the world extending little farther than the ends of their noses, and only vague notions that they are small quills writing a large, if indifferent, history.

Not that these are always mindless. Some value "common sense" or "horse sense" and in the basics may be less foolish than certain determined rote sophisticates and any number of pompous academicians. Some few may read Plato or Camus or otherwise astonish; it does not necessarily follow that he who is poor knows nothing or cares little. On the other hand, you can make boatloads of money and still be a Redneck in your bones, values, and attitudes. But largely, I think—even at the risk of being accused of elitism or class prejudice—the worse components of 'Neckery are found among the unlettered poor.

Attempts to deify the Redneck, to represent his life-style as close to that of the noble savage are, at best, unreal and naïve. For all their native wit—and sometimes they have keen senses of the absurd as applied to their daily lives—Rednecks generally comprise a sad lot. They flounder in perilous financial waters and are mired in the sociopolitical shallows. Their lives are hard: long on work and short on money; full of vile bossmen, hounding creditors, debilitating quarrels, routine disappointments, confrontations, ignorance, a treadmill hopelessness. It may sound good on a country-western record when Tom T. Hall and Waylon Jennings lift their voices, baby, but it neither sounds nor feels good when life is real and the alarm clock's jarring jangle soon must be followed by the time clock's tuneless bells.

Now, the Rednecks I'm talking about are not those counterfeit numbers who hang around Austin digging the Cosmic Cowboy scene, sucking up to Jerry Jeff Walker and Willie Nelson, wearing bleached color-patched overalls, and rolling their own dope, saying how they hanker to go live off the land and then winging off to stay six weeks in a Taos commune before flying back on daddy's credit card. May such toy Rednecks choke on their own romantic pretensions.

No, and I'm not talking about Good Ol' Boys. Do not, please, confuse the two; so many have. A Good Ol' Boy is a Redneck who has acquired a smidgen or much more of polish; I could call him a "former Redneck" except that there ain't no such when you bore bone-deep. One born a 'Neck of the true plastic-Jesus-on-the-dashboard and pink-rubber-haircurlers-in-the-supermarket variety can no more shuck his condition than may the Baptist who, once saved, becomes doctrinarily incapable of talking his way into hell.

The Good Ol' Boy may or may not have been refurbished by college. But bet your ass he's a climber, an achiever, a con man looking for the edge and the hedge. He'll lay a lot of semi-smarmy charm on you, and bullshit grading from middling to high. He acts dumber than he is when he knows something and smarter than he is when he doesn't. He would be dangerous game to hunt. Such parts of his Redneck heritage as may be judged eccentric or humorous enough to be useful will be retained in his mildly self-deprecating stories and may come in handy while he's working up to relieving you of your billfold or your panties. Such Redneck parts as no longer serve him, he attempts to bury in the mute and dead past. And he becomes maniacal when, say, a domestic quarrel causes him to blow his cool enough that those old red bones briefly rise from their interment so that others may glimpse them.

A Good Ol' Boy turns his radio down at red lights so that other drivers won't observe him enjoying Kitty Wells singing through her nose. He carefully says "Negro," though it slips to "Nigra" with a shade much scotch, or even—under stress, or for purposes of humor among close associates—slides all the way down to "nigger." He does not dip snuff or chaw tobacco, preferring cigarettes or cigars or perhaps an occasional sly hip toke of pot. He has forgotten, or tells himself he has forgotten, the daily fear of being truly ragged and dirt poor—and, perhaps, how to ride a horse, or the cruel tug of the cotton sack, or the strength of the laborer's sun. He may belong to a civic club, play golf, travel, own his own shop, or run somebody else's. For a long time he's been running uphill;

Sometimes he doesn't know when he's reached level ground and keeps on struggling. Having fought and sweated for his toehold, he'll likely be quick to kick those who attempt to climb along behind him.

While all Good Ol' Boys have been at least fringe Rednecks, not nearly all Rednecks rise to be Good Ol' Boys. No. Their gizzards don't harbor enough of something—grit, ambition, good fortune, con, education, flint, self-propellants, saddle burrs, chickenshit, opportunity, whatever—and so they continue to breed and largely perpetuate themselves in place, defanged Snopeses never to attain, accumulate, bite the propertied gentry, or smite their tormentors. These are no radicals; though the resentful juices of revolution may ache their bloodstreams, they remain—with rare, crazed exceptions—amazingly docile. They simply can't find the handles of things and drop more than they can pick up.

Though broad generalities deserve their dangerous reputation, one hazards the judgment that always such unreconstructed Rednecks shall vote to the last in number for the George Wallaces or Lester Maddoxes or other dark ogres of their time; will fear God at least in the abstract and Authority and Change even more; will become shade-tree mechanics, factory robots, salesmen of small parts, peacetime soldiers or sailors; random serfs. (Yes, good neighbors, do you know what it is to envy the man who no longer carries the dinner bucket, and hope someday you'll reach his plateau: maybe shill for All-State?) The women of such men are beauticians and waitresses and laundry workers and notions-counter clerks and generally pregnant. Their children may be hauled in joustabout pickup trucks or an old Ford dangling baby booties, giant furry dice, toy lions, nodding doggies and plastered with downhome bumper stickers: "Honk If You Love Jesus," maybe, or "Goat Ropers Need Love Too." Almost certainly it's got a steady mortgage against it, and at least one impatient lien.

We are talking, good buddies, about America's white niggers: the left behind, the luckless, the doomed. It is these we explore: my clay, native roots, mutha culture. . . .

I didn't know I was a Redneck as a kid. The Housenwrights were Rednecks, I knew—even though I was ignorant of the term; couldn't have defined it had I heard it—and so were the Spagles and certain branches of the Halls, the Peoples, the Conines, the many broods of Hawks. These were the raggedest of the ragged in a time when even FDR judged one third of a nation to be out-at-elbows. There was a hopelessness about them, a feckless wildness possible only in the truly surrendered, a community sense that their daddies didn't try as hard as some or, simply, had been born to such ill luck, silly judgments, whiskey thirsts, or general rowdiness as to preclude twitches of upward mobility. Such families were less likely than others to seek church; their breadwinners idled more; their children came barefoot to the rural school even in winter. They were more likely to produce domestic violence, blood feuds, boys who fought their teachers. They no longer cared and, not caring, might cheerfully flatten you or stab you in a playground fight or at one of the Saturday-night country dances held in rude plank homes along the creek banks. Shiftless badasses. Poor tacky peckerwoods who did us the favor of providing somebody to look down on. For this service we children of the "better" homes rewarded them with rock fights or other torments: "Dessie Hall, Dessie Hall / Haw Haw Haw / Your Daddy Never Bathes / But He's Cleaner Than Your Maw."

Ours was a reluctant civilization. Eastland County, Texas, had its share of certified illiterates in the 1930s and later, people who could no more read a Clabber Girl Baking Powder billboard than they could translate from the French. I recall witnessing old nesters who made their laborious "marks" should documents require signatures. A neighboring farmer in middle age boasted that his sons had taught him simple long division; on Saturdays he presided from the wooden veranda of Morgan Brothers General Store in Scranton, demonstrating on a brown paper sack exactly how many times 13 went into 39, while whiskered old farmers gathered for their small commerce looked on as if he might be revealing the internal rules of heaven.

We lived in one of the more remote nooks of Eastland County, in cotton and goober and scrub-oak country. There were no paved roads and precious few tractors among that settlement of marginal farms populated by snuff dippers, their sunbonneted women, and broods of jittery shy kids who might regard unexpected visitors from concealment. We were broken-plow farmers, holding it all together with baling wire, habit, curses, and prayers. Most families were on FDR's relief agency rolls; county agriculture agents taught our parents to card their cotton by hand so they might stuff home-made mattresses. They had less success in teaching crop rotation, farmers feeling that the plot where daddy and granddaddy had grown cotton remained a logical place for cotton still. There were many who literally believed in a flat earth and the haunting pres-ence of ghosts; if the community contained any individual who failed to believe that eternal damnation was a fair reward for the sinner, he never came forward to declare it.

Churches grew in wild profusion. Proud backwoodsmen, their best doctrines disputed by fellow parishioners, were quick to es-tablish their rival rump churches under brush arbors or taberna-cles or in plank cracker boxes. One need have no formal training to preach; the Call was enough, a personal conviction that God had beckoned one from a hot cornfield or cattle pen to spread the Word; this was easy enough for God to do, He being everywhere and so little inclined toward snobbery that He frequently visited the lowliest Eastland County dirt farmer for consultations. Con-verts were baptized in muddy creeks or stock tanks, some flocks— in the words of the late Governor Earl Long of Louisiana—"chunk-ing snakes and catching fevers."

It was not uncommon, when my father was a young man, for righteous vigilantes to pay nocturnal calls on erring wife beaters or general ne'er-do-wells, flogging them with whips and Scriptures while demanding their immediate improvement. Such godly posses did not seek to punish those who lived outside the law, however, should commerce be involved; when times were hard, so were the people. Bootleggers flourished in those woods in my youth, and it was not our responsibility to reveal them. Even cattle thieves were ignored so long as they traveled safe distances to improve their small herds.

My father's house was poor but proud: law-abiding, church-ridden, hardworking, pin-neat; innocent, it seems in retrospect, of conscious evil, and innocent, even, of the modern world. Certainly we had good opinions of ourselves and a worthy community standing. And yet even in that "good" family of work-worn, self-starting, self-designated country aristocrats there were tragedies and explosions as raw as the land we inhabited: My paternal grandfather was shot to death by a neighbor; an uncle went to the pen for carnal knowledge of an underaged girl; my father's fists variously laid out a farmer who had the temerity to cut in front of his wagon in the cotton-gin line, a ranch hand who'd reneged on a promise to pay out of his next wages for having his horse shod, a kinsman who threatened to embarrass the clan by running unsuccessfully for county commissioner a ninth straight time. My father was the family enforcer, handing out summary judgments and corporal punishments to any in the bloodline whose follies he judged trashy or a source of community scorn or ridicule. It was most tribal: Walking Bear has disgraced the Sioux; very well, off with Walking Bear's head.

So while we may have had no more money than others, no more of education or raw opportunity, I came to believe that the Kings were somehow special and that my mother's people, the proud and clannish Clarks, were more special still. A certain deference was paid my parents in their rural domain; they gave advice, helped shape community affairs, were arbiters and unofficial judges. I became a "leader" at the country school and in Bethel Methodist Church, where we took pride in worships free of snake handling or foot washings—although it was proper to occasionally talk in tongues or grovel at the mourners' bench.

I strutted when my older brother, Weldon, returned in his second-hand Model A Ford to visit from Midland, a huge metropolis of 9,000 noblemen in oil, cowboy, and rattlesnake country more than 200 miles to the west. I imagined him a leading citizen there; he had found Success as manager of the lunch counter and fountain at Piggly Wiggly's and announced cowpoke melodies part time over the facilities of radio station KCRS. More, he was a hot-fielding second baseman with the semiprofessional Midland Cowboys baseball team. Any day I expected the New York Yankees to call him up and wondered when they did not.

Weldon epitomized sophistication in my young mind; he wore smart two-toned shoes with air holes allowing his feet to breathe, oceans of Red Rose hair oil, and a thin go-to-hell mustache. In the jargon of the time and the place he was "a jellybean." Where rustics rolled their own from nickel bags of Duke's Mixture or Country Gentlemen, my brother puffed luxurious "ready rolls." When he walked among local stay-at-homes on his rare visits, he turned the heads of milkmaids and drew the dark envied stares of male contemporaries who labored on their fathers' farms or, if especially enterprising, had found jobs at the broom factory in Cisco. He was walking proof of the family's industry and ambition, and he reinforced my own dreams of escape to bigger things.

Imagine my shocked surprise, then, when—in my early teens—I accompanied my family in its move to the City of Midland, there to discover that *I* was the Redneck: the bumpkin, the new boy with feedlot dung on his shoes and the funny homemade haircuts. Nobody in Midland had heard of the Kings or even of the Clarks; nobody rushed to embrace us. Where in the rural consolidated school I had boasted a grade average in the high nineties, in Midland the mysteries of algebra, geometry, and biology kept me clinging by my nails to scholastic survival. Where I had captained teams, I now stood uninvited on the fringes of playground games. My clothes, as good as most and better than some in Eastland County, now betrayed me as a poor clod.

I withdrew to the company of other misfits who lived in clapboard shacks or tents on the jerry-built South Side, wore tattered time-faded jeans and stained teeth, cursed, fought, swigged beer, and skipped school to hang around South Main Street pool halls or domino parlors. These were East Texans, Okies, and Arkies whose parents—like mine—had starved off their native acres and had followed the war boom west. Our drawls and twangs and marginal grammar had more of the dirt farmer or drifting fruit picker in them than of the cattleman or small merchant; our homes utilized large lard buckets as stools or chairs and such paltry art as adorned the wall likely showed Jesus on the cross suffering pain and a Woolworth's framing job; at least one member of almost every family boasted its musician: guitar or banjo or mandolin pickers who cried the old songs while their instruments whined or wailed of griefs and losses in places dimly remembered.

We hated the Townies who catcalled us as shitkickers . . . plow-boys . . . Luke Plukes. We were a sneering lot, victims of cultural shock, defensive and dangerous as only the cornered can be. If you were a Townie, you very much wished not to encounter us unless you had the strength of numbers; we would whip your ass and take your money, pledging worse punishments should the authorities be notified. We hated niggers and meskins almost as much as we hated the white Townies, though it would be years before I knew how desperately we hated ourselves.

In time, deposits of ambition, snobbery, and pride caused me to work exceedingly hard at rising above common Redneckery. Not being able to beat the Townies, I opted to join them through path-ways opened by athletics, debating, drama productions. It was simply better to be in than out, even if one must desert his own kind. I had discovered, simply, that nothing much on the bottom was worth having.

I began avoiding my Redneck companions at school and dodg-ing their invitations to hillbilly jam sessions, pool hall recreations, forays into the scabbier honky-tonks. The truth is, the Rednecks had come to depress me. Knowing they were losers, they acted as such. No matter their tough exteriors when tormenting Townies, they privately whined and sniveled and raged. The deeper their alienations, the smaller they seemed to become physically; except-ing an occasional natural jug-butted Ol' Boy, Rednecks appeared somehow to be stringier, knottier, more shriveled than others. They hacked the coughs of old men and moved about in old men's motions somehow furtive and fugitive. I did not want to be like them.

Nor did I want to imitate their older brothers or fathers, with whom I worked in the oil fields during summers and on weekends. They lived nomadic lives, following booms and rumors and their restless, unguided hearts. It puzzled me that they failed to seek better and more far-flung adventures, break with the old ways and start anew; I was very young then and understood less than all the realities. Their abodes were tin-topped old hotels in McCamey, gasping-hot tents perched on the desert floor near Crane, a crummy tourist court outside Sundown, any number of peeled fading houses decorating Wink, Odessa, Monahans. Such places smelled of sweat, fried foods, dirty socks, the bottom of the barrel, too much sorry history.

By day we dug sump pits, pissanted heavy lengths of pipe, mixed cement and pushed it in iron wheelbarrows ("wheelbars"), chemically blistered our skins while hot-doping new pipeline, swabbed oil storage tanks, grubbed mesquite or other prickly desert growths to make way for new pump stations. We worked ten hours; the pay ranged from seventy to ninety-four cents for each of them, and we strangely disbelieved in labor unions.

There was a certain camaraderie, yes, a brotherhood of the lower rungs; kidding could be rough, raw, personal. Often, however, the day's sun combined with the evening's beer or liquor to produce a special craziness. Then fights erupted, on the job or in beer joints or among roommates in their quarters. Few rules burdened such fights, and the gentle or unwary could suffer real damage. Such people frightened me. They frighten me now, when I encounter them on visits to West Texas beer joints or lolling about a truckstop café. If you permit them to know it, however, your life will become a special long-running hell: *Grady, let's me and you whup that booger's ass for him again.* Often, in the oil patch, one had to act much tougher than the stuff he knew to be in his bones. It helped to pick a fight occasionally and to put the boots to your adversary once you got him down. Fear and rage being first cousins, you could do it if you had to.

But I can't tell you what it's really like, day to day, being a Redneck: not in the cool language of one whom time has refurbished a bit or by analytical uses of whatever sensibilities may have been superimposed through the years. That approach can hint at it in a general way, knock the rough edges off. But it isn't raw enough to put you down in the pit: let you smell the blood, know the bone dread, the debts, the random confrontations, the pointless migrations, or purposeless days. I must speak to you from an earlier time, bring it up from the gut. Somehow fiction is more suited to that.

You may consider this next section, then, to be a fictional interlude . . . or near-fiction, maybe . . . voices from the past . . . essence of Redneck. Whatever. Anyway, it's something of what life

was like for many West Texas people in the late 1940s or early
1950s; I suspect that even today it remains relatively true there and
in other sparse grazing places of America's unhorsed riders: those
who fight our dirtier wars, make us rich by the schlock and dreck
they buy and the usurious interest rates they pay, those who suffer
the invisible rule of deaf masters and stew in their own poor juices.
Those white niggers who live on the fringes out near the very edge
and hope, mostly, to accumulate enough survival techniques to
skate by. What follows is, at once, a story that didn't really happen
and one that has happened again and again.

2.

Me and Bobby Jack and Red Turpin was feeling real good that
day. We'd told this old fat fart bossing the gang to shove his pipeline up his ass sideways, and then we'd hitched a ride to Odessa
and drawed our time. He was a sorry old bastard, that gang boss.
He'd been laying around in such shade as he could find, hollering
at us for about six weeks when we didn't pissant pipe fast enough
to suit him. Hisself, he looked like he hadn't carried nothing heav-
ier than a lunch bucket in twenty years.

What happened had happened in the morning, just before we
would of broke for dinner. Red Turpin was down in the dumps
because the finance company had found him and drove his old
Chevy away. We tried to tell him not to sweat it, that it wasn't
worth near half of what he owed on it, but that never wiped out the
fact that he was left afoot.

The gang boss had been bitching and moaning more than usual
that day. All at once Red spun around to him and said, "I'm gona
git me a piece of yore ass, Mr. Poot, if you don't git offa mine."
Well, the gang boss waved his arms and hollered that ol' Red was
sacked, and Red said, "Fuck you, Mr. Poot. I was a-huntin' a job
when I found this 'un."

Me and Bobby Jack was standing there with our mouths dropped
open when the gang boss started yelling at us to get back to work
and to show him nothing but assholes and elbows. He was jumping around all red in the face, acting like a stroke was on him.

Bobby Jack said, "Shit on such shit as this. Lincoln's done freed the slaves," and about that time he dropped his end of that length of pipe and told that gang boss to shove it.

"Sideways, Mr. Poot," I hollered. And then I dropped *my* end in the dirt.

Mr. Poot squealed like a girl rabbit and grabbed a monkey wrench off the crew truck and warned us not to come no closer. Which would of been hard to do, fast as he was backing up. So we cussed him for seventeen kinds of a fool and pissed on the pipe we'd dropped and then left, feeling free as the blowing wind. I never been in jail long enough to have give thought to busting out, but I bet there'd be some of the same feeling in it.

Out on the Crane Highway we laughed and hooted about calling that old gang boss "Mr. Poot" to his face, which is what we'd been calling him behind his back on account of he just laid around in the shade by the water cans and farted all day. But finally, after four or five cars and several oil trucks passed us up, we kinda sagged. You could see down that flat old highway for about three days, and all there was was hot empty. Red got down in the mouth about his old lady raising hell soon as she learned how he'd cussed his way off the job. Bobby Jack said hell, just tell 'er he got laid off. "Shit," Red said. "She don't care if it's fared or laid off or carried off on a silk piller. All she knows is, it ain't no paycheck next week."

By the time we'd grunted answers to questions and signed papers and drawed our time at the Morrison Brothers Construction Company there in Odessa, and got a few cool 'uns down in a East Eighth Street beer joint, we was back on top. I swear, a certain amount of beer can make a man feel like he could beat cancer. We played the jukebox—Hank Williams, he'd just come out with one that reached out and grabbed you; seems to me like it was "Lovesick Blues," and there was plenty of Tubbs and Tillman and Frizzell—and shot a few games of shuffleboard at two bits a go. It was more fun than a regular day off because we was supposed to be working. I recollect Bobby Jack wallowing a swig of beer around in his mouth and saying, "You know what we doin'? We stealin' time." He looked real pleased.

Bobby Jack danced twice with a heavyset woman in red slacks from Conroe, who'd come out to Odessa on the Greyhound to find her twin sister that had been run off from by a driller. But all she'd found was a mad landlord that said the woman's sister had skipped out on a week's rent and had stole two venetian blinds besides. "I called that landlord a damn liar," the Conroe woman said. "My twin sister don't steal, and she wadn't raised to stealin'. We come from good stock and got a uncle that's been a deputy sheriff in Bossier City, Louisiana, for nearly twenty years."

Bobby Jack had enough nookie on the brain to buy her four or five beers, but all she done was flash a little brassiere strap and give him two different names and tell him about being a fan dancer at the Texas Centennial in 19-and-36. She babbled on about what all she'd been—a blues singer, a automobile dealer's wife, a registered nurse; everything but a lion tamer it seemed like—until Bobby Jack said, "Lissen, hon, I don't care what all you been. All I care about's what you are now and what *I* am. And I'm horny as a range bull with equipment hard as Christmas candy. How 'bout you?" She got in a mother huff and claimed it was the worst she'd ever been insulted. When Bobby Jack reached over and taken back the last beer he'd bought her, she moved over to a table by herself. I didn't care; she'd struck me as a high hat anyway.

A fleshy ol' boy wearing a Mead's Fine Bread uniform straddled a stool by us and said, "Man, I taken a leak that was better'n young love. I still say if they'd *give* the beer away and charge a dollar to piss, they'd make more money." We talked about how once you'd went to take a beer piss, you had to go ever five minutes, where you could hold a good gallon up until you'd went the first time.

Red Turpin got real quiet like he does when he's bothered bad. I whispered to Bobby Jack to keep an eye on the sumbitch because when Red quits being quiet, he usually gets real loud and rambunctious in a hurry. Then, along between sundown and dark, Bobby Jack got real blue. He went to mumbling about owing on his new bedroom set and how much money his wife spent on home permanents and started cussing the government for different things. Bobby Jack had always hated Harry Truman for some reason and blamed him ever time a barmaid drawed a hot beer or he dropped a dime in a crack. Now it seemed like he was working up to blaming Truman for losing him his job. I didn't much care about Harry

Truman either way, but I'd liked President Roosevelt for ending hard times even though ol' Eleanor traipsed all over the world and run with too many niggers. My daddy's people come from Georgia before they settled over around Clarksville, and hadn't none of us ever been able to stomach niggers.

Bobby Jack kept getting bluer and bluer, and I commenced worrying about what he might do. He may be little; but he's wound tight, and I've seen him explode. Finally a flyboy from the Midland Air Base tapped his shoulder and asked if he had a match. Bobby Jack grinned that grin that don't have no fun in it and said, "Sure, airplane jockey. My ass and your face." The flyboy grinned kinda sickly. Before he could back off, Bobby Jack said, "Hey, Yankee boy, what you think about that shitass Harry Truman?" The flyboy mumbled about not being able to discuss his Commander in Chief on account of certain regulations. "I got your Commander in Chief swangin'," Bobby Jack said, cupping his privates in one hand. "Come 'ere and salute 'im." The flyboy set his beer down and took off like a nigger aviator, lurching this way and that.

Bobby Jack felt better for a little bit; I even got him and Red Turpin to grinning a little by imitating Mr. Poot when we'd cussed him. But it's hard to keep married men perked up very long. I married a girl in beautician's college in Abilene in '46, but we didn't live together but five months. She was a Hardshell Baptist and talked to God while she ironed and pestered me to get a job in a office and finish high school at night. She had a plan for me to go on to junior college and then make a tent preacher.

Red Turpin went to the pay phone back by the men's pisser to tell his wife to borrow her daddy's pickup and come get him. He had to wait a long spell for her to come to the neighbor's phone, because Red's had been cut off again, and I could tell right off she wasn't doing a great deal of rejoicing.

"Goddammit, Emma," Red said. "We'll thresh all that shit out later. Come git me and chew my ass out in person. It's cheaper than doin' it long distance." Red and Emma lived in Midland behind the Culligan Bottled Water place. "Lissen," Red said, "I can't do nothin' about it right now. I'll whup his ass when I can find him, but all I'm tryin' to do right now is git a ride home . . . What? . . . Well, all right, goddammit *I* don't like hearing the little fartknocker cry neither. Promise 'im we'll buy 'im another 'un." He listened for a minute, got real red in the face, and yelled, "Lissen, Emma, *just fuck you!* How many meals you missed since we been married? *Just fuck you!*" From the way he banged the phone down I couldn't tell for sure which one of 'em had hung up first. Red looked right through me, and his eyes was hard and glittery. "Some cocksucker stole my kid's trike," he said, and stumbled on back toward the bar.

Two old range cowboys come in about then, their faces like leather that had been left out in the sun, and the potbellied one was right tipsy. He was hollering "*Ahha, Santa Flush!*" and singing about how he was a plumb fool about "Ida Red," which was a song that had been made popular by Bob Wills and the Texas Playboys. He slammed me on the back in a good-natured way and said, "Howdy, stud. Gettin' any strange?"

He grinned when I said, "It's all strange to me," and went on in the pisser real happy. When Red followed the old cowhand in, I just naturally figured he'd went to take a leak. I moseyed over to the jukebox and played "Slippin' Around" by Floyd Tillman, which, when I seen him play the Midland VFW Hall, he said he had wrote on a napkin late one night at a café in Dumas when all between him and starvation was forty-some cents and a bottle of Thunderbird wine.

In a little bit Red Turpin slid back on his stool and started drinking Pearl again, big as you please. About a half a beer later the second cowboy went to the pisser and come out like a cannon had shot him, yelling for a doctor and the po-leece. "They done killed ol' Dinger," he hollered. "I seen that big 'un go in right behind him. They's enough blood in there to float a log."

Four or five people run back toward the pisser; a general commotion started, and I said real quick, "Come on. Let's shuck outta here." But Bobby Jack was hopping around cussin' Red Turpin, asking what the hell he'd did. Red had a peculiar glaze in his eye; he just kept growling and slapping out at Bobby Jack like a bear swatting with his paw at a troublesome bee.

The barkeep run up and said, "You boys hold what you got." He yanked a sawed-off shotgun from under the bar and throwed down on us. "Skeeter," he hollered, "call the po-leece. And don't you damn bohunks move a hair." I wouldn't a-moved for big money.

The old cowboy had been helped out of the pisser and was sitting all addled at a back table, getting the blood wiped off his face. He groaned too loud to be good dead and kept asking, "What happened?" which was the same thing everybody was asking him. He seemed to think maybe a bronc had unhorsed him, and somebody laughed.

The barkeep relaxed his shotgun a smidgen. But when I leaned across the bar and offered him $12 to let us go on our way, he just shook his head and said, "It's gonna cost you a heap more'n that if I hafta blow you a twin asshole."

Two city cops come in, one fatter than the other; hog fat and jowly. They jangled with cuffs, sappers, and all kinds of hardwear; them sumbitches got more gear than Sears and Roebuck. The biggest cop huffed and puffed like he'd run a hill and said, "What kinda new shit we got stirred up here, Frankie?"

The barkeep poked a thumb in our direction and said, "That big ol' red-haired booger yonder beat up a Scharbauer Ranch cowboy." I didn't like the sound of that, on account of the Scharbauers owned everything that didn't belong to God and had the rest of it under lease.

"What about it, big 'un?" the fattest cop asked Red.

"I never hit *him*," Red said.

"Oh, I see," the big cop said. "That feller just musta had bad luck and slipped and fell on his ass in somebody else's blood." You could tell he was enjoying hisself, that he would of poleeced for free.

"I never hit *him*," Red said again. He commenced to cry, which I found disgusting. From the way Bobby Jack looked at me and shook his head I could tell it pissed him off, too.

"Yeah, he did," the barkeep said. "Near as I unnerstan' it, the boomer hit the cowboy without a word passin'. Far as the cowboy knows he might been knocked flat by a runaway dump truck."

"On your feet." The big cop jerked Red off of the barstool. He tightened his grip and lowered his voice and said, "You twitch just one of them fat ol' shitty muscles, big 'un, and I'll sap you a new hat size. And if 'at ain't enough, my partner'll shoot you where you real tender." Red kept on blubbering, whining something about somebody stealing his kid's trike, while the short cop fumbled the cuffs on him; me and Bobby Jack looked away and was careful not to say nothing. One time up in Snyder, I ask this constable what a buddy's fine would be when he was being hauled off for common public drunk, and the sumbitch taken me in, too. Next morning in court I found out the fine for common public drunk: $22 and costs.

The big cop went back and talked to the hurt cowboy awhile and wrote down in a notebook. Now that his health was better the hurt cowboy wanted more beer. The barkeep give him one and said, "On the house, Hoss. Sorry about the trouble."

Then the big cop come walking back to me and Bobby Jack, giving us the hard-eye. He said, "You two peckerwoods holdin' cards in this game?" We naw-sirred him. The barkeep nodded, which I thought it was nice of him not to have told I'd offered a $12 bribe. The big cop looked us over: "Where you boys work at?" We told him Morrison Brothers Construction. "Him, too?" He nodded toward Red, who was standing with his head down and studying his cuffed wrists.

"Well," I said, "I heard he quit lately."

The cop grunted and tapped Bobby Jack on the ass with his billy club and said, "Keep it down to a dull roar, little 'un. I'm tard, and done had six Maggie-and-Jiggs calls. Old ladies throwin' knives and pots at their husbands, or their husbands kickin' the crap out of 'em. I don't wanta come back in this sumbitch till my shift's over and I'm scenting beer."

They taken the old cowboy to the county hospital for stitches. When he passed by, being about half helt up, I seen his face had been laid open like a busted watermelon. I guess maybe Red's ring that he got in a gyp joint in that spick town acrost from Del Rio done it. Just seeing it made my belly swim and pitch. One time at Jal, New Mexico, I seen a driller gouge out a roughneck's eye with a corkscrew when they fell out over wages, and I got the same feeling then, only more so.

The Conroe woman in red slacks was sashaying around, telling everybody with a set of ears how we'd broke a record insulting her just before Red beat up the old cowboy, and you could tell she'd be good at stirring up a lynch mob and would of enjoyed the work. Everybody kept looking at us like they was trying to make up their minds about something. After we'd drank another beer and belched loud to show they wasn't spooking us, and dropped a quarter in the jukebox like nothing had happened, we eased on out the door.

I wanted to hit Danceland on East Second because a lot of loose hair pie hung out there. Or the Ace of Clubs, where they had a French Quarter stripper who could twirl her titty tassels two different directions at once and pick half dollars up off the bar top with her snatch. But Bobby Jack said naw, hell, he reckoned he'd go on home and face the music. I sure was glad I didn't have no wife waiting to chew on my ass and remind me that I owed too much money or had too many kids to go around acting free. I walked with Bobby Jack up to where he turned down the alley running between the Phillips 66 Station and Furr's Cafeteria, which was close to the trailer park where he lived. "Well," Bobby Jack said, "at least ol' Red won't have to worry 'bout gettin' a ride to Midland. He's got him a free bed in the crossbar hotel." We talked a little about checking on how much Red's bail had been set at, but didn't much come of it. To tell the truth, what he had did didn't make much sense and ruined the best part of the night. Without saying so, we kinda agreed he'd brought it on hisself.

I went over to the Club Café and ate me a chicken-fried steak with a bowl of chili beans on the side and listened to some ol' humpbacked waitresses talk about how much trouble their kids was. Next day I caught on with a drilling crew up in Gaines County, and it wasn't but about six weeks more that I joined the Army just in time to see sunny Korea, so I never did learn what all Red got charged with or how he come out.

1974

A Coach for All Seasons

THE FOOTBALL BOYS of Midland High School were anxious and uncertain on that day in 1945 when we met our new coach. Rumors flew that he was half Comanche Indian. Texas boys knew the Comanches to be the fiercest of the warring desert tribes.

Aubra Nooncaster was a fearsome-looking fellow if judged on size alone; his 6-foot, 5-inch frame held 250 pounds so well distributed he appeared almost lean. At 32, he gave the impression he would not do to trifle with. Linebacker Barry Boone took one look and whispered, "I bet he works our blankety-blank fannies off."

All we knew of the coach was that he was freshly out of the U.S. Army Air Corps and World War II. I had no way of knowing that this dark, brooding man who often seemed preoccupied by concerns not visible to the rest of us—my initial impression as a 16-year-old high school junior—would become one of the most important people to touch my life.

Our football squad had drilled for about a week when Coach Nooncaster said: "We don't have as much material as Odessa, Abilene and some others on our schedule. We must work harder than they do to attain results." I was stunned at hearing the truth so baldly spoken; my prior coaches had attempted to persuade our thin squad that we could easily run through oak doors, Notre Dame and the schoolboy opposition.

After we lost our opening game in 1945 by three touchdowns, Coach Noon—as I came to call him—was quick to praise those who had played well and to thank us all for not having quit. This is when I first began to like and appreciate the man. We were accustomed to coaches who raged in losing locker rooms and walked away with dead men's stares. They had not helped my youthful opinion of myself when I was already tired, bruised, beaten and unsure of my worth.

Don't get the notion Coach Noon was soft. At Brownfield, before World War II, in five years he coached his teams to 50 wins in

56 games in a region where football was more nearly a religion than a sport. In a time when all football coaches believed that drinking liquids in practice or during games was harmful, Nooncaster's players went as cotton-mouthed and dehydrated as anyone's. Any player caught in the consumption of carbonated drinks or sweets—conventional no-nos of the period—would rue it while running punishment laps. Long before Vince Lombardi would be noted for saying, "Fatigue makes cowards of us all," Coach Noon was teaching that principle by example under a broiling Texas sun.

But it was in the classroom, rather than on the gridiron or basketball court, that Coach Noon gave me—and my teammates— our biggest surprise. And it was there he would shape me more than I knew.

Learning that he would teach a class in English literature, the football squad stampeded to enroll as if he might be handing out free beer and barbecue. It was assumed that Coach Noon would go easy on us in class to keep us scholastically eligible for service on what Gen. Douglas MacArthur had called "the field of friendly strife." The coddling of schoolboy athletes was a fairly general practice; I had once been credited, in New Mexico, with passing a course I had never enrolled in or attended.

We soon learned that Coach Noon regarded Shakespeare and Shelley at least as seriously as he took the Odessa Bronchos or the San Angelo Bobcats. I was secretly pleased. Though a dismal scholar in the mathematical and physical sciences, I privately cherished literature and history. It would have been folly to reveal those quirks to my contemporaries, many of whom were the most casual of scholars. I already had encountered hazing for the sissy crime of enlisting in a typing course ("Hey, Miss King, hunny! Take a letter!"). Though from childhood I had secretly thirsted to become a writer, precious few knew of my unmanly ambition. Certainly there was little reason for Coach Noon even to suspect it.

One afternoon in class, Coach Noon played a record of himself reciting Kipling's biting "Tommy Atkins," a lament on civilian indifference to soldiers except in time of war. We surreptitiously giggled as he listened to the poem with his eyes closed.

At the record's conclusion, Coach Noon looked up. "Smith, what did that poem mean to you?"

The big tackle in faded blue jeans shuffled in place: "Aw hail, Coach. It don't make much sense to me."

"Green?"

"It don't mean nothin' to me, Coach."

"Brown?"

"Me neither, Coach. I think it's silly."

Around the room it went until Coach Noon called my name: "Me neither, Coach."

Our teacher dropped his head, closed his eyes and said nothing for what seemed five minutes. Then, quietly: "At the conclusion of this year, I hope never again to darken the door of a schoolhouse. Class dismissed."

We deserted the classroom in an enthusiastic clatter. I was somewhere in the pack when Coach Noon's voice stopped me: "Not you, King!"

I flopped back in my seat, wondering about my special crime. Coach Noon approached, shaking a huge finger in my face. His voice trembling, he said, "Smith can sit on his butt in ignorance if he chooses, because he'll inherit a big ranch. Green is the son of a rich oilman who'll take care of him. Brown's family owns this, that and the other thing." I sat, astonished, not understanding the drill. "But *your* father," he said, momentarily grabbing my shirt front, "is a working man just like mine. If you expect to amount to anything, you'll have to do it on your own."

"Yessir," I mumbled.

"You're not using your brains or your talents," he rumbled in a rising voice. "You're better than you show, and that's what makes me so damned mad!"

"Yessir."

"You're going to have to do A work in this class to get a C!" he thundered. "And if you don't do A work, then I'll take it out of your hide on the football field! Understand? Got that?"

He loomed over me, larger and angrier than the Old Testament God. "Yessir," I quaked, and escaped as soon as permitted.

That afternoon in study hall, I bent to my books rather than indulging in the usual horseplay or attempting to sneak off to the boys' room for a forbidden smoke.

I had been having trouble with my father since age 14, staging a noisy rebellion against what I considered his tight leash and restrictive codes. He was a stubborn man who refused to exchange his values for mine.

Shortly after I came under coach Noon's influence, my father and I had an ugly fight from which no winner emerged. (In later years, as I matured and he mellowed, we grew close and loving. In 1945, however, that seemed a dim prospect.)

Following our fight, my father decreed that I could no longer live in his home unless I agreed to his terms. I proudly refused. For several days, I stayed the night at friends' houses, cadging meals where I could. But as word got around of my home troubles, my friends' parents withdrew their hospitalities.

One day after basketball practice, I hid in a small room used to store athletic gear and passed the night in the high school gym. The next day, I smuggled in a few toilet articles and clothes, using the locker-room facilities for my morning shower. It was lonely and wretched but had the virtue of not lasting long—school authorities learned of my unauthorized nest and ordered me out. Coach Noon took me to the Minute Inn, on the edge of the campus; over a cheeseburger and milk shake he'd bought me, he indirectly persuaded me to return home with remarks about respect and responsibility.

The feud with my father continued, however. I sought out the Navy recruiter, lied about my age and attempted to enlist. I learned that, although I claimed to be 17, I would need my father's signature. While I brooded over how to get around that requirement, Coach Noon approached me.

He was manning a push broom, sweating, as he instructed me to walk along with him in the gym. "What's this nonsense I hear that you're trying to join the Navy?"

Well, yes, I had given it some thought.

He snorted and shook his head in exasperation, "No you haven't! You don't know enough to have thought it out!" While I reeled from that assault, he said, "You think war is glamorous. It isn't. Good friends of mine—boys I coached, some only a little older than you—are in their graves now." Suddenly, I knew what he'd been brooding about that I hadn't been able to see. "We haven't seen our last war," he said. "Don't risk it. The military will promise you anything, but once they get you, they own you. They'll do with you as they like." He placed a big hand on my shoulder; I don't know which of us he felt the need to steady. Softly he said, "Stay in school. Learn. Equip yourself. Don't throw your future away."

And then I was looking at his broad back, moving away, bent over the push broom; he moved rapidly, swiping at the floor as if intending to erase something.

For the remainder of the school year, it seems in retrospect, Coach Noon took me on as a personal project. Colorblind, he placed me by his side in the station wagon we used for basketball trips—ostensibly to tell him whether traffic lights were red or green, though now I suspect deeper motives. Once I asked who had written a poem he quoted. He grinned and said, "I fear that's the doggerel according to Nooncaster." That's when I realized I was in the presence of my first flesh-and-blood poet.

Coach seemed to find a lesson or moral in all things. After our star basketballer had fouled out of a close, tense, one-point game, then casually trotted to the locker room to change, I could see Coach Noon doing a slow burn. Later, he said to me privately, "That boy will have trouble in life. He didn't care enough about the outcome of the game or his teammates to stick around. He didn't even show normal curiosity!"

My schoolwork improved; good habits carried over into the spring of 1946. But in the summer, I clashed again with my father. He sighed, surrendered and signed papers permitting me to join the Army; it seemed the only way we might reach an armistice in our private war. Teachers, coaches and members of the Bulldog Boosters gave me a bad time about it. Coach Noon had disappeared for the summer and didn't know.

Soon homesick, I wrote him from a lonely barracks in New Jersey to tell him I wished I had taken his advice. But the letter came off whiny, so I ripped it up. When I returned home on my first furlough and rushed to Midland High School, one coach glared and said, "If you and Bert Stringer hadn't joined the Army, we might have won two more games." Coach Noon failed to censure me. As our brief visit ended, he said simply, "I hope you won't stop reading."

I next saw him in 1954, when I was a sportswriter and getting ready to go East to seek my fortune. He was taping ankles for Pampa High, where he had moved as coach in 1947. When he learned my vocation, he grinned and said, "I should have been nicer to you. You never know who'll wind up passing judgment on you."

I got lost in my career and didn't contact him again for 20 years. Then, on impulse—I think it was because I was trying to teach writing at Princeton and came to a fresh appreciation of how well Nooncaster had taught—I mailed him a copy of my latest book. He retaliated by sending me one of his three published volumes of poetry. We began to exchange long discourses, by letter and telephone, full of midnight philosophies, book talk and those memories aging men cling to.

My vanity was a bit bruised when I learned Coach Noon didn't recall half as much of our association as I did—understandable, as he had taught thousands. Still, I wanted to feel more special because he had been so special to me. I also learned he was not Indian at all, but Dutch-English-Scotch-Irish, and that we had grown up only 16 years apart in Eastland County, the sons of fathers who were poor dirt-farmers and oil-field workers. And I learned that his poetry was very fine indeed, that it haunted me with its rhythms and imagery of weather, attritions, hard-scrabble farming and general melancholy.

"Sequence for Catharisis" is about that terrible day when Coach Noon, then 8 years old, saw his father injured and his 4-year-old brother killed when a wagon pulled by runaway horses flipped over. The poem implies much self-guilt on the part of the older brother who had dallied—"unfit to cope with summer's lassitude and summer's pain"—when instructed to scotch the wagon's wheels with chock blocks. It reads in part:

Oh, God, I never, never will forget
His eyes and how unwillingly he let
My brother go or how his face turned white.
They carried both of them as best they could

To house and bed. My father's legs were crushed.
Then someone cranked a Model T and rushed
To town for help. The others turned to wood.
My brother died before the hour went by.
*My father lived, but maimed, and so did I.**

On several occasions, I arranged to visit Coach Noon, but something—airline trouble, illness—seemed to conspire to prevent it. A few months ago, as he approached 70 and I passed my 54th birthday, the old warriors got together. I felt guilty smoking around him and could no more have called him by his first name than I might address the British Queen as "Lizzie" to her face.

I wanted to tell Coach Noon what a beacon he had been when I was a young lost ship, how much of a sturdy anchor he had provided when I desperately needed a port in the storm. But I turned 16 again, tongue-tied and uncertain, and could not deliver the utterance. Somehow, I fancied it might embarrass him. As we parted on his lawn, however, I screwed up my courage and swallowed the last vestiges of that time when to show honest emotion was thought by my contemporaries to be unmanly. "Coach," I said, "I love you." He gripped my hand, hard, and said, "And I love you too."

Driving away, I looked back on a man who, though now a bit stooped and not quite as quick of eye or limb as formerly, will always stand young and tall in my eyes. Perhaps by the measurements of the age—money, power, prestige—this retired small-town teacher, poet and good family man would not be considered exceptional. But I thought, *There stands a man who did not waste his life nor permit me to entirely waste mine.* I meant it as a living accolade, of course, but we might all die satisfied should we deserve it as an epitaph.

1983

* "Sequence for Catharsis" excerpt from *Amid the Glow of Suns* by A. R. Nooncaster. The Naylor Company: San Antonio. Reprinted by permission of the author.

My Hero LBJ

*How a second-banana politician confronted Lyndon in ele-
vators, airplanes, campaign meetings, and hotel suites, and
captured for good and ill one of the most complex and flam-
boyant political personalities in our history.*

IF ANYTHING SET ME APART from my boyhood contemporaries
in the parched and impoverished area of West Texas where I grew
up, it was a precocious interest in politics. My father, a small dirt
farmer and lay preacher, took me to a political pie supper when
I was nine. I fell completely under the political spell. The idea
of being applauded by a crowd for bragging about yourself,
and maybe getting paid for it besides, fascinated me. A county-
commissioner candidate from our mud-bog precinct, one Arch
Bint, was the Devil's instrument in my case. He paid me the highest
compliment a child may receive from a practicing adult by solemnly shaking my hand, soliciting my vote as if I had one, and
asking if I'd like to help him campaign. Then he gifted me with a
fistful of campaign cards. For days I walked barefoot on the dirt
roads of Eastland County on behalf of some vague justice involving
Arch Bint. Arch Bint's victory sealed my fate. Someday—somehow—I would hitch up with a big-time political hero.

My first recollection of Lyndon Johnson dates back to 1941,
when I was twelve. Johnson, then a Congressman representing a
district many miles to the east of us, was running for the U.S. Senate. One morning I walked the half-mile from our shabby old
farmhouse to the rural-route mailbox. There I found what even
then I recognized as the literature of a political pitchman. The candidate was frozen in the poses I would later get to know so well:
smiling from a platform as folks reached up to shake his hand,
serious as he talked with a rural pharaoh, radiating cheer in the
traditional family photo where hair was slicked down, dresses
starched to a fault, and everybody looked as if he'd stepped out of

a bandbox. What made this campaign pamphlet especially memorable for me was a red-letter pledge bannered across the top:

THE DAY LYNDON JOHNSON MUST VOTE TO SEND YOUR SON
TO FOREIGN WARS, THAT DAY LYNDON JOHNSON
WILL LEAVE CONGRESS AND GO WITH HIM.

With Japan warring on China and Hitler's panzer divisions smashing through Europe it was a dramatic pledge: to a small boy who saw only glory and medals in the bloodletting it was a heroic one.* Standing barefoot by that mailbox a quarter of a century ago, I became an instant LBJ man.

Johnson did not win the Senate seat in 1941. He lost by only 1,200 votes to W. Lee (Pappy) O'Daniel, that sprightly demagogue and hillbilly singer who had emerged from a flour salesman's obscurity to the Texas governorship by shouting radio hosannas in the name of the Old Folks, the Alamo, and Jesus Christ. The Texas Election Bureau prematurely announced that Johnson had won. When a flood of O'Daniel votes came in from the boondocks and pine thickets two or three days later, the reversal came as a bitter disappointment to me.

At this point I had not only never seen Johnson, I had never even heard the sound of his voice. The Depression had lingered on our sandy farm long after the nation had achieved some measure of recovery. We had no money for a luxury item like a radio. I knew LBJ only as a face smiling from posters nailed to fence posts and from stories in week-old newspapers cadged each Sunday from our more affluent neighbors. Yet these so impressed me that once, while helping my father harvest corn, I was prattling enthusiastically about Lyndon Johnson and turned a team of horses so short the flatbed wagon flipped over and very nearly maimed me. "Boy," my father asked, "don't you never think about nothin' but Lyndon Johnson and football?"

---

*Johnson fulfilled his promise. Obtaining leave from the House after Pearl Harbor, he served in the Southwest Pacific for eight months, until President Roosevelt ordered all Congressmen on active duty to return to Washington.

A NEOPHYTE'S GLIMPSE OF POWER

I would not see Johnson for another thirteen years, when he was campaigning for reelection to the U.S. Senate in 1954 (he had been first elected in 1948 by his memorable 87-vote margin). I was then a newspaper reporter deep in oil-and-McCarthy country. Senator Johnson came to Odessa to give a speech. It was a conventional one: service to the good folks of Texas, love of country and faith in the free-enterprise system, the soil, and Heaven's Plan. There were the usual homilies, the same hoary political jokes, the same cardboard poses I had gotten to know in other candidates. I left disappointed by my first glimpse of The Great Man. Besides, boyhood idolatry has a way of vanishing, and Johnson by this time had two strikes against him in my book: he had given Adlai Stevenson only token support in 1952, and he had remained too long silent while the McCarthyites treated us to their national spook show.

But Johnson's Democratic opponent in the primary reawakened my allegiance. Douglas T. Daugherty campaigned in a red fire truck and made speeches that would have frightened George III. He favored quitting the UN, going back to the Hoover Dollar, making deep knee bends to King Oil, and cleaning "the Godless Commies" out of the State Department. I went straightaway to County Democratic headquarters to enroll again in Lyndon Johnson's cause. Through that summer I tacked posters, sealed envelopes, and spoke for Johnson to vest-pocket rallies of ten-folks-and-a-rooster in remote villages like Wink, Crane, and No Trees.

I went to Washington in late 1954 with a freshman Congressman who, after noting my talents in menial tasks, had chosen me for his administrative assistant. Johnson was Texas' senior Senator and blossoming as a national figure. I arrived in Washington assuming that I would be the frequent companion of Speaker Rayburn, Senator Johnson, Mr. Justice Tom Clark, and other Texans who had preceded me to the sources of power. I did not know that "the help" is "the help" in Washington much as it is in the kitchen pantry.

Though I didn't drink coffee at the White House or socialize with Johnson after work, I did see a great deal of the Senator's staff. A neophyte in Washington could have done worse. As Majority

Leader, Johnson had great powers—many of which he had created or assumed for himself. He kept a sensitive finger on Texas politics. He could bestow grand favors. Consequently any Texan who needed to plead a special cause for his constituents or for himself naturally went to LBJ. Since most such matters are handled at the staff level, I worked in those early years with Walter Jenkins, Arthur Perry, Booth Mooney, Bill Brammer, Harry McPherson (Bill Moyers was still in college and unknown to any of us), and other Johnson staffers on a thousand routine chores. I was beer-drinking close to some of them.

I knew of the Lyndon Johnson who hired man-and-wife staff teams because, as one of his secretaries quoted him to me, "I don't want some wife at home cryin' about the cornbread gettin' cold while her husband's busy doin' something for me." Often he drove his employees to the limits of their physical endurance or to drink. He sometimes showered staff workers with gifts, praise, and promises of greatness. He might in anger banish an employee from his sight "forever," later to pay thousands of dollars for the same man's hospital bills, with no prospect of reimbursement. Once he impulsively interrupted a conference with a Texas Congressman to telephone a department store and order several new shirts for George Reedy, on the eve of an extended trip, because "that boy's always runnin' out of white shirts."

He could reduce a secretary to tears because she had failed to locate some airborne Senator by telephone within two minutes, or because she had served him an inferior cup of coffee—later apologizing by saying, as one of the young ladies told me, "Honey, you go to the best beauty shop in town, get the full treatment and tell 'em to send me the bill." This was the Lyndon Johnson who once tossed a speech back to his writers with the instructions to "Put somethin' in there that will make me sound goddamn *humble!*" Ego? There was a time when LBJ gifted any Texas baby named after him with a calf from his ranch. Once a man joined LBJ's staff, however, he would be judged a quisling if ever he spoke of his employer in any but the most flattering of terms, or if he groused about working overtime.

Once in a while I encountered the Senator in the Capitol Building, and if he saw me we might exchange quick nods or a rare smile. Generally, however, he would have another Senator in tow: leaning into his companion's face and speaking with some dreadful urgency that blinded him to mere earthlings. The Johnson who rattled the Capitol's staid walls with mad hoo-hawing and aimless goddamning, crowded you like a pickpocket while he poured on the persuasive goose grease, or who threatened, cajoled, or compromised his way through the political jungles was still to me a shadowy myth composed of corridor whispers, poker-table legends, and newspaper superlatives.

A COOLIE TURNS SOUR

Sometime in 1958 I began to see Senator Johnson a bit more frequently. At one meeting in his office, representatives of a half-dozen executive agencies spent an hour enumerating to several of us the reasons why a new international bridge between the U.S. and Mexico could not be built at El Paso. Johnson crossed his long legs, feet propped up on his desk, and drawled, "Now, boys, you-all spent the last hour tellin' me why we *can't* open up another international bridge. Now I want every one of you to give me one reason why we *can*. Then I want you to get the hell out of here and *open it!*" (They did—and LBJ cut the dedication ribbon.)

I had drinks a couple of times in the Majority Leader's suite in the Capitol along with Texas Congressmen, other administrative assistants, and favored Johnson staffers. In these sessions LBJ's conversation ranged broadly: a current political problem in Texas, chances of passing a Reciprocal Trade bill, an anecdote about Franklin D. Roosevelt, a stinging parody of Dwight D. Eisenhower. (He would screw his face into a frown, mimic Eisenhower's flat, clipped speech, and give us his version of the Eisenhower syntax: "Now, I may not know everything there is about this bill, Senator, and I might make what you might call a *mistake* now and then, but I am what you might call *sincere* about this . . ."). Suddenly he would bark a question at an aide about tomorrow's schedule, turn his head abruptly to ask a Congressman "what you're gonna do to help me and the Speaker when that Education bill comes to the Floor," or grab a telephone to dial another Senator. Sitting under a life-sized oil portrait of himself that was illuminated by indirect

lights, his in-the-flesh person looking down on us from his subtly elevated executive's chair, Senator Johnson was invariably jovial and full of hope. I enjoyed these performances hugely.

I saw the famed Johnson temper for the first time in 1959, during a three-day tour of duty that seemed no longer than a century.

Senator Johnson came to my home district as part of a statewide tour designed to solidify the political base in Texas from which he would seek the Presidential nomination the following year. It fell to my lot to act as "advance man"—the nearest thing the Western World has to a Chinese coolie. The advance man arranges for halls, podiums, luncheons, or dinners, keys to the city, press conferences, hotel accommodations, rendezvous between the visiting pooh-bah and his local political underlings, or a pitcher of water for the dignitary's bedside table. He referees disputes over who will sit where at ceremonial functions, and tries to discourage bores or potential troublemakers who might embarrass the Official Presence. Johnson's own staff attended to many of these details, but as resident coolie I was responsible for being on hand to guide everyone through the proper jig-steps.

At his first appearance, on the mezzanine floor of a downtown hotel where he spoke to about a hundred local leaders and their wives, Senator Johnson's performance could have served as a blueprint for the Compleat Cornpone Politician. He was charming, relaxed, and lean. He slouched on the podium, grinning boyishly, pulling at his ear, saying how grand it was for "me and Lady Bird to get out of the steel and stone of the cities and come back here to feel the soil of home under our feet, and draw close to all the things we hold dear while we gaze on the Texas moon." He invited all hands to "drop by and see us when you're in Washington." He reported that the coffeepot was always on, and added that "sometimes Bird bakes a buncha little cookies in the shape of the State of Texas to go with the coffee." (This earned a standing ovation and Rebel yells.) He confessed to vast stores of humility, giving credit for "whatever I may amount to" in equal measure to Celestial Beings, his mother, and everybody present. When he had finished he ambled off to mingle with the crowd, pressing flesh, cooing low, kissing old ladies on the cheek as if he had flushed a covey of favored maiden aunts. Then the party broke up and the Senator's official group retired toward his suite for a brief rest before the evening's scheduled dinner.

With the closing of the elevator door LBJ's sunny smile gave way to thunderstorm expressions. "Goddammit," he said by way of openers, "nobody told me I was supposed to make a *speech!* Didn't know it until I saw the damned podium. Up till then I thought it was just gonna be coffee, doughnuts, and bullshit!" He stared at me down to the blood. "Why in hell didn't you *tell* me they expected a speech out there? You think I'm a mind reader? Hah?" I didn't think "Yes" was the proper answer, but I was mortally afraid to say "No." So I said nothing.

Within the next twenty-four hours Senator Johnson had berated me and his staffers because (1) his hotel bed was too short and "I have to scrooch my legs up until I fold up like a goddamn accordion"; (2) nobody could locate Senator Dick Russell of Georgia on the telephone at the snap of a finger; (3) we were late for three consecutive appointments because "half of you are crawlin', half of you are walkin', and *none* of you are runnin'," and (4) he couldn't immediately find his reading spectacles. In another town where a press conference had been scheduled (and to which I had clearly heard Johnson agree the day before in a rare cheerful moment) the Senator claimed knowledge of it only as he entered the hotel where local reporters waited. He blew up in the lobby and threatened not to appear. He was finally steered into the hotel ballroom, but not before his histrionics caused passersby to congregate and investigate the commotion. One reporter repeatedly baited Johnson with hostile questions. Finally, ignoring him completely, Johnson silently pointed to somebody else. When the heckler persisted the Senator snapped, "That's it. Thank you, boys." He plunged out of the ballroom, the rest of us chasing along, though handicapped by not having heard the starter's gun.

In the elevator the Senator's first words were: "Which one of you do I thank for *this* little lynching?" No one stepped forward to claim the medal. Those were Johnson's last words for the next fifteen minutes as he brooded silently, staring at the television set in his room. The rest of us stared and brooded with him. I was terrified that I might have to sneeze.

Maybe there is something about Lyndon B. Johnson and elevators not apparent to the eye. Some of his greatest conniptions have been thrown there. Likely, however, this is true because elevators happen to be the first place he is able to drop the necessary public poses and give vent to human frustrations. At any rate, my one head-to-head battle with Johnson started in an elevator the night before he would mercifully leave our district. Following a dinner where he had flashed his usual mixture of country charm and worldly knowledge, the Senator barked directly at me: "Who was that redheaded son-of-a-bitch set two chairs down from me?" I groped for the red-headed SOB's identity, but at that moment I could not have read my own name off a billboard. "Who-*ever* he was," Johnson said, "I don't want that goofy SOB sittin' in the same room with me again. Ruined mah whole night . . ." He trailed off into mumbles, glaring.

The hour was late. I was tired, and just about one more harsh word away from tears or running off from home. In his room the Senator was unhappy because a delegation of local citizens required entertainment. I would have gladly done the job. It required nothing more strenuous than pouring a little whiskey, laughing at the punch lines of old jokes, and massaging shriveled egos. Senator Johnson, however, assigned this choice duty to his own permanent staff people. He thrust a slip of paper in my hand. Just before plunging into the bathroom he said, "I want these people in that *exact* order." The note required two telephone calls to Washington, one to New York, one to Austin, and two or three more to small Texas towns. There wasn't a telephone number on the slip. I sat on my hands and let my juices boil. When the Senator entered the room he gave me one quick glance. Then he asked the room-at-large to whom he had given the note. Eventually all eyes turned my way. It was like standing in front of a firing squad.

I'm sure my voice trembled as I said, "I'm tired of being your lackey while your staff people sit on their rumps and drink whiskey. I've got *my own* man to lackey for." (The last sentence was spoken with some strange, hot pride—which shows what being a second-banana politician will do for your sense of values.) I have the vague recollection that somebody dropped an ashtray. One of

Johnson's staffers suddenly snatched the note from my hand and whisked it away, presumably to the nearest telephone.

I am unable to recall the Senator's immediate reaction to the mutiny. Everyone seemed frozen in place. My ears throbbed blood as I plunged from the room. A friend stumbled out behind me, eyes wide and face pale. I would hesitate to quote him exactly, but I think he called on his Lord in a hoarse voice and asked if I had lost my goddamned mind. While I raved about holding Senator Johnson's hat, carrying his bags, and being treated like a stepchild, my friend made frantic shushing sounds and waved his hands as if he might be flagging the Greyhound. He desperately begged that I go someplace to "get a beer, cool off, and for God's sake stay out of Lyndon's sight."

I cooled off enough to worry about whether I'd lose my $16,000 a year job, then returned to a night of feverish sleep. About daylight the next morning the telephone in my room rang.

"You had your coffee yet?"

I said no.

"Come on up and have some," Lyndon Johnson said.

The Senator was in a figured robe. The morning newspaper was scattered about the floor and on the coffee table. He greeted me with a grunt that sounded half-friendly, then poured some coffee and handed it over. Just as I took the cup he said, "You can get kinda salty, can't you?" Then he grinned. My mumbled response consisted of mere sounds without any form resembling known words. The Senator took my arm and stood nose-to-nose, breathing on my eyeglasses. He talked about how "young fellas" like me make big politicians tick. He himself had been secretary to a Congressman, he said, in 19-and-32.

Then he settled on the couch and for perhaps the next half-hour entertained me with memories of New Deal days, and of his Texas boyhood, and praise of my boss. He spoke of how dedicated his staff was to him, and of how very much he loved his staff. He offered free advice ("You oughta get a law degree, young man like you. Come in handy no matter *what* profession you follow"), asked my opinion on whether a local politician had Congressional ambitions "enough that it won't let him sleep nights." Then he so adroitly maneuvered me out of the room with a darting little series of back-pats, soothing clucks, and handclasps that I was in the elevator before I fully realized the audience was over.

I soon came back, though. For when the Senator departed for the airport, I found myself struggling with the bellhop for the honor of carrying his bags.

BEDDING DOWN WITH MOSSBACKS

Some admiring newspapermen, many Southern Congressmen, and almost all Johnson staffers thought LBJ would be nominated for President in 1960. I disagreed. Unwisely I said so a few times. When the word got around, one of Johnson's key advisers met me over lunch to suggest a little more diplomacy. "You're from Texas," he pointed out. "It couldn't help the Senator, it couldn't help your Congressman, and it couldn't help *you personally* if you went around saying 'Johnson can't win.'" Though this sounded a little like a threat, it also sounded a lot like the truth.

In early 1960, Johnson-for-President headquarters opened in Washington's Ambassador Hotel. Walter Jenkins, Johnson's long-time administrative assistant, solicited my "volunteer" help at the campaign headquarters at nights and on weekends. The Senator, Jenkins said, would not be a candidate of record. He might even issue statements from time to time disavowing Presidential ambitions. Meanwhile, the Humphreys, Stevensons, Kennedys, and Symingtons would, perhaps, knock themselves off in Presidential primaries.

I was but one of many "volunteers," many of them from Capitol Hill and almost all of them with Texas roots, who pioneered the Johnson Presidential effort. No doubt I had more inner conflicts and reservations than most. I did not believe that Senator could be nominated because of sectional limitations, and I was personally attracted to Jack Kennedy.

By 1960 my feelings about Johnson were ambivalent—I admired him on the one hand and couldn't tolerate him on the other. As a working politician I admired his art in steering legislation through Congress at a time when he could have frustrated Presi-

dent Eisenhower by tying up the legislative machinery. But he refused the obstructionist role, saying that "any jackass can kick
down a barn but it takes a carpenter to build one."

In fact, he saved Eisenhower's legislative chestnuts time after
time. It seemed apparent, however, that many of Senator Johnson's
shows suffered from overdirection. Often I was amazed that the
national press (to say nothing of Republicans) didn't blow the
whistle on his more obviously staged dramas. He seldom called a
record vote until his pulse takers had determined that he had
enough votes to win. He often stashed two or three or four "safe"
Senators away in the Senate cloakroom, rushing these loyal reserves in to win a cliff-hanger at the most dramatic moment. LBJ
knew that the more powerful and effective he could *appear*, the
more powerful and effective he would *be*.

Politicians, like sleight-of-hand artists, must create certain illu-
sions: there is simply not enough legitimate, workable magic to
satisfy the customers. Any show—however well-staged or smoothly
presented—requires a lot of honest toil behind the scenes before it
approaches perfection. Johnson's did. But in the matter of exercis-
ing national partisan leadership, or in performing real political services in Texas (emotionally, I confess unshamedly, almost as important to me as all the Senate productions in the world) my boyhood
hero was sadly disappointing. It was not merely that he failed to be
liberal, not even that he had voted against anti-lynch legislation in
the late 1940s, or that he sang praises to the 27½ per cent oil-
depletion allowance under which the rich get richer and the poor
pay taxes. As a working pol, I could understand his dilemma. He
represented a state largely oriented toward the southern viewpoint,
a state where schoolboys are taught that oil is the backbone of the
economy and is, therefore, sacred. What disappointed me most
about Johnson was that he threw his considerable weight and prestige into the camp of mossbacks who held Texas as if it were their
own grand duchy.

The Texas Establishment has opposed social reforms to the extent of perpetuating oppression, ignorance, and poverty. Even today, Texas ranks at or near the bottom of the 50 states in aid to the
blind, aged, and mentally ill, and in almost all social services.

Texas Governors have routinely vetoed appropriations to improve hospitals, libraries, prisons, and old-age pensions. They have cheerfully signed "right-to-work" laws and harsh segregation measures. Legislators have urged soak-the-poor taxes on bread, work clothes, and medicines. They have permitted loan sharks to charge usurious rates and have refused to enact any laws protecting the state's thousands of migratory farm laborers who are carted from farm to hovel in open cattle trucks. They have openly cavorted with the fat-cat lobbyists. They have damned the federal government for foreign aid, aid to education, the antipoverty program, and the Peace Corps. I am not speaking here of John Birch Republicans nor even of Eisenhower ones, but of Tory Democrats who have made the wheels of influence go in Texas.

If any man had the power and finesse to move Texas toward a more moderate, enlightened political climate it was Lyndon Johnson. He chose not to use his talents in that direction at all. He did not stay on the sidelines while the liberals fought desperately for survival (as he might have done) but he invariably cast his lot with the Tories. He saw the labor-liberal bloc as a rising threat to his grip on Texas. Time after time he fused patchwork coalitions that effectively crushed liberal hopes of gaining a voice in the Democratic party. Working within the framework of the Establishment—*i.e.*, the Governor, the State Democratic Executive Committee, and local political bosses—Lyndon Johnson got what he wanted. What he wanted was, simply, control.

VISITING BARONS

A typical display of Johnson's tactics occurred at the Democratic state convention in Fort Worth in 1956. As in past years, Johnson and crusty old Speaker Sam Rayburn arrived from Washington like visiting feudal barons. They received in their hotel rooms, and if you had business to transact you sought them out with a smile on your face. They brought along a coterie of Texas Congressmen to use in the same way that they used office runners and legislative aides in Washington. The Congressmen, taking to heart speaker Rayburn's advice—"The best way to get along is to go along"—

fanned out to their respective home-district delegations to act as Johnson's eyes and ears. Most of them were so conservative they did not fully approve of indoor plumbing.

These Congressmen were on friendly, first-name terms with the yahooing Main Street merchants, bankers, oil barons, labor-hating farmers, and xenophobic ranchers who were delegates to the convention. If the Congressmen heard rumors that a certain delegate was flirting with "the Red Hots" (LBJ's private name for the liberals) they rushed to pass the word. More than one delegate who had "flirted with the Red Hots" found himself confronted by his banker, preacher, lawyer, Congressman, brother, or anyone else who might hold some financial or emotional claim on him. Most were happy to scurry back into the fold after being exposed to "The Treatment."

In 1956 numerous counties sent contesting delegations to the state convention—liberal and conservative groups both claiming to be "official." The handpicked credentials committee invariably, of course, certified the conservatives.

El Paso County Judge Woodrow Wilson Bean was chairman of a liberal delegation. No stranger to ambition, he badly wanted his delegation seated, but knew this would take some special miracle. He set out to fashion one. Judge Bean went to Johnson and propositioned him: See that my El Paso liberals are seated and I'll deliver their votes to you. Senator Johnson saw the opportunity to woo away a delegation everyone considered firmly committed to the liberals, and at the same time acquire a pipeline into the Red Hot camp for future purposes. He told Bean that a floor fight was in prospect over whether to seat the huge Houston liberal or conservative delegation. Would Bean's liberals be willing to vote for the Houston conservatives as the price for their own seats? Judge Bean said they would. Johnson picked up the telephone, and very shortly the credentials committee certified the El Paso liberals.

Judge Bean had outpromised himself. Deeply committed to liberal causes, the El Paso delegates balked at opposing their Houston counterparts. One angrily stormed, "I didn't come down here for the pleasure of being Lyndon Johnson's rubber stamp." In a turbulent session behind locked doors the delegates reminded themselves that their purpose was to rid the state of "Dixiecrats masquerading as Democrats." Bean couldn't deal with the mutiny. He did not, however, pull up lame by rushing to Senator Johnson with a full confession.

He didn't need to. Johnson had eyes in the back of his head, it would soon seem to Bean. Through one of his many agents the Senator learned of the El Paso rebellion. When Bean arrived, Johnson said, "Judge, I hear you've decided not to go along with me on the Houston delegates."

"I'd like to, Lyndon," Bean said. "But I'm having a little trouble with some of the boys. You know how boys kick up their heels when they get away from home."

"Well, can you deliver 'em or not?"

"I can try, Senator."

"Trying don't count," Johnson snapped. "You with me or against me?"

"Well, I tell you," Bean said, "it looks like we'll be forced to go the other way, Senator."

Johnson poked a finger into the Judge's chest. "Woodrow Bean," he said. "I'm gonna give you a little three-minute lesson in integrity. And then I'm gonna *ruin* you!"

The Senator lectured Bean for approximately three minutes on the virtues of loyalty, courage, dealing honorably, and of being a true friend to Lyndon Johnson. Whereupon he *reconvened* the credentials committee after it had permanently adjourned, a perfect sign of his iron hold on the convention. One hour later Bean's troops had been shorn of their credentials and replaced by conservative delegates. Judge Bean joined other dissidents in a fruitless "rump session" at a nearby cowbarn.

JOHNSON FOR PRESIDENT

It was the memory of his home-state tactics that made me the least joyful "volunteer" at Johnson-for-President headquarters in 1960. His preconvention campaign, as it turned out, was a shambles. Nobody seemed to be in charge of Johnson's headquarters in Washington. The co-chairmen (John Connally, later Governor of Texas, and Oscar Chapman, one-time Interior Secretary under Harry S. Truman and a sugar lobbyist) were theoretically in charge. Perhaps they occupied themselves diligently elsewhere, but they were seldom seen in headquarters. In their absence nobody assumed command. Volunteers milled about without purpose or assignment. A half-dozen of us who had practiced the craft of politics for years sat idly by while "policy decisions" were made—or pretended to be made—by a handful of old biddies I knew largely from seeing their pictures on the society page.

Once I tried to get some direction from the man said to be nominally in charge: Marvin Watson, then a Texas steel executive on loan to Johnson and now a top White House aide. Watson cheerfully confessed that he hadn't much notion of what we might do to help. Then he continued dictating a letter to some agitated Dixie mystic who had written in about "the nigger problem." Watson solemnly explained that Lyndon B. Johnson's "roots are in the South and his heart is with the South." He mentioned the Senator's heroic old Confederate soldier granddaddy.

Eventually, about all I found to do was dictate letters of the same type. Almost all of Johnson's mail came from the south or the flatlands Midwest. Much was written on lined tablet paper or in a palsied hand. Many letters were Doomsday tracts of the type handed out on street corners by trembling, popeyed prophets. Others were directed against John F. Kennedy as "the Pope's candidate," or railed against plots by the UN to take over the Pentagon, or spoke of Alaskan concentration camps being prepared for the enemies of Hubert Humphrey. Obviously, there was not a delegate vote in a carload of such correspondents. Just as obviously, LBJ was at that stage the candidate of Tory Democrats of the world.

Johnson's advisers mistakenly assumed that tactics successful in Texas would prove workable nationally. In Texas you cuddled to the Establishment by making alliances of convenience. You used your Congressional influences where they best served, by manipulating young legislators eager for seats in close proximity to the Congressional leaders, or by logrolling with cynical, horse-trading old pro pols. Thus did Johnson partisans set out to form a coalition of Dixiecrats, aging New Dealers whose visions had dimmed even

as their paunches had increased, and Congressmen or Senators thought to be susceptible to suggestion because of the vast influence of Johnson and Rayburn.

I suggested to Walter Jenkins that somebody needed to take the campaign firmly in hand. Jenkins listened a bit impatiently to my complaints. Perhaps it is well my advice was offered free, for he seemed not to set a high value on its worth. "The Senator's got a world of faith in John Connally," he said. Then he pointedly added, "I have, too." He blandly said that Johnson would capture all the southern states, that old New Deal cronies would deliver "a lot of votes in the North and East not apparent on the surface," and that endorsements had been lined up from congressional powers "all across the nation." (Asked for examples, Jenkins named Representative Ralph Rivers of Alaska and Senator Thomas Dodd of Connecticut.) He said Johnson would "naturally appeal" in Western states such as "New Mexico, Arizona, and Wyoming." He even claimed certain influences for Senator Johnson in California, adding that "the Senator worked out there as a young man for a couple of years—running an elevator in an office building." Thereafter, I privately thought of Johnson's campaign headquarters as "Disneyland East."

Typical of these elusive "supporters" was Senator Gale McGee of Wyoming. In May of 1960, with the national convention about two months away, Jenkins asked me to accompany a Texas Congressman, another from Alaska, and a former congressional delegate from Hawaii, into Wyoming. Our assignment was to see to it that the state Democratic convention adopt a motion binding delegates to the national convention under a unit rule—meaning that all delegates, regardless of their personal preferences, would be under instruction at the national convention to vote for the candidate earlier endorsed at the state level. Walter Jenkins was certain that in Wyoming that man would be Johnson.

"Go see Gale McGee," Jenkins ordered. "He'll cooperate one hundred percent." He exhibited the latest issue of *Time* quoting Senator McGee on Senator Johnson: "He'd make a hell of a President." When I saw him Senator McGee chatted pleasantly with me, praised Johnson, and gave the name of his local campaign manager in Casper who "will give you anything we've got."

In Casper, I asked Senator McGee's man what we might do toward locking up Wyoming's delegates under the unit rule. He was abashed; why, he'd been instructed to be strictly impartial; he couldn't take sides because Senator McGee was adopting a "hands-off" policy. I told him this was news to me and no doubt would be news to Senator Johnson.

After two days of politicking in Wyoming, it was apparent that Washington had misjudged the situation. Almost everyone favored Kennedy, including State chairman Teno Roncalio, who would control the delegation's fifteen votes. In these circumstances the unit rule could be disastrous to Johnson's hopes.

When we conveyed this news to Jenkins, he suggested that we should reverse ourselves. Rather than seeking to "solidfy and harmonize" delegates under the unit rule, we should fight to "preserve the independence of the individual delegate." In that way we might salvage anywhere from four to seven of the fifteen Wyoming votes. Jenkins was especially shocked when he learned that if Senator McGee favored Johnson, he had managed to keep it a secret from everyone in Wyoming—including his campaign manager. Later, after he counseled with Senator McGee, Jenkins called us to say there was no worry on *that* score. McGee would fly in to Wyoming to help us fight against the unit rule.

Senator McGee flew in, all right. But if he did any fighting for us he kept that a secret, too. He also kept a protective cordon of aides and friends about him and, when finally cornered as he left a downtown restaurant, he said smoothly that all the delegates were his friends, that his friends were split up among the numerous good men seeking the nomination, and that he just couldn't find it in his heart to disappoint any of his friends. So he would stay "neutral."

In the end, only the efforts of Governor Joe Hickey kept the Wyoming convention from going for Kennedy under the unit rule. Hickey, we tardily discovered, favored LBJ for the nomination. So we escaped from Wyoming with five firm Johnson votes, two more "possibles," and our scalps.

The last act in this melodrama came two months later on the floor of the Los Angeles convention. With Kennedy only eleven votes short of the nomination, Ted Kennedy approached the Wyoming delegation, where Kennedy was known to have eight and a half solid votes; Johnson had six, and one-half vote remained loyal to Adlai Stevenson. Suddenly one of Wyoming's leaders broke away from a frantic huddle with Ted Kennedy, hopped on a chair, and held up four fingers to the delegates. "Give me four votes!" he begged. "We can put him over the top! *Please* give me four votes!" Hastily the Wyoming delegates decided to write themselves a footnote to history. Chairman Roncalio proudly spoke of the honor that was his as Wyoming cast all fifteen of its votes for John F. Kennedy.

In the roar greeting the announcement, I kept my eyes on the man who had begged for four votes. He was jumping up and down, slapping a beaming Ted Kennedy on the back, apparently beside himself with joy. I recognized him as our old friend Senator Gale McGee.

INCIDENT IN EL PASO

Once the Kennedy-Johnson ticket had been nominated, their preconvention staffs joined for the battle against Nixon and Lodge. With the Kennedy forces in charge of the campaigning, conditions were much improved. Any campaign knows errors that could be authored only by green gremlins. A few boners cropped up after the Kennedy-Johnson fusion of staffs. None, however, was as glaring as those occurring among LBJ's preconvention forces. If you had a suggestion, you'd get a full hearing. Nobody attempted to sweep bad news under the rug. We were better organized and more professional.

One of the first stops was scheduled for El Paso, Texas—my home territory. I was sent ahead to assist in local tub-thumpings and physical preparations. Johnson reminded Texas Congressmen that the six-city tour of Texas would be Kennedy's first real exposure in our state. "I've gotta carry Jack Kennedy on my back in Texas," he said. "I don't want anything going wrong down there." One of the Congressmen remarked that Johnson appeared more "down-in-the-mouth" than he had ever seen him. Official Washington wondered how LBJ would accommodate his bombastic personality to standing in young Jack Kennedy's shadow. GOP partisans taunted Johnson by parodying his campaign slogan: "Half the way with LBJ."

On the night of Sunday, September 11th, Johnson flew in from an engagement in Detroit. The crowd at El Paso International Airport would have warmed any advance man's heart. We had 20,000 cheering and clacking on cue when LBJ's plane touched down. He was supposedly only twenty minutes ahead of the Kennedy plane, which was flying in from California. Along with my Congressman, local officials, and Speaker Rayburn (who had arrived in El Paso a few hours earlier), I lined up at the foot of the ramp for the official greeting. Johnson was obviously delighted with the enthusiastic crowd. He called to old friends while posing on the ramp, and cracked good-natured jokes to the photographers. Before he could step down to the speaking platform, someone called that Kennedy wanted the Senator on the airplane radio. Johnson disappeared inside. Twenty minutes later he had not returned. I was sent to see what had gone wrong.

Johnson was making it very clear. Kennedy had left California late and would be another hour in arriving. Meanwhile, he suggested that Johnson remain aboard his own plane. Johnson was in an uproar. In poolroom language he fumed because Kennedy was late, because he had been quarantined in his own aircraft, and he predicted that "the damn crowd will be gone when he gets here." Congressman Homer Thornberry and others tried in vain to soothe him. I told Lloyd Hand, a Johnson aide, that local officials were also fearful of losing the crowd unless we got the Vice-Presidential nominee on the platform. Somebody, I suggested, should pass this word. Hand suggested that I pass it. Foolishly, I did. Johnson poked a finger at me in a quick, stabbing motion and barked, "You get outta here!" As I retreated he demanded that the door be closed after me.

Five minutes later the door opened and Johnson led his entourage out. Though he acknowledged cheers with a wave of his hat, his smile seemed strained. Someone had prevailed on Johnson to call Kennedy's plane, explain the situation, and request permission to get out. Permission was granted. Having to *ask*, however, had not noticeably improved Senator Johnson's personality. He fidgeted on the platform while a dozen Congressmen and state officials made war-whooping partisan speeches. When Senator Kennedy arrived he spoke briefly, after LBJ had introduced him, inviting the crowd to his speech the following morning in El Paso Plaza. Johnson sat glumly on the platform, apparently in a thoughtful study of his shoes. Leaving the airport Johnson was further unsettled when the crowd spilled from behind restraining barriers, surged against the nominees as they made for waiting automobiles, and almost swept Mrs. Johnson off her feet. She clutched at her husband and said something, her face white. I heard Johnson snap, "For God's sakes, clear a path! Somebody's gonna get killed."

The Hotel Cortez was so crowded with cheering hordes we could hardly force our way into the elevators. I was pushed into an elevator and wedged between Kennedy and County Judge Woodrow Bean. Bean was babbling about the moment being "the greatest in Texas history" while JFK silently smiled and nodded.

The floor where Kennedy and Johnson had been booked proved to be a madhouse. Much of the crowd had eluded special policemen stationed on the stairs. Seeing the confusion Kennedy said quickly to the elevator operator, "Close the door." This done he ordered, "Stay here until they're dispersed." Somebody handed Kennedy an orange. He began to peel and eat it, cupping the peelings in his hand until I relieved him of them. When no one was looking I slipped them into Judge Bean's coat pocket.

Unfortunately, Johnson's elevator operator had dumped him into the milling crowd in the hall and he took another buffeting. By the time we arrived in Kennedy's "Presidential Suite," Senator Johnson was waiting there in a new rage. "Goddamnit," he yelled to Lloyd Hand, "where's Speaker Rayburn?" Hand said that "he was in the hall a couple of minutes ago." LBJ said, "I don't give a damn where he was a couple of minutes ago! I asked you where he is *now!*"

Hand disappeared to hunt the Speaker. Kennedy sat on a couch to eat his orange. My Congressman, Slick Rutherford, sat down by him. While they talked, I approached to take pictures to be used in the campaign. Kennedy quickly hid the orange, and gave my Congressman his full attention. After I'd finished taking pictures he resumed eating the orange.

A Kennedy staffer began clearing the room, now overflowing with local officials and unknown gawkers. He was pushing me out also (the camera leading him to think I was a newspaper photographer) until Kennedy called, "No, he's with us." I then asked Senator Kennedy to pose with my Congressman, Senator Johnson, and Speaker Rayburn. Kennedy nodded, and called across the room now free of hangers-on: "Lyndon!"

Johnson was in Sam Rayburn's face, crying out some terrible woe and emphatically poking the Speaker's chest with that stabbing forefinger. The Speaker looked tired and faintly agonized.

Kennedy called again: "Senator Johnson!" Still no answer. Lloyd Hand plucked furtively at Senator Johnson's sleeve. LBJ whirled on him: "Can't you see I'm talkin' with the Speaker, goddamnit?"

"We need you for a picture," Senator Kennedy called.

Johnson snorted a pithy expletive.

Kennedy grinned. He said, "Settle down, Lyndon. It's a long time until November."

1966

Leavin' McMurtry

A LITTLE OVER A YEAR AGO (1972) the movie folk came to Texas—to Bastrop—to film Larry McMurtry's *Leaving Cheyenne*, which remains my favorite among that good writing man's novels of the old home state. *Life* magazine offered me money to write what I saw of Tinseltown's efforts to capture McMurtry's Texas on film. Perhaps foolishly, I took it.

About a month later, while I was accomplishing some real serious mid-afternoon research over beer at Scholz's in Austin, a New York lawyer tracked me down to report a death in the family: *Life*, as of two hours earlier, had expired. But to assuage my grief, I could keep the money.

I also kept my notes and memories against the day when *Molly, Gid, and Johnny*—the shooting title—might be loosed upon an unsuspecting world. Well, neighbors, it soon will be, under the title *Lovin' Molly* (which won out, at the final gun, over *The Wild and the Sweet*) and unless you are careful you soon may find yourself trapped with it in some Texas theater. Should you find more than a modicum of true Texas in the film—excluding John Henry Faulk's bit role—why, then, I'll buy you a two-dollar play purty. *Lovin' Molly* has no sense of Time or Place: a curious development, indeed, when you consider that Larry McMurtry's writing strength derives from evoking Time-and-Place about as well as you will find it done this side of Faulkner.

McMurtry writes of a real and human Texas. It is that part I know best—"My blood's country and my heart's pastureland," he puts it—where the land is flat, the people narrow, and their small, pinched lives beyond even Hollywood redemptions. Tales of "legendary" Texas, blessedly, are not McMurtry's cup of Pearl: not for him blazing six-guns, noble Pioneers taming the land by killing Indians, granite-jawed sons of the Alamo, the excesses of the Big Oil New Rich—all those characters and situations which long ago passed across the great divide of willing suspension of disbelief to take firm root in Cliché Land.

What I like about McMurtry is that he sees those hypocrisies, attritions, perversions, and absurdities common to the universal human condition and then isn't afraid to admit, in print, that they exist even in Texas Our Texas. Not all "Texas writers" are entirely bold in telling truths on the home-folks, a condition reflecting our Boosterism Heritage, traditional Yahoo-ism, and dogged, un-natural institutional and family pressures to conform: to put a good face on all things Texas and Texan and to unite against critics from within or without. Introspection has never been highly prized in the land of my birth, or hard looks at why we operate as we do or feel as we feel. For too many years writing was considered "woman's work" by most Texans and still is by some.

Our writing antecedents, including the revered J. Frank Dobie, too often hurrahed or gung-hoed and looked away from painful truths. Younger "Texas writers" are more honest than their elders. McMurtry, now a doddering 38, got in the truth-telling business early: *Leaving Cheyenne* was written at a precocious 23. He knows more truths now than he knew then, and has recently said of the book that it often seems to him the gropings of a somewhat dreamy very young man. Still: it's a fine job; it rings true in the basics.

Not that I never quarrel with McMurtry. He sometimes harbors a touch too much romanticism, especially in his early work. His women strike me as a bit much, too heroic and long-suffering and strong. Too *good*. He sees 'em tough, but seldom does he see 'em mean. And Texas probably has as many mean, bitchy, neurotic women as any place on earth, with the possible exception of Man-hattan; there, of course, they've gathered from all points of the compass, while our own crop is largely home-grown. McMurtry recognizes their ability to fight back, to survive in tough country, and knows that Texas women may often be stronger than their men. But I think he misses the extent to which large numbers purely enjoy wrecking and plundering and flashing their stingers.

And in *The Last Picture Show*, it's my feeling that McMurtry too gently judges what a small town would tolerate should word get around that a high school kid was regularly diddling the coach's wife—especially in the 1950s. There are just too many busy bodies and bored avengers to permit anything short of catastrophe in retribution. I believe one—or several—bad things would have happened: the coach would have been fired, his wife would have been chased out of town, and the cuckolded would have killed (1) the student and/or (2) the wife.

But no matter. McMurtry writes of Texas and Texans as well, or better, than anyone and with a rare honest bite. If I green with envy at the thought of a fellow-author's Texas book, it's McMurtry's *In a Narrow Grave: Essays on Texas*. That high standard will last awhile. So he is a favorite with me, and I am saddened and angry when—as in *Lovin' Molly*—I find him foully used. Let us fade, now, into the recent past—back to Austin and Bastrop, in November and December, 1972—to discover how professional film folks could have so botched and perverted McMurtry's Texas.

Arriving at Austin's Chariot Inn, I found the film company from technicians to Biggies—Director Sid Lumet, "Stars" Tony Perkins, Beau Bridges, Blythe Danner, Edward Binnes—understandably torpid in their enthusiasms toward the local culinary arts. Like starving Prisoners of War, they sat over their burned steaks or soggy tacos dreaming of the ideal: bagels and lox, frog's legs provençale paysanne, duckling a l'orange with wild rice, vichyssoise. When one of their number, fresh off the airplane from New York, recounted his recent dinner—artichokes Juan-les-Pins, soup aux Choux paysanne, caviar and cucumber aspic and, maybe, candied Yak's rump or salt-pickled hummingbird tongue—much of his audience cheered; others wept into their neglected barbecue.

The scene offered my first clue to the immediate future. "Billie Lee"—I said to writer William Brammer—"do you reckon people who don't appreciate chicken-fried steak with cream gravy can do justice to McMurtry on film?"

"Naw," he said. "No way. I bet they don't even drink Dr. Pepper."

I kept that in mind when Producer Steve Friedman offered the opportunity to invest a few thousand in his upcoming production.

Leaving Cheyenne is a triangular love story spanning 40 years, set in Wichita Falls country with side excursions to Fort Worth's

old North Side bars and smelly cattle pens and to the Panhandle's taller points. It is a story of small ranchers and their evolutions forward from the 1920s. You get this bleak sense of landscape, of drought and semi-arid soil, of prayers sent to high, dry skies pleading for enough rain that the cattle won't finish skinny at market time. True, the family patriarch disturbs his own son, Gid Fry (Tony Perkins), by diversifying with a little wheat. What McMurtry is telling us is that even in 1925 *some* Texans knew that cattle wouldn't make it forever, that the last Big Herd had passed, that one day irrigated farming and perhaps even oil wells would come. But he obviously intended a yarn of cattle country and of the last stubborn independent men in it; he well-clued the reader that his people wore coiled hats, boots, jeans, and retained a certain fierce saddleback pride.

So director Sid Lumet trots everybody out in clod-hoppers and bib-overalls; they plant and reap as if in the best bottomlands of the rich Mississippi Delta.

First day on location I said to Producer-Screen Writer Friedman: "Jesus, Steve, what's all this sowing-and-reaping shit about?" He didn't understand the question. I said, "Look, you've got scenes bustin' wild broncs, shippin' cattle, birthin' calves. And folks just didn't *do* those things, back then, while rigged out in Li'l Abner overalls. Texans—especially North and West—surrendered most reluctantly to the plow. Up there in cowboy country, people simply wouldn't have gone around 50 years ago dressed like Arkies on the way to pick prunes in California."

"So?"

"So, goddamn it, there was a beginning *shame* to farming up there. It wasn't considered quite . . . manly. It broke with tradition. And if anything would make them uneasy, it would be cracking tradition. They would have—and did—cling to their cattle-man's garb."

"Yeah?"

"Yeah! See Steve, the difference between ranching and farming is . . . well, hell . . . between riding, I guess, and walking. Between *being* served by animals, or *serving* them. Understand?"

The producer-writer stared into the distance. "I see what you mean," he said, in a way perfectly indicating that he did not.

They had a fence-mending scene. Tony Perkins held a post atop the good earth while his buddy and hired man Johnny (Beau Bridges) whomped on it with a sledgehammer.

"Jesus, Steve," I said, "the goddamn ground's near to *rock* just below top soil. You couldn't hammer fence posts in the ground!"

"How would you do it, then?"

"You'd use post-hole diggers! You'd have to dig deep, and you'd feel the shock all through your body. And when you'd finished your back would ache like you'd been kidney punched. But you'd know the fence would *hold*. It would turn back a stud horse trying to reach a mare in heat. Christ, even if you *could* hammer a fence post in the ground, the damn thing would collapse the minute you strung wire and pulled it tight."

"So who's gonna know?," Friedman asked. "How many movie-goers ever saw a fence made?"

Gid and Johnny—buddies, and rivals for Molly's bed and love—had a fight on a cattle car while transporting their lowing charges to Fort Worth market. Each accused the other of having first slept with Molly and then of failing to make an honest woman of her via matrimony.

It was the sissiest, most awkward fight I've seen outside Elaine's—which is where New York's high-rent literati gather to juice, backbite, screech and scratch out their professional frustrations or petty jealousies.

I sought out Director Lumet: "Jesus, Sid, that fight scene's a real pussy-cat. It just won't do."

Lumet chuckled: "That's my point. We're getting away from the obligatory standard Texas *machismo*."

"You're wrong," I said. "See back then, two guys fighting over the honor of their mutual girl friend would be as mean and unreasoning as rattlesnakes. They'd literally beat shit and blood out of each other."

"But these guys are *good friends*," Lumet said.

"Beg your pardon, Sid, but that's why it'd be so fierce. The only way it'd be worse is if they were brothers. In which case somebody might be seriously maimed."

"We're trying to reject the old myths," Lumet said.

I said, "Look, I appreciate that. I'm sick of tough, tall Texans myself. And I feel about half-foolish insisting on blood. But given the emotional circumstances, I think blood would flow."

The director smiled and touched my arm, forgiving my standard Texas parochialism. He moved away before I could say that the most damage I had ever inflicted, or *had* inflicted, came in fist-fights with a good friend or two. Except the time when I was 15, and had a bloody knock-down with my father.

Over drinks that night I tried to persuade Friedman. "It's funnier Sid's way," he said.

"Maybe so, baby. But it ain't real."

One finally grew weary of approaching the film folk with un-solicited advice. Also, it got more difficult to slip up on their blind sides. When they spotted that certain outraged gleam or heard the beginning echos of "Jesus, Steve," or "Jesus, Sid," they moved with all deliberate speed to safer quarters. Lumet reached the point of fleeing the Chariot Inn bar should he discover me in it.

At great expense to my soul I said nothing when a 1945 scene presented a Rural Route mail carrier *not* in khakis or tattered blue jeans but in a sparkling, tailored U.S. Mail costume which even Houston's city letter-carriers would not adopt until years later.

I held my tongue when Gid and Johnny abandoned the Fry place to briefly cowboy in "the Panhandle"—maybe five minutes worth on film—where they were constantly in the company of lush Delta growths, lakes, and rivers.

I stood silently when Molly, accepting a telegram telling of her son's death in World War II, expressed her grief in front of a pastel-hued building which no Texas town had that early. Nor did I com-plain that she supported herself by clutching a huge, modern red-and-white stop sign even though stop signs in them days, pardner, were teensie-tiny and announced themselves in blacks and yellows.

I said not a word when Mr. Fry, son Gid, and buddy Johnny sat on horses near a cattle-loading chute—*outside* the corral—to chat of their market worth while, apparently, the cattle accommodat-ingly loaded themselves.

Watching the filming and the daily rushes, one knew the final product would offer no sense of place: that geography, somehow, was being judged unworthy of attention. Throughout *Lovin' Molly* people canter by horse, wagon, buggy, or pickup-truck to this ranch or that farm or another town, without any sense of direction; you don't know if a given trip implies a journey of a hundred yards or an equal number of miles: all you know is that wherever people go—whether to Fort Worth or to the Panhandle or to an adjoining spread—the landscape is as unvarying as the moon's. Though it all looks as if it might yield 40 bales to the acre.

I grin and am warmed by recollecting an Early-Dewline warning flashed by Amarillo's Buck Ramsey. Ole Buck for years was the quintessential Texas cowboy; he rode for wages, fought in bars, and his neck was red. Some years ago Buck Ramsey's horse tricked him off, stomped him, and dragged him far enough that Buck has since been assigned a wheelchair. This cut down on Buck's riding and fighting, though not on his drinking or sense of humor. As a side effect, Buck was caused to read and mull Camus, Dickens, Twain, McMurtry and better. So when I called Buck Ramsey one night to inform that *Leaving Cheyenne* would soon be filmed near Austin, Buck gave the perfect literary criticism: "Shit, when will them folks learn not to film cowboy stories down yonder in that damn swamp country?"

Stars, producer, and director jangled in anticipation of Larry McMurtry's heralded visit to the shooting location. He disappointed them by arriving in Austin after the day's wrap. Though McMurtry had—and has—no responsibility for the flick, other than having sold its screen rights, Lumet and Friedman sought him out for dinner and to court his good will. McMurtry, who does not flower in the presence of excessive praise, squirmed and wouldn't look anybody in the face while being told of what a grand, perfect "vehicle" he had provided.

"You know what your book's about?" Lumet curiously asked.

Startled, McMurtry said something sounding like er-ah-whonk-oh.

Lumet leaned in, grasping McMurtry's arm, frowning to show Deep Artistic Insight: "Larry, it's about . . . well, it's about . . . *the glory of no reward!*"

"Hmmmmmmmmmmm," McMurtry perfectly responded, failing to look up from his cucumber salad.

Later, McMurtry witnessed the latest daily rushes flown down from New York processings: rough cuts and retakes of scenes put on celluloid three, four days earlier. Often he snorted or muttered to himself.

By now they were filming some scenes from the 1960s portion of the book, when the principals have aged 40 years over the film's beginning. Tony Perkins, who in the opening reel appeared much too used and scabby for the 23-year-old he portrayed, now appeared to be about two years older than Christianity: possibly the worst make-up job since Nixon's in that first debate against Kennedy; he spoke in a voice cracking near to a yodel, and exaggerated the shakings of terminal palsy. In the darkness of the Chariot Inn's makeshift screening room, generally a meeting place of Lions and Rotarians, McMurtry took one look and grunted like somebody had poked his ribs with a pitchfork.

He suffered the sissy mock fistfight, Blythe Danner's pitiful attempts at a West Texas accent (it sounded as if it had been shipped in from Philadelphia by way of Pascagoula), and a 1925 scene where Gid and Molly, semi-sensually roistering in an open field, groped in passion near a fresh cow-plop obviously and recently tracked by a 1972 giant-type tri-wheeler. When a scene depicting "the Panhandle" revealed green foliage, and many running brooks, McMurtry breathed: "Is that Vietnam, or Missouri?"

McMurtry talked near to dawn in a motel room with old Texas friends, instructing how, for all their millions, movie folk seemed to possess natural talents for being unable to distinguish asses from elbows. He philosophized that, well, hell, you wrote something and then you moved on to write something else and the devil take the hindmost.

As a perfect counterpoint to the Technicolor turkey then in the making, he reported on his old cattleman daddy, who—aged, ill, long past any hopes of Big Herds—had freshly battled a mad cow to at least a moral victory though suffering a bootful of blood and a major fracture. It was a symbolic story, almost as poignant as the old yarn of the dying Indian tribe buying a Longhorn steer and then killing it the way they—and their ancestors—had once killed countless buffalo. And I thought it an affirmation of that which McMurtry writes about: life's natural attritions, and inevitable change, and the stubborn surrenderings they force. You knew damn well that tough old Jeff McMurtry hadn't worn bib-overalls— or given a thought one way or another to Texas *machismo*—in playing out one of the final, natural dramas of a hard-scrabble ranch life.

One night on location outside Bastrop, as a few dozen of us shivered in a chill wind and klieg lights, I cornered a big, cheerful, robust native-Texan rancher who supplied cattle and horses for *Lovin' Molly* and also was being paid as a technical advisor. True, he had taught the principal actors how to mount horses without appearing totally foolish or getting hurt, how to toss a rope or to saddle-up and other "techniques" that were to him second nature, but how—I asked—could he permit the make-believe cowboys to miss or misinterpret so much, to commit so many dozens of small boo-boos he certainly must have recognized?

He was a good ole boy, not without a certain country ambition, and we'd poured enough booze together that I knew he owned more smarts than he'd publicly revealed. He lowered his voice and carefully checked for outsiders: "Listen" he said, "them people payin' me $3600 for six weeks a-work. And I got three buttons to educate. This is the best and quickest money I ever seen. Maybe, you know, them people may come back down here from New York to make another picture one day. You want me to screw up easy money by quarrelin' with 'em *now*? Whatever pleases *them* people, cousin, just tickles me plumb to death . . ."

All prevailing deceptions were not hatched by Texans. Governor Preston Smith and several state legislators "starred" in a cattle auction scene ending with the auctioneer crying out, "Sold for forty dollars to Preston Smith." I remarked to Producer Friedman that the scene didn't appear all that vital to moving his story line. He grinned: "Well, it never hurts to politick with the politicians. Meanwhile, when we need cooperation from the authorities— well, this scene hasn't hurt us."

I said, "And there's always the cutting room floor. You can always decide during the final editing that maybe Governor Smith's scene is expendable."

Friedman laughed: "You're pretty damn smart for a Texan. You sure there's not a little New York hustler somewhere in your bloodline?"

P.S.: If Preston Smith made the movie as released, I neither saw him nor heard his name.

Beau Bridges, cast as the happy-go-lucky Johnny, noted that many real-life cowboys chewed tobacco. Concluding that perhaps Johnny would take a chaw, too, he wrote that bit into his part. "A guy passed me some of this stuff that looked like a pressed rag," he said, "and I chewed it and nearly passed out." By now Director Lumet loved the tobacco-chawin' idea, and Bridges was stuck with it. He tried substitutes: licorice, black bubble gum; nothing seemed to work but the real thing. Beau spent a lot of off-camera time rinsing out his mouth, and gagging.

The cast and crew grumbled of a spartan social life. One night a party was arranged in the home of a congenial Austin man who supplied booze, music, deposits of minor dope, and friendly girls attracted to the possibility of meeting Tony Perkins. It was the flop of Austin's social season: only the technicians among the film folk appeared, and after nervous introductory drinks and chatter they segregated themselves to talk of Joe Namath, cream cheese, the New York Giants, and how wonderful it would be to see the spires of Manhattan.

Since Producer Friedman had made much—in press conferences and local speeches—of how at home New Yorkers were being made to feel in Texas, I asked one of the crewmen—by then drunk—what he really thought of the cowboy life and the region. "I get enough of these salt-of-the-earth types in a hurry," he said. "Hell, they don't even know what *stick*-ball is!"

Finally, it was over. At the cast party—attended, again, only by technicians and, this time, Beau Bridges from among the "stars"— there were mutters that anti-Semitism had been felt in Bastrop. "How so?" "Well," said an assistant producer, "when we needed to lease farms or ranches or equipment for certain scenes, people tried to hold us up. And one old rancher said to me, 'Listen, you New York Jews come in here and git rich makin' fun of us and try to git out for six-bits.' I can't say I won't be happy to get home."

I saw McMurtry last summer, shortly after he'd witnessed the first rough-cut screening of *Lovin' Molly*; he was in a state of mild shock.

"It's simply dreadful," he said. "Tony Perkins plays a swishy boy until the final reel, and then suddenly he's older than rocks or water. The old-age make-up on everybody is simply grotesque. There's no sense of direction: Lumet apparently shot the thing in track shoes—zip, zip, zip. People at the screening kept laughing in all the wrong places, and some walked out. Near the interminable end, I realized a woman behind me had been crying for 20 minutes. I wondered what kind of woman would cry at such a film. When I risked a look behind me, it was my agent."

With some 20 minutes clipped from the original cut—mercifully, most of it in the mismanaged "old age" sequences—Columbia Pictures held a recent New York screening.

I was surprised to find Larry McMurtry sitting alone near the front row. "Glad to see you," he said. "I'll probably need your moral support."

What in hell was he doing there?

"Well, I've been asked to write a review for *The New York Times*." We laughed for the only time that day.

The longer the film ran, the lower McMurtry sank in his seat: "It's not so bad if you see only the top half of the screen." We suffered it all again: sowings and reapings, technical boo-boos, lush growths and rivers allegedly indigenous to Panhandle country; Blythe Danner clasping a bloody, wet, new-born calf to her generous bosoms and then—yes!—*kissing* it. McMurtry covered his face with his hands; his shoulders shook. I don't know if he was giggling or crying. We felt no sense of how hard-scrabble ranch life might be on the high Texas plains; received no notions of sand-storms, summer parchings, winter freezes, wild lonesome winds, or incessant jangling country tunes.

We escaped to a bar, drinking silently and shaking our heads.

I asked McMurtry what he intended to call his review for *The New York Times*. He perked up and smiled for the first time in two hours. "I'm gonna call it," he said, "'Leavin' Lumet.'"

1973

The Lost Frontier

As THE NATION MOVED WEST seeking new frontiers, Texas, a rude young empire won in blood, was inhabited by restless and adventurous men chasing their own special dreams. One of these was Oliver Loving, a legendary cattleman who, passing through the barren reefs adjoining New Mexico in 1867, was shot, scalped, and left for dead. He crawled eighteen miles, chewing an old leather glove for sustenance, and emptied his pockets of valuables to a roving band of Mexican traders against assurance that he would be packed in charcoal and returned East to Weatherford— almost five hundred miles—for burial. It was perhaps typical of the breed, the period, and the place that Oliver Loving stubbornly refused to die until he had arranged his own terms.

Our literature and our legends abound with tales of the frontier spirit, of men who lived out of saddlebags or sod huts, carving and sweating a new civilization in which they attended their own fractures, made their own rules, and raised their sons to independent and taciturn ways. In 1893, twenty-six years after Oliver Loving's death, a county bordering on New Mexico in the westernmost part of Texas was named after him. Loving County today is the most sparsely populated county in the contiguous United States, 647 square miles with 150 people scattered among 451 producing oil wells. This is land no less desolate than in an earlier time, and it is reasonable to suspect that the folks who remain here—the sons and daughters of gritty dry-gulch farmers, wild-horse tamers, and oil-field roustabouts—would naturally retain their forebears' adventuresome pioneer spirit, coupled with their own stubborn dreams of self-fulfillment.

Once the nation drew its strength from these lower regions, masses of individual songs melding into one symphony of hope and pride and individual doing. Now so much in America seems to have homogenized and dulled us that it is not too much to imagine that one day soon we shall all sound like Jack Lescoulie. Perhaps out on those few old frontiers where there is still elbowroom, we can rediscover charms, virtues, and vitalities that speak well of our roots and suggest options for our futures. These are the hopes, at least, that one can bring to an examination of Loving County.

The best place to meet Loving County's last frontiersmen is in the town of Mentone, and more specifically in Keen's Café, popularly known as "Newt's and Tootsie's." Keen's is the only place in all the county where one may purchase a beer—or anything else of value, though they do sell marriage licenses across the street at the squat county courthouse. On this boiling day, Weepin' Willie Nelson is warning on Newt Keen's jukebox of all the gratuitous troubles love provides when another kind of trouble—wearing a big-brimmed hat and a snub-nosed pistol—clatters through the front screen door.

Granville Lacy, ruddy-faced to the bone, is toting the snub-nosed pistol under the aegis of the Texas Liquor Control Board. He has driven from Odessa across seventy-eight miles of burning desert sands—past oil-well pumps, nodding in their rich extractions like gentled rocking horses, and past infrequent hardscrabble ranches—to serve a seven-day suspension notice of the beer permit entrusted to Keen's Café.

Newt Keen, proprietor, is a graying former cowboy with jug ears and a sly country grin that says he knows the joke and the joke is not on him. He seems to harbor some secret mirth, a submerged mysterious bubbling that has survived tornado funnels, droughts, bedroll rattlesnakes, rodeo fractures, and the purchase of a ranch from a salty old pioneer woman who, it developed, did not own a ranch to sell. Equipped by seasoning and history to expertly sense disaster in its many forms, Newt, on spotting the lawman, mumbles, "Oh, hail far! It's liable to get a whole lot drier around here."

Newt greets the liquor agent aloud, however, as if in the hire of Welcome Wagon: "Come in! Come in! Y'all been gettin' any rain over your way?" He crashes about in scuffed cowboy boots, his body a tad stooped as if permanently saddlesore, and offers the lawman a mug of thick coffee.

Granville Lacy sits at one of the two rickety counters between a factory-tooled sign instructing: *America, Love It or Leave It!* and a homemade sign running alternately uphill and down, as if maybe it had been painted in the dark: *Our Beer License Depends on Your Good Conduct.* The six other customers in the café, which seats a maximum of twenty, watch the lawman with obvious distaste and apprehension.

"Mr. Keen," the lawman says, "I've got some papers to serve on you."

Conveniently deaf, Newt gestures toward the coffee he's poured Lacy: "You want me to cripple that with a little dab of cream? Looks like it was dredged up from the Pecos River bottom." A headshake. Newt tries again: "How's them two big old boys of yours? They doing all right?" Above the counter are likenesses of Newt's own two older sons, Vietnam veterans, proudly in uniform.

The liquor agent unfurls and crackles his official documents: "Now, Mr. Keen, this temporary suspension begins next Monday. . . ." But Newt is clomping across the wooden floor to replenish beer supplies and honor orders for cheeseburgers or chicken-fried steaks with cream gravy.

Agent Lacy inspects his papers while Newt relays food orders to his red-haired wife, Tootsie, who retains a high faith in bee-hive hairdos. The jukebox has fallen dumb, permitting the lawman to better sample a united community hostility among the oil-field workers and ranchers. It is one thing to retard the flow of alcoholic comforts in any one of Manhattan's countless aid stations—or even one of Odessa's—but it is quite a deeper sin to dry up the only watering hole in all of Loving County. Newt and Tootsie dispense approximately fifty cases of beer each week; a shutdown theoretically would meanly deprive every man, woman, and child in the county of eight bottles or cans. Better Granville Lacy had come to town to poison the water, which leads one to believe that Sheriff Elgin (Punk) Jones—who reported the infraction—will have to pay for his nefarious deed.

When Newt Keen next passes within range, the liquor agent reads in a low monotone: . . . *did on the some-oddth day of August 1971, in violation of section this, paragraph so-and-so . . .* Newt shuffles, pulls an ear, shoots concerned glances at Tootsie. She attends her griddle with jerky motions of anger, slapping hamburger patties with unusual vigor. . . . *nor sell, nor give, nor consume, nor allow to be consumed, any alcoholic beverage on said premise until* . . . Wearing the abashed grin of an erring schoolboy, Newt laboriously scratches his signature.

Newt's formal surrender seemingly reassures the lawman, who jovially says, "Now I got another complaint. You've got four beer signs outside, and you're not allowed but two."

"*Four?* I can't count but three."

"Naw, four. Your main sign counts as two. One for each side of the sign."

Newt, uncertain of the bureaucratic bogs, says, "Well, what's the big gripe?"

"Congestion."

Newt is mute and uncomprehending. This is happening to him in downtown Mentone—population forty-four—where from any vantage point one can see for three days in all directions and still have nothing to tell. He gazes across all that empty territory until his eyes lock on a distant windmill. "Well," he finally drawls, "I sure would hate to cause any traffic jams." When the locals snigger over their well-ketchuped home fries, the lawman reddens. "We've got no choice but to enforce the law. It's an old law the church folks got passed back in the '30s." He makes it out the door unaided by any understanding nods.

Before the lawman's dust departs, all the customers compete to damn the prying old government. Warren Burnett, a prominent Texas lawyer who has paused at the café in midpassage to El Paso, offers to represent Newt for free should he wish to fight the suspension order: "We'll claim cruel and unusual punishment! A man could die of thirst out here. Hell, Newt, your place is more than a community center—it's an *outpost*, by God, offering new beginnings and shelter against the elements. . . ."

"Do it, Newt," Tootsie said.

"Naw, I got to live with that old boy. Besides, this ain't his fault."

"Well," the lawyer said, "come next Monday it'll be a long hot path to beer. So whose fault is it?"

Newt drawls it out like *Gunsmoke*'s Festus: "Accordin' to that batch of official papers, it's mine!" After the laughter abates, he says, "Aw, one night a while back we got to dancing and barking at the moon in here and well, maybe we run a little past closing time.

Mister, I been in this country since the sun wasn't no bigger than a orange and there wasn't no moon a-tall and windmills wasn't but waist-high, and I've learnt that when you can *sell* something out here—you better not worry about what time it is."

Tootsie says: "That ain't the whole story."

"Well, OK, mama. Awright, I *was* dranking nearly as much as I was selling and business wasn't too bad. The sheriff—old Punk Jones—he come in and caught me and snitched to the liquor board."

"You oughta run for sheriff yourself, Newt," one of the locals suggests.

"Naw sir," Newt says. "I ain't gonna say a mumblin' word against old Punk—right on up to election day." Appreciating the laughter, he fishes in icy waters and pops himself a beer. "Punk, he don't have nothing to do but enforce the closing laws in this one little old place, and I sure wouldn't wanta interfere with law and order here in Loving County."

The dominant political strain in Loving County runs to an abiding conservatism. The natives—well-off and poor alike—reject anything smacking of charity, and so they regard federal aid as being no less poisonous than the ever-present rattlesnake. When a federal court instructed every county in Texas to participate in the Family Food Assistance Program for the poor, Loving County Judge W. T. (Bill) Winston said: "We don't need it, we don't want it, and we can't use it if we're forced to take it." Snorting and jiggling his beer glass in Newt's and Tootsie's now, Judge Winston gloomily says, "They finally forced it on us. We've got nine people getting it—seven in one family. And *they're* Mexicans." When the Department of Health, Education and Welfare ordered the county either racially integrate Mentone's sixteen-pupil school or lose its federal money, Judge Winston fired off a terse letter informing Washington that Loving County: (1) had no black residents, (2) had never received a dime's worth of federal school aid, and (3) didn't covet any.

Television has brought the problems of New York, Watts, and Saigon to the attention of the neglected territory. Everybody worries about blacks or dope or crime or the Vietcong just as if they had some. Newt Keen no longer goes off and leaves his café doors unlocked to accommodate stray customers because "you can't tell when somebody might come over from Monahans or Pyote and clean you out." But the Mentone jail has not had a customer in seven years, and Loving County's crime wave last year consisted of a profitless burglary of the schoolhouse and the theft of several rolls of steel cable from an oil lease.

Ann Blair, a pretty young blond who works in the courthouse for her mother, county clerk Edna Clayton, frets that the outside world may taint her two small children. "Let's face it, it's boring here for adults, but there's no better place to raise kids," says Ann, a graduate of Odessa Junior College. "We have a good family life. My fifth-grade boy has learned work and the value of a dollar. When I went off to college, I saw wild kids and all kinds of temptation. And it's so much worse now, with drugs and sex crimes."

Inconvenience is taken for granted. The nearest moviehouse, beauty shop, physician, lawyer, bank, weekly newspaper, cemetery, or grocery store is from fifty-five to ninety round-trip miles away. Fifteen of sixteen Mentone School pupils are bused in from six to sixty miles away. Sixth graders and above are bused almost eighty round-trip miles to Wink.

Despite the riches of oil and gas under the earth, each Loving County family must provide its own bottled-gas system. And there is no public water supply. Water is hauled in a tank from Pecos at fifty cents per barrel. Even cattle balk at drinking the brackish product of the Pecos River, long ago polluted by potash interests in upstream New Mexico, a fact that, surprisingly, no one here rails against even though their forebears always raised hell at anything—fences, sheep herds, squatters—infringing on their freedoms or presuming to prosper at their expense.

The land is stark and flat and treeless, altogether as bleak and spare as mood scenes in Russian literature, a great dry-docked ocean with small swells of hummocky tan sand dunes or humpbacked rocky knolls changing colors with the hour and the shadows: reddish brown, slate gray, bruise colored. But it is the sky—God-high and pale, like a blue chenille bedspread bleached by seasons in the sun—that dominates. There is simply *too much* sky. Men grow small in its presence and—perhaps feeling diminished—they sometimes are compelled to proclaim themselves in wild or berserk ways. Alone in those remote voids, one may suddenly half believe he is the last man on earth and go in frantic search of the tribe. Desert fever, the natives call it.

And while the endless dry doomed land and eternal sky may bring on the fever, so, too, can the weather. The wind, persistent and unengageable for half the year, swooshes unencumbered from the northernmost Great Plains, howling, whining, singing off-key and covering everything with a maddening grainy down. Court records attest that during the windy seasons the natives are quicker to lift their voices, or their fists, or even their guns, in rage.

The summer sun is as merciless as a loan shark: a blinding, angry orange explosion baking the land's sparse grasses and quickly aging the skin. In winter there are nights to ache the bone; cold, stinging lashings of frozen rain. Yet even the weather is not the worst natural enemy. Outside the industrial sprawl of the prairie's mini-cities—on the occasional ranches or oil leases or in the flawed little country towns—the great curse is boredom. Teenagers in the faded jeans and glistening ducktail hairstyles of another day wander in restless packs to the roller rink or circle root beer stands sounding their mating calls by a mighty revving of engines. Old men shuffle dominoes in the shade of service stations or feedstores. There is the television, of course, and the joys of small-town gossip—and in season a weekly high school football game may secretly be considered more important than even Vacation Bible School. Newt Keen laments the passing of country socials where people reveled all night at one ranch house or another: "Now you got to go over to Pecos to them fightin' and dancin' clubs. But, you know, it ain't near as much fun to fight with strangers."

The young and the imaginative in Loving County are largely disaffected, strangers in Jerusalem. And those who can, move on when they can. Today's desert youths belong to a transitional generation. Born to an exhausted frontier where there are no more Dodge Citys to tame, no more wild rivers to ford, no more cattle trails to ride or oil booms to follow, theirs is a heritage beyond preserving. The last horseman has passed by, leaving only myths and fences. Industrialization has come and gone: having drilled the robbed the earth, the swaggering two-fisted oil boomer, heir apparent to the earlier cowboy or Indian fighter, has clattered off to the next feverish adventure, leaving behind sterile sophisticated pumps and gauges and storage tanks that automatically record their own dull technological accomplishments. Only the land remains, the high sky, the eerie isolation. The wind hums mocking tunes of loss and the jukeboxes echo it: "*Just call Lonesome-seven-seven-two-oh-three . . .*" "*I'd trade all of my tomorrows for just one yesterday. . . .*"

The songs are of rejection, disappointment, aborted opportunities . . . of finishing second. And the music is everywhere, incessantly jangling, the call of the lonely. Even many graybeards who have trimmed back their dreams—if they ever had any—cannot sit still unless the jukebox or radio is moaning to them of old loves lost, of the tricks of the wicked cities, of life's rough and rocky traveling. Few know that the music says more about them than they say of themselves.

The young sense the loss of a grander and more adventurous past. It is these—the young and those who secretly know they never will be truly young again—who prove most susceptible to fits of desert fever. And so they sometimes go lickety-splitting down the rural highways at speeds dizzy enough to confuse the ambidextrous, running like so many Rabbit Angstroms, leaving behind a trail of sad country songs, beer vapors and the echo of some feverish, senseless shout. Some may find themselves at dawn howling in the precincts of a long-forgotten girl friend, or tempting the dangers of "fightin' and dancin' clubs" with names like Blue Moon Bar or Texas Taddy Jo's. Some keep running: to the army or to a Fort Worth factory or maybe to exotic Kansas City. Others, their fevers cooled and with no place to go, drive back slowly—a bit sheepishly—to rejoin the private chaos and public tediums of their lives.

Newt Keen's son Jack begins to boot stomp across the wooden floor in a jukebox dance with a tall visiting airline hostess. Jack is dipping snuff and wearing an outsized silver belt buckle he has won riding bulls. Over the whines and thumps of the music he regrets that after next weekend he can't rise at four thirty each morning to cowboy on one of the area ranches because school is imminent. Jack does not appear to be real partial to school, where they take a dim view of twelve-year-old eighty-three-pound boys who appreciate snuff more than arithmetic. To somebody who first dipped at age five, who slew his first snake at seven, and who is impatient to ramrod his own ranch, the arbitrary restrictions on scholars can be mighty vexing.

Tootsie worries about her son. "Till school takes up, Jack's the only kid in Mentone. The rest live on ranches or oil leases. All he's ever been around is adults and he don't get along real well with kids." Jack proves his mother right on the second day of school, decking another boy who has earned his disapproval. Jack's reward is three licks from the principal's paddle. "It stung," he admits, taking a pinch of Copenhagen from his personal tin. "I got to sign the paddle, though. You ain't allowed to sign it unless you been whupped with it."

"What'd you hit that boy for?" Tootsie demands.

Busy roping a cane-bottomed chair, Jack says, "Aw, he's about half silly."

"Yes, but what'd he *do*, look at you cross-eyed? Jack, dammit, stop roping them chairs. This ain't no rodeo arena."

Disengaging his lariat, Jack says, "He put his hands on my book."

"Oh," Tootsie says, apparently mollified.

Newt is amused. "Jack despises school much as I do a rattlesnake. He swears he's gonna quit when he gits to sixth grade."

"Or the seventh," Jack says. "Maybe the eighth."

"Why, Jack," Newt says, "you're liable to wind up a full professor. What's got into you?"

The boy, vaguely embarrassed, tilts his western hat over his eyes: "Mr. Knott says sixth grade ain't enough any more."

Charles Knott, forty-three, is the new schoolteacher in Mentone. When asked why in mid-career he has deserted El Paso's modern school system for the lesser ecstasies of Loving County, he says, "I like small towns. I had thirty-odd kids to the class in El Paso, damn few of them Anglos. The kids here are eager. You take little Jack Keen. Now, he may wind up ranching and live here all his life. If he wants that—well, fine. But he ought to have options. He ought to know that another life exists. You know, kids from small towns—well, there just seems to be more *to* them. I grew up in a little old East Texas town—one picture show and a one-gallus night watchman. And a higher percentage of the kids there made it than ever will make it in El Paso. They were more aware of themselves, aware of life. Maybe it's nurturing their isolation, having time to think things through. Whatever, I think small-town kids use more of their potential."

The next day, as school lets out, Tootsie is gazing through the shimmying heat waves when suddenly she says, *"My Lord*, little Jack must be sick. Yonder he comes wagging his school books *home* with him." Apparently she doesn't realize that Jack may have a growing dream.

Day after day, as the suspension lengthens, the mood in Newt and Tootsie's beerless free-enterprise café grows more and more subdued. Since the suspension, Sheriff Punk Jones—who rose to his present eminence after serving as courthouse janitor—has begun to hear rumors that a disgruntled Newt Keen might oppose him on the ballot after all. A good country politician who knows that a handful of votes might return a sheriff to mopping the courthouse, Punk Jones begins to stress the vast stores of bookwork attending his office; it is well known that Newt's painfully concocted customers' checks for chili or cheeseburgers require more translations than the Rosetta Stone.

In the café, customers are infrequent. Those who drop in jangle around aimlessly, some lamenting the lack of liquid comforts with the sorrow of one whose dog has died. Tootsie sits at a table near the soundless jukebox, making do with coffee. Abruptly she says to her husband behind the counter, "Newt, what we doing in this fool café business anyhow?"

"Well, hon, I just got plain tard of being governor, and the gold-mining business was boring me."

Irked, Tootsie helplessly shakes her head. Daring for once to question life's random assignments, her reward is another of Newt's drawling jokes. One has the impression she suddenly requires answers to questions that did not exist for her before. Some-

thing in the restless sweeping of her eyes hints that she has come on some new, if myopic, vision.

"We've made a living," Newt defends, walking over and putting a quarter in the jukebox.

"Yeah," Tootsie says. "I don't buy a whole lot of diamonds."

"Naw, mama, but you don't live in some old line shack and cook for the range camp neither." They are silent while Willie Nelson sings of how "it's a Bloody-Mary mornin' since baby left me without warnin' sometime in the night. . . ." "Say," Newt says, "you remember when we was fresh married and lived in that old dirt-floor dugout?" Tootsie nods, smiling, her face softened by some special old memory. "Well, hon, I always wanted to ask you something about that: when you snuggled up so close to me that first winter, was it on account of you loved me so much or because you was scared of the rats?"

In a monotone as flat as sourdough biscuits, she says, "I was scared of the rats." They look at each other and laugh.

"All this will straighten out in a day or two," Newt promises, seeming to have missed the point of her question, her mood. "Hail, we got more food business than we do beer sales."

He shuffles over and sits at the table beside Tootsie, who is stirring her mug of thick coffee. The two of them gaze out the screen door at the lost frontier. Nothing, absolutely nothing, is moving on the ribbon-straight highway. They sit and stare, their faces in repose as melancholy as a plain old three-chord hurtin' country song, while Eddy Arnold croons to them of big bouquets of roses.

Something old and precious and a close kinsman to steel—some abiding chemistry of hope and grit—seems to have disappeared from the frontier blood. The men who shaped and settled this desolate waste relied on a fierce, near-savage independence coupled with a vision that made them feel captains of their own fate. That vigor, that vision, is gone now, as exhausted as the frontier itself.

It is sad to see people so tamed and hobbled and timid and dreamless in a land born wild. The descendants of the old breed may roar like wounded lions at distant menaces—the pretensions of sociologists, the pious prattlings of politicians, the mod and the unfamiliar—but they grapple ineffectually with their immediate concerns: their boredoms, small, mean jobs, polluted rivers, and officious bureaucrats. In the old days the people simply would not have tolerated the closing down of their only communal outpost: no, they would have told Punk Jones that they would drink when thirsty, by God, no matter the preferences of some chair-bound Austin bureaucrat with nothing better to do than sign suspension orders. This lethargic acceptance of fate's happenstance gifts, with no more than a shrug or a token gripe, gives one the sense of being a visitor at a wake, of witnessing some final burial of the spirit, of watching people without purpose merely getting through another day. Frontiers were made for better uses.

Still, one does encounter qualities to admire and enjoy here. A withered rancher who will identify himself only as Jesse contentedly saws into one of Tootsie's steaks and says, "This country's soothin'. The country's *close* to you out here. You feel a kinship with it. It don't have no boundaries." Newt Keen says of his neighbors: "We come together like a family when there's trouble. You take over here in Kermit"—he jerks a thumb toward the highway— "this stranded family stopped at a church one Sunday to ask for a little food and gas money. All they got was a promise the congregation would pray for 'em. Well, they limped on over here. We supplied 'em a big box of groceries and took up a collection for gas."

There is little Jack Keen, who probably has spunk and survival instincts superior to most children and surely has more room to discover himself. Some essence of the pioneer woman's endurance survives in Tootsie. Newt is improbably cheerful in a time full of frowning; he at once preserves the old colloquialisms and speaks a native American poetry.

That much has survived and must be clung to. But over the years, generation by generation, the resources and the spirit of Loving County have been dried up, and there is a lesson to be learned here. As in the nation as a whole, each generation spoke much and thought little of the future requirements of its heirs. Hereafter we must plan far better with far less.

1972

AFTERWORD

Newt Keen ran afoul of personal ambition. In the same week that a certain key issue of *Life* made its appearance, Newt upped and announced for sheriff against his old tormentor, Punk Jones. Since Warren Burnett and I perhaps had a bit to do with that decision, telling Newt how he was sore needed in public office when we took on a shade too much beer, we sent him twenty-five dollars each and our good wishes. Newt Keen was accused of a lavish campaign financed by outside interests and he lost, fifty-three to thirty-eight. In mid-1973, Newt sold his café and took a job in Pecos.

Playing Cowboy

WHEN I WAS YOUNG, I didn't know that when you leave a place, it may not be forever. The past, I thought, had served its full uses and could bury its own dead; bridges were for burning; "good-bye" meant exactly what it said. One never looked back except to judge how far one had come.

Texas was the place I left behind. And not reluctantly. The leave-taking was so random I trusted the United States Army to relocate me satisfactorily. It did, in 1946, choosing to establish in Queens (then but a five-cent subway ride from the clamorous glamour of Manhattan) a seventeen-year-old former farm boy and small-town sapling green enough to challenge chlorophyll. The assignment would shape my life far more than I then suspected; over the years it would teach me to "play cowboy"—to become, strangely, more "Texas" than I had been.

New York offered everything to make an ambitious kid dizzy; I moved through its canyons in a hot walking dream. Looking back, I see myself starring in a bad movie I then accepted as high drama: the Kid, a.k.a. the Bumptious Innocent, discovering the theater, books, a bewildering variety of nightclubs and bars; subways and skyscrapers and respectable wines. There were glancing encounters with Famous Faces: Walter Winchell, the actor Paul Kelly, the ex-heavyweight champion Max Baer, bandleader Stan Kenton. It was easy; spotting them, I simply rushed up, stuck out my hand, sang out my name, and began asking personal questions.

Among my discoveries was that I dreaded returning to Texas; where were its excitements, celebrities, promises? As corny as it sounds, one remembers the final scene of that bad movie. Crossing the George Washington Bridge in a Greyhound bus in July 1949—Army discharge papers in my duffel bag—I looked back at Manhattan's spires and actually thought, *I'll be back, New York.* I did not know that scene had been played thousands of times by young men or young women from the provinces, nor did I know that

New York cared not a whit whether we might honor the pledge. In time, I got back. On my recent forty-sixth birthday, it dawned that I had spent more than half my life—or twenty-four years—on the eastern seaboard. I guess there's no getting around the fact that this makes me an expatriate Texan.

"Expatriate" remains an exotic word. I think of it as linked to Paris or other European stations in the 1920s: of Sylvia Beach and her famous bookstore; of Hemingway, Fitzgerald, Dos Passos, Ezra Pound, and Gertrude Stein Stein Stein. There is wine in the Paris air, wine and cheese and sunshine, except on rainy days when starving young men in their attics write or paint in contempt of their gut rumbles. Spain. The brave bulls. Dublin's damp fog. Movable feasts. *That's* what "expatriate" means, so how can it apply to one middle-aged grandfather dodging Manhattan's muggers and dogshit pyramids while grunting a son through boarding school and knocking on the doors of magazine editors? True expatriates, I am certain, do not wait in dental offices, the Port Authority Bus Terminal, or limbo. Neither do they haunt their original root sources three or four times each year, while dreaming of accumulating enough money to return home in style as a gentlemanly rustic combining the best parts of J. Frank Dobie, Lyndon Johnson, Stanley Walker, and the Old Man of the Mountain. Yet that is my story, and that is my plan.

I miss the damned place. Texas is my mind's country, that place I most want to understand and record and preserve. Four generations of my people sleep in its soil; I have children there, and a grandson; the dead past and the living future tie me to it. Not that I always approve it or love it. It vexes and outrages and disappoints me—especially when I am there. It is now the third most urbanized state, behind New York and California, with all the tangles, stench, random violence, architectural rape, historical pillage, neon blight, pollution, and ecological imbalance the term implies. Money and mindless growth remain high on the list of official priorities, breeding a crass boosterism not entirely papered over by an infectious energy. The state legislature—though improving as slowly as an old man's mending bones—still harbors excessive, coon-ass, rural Tory Democrats who fail to understand that 79.7 percent of Texans have flocked to urban areas and may need fewer farm-to-market roads, hide-and-tick inspectors, or outraged orations almost comically declaiming against welfare loafers, creeping socialism, the meddling ol' feds, and sin in the aggregate.

Too much, now, the Texas landscape sings no native notes. The impersonal, standardized superhighways—bending around or by most small towns, and then blatting straightaway toward the urban sprawls—offer homogenized service stations, fast-food-chain outlets, and cluttered shopping centers one might find duplicated in Ohio, Maryland, Illinois, or Anywhere, U.S.A. Yes, there is much to make me protest, as did Mr. Faulkner's Quentin Compson, of the south—"I *don't* hate it. I don't hate it, I *don't.* . . ." For all its shrinkages of those country pleasures I once eschewed, and now covet and vainly wish might return, Texas remains in my mind's eye that place to which I shall eventually return to rake the dust for my formative tracks; that place where one hopes to grow introspective and wise as well as old. It is a romantic foolishness, of course; the opiate dream of a nostalgia junkie. When I go back to stay—and I fancy that I will—there doubtless will be opportunities to wonder at my plan's imperfections.

For already I have created in my mind, you see, an improbable corner of paradise: the rustic, rambling ranch house with the clear-singing creek nearby, the clumps of shade trees (under which, possibly, the Sons of the Pioneers will play perpetual string-band concerts), the big cozy library where I will work and read and cogitate between issuing to the Dallas *Times-Herald* or the Houston *Post* those public pronouncements befitting an Elder Statesman of Life and Letters. I will become a late-blooming naturalist and outdoorsman: hiking and camping, and piddling in cattle; never mind that to date I have preferred the sidewalks of New York, and my beef not on the hoof but tricked up with mushroom sauces.

All this will occur about one easy hour out of Austin—my favorite Texas city—and exactly six miles from a tiny, unnamed town looking remarkably like what Walt Disney would have built for a cheery, heart-tugging Texas-based story happening about 1940. The nearest neighbor will live 3.7 miles away, have absolutely no children or dogs, but will have one beautiful young wife, who adores me; it is she who will permit me, by her periodic attentions, otherwise to live the hermit's uncluttered life. Politicians will come to my door hats in hand, and fledging Poets and young Philosophers. Basically, they will want to know exactly what is Life's Purpose. Looking out across the gently blowing grasslands, past the grazing blooded cattle, toward a perfect sunset, with even the wind in my favor, and being the physical reincarnation of Hemingway with a dash of Twain in my mood, I shall—of course—be happy to tell them.

Well, we all know that vast gap between fantasy and reality when True Life begins playing the scenario. Likely I will pay twice to thrice the value for a run-down old "farmhouse" where the plumbing hasn't worked since Coolidge, and shall die of a heart attack while digging a cesspool. The nearest neighbor will live directly across the road; he will own seven rambunctious children, five mad dogs, and an ugly harridan with sharp elbows, a shrill voice, and a perverse hatred for dirty old writing men. The nearest town—less than a half mile away and growing by leaps, separated from my digs only by a subdivision of mock Bavarian castles and the new smeltering plant—will be made of plastics, paved parking lots, and puppy-dog tails. The trip to Austin will require three hours if one avoids rush-hour crushes; when I arrive—to preen in Scholz Garten or The Raw Deal or other watering holes where artists congregate—people will say, "Who's that old fart?" Unfortunately I may try to tell them. My books will long have been out of print; probably my secret yearning will be to write a column for the local weekly newspaper. Surrounded by strangers, memories, and galloping growth, I shall sit on my porch—rocking and cackling and talking gibberish to the wind—while watching them build yet another Kwik Stop Kwality Barbecue Pit on the west edge of my crowded acreage. Occasionally I will walk the two dozen yards to the interstate highway to throw stones at passing trucks; my ammunition will peter out long before traffic does. But when I die digging that cesspool, by God, I'll have died at home. That knowledge makes me realize where my heart is.

But the truth, dammit, is that I feel much more the Texan when in the East. New Yorkers, especially, encourage and expect one to perform a social drill I think of as "playing cowboy." Even as a young soldier I discovered a presumption among a high percentage of New Yorkers that my family owned shares in the King Ranch and that my natural equestrian talents were unlimited; all one needed to affirm such groundless suspicions were a drawl and a grin. To this day you may spot me in Manhattan wearing boots and denim jeans with a matching vest and western-cut hat—topped by a furry cattleman's coat straight out of Marlboro Country; if you've seen Dennis Weaver play McCloud, then you've seen me, without my beard.

Never mind that I *like* such garb, grew up wearing it, or that I find it natural, practical, and inexpensive; no, to a shameful degree, I dress for my role. When I learned that Princeton University would pay good money to a working writer for teaching his craft—putting insulated students in touch with the workaday salts and sours of the literary world—do you think I went down there wrapped in an ascot and puffing a briar pipe from Dunhill's? No, good neighbors, I donned my Cowboy Outfit to greet the selection committee and aw-shucksed and consarned 'em half to death; Easterners just can't resist a John Wayne quoting Shakespeare; I've got to admit there's satisfaction in it for every good ol' boy who country-slicks the city dudes.

New Yorkers tend to think of Mississippians or Georgians or Virginians under the catchall category of "southerners," of Californians as foreigners, and of Texans as the legendary Texan. We are the only outlanders, I think, that they define within a specific state border and assign the burden of an obligatory—i.e., "cowboy"— culture. Perhaps we court such treatment; let it be admitted that Texans are a clannish people. We tend to think of ourselves as Texans no matter how long ago we strayed or how tenuous our home connections. When I enter a New York store and some clerk— alerted by my nasal twang—asks where I am from, I do not answer "East Thirty-second Street," but "Texas," yet my last permanent address there was surrendered when Eisenhower was freshly President.

More than half my close friends—and maybe 20 percent of my overall eastern seaboard acquaintances—are expatriate Texans: writers, musicians, composers, editors, lawyers, athletes, show-folk, a few businessmen, and such would-be politicians or former politicians as Bill Moyers and Ramsey Clark. Don Meredith, Liz Smith, Judy Buie, Dan Jenkins, you name 'em, and to one degree or another we play cowboy together. Many of us gather for chili suppers, tell stories with origins in Fort Worth or Odessa or Abilene; sometimes we even play dominoes or listen to country-western records.

There is, God help us, an organization called The New York Texans, and about 2,000 of us actually belong to it. We meet each March 2—Texas Independence Day—to drink beer, hoo-haw at each other in the accents of home, and honor some myth that we can, at best, only ill define. We even have our own newspaper, published quarterly by a lady formerly of Spur, Texas, which largely specializes in stories bragging on how well we've done in the world of the Big Apple. Since people back home are too busy to remind us of our good luck and talents, we remind ourselves.

No matter where you go, other Texans discover you. Sometimes they are themselves expatriates, sometimes tourists, sometimes business-bent travelers. In any case, we whoop a mutural recognition, even though we're strangers or would be unlikely to attract each other if meeting within our native borders. Indeed, one of the puzzling curiosities is why the Dallas banker, or the George Wallace fanatic who owns the little dry-goods stores in Beeville, and I may drop all prior plans in order to spend an evening together in Monterrey or Oshkosh when—back home—we would consider each other social lepers. Many times I have found myself buddy-buddying with people not all that likable or interesting, sharing Aggie jokes or straight tequila shots or other peculiarities of home.

If you think that sounds pretty dreadful, it often is. Though I am outraged when called a "professional Texan," or when I meet one, certainly I am not always purely innocent. Much of it is a big put-on, of course. We enjoy sharing put-ons against those who expect all Texans to eat with the wrong fork, offer coarse rebel yells, and get all vomity-drunk at the nearest football game. There is this regional defensiveness—LBJ would have known what I mean— leading us to order "a glass of clabber and a mess of chitlins" when faced by the haughty ministrations of the finest French restaurants. (My group does, anyway, though I don't know about the stripe of Texan epitomized, say, by Red Reed; that bunch has got so smooth you can't see behind the sheen.) I hear my Texas friends, expatriates and otherwise, as their accents thicken and their drawls slow down on approaching representatives of other cultures. I observe them as they attempt to come on more lordly and sophisticated than Dean Acheson or more country than Ma and Pa Kettle, depending on what they feel a need to prove.

That they (or I) need to prove anything is weird in itself. It tells you what they—yes, the omnipotent They—put in our young Texas heads. The state's history is required teaching in the public schools, and no student by law may escape the course. They teach Texas history very much fumigated—the Alamo's martyrs, the Indian-killing frontiersmen, the heroic Early Day Pioneers, the Rugged Plainsmen, the Builders and Doers; these had hearts pure where others were soiled—and they teach it and teach it and teach it. I came out of the public schools of Texas knowing naught of Disraeli, Darwin, or Darrow—though well versed in the lore of Sam Houston, Stephen F. Austin, Jim Bowie, the King Ranch, the Goodnight-Loving Trail over which thundered the last of the big herds. No school day was complete but that we sang "The Eyes of Texas," "Texas our Texas," "Beautiful Texas." I mean, try substituting "Rhode Island" or "North Dakota," and it sounds about half-silly even to a Texan. We were taught again and again that Texas was the biggest state, one of the richest, possibly the toughest, surely the most envied. Most Americans, I guess, grow up convinced that their little corners of the universe are special; Texas, however, takes care to institutionalize the preachment.

To discover a wider world, then, where others fail to hold those views—to learn that Texans are thought ignorant or rich or quite often both, though to the last in number capable of sitting a mean steed—is to begin at once a new education and feel sneaky compulsions toward promoting useless old legends. Long after I knew that the Texas of my youth dealt more with myth than reality, and long past that time when I knew that the vast majority of Texans lived in cities, I continued to play cowboy. This was a social and perhaps a professional advantage in the East; it marked one as unique, permitted one to pose as a son of yesterday, furnished a handy identity among the faceless millions. In time one has a way of becoming in one's head something of the role one has assumed. Often I have actually felt myself the reincarnation or the extension of the old range lords or bedroll cowpokes or buffalo hunters. Such playacting is harmless so long as one confines it to wearing costumes or to speech patterns—"I'm a-hankerin' for a beefsteak, y'all, and thank I'll mosey on over to P. J. Clarke's"—but becomes counterproductive unless regulated. Nobody has been able to coax me atop a horse since that day a dozen years ago when I proved to be the most comic equestrian ever to visit a given riding stable on Staten Island. Misled by my range garb, accent, and sunlamp tan, the stable manager assigned what surely must have been his most spirited steed. Unhorsed after much graceless grabbing and grappling, I heard my ride described by a laughing fellow with Brooklyn in his voice: "Cheez, at foist we thought youse was a trick rider. But just before youse fell, we seen youse wasn't nothing but a shoemaker."

Though I wear my Texas garb in Texas, I am more the New Yorker there; not so much in my own mind, perhaps, as in the minds of others. People hold me to account for criticisms I've written of Texas or accuse me of having gone "New York" in my thinking or attitudes. "Nobody's more parochial than a goddamn New Yorker," some of my friends snort—and often they are right. I, too, feel outraged at Manhattan cocktail parties when some clinchjawed Easterner makes it clear he thinks that everything on the wrong side of the George Washington Bridge is quaint, hasn't sense enough to come in from the rain, and maybe lacks toilet training. Yet my Texas friends have their own misconceptions of my adopted home and cause me to defend it. They warn of its violent crime, even though Houston annually vies with Detroit for the title of "Murder Capital of the World." They deride New York's slums and corruptions, even though in South El Paso (and many another Texas city) may be found shameful dirt poverty and felonious social neglect, and Texas erupts in its own political Watergates—

banking, insurance, real estate scandals—at least once each decade. So I find myself in the peculiar defense of New York, waving
my arms, and my voice growing hotter, saying things like "You
goddamn Texans gotta learn that you're not so damned special. . . ." *You* goddamn Texans, now.

My friends charge that despite my frequent visits home and my
summering on Texas beaches, my view of the place is hopelessly
outdated. Fletcher Boone, an Austin artist and entrepreneur—
owner of The Raw Deal Cafe—was the latest to straighten out my
thinking. "All you goddamn expatriates act like time froze somewhere in the nineteen-fifties or earlier," he said. "You'd think we
hadn't discovered television down here, or skin flicks, or dope.
Hell, we grew us a *President* down here. We've got tall buildings
and long hairs and some of us know how to ski!" Mr. Boone had
recently visited New York and now held me to account for its sins:
"It's mental masturbation. You go to a party up there, and instead
of people making real conversation, they stop the proceedings so
somebody can sing opera or play the piano or do a tap dance. It's
show biz, man—buncha egomaniacal people using a captive audience to stroke themselves. Whatta they talk about? 'I, I, I. Me, me,
me. Mine, mine, mine.'" Well, no, I rebut; they also talk about
books, politics, and even *ideas*; only the middle of these, I say, is
likely to be remarked in Texas. Boone is offended; he counter-
attacks that Easterners do not live life so much as they attempt to
dissect it or, worse, dictate how others should live it by the
manipulations of fashion, art, the media. We shout gross generalities, overstatements, "facts" without support. I become the Visiting Smart-ass New Yorker, losing a bit of my drawl.

Well, bless him, there may be something to Fletcher Boone's
charge as I found recently when I returned as a quasi-sociologist. It
was my plan to discover some young, green blue-collar or white-
collar, recently removed to the wicked city from upright rural up-
bringings, and record that unfortunate hick's slippages or shocks.
Then I would return to the hick's small place of origin, comparing
what he or she had traded for a mess of modern city pottage; family graybeards left behind would be probed for their surrogate
shocks and would reveal their fears for their urbanized young. It
would be a whiz of a story, having generational gaps and cultural

shocks and more disappointments or depletions than the Nixon White House. It would be at once nostalgic, pitiful, and brave; one last angry shout against modernity before Houston sinks beneath the waves, Lubbock dries up and blows away for lack of drinking water, and Dallas-Fort Worth grows together as firmly as Siamese twins. Yes, it would have everything but three tits and, perhaps, originality.

Telephone calls to old friends produced no such convenient study. Those recommended turned out to have traveled abroad, attended college in distant places, or otherwise been educated by a urban, mobile society. A young airline hostess in Houston talked mainly of San Francisco or Hawaii; a bank clerk in Dallas sniggered that even in high school days he had spent most of his weekends away from his native village—in city revelry—and thought my idea of "cultural shock" quaint; a petrochemical plant worker failed to qualify when he said, "Shit, life's not all that much different. I live here in Pasadena"—an industrial morass with all the charms and odors of Gary, Indiana—"and I go to my job, watch TV, get drunk with my buddies. Hail, it's not no different from what it was back there in Monahans. Just more traffic and more people and a little less sand." I drove around the state for days, depressed by the urbanization of my former old outback even as I marveled at its energy, before returning to New York. Where I might feel, once more, like a Texan: where I might play cowboy; dream again the ancient dreams.

It is somehow easier to conjure up the Texas I once knew from Manhattan. What an expatriate most remembers are not the hardscrabble times of the 1930s, or the narrow attitudes of a people not then a part of the American mainstream, but a way of life that was passing without one's then realizing it. Quite without knowing it, I witnessed the last of the region's horse culture. Schoolboys tied their mounts to mesquite trees west of the Putnam school and at noon fed them bundled roughage; the pickup truck and the tractor had not yet clearly won out over the horse, though within the decade they would. While the last of the great cattle herds had long ago disappeared up the Chisholm or the Goodnight-Loving Trail, I would see small herds rounded up on my Uncle Raymond's Bar-T-

Bar Ranch and loaded from railside corrals for shipment to the stockyards of Fort Worth—or "Cowtown," as it was then called without provoking smiles. (The rough-planked saloons of the brawling North Side of "Cowtown," near the old stockyards, are gone now save for a small stretch lacquered and refurbished in a way so as to make tourists feel they've been where they ain't.) In Abilene, only thirty-two miles to the west, I would hear the chants of cattle auctioneers while smelling feedlot dung, tobacco, saddle leather, and the sweat of men living the outdoor life. Under the watchful eye of my father, I sometimes rode a gentle horse through the shinnery and scrub oaks of the old family farm, helping him bring in the five dehorned milk cows while pretending to be a bad-assed gunslinger herding longhorns on a rank and dangerous trail drive.

But it was all maya, illusion. Even a dreaming little tad knew the buffalo hunters were gone, along with the old frontier forts, the Butterfield stage, the first sodbusters whose barbed wire fenced in the open range and touched off wars continuing to serve Clint Eastwood or James Arness. This was painful knowledge for one succored on myths and legends, on real-life tales of his father's boyhood wanderings in a covered wagon. Nothing of my original time and place, I felt, would be worth living through or writing about. What I did not then realize (and continue having trouble remembering) is that the past never was as good as it looks from a distance.

The expatriate, returning, thus places an unfair burden upon his native habitat: He demands it to have impossibly marked time, to have marched in place, during the decades he has absented himself. He expects it to have preserved itself as his mind recalls it; to furnish evidence that he did not memorize in vain its legends, folk and folklore, mountains and streams and villages. Never mind that he may have removed himself to other places because they offered rapid growth, new excitements, and cultural revolutions not then available at home.

We expatriate sons may sometimes be unfair: too critical; fail to give due credit; employ the double standard. Especially do those of us who write flay Texas in the name of our disappointments and melted snows. Perhaps it's good that we do this, the native press being so boosterish and critically timid; but there are times, I suspect, when our critical duty becomes something close to a perverse pleasure. Easterners I have known, visiting my homeplace, come away impressed by its dynamic qualities; they see a New Frontier growing in my native bogs, a continuing spirit of adventure, a bit of trombone and swashbuckle, something fresh and good. Ah, but they did not know Texas when she was young.

There is a poignant tale told by the writer John Graves of the last, tamed remnants of a formerly free and proud Indian tribe in Texas: how a small band of them approached an old rancher, begged a scrawny buffalo bull from him, and—spurring their thin ponies—clattered and whooped after it, running it ahead of them, and killed it in the old way—with lances and arrows. They were foolish, I guess, in trying to hold history still for one more hour; probably I'm foolish in the same sentimental way when I sneak off the freeways to snake across the Texas back roads in search of my own past. But there are a couple of familiar stretches making the ride worth it; I most remember one out in the lonely windblown ranch country, between San Angelo and Water Valley, with small rock-dotted hills ahead at the end of a long, flat stretch of road bordered by grasslands, random clumps of trees, wild flowers, grazing cattle, a single distant ranch house whence—one fancies— issues the perfume of baking bread, simmering beans, beef over the flames. There are no billboards, no traffic cloverleafs, no neon, no telephone poles, no Jiffy Tacos or Stuckey's stands, no oil wells, no Big Rich Bastards, no ship channels threatening to ignite because of chemical pollutions, no Howard Johnson flavors. Though old Charley Goodnight lives, Lee Harvey Oswald and Charles Whitman remain unborn.

Never have I rounded the turn leading into that peaceful valley, with the spiny ridge of hills beyond it, that I failed to feel new surges and exhilarations and hope. For a precious few moments I exist in a time warp: I'm back in Old Texas, under a high sky, where all things are again possible and the wind blows free. Invariably, I put the heavy spurs to my trusty Hertz or Avis steed: go flying lickety-split down that lonesome road, whooping a crazy yell and taking deep joyous breaths, sloshing Lone Star beer on my neglected dangling safety belt, and scattering roadside gravel like bursts of buckshot. Ride 'im, cowboy! *Ride* 'im. . . .

1975

The Old Man

While we digested our suppers on The Old Man's *front porch, his grandchildren chased fireflies in the summer dusk and, in turn, were playfully chased by neighborhood dogs. As always, The Old Man had carefully locked the collar of his workday khakis. He recalled favored horses and mules from his farming days, remembering their names and personalities though they had been thirty or forty years dead. I gave him a brief thumbnail sketch of William Faulkner—Mississippian, great writer, appreciator of the soil and good bourbon—before quoting what Faulkner had written of the mule: "He will draw a wagon or a plow but he will not run a race. He will not try to jump anything he does not indubitably know beforehand he can jump; he will not enter any place unless he knows of his own knowledge what is on the other side; he will work for you patiently for ten years for the chance to kick you once." The Old Man cackled in delight. "That feller sure knowed his mules," he said.*

SONS RARELY GET TO KNOW their fathers very well, less well, certainly, than fathers get to know their sons. More of an intimidating nature remains for the father to conceal, he being cast in the role of example-setter. Sons know their own guilty intimidations. Eventually, however, they graduate their fears of the lash or the frown, learn that their transgressions have been handed down for generations. Fathers are more likely to consider their own sins to have been original.

The son may ultimately boast to the father of his own darker conquests or more wicked dirkings: perhaps out of some need to declare his personal independence, or out of some perverted wish to settle a childish score, or simply because the young—not yet forged in the furnace of blood—understand less about that delicate balance of natural love each generation reserves for the other.

Remembering yesterday's thrashings, or angry because the fathers did not provide the desired social or economic advantages, sons sometimes reveal themselves in cruel ways.

Wild tigers claw the poor father for failures real or imagined: opportunities fumbled, aborted marriages, punishments misplaced. There is this, too: a man who has discovered a likeness in his own image willing to believe (far beyond what the evidence requires) that he combines the natural qualities of Santa Claus, Superman, and the senior Saints, will not easily surrender to more mature judgments. Long after the junior partner has ceased to believe that he may have been adopted, or that beating-off will grow hair on the hand while the brain slowly congeals into gangrenous matter, the father may pose and pretend, hiding bits and pieces of yesterday behind his back. Almost any father with the precious stuff to care can adequately conceal the pea. It is natural in sons to lust—yes, to *hunger* for—an Old Man special enough to have endowed his progeny's genes with genius and steel. Or, failing the ideal, to have a father who will at least remain sturdy, loyal, and *there* when life's vigilantes come riding with the hangman.

You see the fix the poor bastard is in, don't you? He must at once apologize and inspire, conceal and judge, strut and intervene, correct and pretend. No matter how far he ranges outside his normal capabilities, he will remain unappreciated through much of the paternal voyage—often neglected, frequently misread, sometimes profaned by his own creation. For all this, the father may evolve into a better man: may find himself closer to being what he claims, a strong role having ways of overpowering the actor. And if he is doubly blessed, he may know a day when his sons (by then, most likely, fathers themselves) will come to love him more than they can bring themselves to say. Then, sometimes, sons get to know their fathers a bit: perhaps a little more than nature intended, and surely more than yesterday would have believed.

There was that blindly adoring period of childhood when my father was the strongest and wisest of men. He would scare off the bears my young imagination feared as they prowled the night outside our Texas farmhouse, provide sunshine and peanut butter, make the world go away. I brought him my broken toys and my skinned knees. He did imitations of all the barnyard animals; when we boxed he saw to it that I won by knockouts. After his predawn winter milkings, shivering and stomping his numb feet while rushing to throw more wood on the fire, he warned that tomorrow morning, by gosh, he planned to laze abed and eat peach cobbler while his youngest son performed the icy chores.

He took me along when he hunted rabbits and squirrels, and on alternate Saturdays when he bounced in a horse-drawn wagon over dirt roads to accomplish his limited commercial possibilities in Putnam or Cisco. He thrilled me with tales of his own small-boy adventures: an odyssey to Missouri, consuming two years, in covered wagons pulled by oxen, fordings of swift rivers, and pauses in Indian camps where my grandfather, Morris Miles King, smoked strong pipes with his hosts and ate with his fingers from iron kettles containing what he later called dog stew. The Old Man taught me to whistle, pray, ride a horse, enjoy country music, and, by his example, to smoke. He taught that credit-buying was unmanly, unwise, and probably unforgivable in Heaven; that one honored one's women, one's flag, and one's pride; that, on evidence supplied by the biblical source of "winds blowing from the four corners of the earth," the world was most assuredly flat. He taught me the Old Time Religion, to bait a fishhook or gut a butchered hog, and to sing "The Nigger Preacher and the Bear."

I had no way of knowing what courage was in the man (he with no education, no hope of quick riches, no visible improvements or excitements beckoning to new horizons) to permit him to remain so cheerful, shielding, and kind. No matter how difficult those Depression times, there was always something under the Christmas tree. When I was four, he walked six miles to town in a blizzard, and returned as it worsened, carrying a red rocking chair and smaller gifts in a gunnysack. Though he had violated his creed by buying on credit, he made it possible for Santa Claus to appear on time.

I would learn that he refused to accept the largess of one of FDR's recovery agencies because he feared I might be shamed or marked by wearing to school its telltale olive drab "relief shirts." He did accept employment with the Works Progress Administration, shoveling and hauling wagonloads of dirt and gravel for a road-building project. When I brought home the latest joke from the rural school—"WPA stands for 'We Piddle Around'"—he delivered a stern, voice-quavering lecture: *Son, the WPA is a honest way some poor men has of makin' their families a livin'. You'd go to bed hungry tonight without the WPA. Next time some smart aleck makes a joke about it, you ought to knock a goddamned whistlin' fart out of him.*

Children learn that others have fathers with more money, more opportunity, or more sophistication. Their own ambitions or resentments rise, inspiring them to reject the simpler wants of an earlier time. The son is shamed by the father's speech, dress, car, occupation, and table manners. The desire to flee the family nest (or, at bottom, to soar higher in it; to undertake some few experimental solos) arrives long before the young have their proper wings or before their parents can conceive of it.

The Old Man was an old-fashioned father, one who relied on corporal punishments, Biblical exhortations, and a ready temper. He was not a man who dreamed much, or who understood that others might require dreams as their opium. Though he held idleness to be as useless and as sinful as adventure, he had the misfortune to sire a hedonist son who dreamed of improbable conquests accomplished by some magic superior to grinding work. By the time I entered the troublesome teen-age years, we were on the way to a long dark journey. A mutual thirst to prevail existed—some crazy stubborn infectious contagious will to avoid the slightest surrender.

The Old Man strapped, rope-whipped, and caned me for smoking, drinking, lying, avoiding church, skipping school, and laying out at night. Having once been very close, we now lashed out at each other in the manner of rejected lovers on the occasion of each new disappointment. I thought The Old Man blind to the wonders and potentials of the real world; could not fathom how current events or cultural habits so vital to my contemporaries could be considered so frivolous, or worse. In turn, The Old Man expected me to obediently accept his own values: show more concern over the ultimate disposition of my eternal soul, eschew easy paths when walking tougher ones might somehow purify, be not so inquisitive or damnfool dreamy. That I could not (or would not) comply puzzled, frustrated, and angered him. In desperation he moved from a "wet" town to a "dry" one, in the foolish illusion that this tactic might keep his baby boy out of saloons.

On a Saturday in my fifteenth year, when I refused an order to dig a cesspool in our backyard because of larger plans downtown, I fought back: it was savage and ugly—though, as those things go, one hell of a good fight. Only losers emerged, however. After that we spoke in terse mumbles or angry shouts, not to communicate with civility for three years. The Old Man paraded to a series of punishing and uninspiring jobs—night watchman, dock loader for a creamery, construction worker, chicken-butcher in a steamy, stinking poultry house, while I trekked to my own part-time jobs or to school. When school was out I usually repaired to one distant oil field or another, remaining until classes began anew. Before my eighteenth birthday, I escaped by joining the Army.

On the morning of my induction, The Old Man paused at the kitchen table, where I sat trying to choke down breakfast. He wore the faded old crossed-gallus denim overalls I held in supreme contempt and carried a lunch bucket in preparation of whatever dismal job then rode him. "Lawrence," he said, "is there anything I can do for you?" I shook my head. "You need any money?" "No." The Old Man shuffled uncertainly, causing the floor to creak. "Well," he said, "I wish you good luck." I nodded in the direction of my bacon and eggs. A moment later the front door slammed, followed by the grinding of gears The Old Man always accomplished in confronting even the simplest machinery.

Alone in a Fort Dix crowd of olive drab, I lay popeyed on my bunk at night, chain-smoking, as Midland High School's initial 1946 football game approached. The impossible dream was that some magic carpet might transport me back to those anticipatory tingles I had known when bands blared, cheerleaders cartwheeled sweet, tantalizing glimpses of their panties, and we purple-clads whopped and clattered toward the red-shirted Odessa Broncos or the Angry Orange of San Angelo. Waste and desolation lived in the heart's private country on the night that opening game was accomplished on the happiest playing field of my forfeited youth. The next morning, a Saturday, I was called to the Orderly Room to

accept a telegram—a form of communication that had always meant death or other disasters. I tore it open with the darkest fantasies to read: MIDLAND 26 EL PASO YSLETA 0 LOVE DAD. Those valuable communiqués arrived on ten consecutive Saturday mornings.

With a ten-day furlough to spend, I appeared unannounced and before a cold dawn on the porch of that familiar frame house in Midland. The Old Man rose quickly, dispensing greetings in his woolly long-handles. "You just a First Class Private?" he teased. "Lord God, I would a-thought a King would be a General by now. Reckon I'll have to write ole Harry Truman a postcard to git that straightened out." Most of the time, however (when I was not out impressing the girls with my PFC stripe) a cautious reserve prevailed. We talked haltingly, carefully, probing as uncertainly as two neophyte pre-med students might explore their first skin boil.

On the third or fourth day, The Old Man woke me on the sleeping porch, lunch bucket in hand. "Lawrence," he said, "your mother found a bottle of whiskey in your suitcase. Now, you *know* this is a teetotal home. We never had a bottle of whiskey in a home of ours, and we been married since 19-and-11. You're perfectly welcome to stay here, but your whiskey's not." I stiffly mumbled something about going to a motel. "You know better than that," The Old Man scolded. "We don't want you goin' off to no blamed motel." Then, in a weary exasperation not fully appreciated until dealing with transgressions among my own offspring: "Good *God*, son, what makes you want to raise old billy hell all the time?" We regarded each other in a helpless silence. "Do what you think is right," he said, sighing. "I've done told you how me and your mother feel." He went off to work: I got up and removed the offending liquids.

The final morning brought a wet freeze blowing down from Amarillo by way of the North Pole. The Old Man's car wouldn't start; our family had never officially recognized taxis. "I'll walk you to the bus station," he said, bundling in a heavy sheepskin jumper and turning his back, I suspect, so as not to witness my mother's struggle against tears. We shivered down dark streets past homes of my former schoolmates, by vacant lots where I played softball or slept off secret sprees, past stores I remembered for their bargains in Moon Pies and then Lucky Strikes and finally Trojans. Nostalgia and old guilts blew in with the wind. I wanted to say something healing to The Old Man, to utter some gracious good-bye (the nearest thing to retroactive apologies a savage young pride would permit), but I simply knew no beginnings.

We sat an eternity in the unreal lights of the bus station among crying babies, hung-over cowboys, and drowsing old Mexican men, in mute inspection of those dead shows provided by bare walls and ceilings. The Old Man made a silent offering of a cigarette. He was a vigorous fifty-nine then, still clear-eyed, dark-haired, and muscular, but as his hand extended that cigarette pack and I saw it clearly—weather-cured, scarred, one finger crooked and stiff-jointed from an industrial accident—I suddenly and inexplicably knew that one day The Old Man would wither, fail, die. In that moment, I think, I first sensed—if did not understand—something of mortality; of tribes, blood, and inherited rituals.

At the door to the bus, The Old Man suddenly hugged me, roughly, briefly: not certain, perhaps, such an intimacy would be tolerated by this semi-stranger who bore his name. His voice broke as he said, "Write us, son. We love you." I clasped his hand and brushed past, too full for words. For I knew, then, that I loved him, too, and had, even in the worst of times, and would never stop.

We took a trip last summer, one The Old Man had secretly coveted for a lifetime, though, in the end, he almost had to be prodded into the car. "I hate like the devil to leave Cora," he said of his wife of almost six decades. "She's got to where her head swims when she walks up and down the steps. She taken a bad spill just a few weeks ago. I try to stay close enough to catch her if she falls."

The Old Man did not look as if he could catch much of a falling load as he approached eighty-three. Two hundred pounds of muscle and sinew created by hard work and clean living had melted to a hundred-sixty-odd; his senior clothing flapped about him. He had not worn his bargain dentures for years, except when my mother insisted on enforcing the code of some rare social function, because, he complained, they played the devil with his gums, or gagged him, or both. The eagle's gleam was gone from eyes turned watery and rheumy; he couldn't hear so well anymore; he spoke in a wispy voice full of false starts and tuneless whistles requiring full attention.

He was thirteen years retired from his last salaried job, and he had established himself as a yard-tender and general handyman. He mowed lawns, trimmed hedges, tilled flower beds, grubbed stumps, painted houses, performed light carpentry or emergency plumbings. In his eightieth year, my mother decreed that he might no longer climb trees for pruning purposes. Though he lived with that verdict, his eyes disapproved it just as they had when his sons dictated that he might no longer work during the hottest part of the desert summer days. The Old Man surrendered his vigor hard, each new concession (not driving a car or giving up cigarettes) throwing him into a restless depression. He continued to rise each morning at five, prowling the house impatiently on rainy days, muttering and growling of all the grass that needed mowing or of how far behind Midland was falling in unpainted fences. At such times he might complain because the Social Security Administration refused him permission to earn more than $1,200 annually while continuing to merit its assistance: he sneaked in more work by the simple expediency of lowering his prices. Except on the Sabbath (when, by his ethic, the normal joy of work translated to sin), he preferred the indoors only when eating or sleeping. He had long repaired to a sleeping porch of his own creation, where it was always twenty degrees cooler in winter and correspondingly hotter in the summertime; one of the curses of modernity, he held, was "refrigerated air."

On my mother's reassurances that she would spend a few days with her twin sister, we coaxed The Old Man into my car. Years earlier, I had asked him whether he wanted to see some particular place or thing and whether I might take him there. To my surprise (for The Old Man had never hinted of secret passions), he said yes, he had wanted since childhood to visit the State Capitol in Austin and the Alamo in San Antonio: he had read of them in books his mother had obtained when his father's death had cut off his schooling. I had long procrastinated. Living in the distant Sodoms and Gomorrahs of the East, I wandered in worlds alien to my father in search of ambitions that surely mystified him. There were flying trips home: an hour's domino-playing here, an evening of conversation there. Then the desert would become too still, dark, and forbidding: I would shake his worn old hand, mutter promises and excuses, grab a suitcase; run. Last summer my wife effectively nagged me to deliver on my old pledge. And so, one boiling morning in July, we departed my father's house. He sat beside me on the front seat, shrunken and somehow remote, yet transmitting some youthful eagerness. The older he had grown, the less The Old Man had ever troubled to talk, contenting himself with sly grins or solemn stares so well-timed you sometimes suspected he heard better than advertised. Deliver him a grandchild to tease and he would open up: "Bradley Clayton King, I hear turrible things on you. Somebody said you got garments on your back, and you have ancestors. And word come to me lately that you was seen hesitatin' on the doorstep." With others, however, he was slow to state his case.

Now, however, we had hardly gone a mile before The Old Man began a monologue lasting almost a week. As we roared across the desert waste, his fuzzy old voice battled with the cool cat's purr of the air conditioner; he gestured, pointed, laughed, praised the land, took on new strentgth.

He had a love for growing things, a Russian peasant's legendary infatuation for the motherland; for digging in the good earth, smelling it, conquering it. "Only job I ever had that could hold a candle to farmin'," he once said, "was blacksmithin'. Then the car come along, and I was blowed up." Probably his greatest disappointment was his failure as a farmer—an end dictated by depressed prices in his most productive years, and hurried by land worn down through a lack of any effective application of the basic agrarian sciences. He was a walking-plow farmer, a mule-and-dray-horse farmer, a chewing-gum-and-bailing-wire farmer. If God brought rain at the wrong moment, crops rotted in the mud; should He not bring it when required, they baked and died. You sowed, tilled, weeded, sweated: if Heaven felt more like reward than punishment, you would not be forced to enter the Farmer's State Bank with your soiled felt hat in your hand.

World War II forced The Old Man off the family acres: he simply could not reject the seventy-odd cents per hour an oil company promised for faithful drudgery in its pipeline crew. And he felt, too, deep and simple patriotic stirrings: perhaps, if he carried enough heavy pipe quickly enough, the fall of Hitler and Tojo might be hastened. He alternately flared with temper fits and was quietly reflective on the fall day in 1942 when we quit the homestead he had come to in a covered wagon in 1894; later, receiving word of the accidental burning of that unpainted farmhouse, he walked around with tears in his eyes. He was past seventy before giving up his dream of one day returning to that embittered soil, of finally mastering it, of extracting its unkept promises.

As we left behind the oil derricks and desert sandhills last summer, approaching barns and belts of greenery, The Old Man praised wild flowers, dairy herds, shoots of cotton, fields of grain. "That's mighty good timberland," he said. "Good grass. Cattle could bunch up in them little groves in the winter and turn their backsides to the wind." He damned his enemies: "Now, Johnson grass will ruin a place. But mesquite trees is the most sapping thing that God lets grow. Mesquites spreads faster than gossip. A cow can drop her plop on a flat rock, and if she's been eatin' mesquite beans they'll take a-holt and grow like mornin' glories."

One realized, as The Old Man grew more and more enthusiastic over roadside growths and dribbling little creeks, just how fenced-in he had been for thirty years; knew, freshly, the depth of his resentments as gas pumps, hamburger outlets, and supermarkets came to prosper within two blocks of his door. The Old Man had personally hammered and nailed his house together, in 1944, positioning it on the town's northmost extremity as if hoping it might sneak off one night to seek more bucolic roots. Midland had been a town of maybe 12,000 then; now it flirted with 70,000 and the Chamber of Commerce mindlessly tub-thumped for more. The Old Man hated it: it had hemmed him in.

We detoured to Eastland County so he might take another glimpse of the past. He slowly moved among the tombstones in a rural cemetery where his parents rested among parched grasses and the bones of their dear friends: people who had been around for the Civil War; God-fearing, land-grubbing folk who had never dreamed that one day men would fly like birds in the sky or swim like fishes beneath the sea. Though he had on his best suit, he bent down to weed the family plot. I kneeled to help; my young son joined us. We worked in silence and a cloaking heat, sharing unspoken tribal satisfactions.

We drove past stations he recognized as important milestones: "Right over yonder—the old house is gone now, been gone forty years—but right there where you see that clump of them blamed mesquites, well, that was where your brother Weldon was borned. 19-and-15, I reckon it was. We had two of the purtiest weepin' willers you ever seen. I had me a dandy cotton crop that year." We climbed an unpaved hill, the car mastering it easily, where the horses or mules of my youth had stained in harness, rolling their eyes under The Old Man's lash. "This durn hill," he said. "I come down it on a big-wheel bicycle I'd borrowed when I was about fifteen. First one I'd seen, and I was taken with it. Didn't know no more about ridin' it than I did about 'rithmetic. Come whizzin' down so fast my feet couldn't match them pedals: didn't have *sense* enough to coast. Wellsir, I run plumb over in the bar-ditch and flipped over. It taken hair, hide and all." He laughed, and the laugh turned into a rasping cough, and the cough grew so violent that veins hammered at the edge of his sparse hair, and the old face turned crimson. Through it all he joyously slapped his leg.

We stopped for lunch in a flawed little village where my father had once owned a blacksmith shop. The café was crammed by wage hands and farmers taking their chicken-fried steaks or bowls of vegetable soup seriously, men who minutely inspected strangers and muted their conversations accordingly. Weary of the car and the road, The Old Man chose to stand among the crowded tables while awaiting his order. He was grandly indifferent to the sneaked upward glances of the diners, whose busy elbows threatened to spear him from all sides, and to the waitress who, frowning, danced around him in dispensing hamburgers or plates of hot cornbread. "Tell Grand Dad to sit down," my teen-age daughter, Kerri, whispered. "He's all right," I said. "Well, my *gosh*! At least tell him to take off his *hat*!"

The Old Man startled a graybeard in khakis by gripping his arm just in time to check the elevation of a spoonful of mashed potatoes. "What's your name?" he inquired. The old nester's eyes nervously consulted his companions before he surrendered it. "Don't reckon I know you," my father said. "You must not of been around here long." Twenty-some years, the affronted newcomer mumbled. "I had me a blacksmith shop right over yonder," The Old Man said. He pointed through a soft-drink sign and its supporting wall. "It was in the 1920s. My name's Clyde King. You recollect me?" When the old nester failed the quiz, my father abandoned him to his mashed potatoes. "What's *your* name?" he inquired of a victim mired in his blackberry pie. My twelve-year-old son giggled; his sister covered her humiliated face.

He walked along a diminutive counter of ketchup bottles, fruit pies, and digestive aids, reading only those faces grizzled enough to remember. An aging rancher, deep in his iced tea, nodded: "Yeah, I remember you." The Old Man pumped his hand, beaming. "I was just a kid-of-a-boy," the rancher said. "I was better acquainted with your brother Rex. And the one that run the barbershop. Claude, wasn't it? Where they at now?" The Old Man sobered himself: "Well, I buried 'em within three weeks of one another last month. Claude was seventy-eight and Rex was seventy-four. I'm the only one of the King boys still kickin'. Oldest of the bunch, too. If I live to the eighteenth day of next February, the Lord willin', I'll be eighty-three year old." "Well, you look in right good shape," the rancher said.

When The Old Man sat down at our booth my daughter asked, too sweetly, "Grand Dad, you want me to take your hat?" He gave her an amused glance, a look suggesting he had passed this way before. "Naw," he said. "This a-way, I know where it's at if this café catches a-fire and I need it in a hurry." Then he removed the trespass to his outer knee and slowly crumbled crackers into the chili bowl before bending to feed his toothless face.

His bed was empty when I awoke in an Austin motel shortly after sunrise. He could be seen in contemplation of the swimming pool, turning his direct gaze on all who struggled toward their early jobs. Conversing with a black bellhop when I claimed him, he was full of new information: "That nigger tells me he averages a dollar a head for carryin' suitcases. I may buy me some fancy britches and give him some competition. . . . Folks sure must be sleepyheaded around here. I bet I walked a mile, and didn't see two dozen people. . . . Went over yonder to that Governor's Mansion and rattled the gate and yelled, but didn't nobody come to let me in." "Did you *really*?" I asked, moderately appalled. "Thunder, yes! I'm a voter. Democrat, at that." Then the sly country grin flashed in a way that keeps me wondering in the night, now, whether he really had.

We entered a coffee shop. "Lord God," The Old Man said, recoiling from the menu. "This place is high as a cat's back. You mean they git a dollar eighty-five for two eggs and a little dab a bacon?" I smiled: how much did he think our motel room had cost? "Well, the way things is now, I expect it run ten or twelve dollars." No, the price had been thirty dollars. His old eyes bulged: "For one *night*? Lord God, son, let's git us a blanket and go to the wagon yard!"

"This here's a heap bigger place than I thought it would be," he said in a hushed voice as he inspected the polished chambers of the Texas House of Representatives. He read the faces of past governors hanging in the rotunda, pointing out his favorites (selecting three good men and two rank demagogues). He stood shyly, not having to be reminded to remove his hat, when introduced to a few stray legislators and when led into Governor Preston Smith's office.

Probably he was relieved to find the Governor was absent, for The Old Man had never prospered in the company of "big shots": a big shot may be defined as one who wears neckties in the middle of the week or claims a title; I was never certain what fine distinctions The Old Man made in his mind between a United States Senator and a notary public.

He marveled at the expanse of grass on the Capitol grounds, inspected its flower beds, inquired of an attendant how many gallons of water the grounds required each day, and became stonily disapproving when the hired hand did not know. In the archives of the General Land Office, he painstakingly sought out the legal history of that farm his father had settled in the long ago. He was enchanted by the earliest maps of Texas counties he had known as a boy.

That night he sat on his motel bed recalling the specifics of forgotten cattle trades, remembering the only time he got drunk (at age sixteen) and how the quart of whiskey so poisoned him that he had promised God and his weeping mother that, if permitted to live, he would die before touching another drop. He recited his disappointment in being denied a preacher's credentials by the Methodist hierarchy on the grounds of insufficient education. "They wanted note preachers," he said contemptuously. "Wasn't satisfied with preachers who spoke sermons from the heart and preached the Bible pure. And that's what's gone wrong with churches."

A farmhand and apprentice blacksmith, he had not been smitten blind by his first encounter with my mother-to-be at a country social. "I spied another girl I wanted to spark," he grinned. "Next day, I seen that girl and several others go into a general store by the blacksmith shop. I moseyed over like I was out of chewin' tobacco. Lord God, in the daylight that girl was ugly as a mud fence! I couldn't imagine wakin' up to that of a-mornin'." He laughed: "Then I taken a second look at Cora—she was seventeen—and she had the purtiest complexion and eyes and . . . well, just *ever*thing." Scheming to see her again, he pep-talked his faint heart to encourage the boldness to request a date.

"Didn't seem like I'd ever do it," he confessed. "I'd go up to her at socials or church and make a bow and say, 'Miss Cora.' And she would bob me a little curtsy and say, 'Mister Clyde.' Then I'd stand there like a durned lummox, fiddlin' with my hat, and my face

would heat up, and I couldn't think of a consarned thing to say."
He laughed in memory of the callow swain that was. "It was customary in them days for young women to choose young men to lead singin' at church. I know within reason, now, that it was to help tongue-tied young hicks like myself, but I was pea-green then, and didn't know it. One night Cora picked me. Lord God, it excited me so that I plumb forgot the words to all the hymns I knowed." One could see him there in that lantern-lighted plank church, stiff in his high collar and cheap suit, earnest juices popping out on his forge-tanned forehead, sweet chaos alive in his heart. His voice would have quavered as he asked everyone to please turn to Number One-Forty-Three, while matchmaking old women in calico encouraged him with their wise witch's eyes and young ladies with bright ribbons in their hair giggled behind fluttering fans advertising Sunday School literature or pious morticians.

"Somehow I stumbled through it. Never heard a word the preacher said that night: I was tryin' to drum up nerve to approach Miss Cora, you see. Quick as the preacher said 'Amen' to his last prayer, I run over fat women and little kids to git there before I got cold feet: 'Miss Cora, may I have the pleasure of your company home?' When she said, 'Yes, if you wish,' my heart pounded like I was gonna faint!

"Her daddy—ole man Jim Clark, *Lord God*, he was a tough case!—he didn't allow his girls to ride in no buggies. If you wanted to spark a Clark girl, you had to be willin' to walk. Wellsir, I left my team at the church. Walkin' Cora home I asked if I could pay a call on her. I never dated no other woman from then on. There was another young feller had his eye on Cora. Once I had paid her three or four courtin' calls, I looked him up to say I didn't want him tryin' to spark her no more. Because, I said, I had it in mind to marry her. 'What'll you *do* about it?'—he got his back up, you see. I said, 'Whatever I *got* to do. And if you don't believe me, by God, just you try me!' He never give me no trouble."

The Old Man revealed his incredulous joy when, perhaps a year later, his halting proposal had been accepted. "Do you remember what you said?" my intrigued daughter asked. "Durn right! *Ought* to. I practiced on it for some weeks." He laughed a wheezing burst. "We had just walked up on her daddy's porch one evening and I said"—and here The Old Man attempted again the deeper tones of youth, seeking the courtly country formality he had brought into play on that vital night, reciting as one might when called upon in Elocution Class in some old one-room schoolhouse—"'Miss Cora, I have not got much of this world's goods, and of education I haven't none. But I fancy myself a man of decent habits, and if you will do me the honor of becoming my wife, I will do the best I can by you for always.'" He bowed his head, hiding his tears. "Grand Dad," my daughter asked, "did you kiss her?" "Lord God, *no!*" The Old Man was sincerely shocked, maybe even a bit outraged: "Kissin' wasn't took lightly in them days."

Between Austin and San Antonio we drove through San Marcos; a prominent sign proclaimed that Lyndon B. Johnson had once earned a degree at the local teachers' college. "That's a mighty fine school," The Old Man said. I remained silent. "Yessir," he said, "a *mighty* fine school." Only the purring air conditioner responded. The Old Man shifted elaborately on the seat. "Why, now, I expect that school's as good a school as the Newnited States has." By now he realized that a contest was joined: whatever joke he wished to make must be accomplished in the absence of my feeding straight-line. "I doubt if that Harvard outfit up yonder could hold a candle to this school," he said. "I expect this school would put that Harvard bunch in the shade." My son, less experienced in such games, provided the foil: "Grand Dad, why is it such a good school?" "*Got* to be," The Old Man said. "It learned ole Lyndon to have sense enough to know he couldn't get elected again." He enjoyed his chortle no less for the delay.

"Didn't you like President Johnson?" my son asked.

"Naw. LBJ told too many lies. I wouldn't a-shoed horses on credit for him."

"Who was your favorite President?"

"Harry Truman. Harry wasn't afraid to take the bull by the horns. Wasn't no mealymouth goody-goody in him like in most politicians. Ole Ike, now, they blowed him up like Mister Big and all he ever showed me was that silly grin."

"Did you ever vote for a Republican?" my son asked.

"Yeah, in 19-and-28. Voted for Herbert Hoover. And he no more than put his britches on the chair till we had a Depression. I promised God right then if He wouldn't send no more Depressions, I wouldn't vote for no more Republicans."

"Do you think God really cares who's President?" I asked.

"I reckon not," The Old Man said. "Look at what we got in there now."

What did The Old Man think of this age of protest and revolt?

"It plagues me some," he admitted. "I got mad at them young boys that didn't want to fight in Vietnam. Then after the politicians botched it so bad nobody couldn't win it, and told lies to boot, I decided *I* wouldn't want to risk dyin' in a war that didn't make sense."

It was suggested that no wars made sense.

"Maybe so," The Old Man said. "Bible says, 'Thou Shalt Not Kill.'" Still yet, the Bible's full of wars. Bible says there'll be wars and rumors of wars. I don't think war is what all the ruckus is about, though. I think young people is just generally confused."

Why?

"They don't have nothing to cling to," he said; they had been raised in whiskey homes; their preachers, teachers, politicians, and daddies had grown so money-mad and big-Ikey nothing else counted. Too much had been handed today's kids on silver platters: they got cars too soon and matching big notions. They went off chasing false gods. Well, didn't guess he much blamed 'em: they didn't have nothing waiting at home except babysitters, television, and mothers that cussed in mixed company or wore whiskey on the breath.

"I seen all this coming during the Second World's War," The Old Man said. "People got to moving around so much with good cars. Families split up and lost their roots. The main thing, though, was the women. Women had always stayed home and raised the kids: that was their job. It's just nature. And the man of the family had to be out scratchin' a living. But during that Second World's War, women started workin' as a regular thing and smokin' and drinkin' in public. Triflin' started, and triflin' led to divorces. I knowed then there was gonna be trouble because *somebody's* got to raise the kids. You can't expect kids to turn out right if you shuffle 'em off to the side." There was little a divorced man could say.

"I'm thankful I raised my family when I did," he said. "World's too full of meanness and trouble these days. Ever' other person you meet is a smart aleck, and the other one's a crook. Them last few years I was workin' for wages, there wasn't one young feller in fifty willin' to work. All they had in mind was puttin' somethin' over on somebody. Down at the creamery docks, the young hands would slip off to play cards or talk smut or sit on their asses any time the bossman wasn't standin' over 'em. They laughed at me for givin' a honest day's work. I told 'em I'd *hired out* to work, by God. I wouldn't a-give a nickel for any of 'em. Didn't put no value on their personal word. I'd lift them heavy milk crates—lift a dozen to their one—and when the drivers come in and their trucks had to be swamped out and cleaned, I'd look around and be the only hand workin'." He shook his head. "They didn't care about nothin'. Seemed like life was . . . well, some kind of a joke to 'em.

"Now," he said, "I think the niggers is raisin' too much sand. Maybe I'd be raisin' ole billy myself if I'd been kinda left out of it like them. I dunno: it's hard to wear the other feller's shoes. But I just wasn't raised up to believe they're supposed to mix with us. It don't seem natural."

"Dad!" I said. "*Dad* . . . Dad . . ."

"Oh, I know," he said. Impatience was in his voice. This was an old battle fought between us many times without producing a victor—even though we had selectively employed the Bible against each other.

"You still mowing Willie's lawn?" I asked.

"Ever' Thursday." The Old Man said. "Durn your hide," he chuckled. Then: "Naw. Willie's moved off to Houston or some place." Willie was a male nurse and had been the first black man to move into my father's neighborhood eight years earlier. Not long after that community despoiling, I visited home: great were the dire predictions having to do with Willie's staying in his place. Six months later, we were sitting on the front porch. The black man walked into the yard. "Hey there, Old Timer," he said.

I stiffened: surely The Old Man would burn a cross, bomb a school, break into "The Nigger Preacher and the Bear."

Instead he said, mildly, "How you, Doctor?"

"Can you do my lawn a couple days early next week? I'm having some people over for dinner Tuesday night."

"Reckon so," The Old Man said. "Whatcha gonna have to eat?"

The black man smiled and said he thought he might burn some steaks on the grill.

"You can *tip* me one of them beefsteaks," The Old Man said, looking mischievous. "I'm a plumb fool about beefsteak."

They laughed; the black man complimented my father on his flower beds before giving him instructions on exactly how he wanted his shrubbery trimmed. The Old Man walked with him across the street to inspect the particulars. When he returned to ease back into his chair, I said—affecting the flattest possible cracker twang—"Boy Hidy, if that chocolate-coated sumbitch don't stay in his *place* . . ." The Old Man's grin was a bit sheepish. "I wouldn't mind 'em if they was all like old Willie," he said. "He works hard, he keeps hisself clean, to my knowledge he don't drink and I don't believe he'd steal if he was hungry." Then came one of those oblique twists of mind of which he was capable: "I don't take his checks though. I make 'im pay cash."

Now, some years later, we were approaching San Antonio: "I always figgered this for just another little ole Meskin town except for havin' the Alamo," he said. Soon he was marveling at the city's wonders, at the modern office buildings, old Spanish-style homes, green parks and easy-riding rivers. The Old Man happily waved to passing paddle boats as we idled under a tree at a riverfront café, laughing through the tears at himself when—mistaking a bowl of powerful peppers for stewed okra—he spooned in a country mouthful requiring a hard run on all available ice water.

He approached the Alamo with a reverence both enthusiastic and touching. "Right here," he proclaimed—pointing to a certain worn stone slab—"is where Travis drawed a line with his sword and told all the boys willin' to die for the right to step across. All of 'em stepped across except Jim Bowie, who was sick on a cot, and he had his buddies *carry* him across." Just why he had selected that particular stone not even historians may attest: the much-restored Alamo must make do with the smaller original artifacts and the wilder romanticisms. Indeed, where much of the blood was spilled, a prestige department store now stands.

He moved among display cases containing precious bits and

pieces of a more vigorous time: wooden pegs serving purposes later to be preempted by metal hinges, square-headed nails, early Colt firearms, crude chisels and hand-operated bellows, arrowheads, saddlebags, oxen yokes, tintype photos, the earliest barbed wire, a country doctor's bag with crude equipment such as an old uncle had carried in the long ago. He assembled his descendants to explain the uses of each relic, carefully associating himself—and his blood's blood—with that older time and place. He came to a new authority; his voice improved. Soon a group of tourists followed him about, the bolder ones asking questions. The Old Man performed as if he had been there during the siege. Choosing a spot on the outer walls, he said with conviction that "right over yonder" was where the invaders had fatally broken through. ("Daddy," my daughter whispered, "will you *please* get him to stop saying 'Meskin'?")

Taking a last look, he said, "Ma bought me a book on the Alamo. I must of read it a hundred times. I read how them damn Meskins done Travis and his brave boys, how ole General Santa Anna had butchered all them Texas heroes, and I promised myself if I ever seen one of them greaser sons-a-bitches, why, I'd kill him with my bare hands." He laughed at that old irrationality. "But did you notice today, half the people in that Alamo was *Meskins*? And they seemed to think just as much of it as we do."

Now it was late afternoon. His sap suddenly ran low; he seemed more fragile, a tired old head with a journey to make; he dangerously stumbled on a curbstone. Crossing a busy intersection, I took his arm. Though that arm had once pounded anvils into submission, it felt incredibly frail. My children, fueled by youth's inexhaustible gases, skipped and cavorted fully a block ahead. Negotiating the street, The Old Man half-laughed and half-snorted: "I recollect helpin' you across lots of streets when you was little. Never had no notion that one day you'd be doin' the same for me." Well, I said. Well. Then: "I've helped that boy up there"—motioning toward my distant and mobile son—"across some few streets. Until now, it never once occurred that he may someday return the favor." "Well," The Old Man said, "he will if you're lucky."

Three o'clock in an Austin motel. The Old Man snores in competition with jet aircraft. On an adjoining bed his grandson's measured breathing raises and lowers a pale banner of sheets. Earlier, the boy has exorcised his subconscious demons through sheet-tugging threshings and disjointed, indistinct private cries. The Old Man snores on, at peace. *Night battles never plagued me,* he once said in explaining his ability to sleep anyplace, anytime. *I never was one to worry much. What people worry about is things they can't do nothin' about. Worryin' always seemed like a waste to me.*

The bridging gap between the two slumbering generations, himself an experienced insomniac, sits in the dark judging whether he would most appreciate a cold six-pack or the world's earliest sunrise. Out of deference to The Old Man, he has known only limited contacts with those bracing stimulants and artificial aids for which his soft polluted body now begs. The only opium available to him is that hallucinogenic agent the layman calls "memory"—a drug of the most awful and powerful properties, one that may ravish the psyche even while nurturing the soul. Stiff penalties should be affixed to its possession, for its dangerous components include disappointing inventories, blocked punts, lumpy batters, and iron buckets of burden. It is habit-forming, near-to-maddening in large doses, and may even grow hair on the palms.

I remembered that we had compromised our differences in about my twentieth year. My own early assumption of family responsibilities proved healing: in the natural confusions of matrimony, one soon came to appreciate The Old Man's demanding, luckless role. Nothing is so leavening to the human species as to gaze upon the new and untried flesh of another human being and realize, in a combination of humility, amazement, and fear, that you are responsible for its creation and well-being. This discovery is almost immediately followed by a sharply heightened appreciation of more senior fathers.

We discovered that we could talk again. Could even sit at ease in long and mutually cherished silences. Could civilly exchange conflicting opinions, compete in dominoes rather than in more deadly games, romp on the lawn with our descendants, and share each new family pride or disappointment. For some four years in the early 1950s, we lived in close proximity. The Old Man came to accept my preference for whiskey as I came to accept his distaste for what it represented; he learned to live with my skeptic's atheism as I came to live with his belief that God was as tangible an entry as the Methodist Bishop.

The Old Man was sixty-six and I was twenty-five when I went away for good. There were periodic trips back home, each of them somehow more hurried, fleeting, and blurred. Around 1960, it dawned on me that The Old Man and his sons had, in effect, switched roles. On a day I cannot name, he suddenly and wordlessly passed the family crown. Now the sons were solicited for advice or leadership, and would learn to live uneasily in the presence of a quiet and somehow deeply wrenching paternal deference. (*Weldon, you reckon it would be all right if I got a better car?* Well, now, Dad, I believe I'd go slow on that. Maybe you don't see and hear well enough to drive in traffic very much. *Lawrence, what would you say to me and your mother goin' back to the farm?* Now, Dad, why in the world? People have been starving off those old farms for fifty years. What would you do out there in the sticks, miles from a doctor, if you or Mother got sick?)

The heart of the young blacksmith continued to beat in that shrinking frame, however. He could not drive a car anymore; he nodded off in the middle of the sermon at Asbury Methodist; meddlers had barred him from climbing trees. He remained very much his own man, however, in vital areas. Living by his sweat, The Old Man saved an astonishing amount of his paltry pensions and earnings, fiercely guarded his independence, took pride in his age, seldom rode when he could walk, tended the soil, ate well, and slept regularly.

On that motel bed slept a man who, at age twelve, had fallen heir to the breadwinner's role for a shotgun-widowed mother and eight younger siblings. He had accepted that burden, had discharged it without running off to sea: had drawn on some simple rugged country grace and faith permitting him no visible resentments then or later. He had sweated two family broods through famines and floods, Great Depressions and World Wars, industrial and sociological revolutions. Though a child of another century, really, he walked through the chaos and tediums of his time as determinedly—as Faulkner wrote of women passing through grief and trouble—"able to go through them and come out on the other side."

The faintest dawn showed through the windows when The Old Man sat up in bed, yawning: "Lord God, is it dinner time? *Must* be, you bein' awake!" He examined my face: "Didn't you get no sleep?" Some. "How much?" Three or four hours, I lied. "You ain't gonna live to see fifty," The Old man predicted. "What you ought to do is buy you a cotton farm and work it all day. I bet you'd sleep at night, then."

He almost hopped into his trousers from a standing position, amazingly agile in that fresh hour he most cherished. Noting my inspection he asked, "Reckon you can do that at eighty-two?" Hell, I said, I can't do it at forty-one; The Old Man celebrated this superiority with a pleased grin. The previous night he had insisted on playing dominoes past midnight in the home of a favorite nephew, Lanvil Gilbert, talking it up like a linebacker: *Say you made five? Why, that makes me so mad I'll play my double-five— and gimme fifteen while you got your marker handy. . . . I forgot to tell you boys I run a domino school on the side. Got a beginner's class you might be able to git in.* Back at the motel, he had again explored the distant past until his grandchildren yawned him to bed. *Old Man*, I thought, *what is the secret? What keeps you interested, laughing, loving each breath?* I remembered his enthusiastic voice on the telephone when I told him I had given my son his middle name: "I'm puttin' a five-dollar bill in the mail to buy him his first pair of long pants. Put it up and keep it. I want that exact five-dollar bill to pay for my namesake's first long pants." Grand satisfactions had visited his face earlier on our Austin trip when my son brought him a gigantic three-dollar pocket watch. The boy had shoved it at him—"Here, Grand Dad, this is for you, I bought it out of my allowance"—and then had moved quickly away from the dangers of sentimental thanks and unmanly hugs.

As we started down to breakfast, The Old Man said, "Why don't we take Bradley Clayton with us?" Sure, if he wants to go.

The Old Man gently shook the boy. "Namesake," he said. "Wake up, namesake, you sleepyhead." The boy rolled over with reluctance, blinking, trying to focus. "Git up from there," The Old Man said in feigned anger. "Time I was your age, I had milked six cows and plowed two fields by this time-a-day."

"*What?*" the boy said, incredulous.

"I'll make you think *what*!" The Old Man said, then repeated his improbable claim.

The boy, pulling his wits together, offered The Old Man a sample of the bloodline's baiting humor: "Was *that* what made you rich?"

The Old Man whooped and tousled the boy's hair, then mock-whipped him toward the bathroom.

We talked late on my final night. The Old Man sat in his jerry-built house, on a couch across from a painting of Jesus risking retina damage by looking directly into the celestial lights. Pictures of his grandchildren were on the walls and on the television top, along with a needlework replica of the Dead Kennedys appearing to hover over the U.S. Capitol, and a Woolworth print depicting a highly sanitized village blacksmith. One of his sons, thinking to please The Old Man, had given him the latter: while he appreciated the thought, he had been amused by the artist's concept. "Lord-a-mercy," he had chuckled, "the feller that painted that thing never *seen* a horse shod or a blacksmith shop either one." The painting revealed a neat, sweatless man effortlessly bending a horseshoe as he worked in an imposing brick edifice surrounded by greenery, while little girls in spotless dresses romped happily among gleaming anvils possibly compounded of sterling silver. The Old Man enjoyed comparing it with the realities of a photo made in the 1920's, showing him grease-stained and grimy in a collapsing wooden structure filled with indescribable debris.

His hands—always vital to his lip movements—swooped and darted, described arcs, pointed, performed slow or vigorous dances according to the moment's chin music. Just before bed, I asked in a private moment whether he had any major regrets. "Two," he said. "I wish I could of done better financially by your mother. I never meant for her to have such a hard life. And I wish I could of went to school."

On the morning of my departure, he was spry and fun-filled. Generally such leave-takings were accomplished in tensions and gloom; for a decade the unspoken thought had hovered that this might be the final goodbye. Last July, however, that melancholy tune was but faintly heard: The Old Man was so vigorously alive that I began to think of him as a sure centenarian. I left him standing on the front porch, wearing his workman's clothes, shaking a friendly fist against what he would do if I didn't write my mother more often.

Six weeks later, he gathered a generous mess of turnip greens from his backyard vegetable garden, presenting them to his wife with the request that she concoct her special cornbread. A few hours after his meal, he became dizzy and nauseated. "I just et too many of them turnip greens," he explained to his wife. Persuaded to the hospital for examination and medications, he insisted on returning home on the grounds he had never spent a night in a hospital bed and he was too old to begin. The next morning, in great pain, he consented to again be loaded into my brother's car.

The Old Man mischievously listed his age as "sixteen" with a crisp hospital functionary filling out the inevitable forms. He ordered nurses out when a doctor appeared, extracting a promise from my brother that "no womenfolks" would be permitted to intimately attend him. When the examining physician pressed his lower abdomen, The Old Man jerked and groaned. "Is that extremely sore, Mr. King?" Well, yes, it was a right-smart sore. "How long has it been that way?" About ten days, he reckoned. "Why didn't you tell me?" my exasperated brother inquired. The old eyes danced through the pain: "Wouldn't a done no good, you not bein' no doctor."

He consented to stay in the hospital, though he did complain that his lawnmower and supporting tools had been carelessly abandoned: would my brother see that they were locked in the backyard tool shed? Then he shook my brother's hand: "Weldon, thank you for everything." He shortly lapsed into the final chills and fevers, and before I could reach home he was gone. I saw him in his final sleep, and now cannot forget those magnificently weathered old hands. They told the story of a countryman's life in an eloquent language of wrinkles, veins, old scars and new. The Old

Man's hands always bore some fresh scratch or cut as adornment, the result of his latest tangle with a scrap of wire, a rusted pipe, a stubborn root; in death they did not disappoint, even in that small and valuable particular. No, it is not given to sons to know everything of their fathers—mercifully, perhaps—but I have those hands in my memory to supply evidence of the obligations he met, the sweat he gave, the honest deed performed. I like to think that you could look at those hands and read the better part of The Old Man's heart.

Clyde Clayton King lived eighty-two years, seven months, and twenty-five days. His widow, four of five children, seven of eight grandchildren, six great-grandchildren, and two great-great-grandchildren survive. His time extended from when "kissin' wasn't took lightly" to exhibitions of group sex; from five years before men on horseback rushed to homestead the Cherokee Strip to a year beyond man's first walk on the moon; from a time when eleven of twelve American families existed on average annual incomes of $380 to today's profitable tax-dodging conglomerates; from the first presidency of Grover Cleveland to the mid-term confusions of Richard Nixon. Though he had plowed oxen in yoke, he never flew in an airplane. He died owing no man, and knowing the satisfaction of having built his own house.

I joined my brother and my son in gathering and locking away The Old Man's tools in that backyard shed he had concocted of scrap lumbers, chipped bricks, assorted tins and reject roofing materials. Then, each alone with his thoughts, we moved in a concert of leaky garden hose and weathered sprinklers, lingering to water his lawn.

1971

PART II

Other Echoes

The Battle of Popcorn Bay

THE DUST OF TWENTY-FIVE YEARS has settled over Pearl Harbor. Now and then a history book reference or a visit from some balding old Army buddy recalls my generation's war in millions of households. Then children all over America, like my own teenaged daughter, ask the old question, "Daddy, what did *you* do in the War?"

Presumably this innocent query holds no terror for Audie Murphy, Dwight D. Eisenhower, or most of their 15,000,000 World War II comrades-in-arms. But for others (war profiteers, Lord Haw Haw, myself) it is a dubious proposition. With Van Johnson and other MGM-based Doolittle Raiders, I spent *Thirty Seconds over Tokyo*. I parachuted into Occupied France with O.S.S. Captain Alan Ladd and hit a dozen Pacific beaches behind Sergeant John Wayne. ("Come on, you Devildogs! Do you want to live forever?") I suffered the perils of the Merchant Marine with Humphrey Bogart in *Action in the North Atlantic*. In Italy I took *A Walk in the Sun* with Dana Andrews, Richard Conti and Lloyd Bridges. In Europe I was menaced by the cold, monocled presence of Nazis Eric von Stroheim and Otto Kruger, who listened to Wagner above the screams of their torture victims. In the Pacific I confronted evil, slit-eyed fanatical Japanese officers such as Richard Loo, Benson Fong, or Phillip Ahn, all graduates of UCLA.

We hit our objectives each Saturday afternoon at exactly 1300 hours, when the box office opened in the shabby movie house in Jal, New Mexico. Ahead lay darkness, danger and a gory glory; to the rear was only the ominous crackling of the popcorn machine. Outside, our air raid warden fathers kept their sand buckets handy while searching the skies for enemy aircraft. Jal, perhaps because it was in close proximity to the county seat, only 39 miles from Hobbs Army Air Field and 5,260 miles from Tokyo, was among top Axis targets.

Cynics might have you believe that Hollywood cranked out its tank-burners for mere money: six motion picture companies simultaneously sought to establish title priority on *Remember Pearl Harbor*; among Hollywood's sacrifices in the mobilization effort was abandonment of the annual Santa Anita Handicap. Studios sent out press releases bravely telling how Movieland was making-do with second-hand lumber and nails in constructing sets. Others might recall that MGM's Louis B. Mayer was so upset by Hirohito's sneak attack he only earned $949,765 in 1942 salaries.

Such cynics argue that in the dull prewar years movie attendance had dropped from 85,000,000 to 55,000,000 despite gimmicks like Bank Nite, Bingo, and Free Dishes. Movie moguls, they claim, were quick to discern how promptly war epics turned a homefront buck. I would not have believed these slanders any more than I would have believed Captain Robert Mitchum smoked reefers. It *is* true that picture making, like gestation, normally required nine months from conception to delivery—but that wartime quickies hit the screen in forty-five to ninety days. One actually made the trip from idea to film can in nine days.*

But for us the emotional involvement was total. When houselights came up following the gathering of the last dastardly Nip to his ancestors, or after Dana Andrews had avenged resistance fighters who burst into patriotic songs in front of Nazi firing squads, I was ready for anything. Nor was I the only Homefront Commando magically transported to distant battles. Once, giving Popcorn Bay support to Duke Wayne in hand-to-hand combat against several dozen Japanese infantrymen, Bood Reed swung an early-day karate chop that fractured Ode Joiner's nose. When Bonita Granville refused to romance a whole squad of Storm Troopers and provide future warriors for the Fatherland, wicked Nazis chained her to a post and flogged the poor girl until her blouse ripped. The chief emotion stirred among us desert youth by Nazi maltreatment of Miss Granville's cleavage was burning patriotism.

---

* Later on, a film distributor would say of wartime movies, "Every night was Saturday night. You could open up a can of sardines and there would be a waiting line to get in. Only sardines wouldn't have smelled as bad."

Typical American superiority was exhibited in a film called *The Fighting Seabees*, in which GI's manning cumbersome bulldozers routed a company of mobile Japanese tanks before dismounting to out-bayonet surviving Nips by a ratio approximating 6 to 1. In *Bataan* a mere dozen Occidental heroes withstood repeated assaults of what had to be a brigade of bowlegged, bucktoothed sadists. *Sahara* saw Humphrey Bogart and a ragtag band of tank soldiers, stranded at an oasis, fight a world's champion sandstorm and a whole Nazi battalion. Perhaps the highpoint of American superiority was reached by Errol Flynn in *Desperate Journey*. Errol outwitted Gestapo Colonel Raymond Massey to the extent that he blew up a lion's share of Germany right under Massey's nose, then escaped in a commandeered Nazi plane while saying to himself: "Now for Australia—and a crack at those Japs." (Music up and out; the sun shines on Flynn's smile.) Dennis Morgan as a Flying Tiger hero in *God Is My Co-Pilot* confessed to Priest Alan Hale that he had killed a hundred men. Father Hale said substantially what Joe Louis (possibly with coaching from Public Information Officers) had said earlier, and more briefly: "We'll win 'cause we're on God's side." By this logic, one must assume that God was with Hitler up to a point, but switched sides during the siege of Stalingrad.

The Greasepaint War gave the screen some of its most despicable villains. There was nothing a ratfink Jap or bullying Kraut wouldn't do to the clean-cut kid next door. Richard Jaeckel as the sixteen-year-old Marine, "Chicken," in *Guadalcanal Diary*, coughed while learning to smoke. His pithier expletives were suited to Robin the Boy Wonder, and he died a hero's clean death only after speaking well of Country, God and Mother; his corpse was blond and smiling. In *So Proudly We Hail*, the enemy indiscriminately strafed our hospitals, walking wounded including Sonny Tufts, Red Cross doughnut trucks, unarmed medics, wretched refugees who looked like the Hundred Neediest Cases, and Paulette Goddard. Our bombers, on the other hand, spared all civilians, cathedrals, and Works of Art.

German spies and Gestapo agents may have fooled the Allied High Command through the opening reels, but our intelligence forces at Popcorn Bay spotted them on sight. Peter Lorre was sneakily sinister as he crept around in the shadows of waterfront cafés; Sydney Greenstreet was so openly and arrogantly evil you felt he might write J. Edgar Hoover a catch-me-if-you-can letter. George Sanders tried to trick us with polished charm, but his clipped hair and a dueling scar from the University of Heidelberg gave him away at Popcorn Bay. Walter Slezak's double-dealing was masked behind a catlike purr and the manner of a clown, though in the end he was revealed as just another blubbering tub of rancid Gestapo cowardice.

But Hollywood saved its choice haymakers for the Japs. Even before that day of infamy, Hollywood saw special horrors in the "yellow monsters"—as Scotland Yard inspectors called them in *The Mask of Fu Manchu*. Boris Karloff, as Fu himself, pledged to "wipe the whole accursed white race from the face of the earth"; his followers were urged to "kill the white men and mate with their women." In *Cry Havoc* the primary goal of Japanese invaders on Bataan seemed to be the charms of a detachment of Army nurses that included Ann Sothern, Joan Blondell, Margaret Sullivan, and Ella Raines.

My friend Bobby Dyer came unglued the afternoon we saw *The Sullivans*, a story of five Boston brothers who went down on the same battleship early in the war. At final fade-out the tagalong kid of the family could be seen running Heavenward ("Hey, wait for me!") toward his four brothers, who were grinning at him from the fleeciest cloud that special effects could create. It was more than Bobby could take; personally, I doubt if even Adolf Eichmann could have stood it. Bobby, two years older than the rest of us, gave his parents no peace until they signed permissive papers. Within ten days San Diego Naval Training Station had gained a new Boot, and the Jal Panthers had lost a 127-pound wingback.

Sometimes Hollywood seemed to get its moral preachments tangled. In one epic, a kindly priest took a rock in hand and crushed a Nazi's skull. A short "documentary," *Conquer by the Clock*, gave us a munitions factory girl who, through sneaking time for a cigarette in the ladies' room, sends a dead cartridge to a soldier and the soldier to his death. This failed to suggest—as James Agee wrote in *The Nation*—"that the same thing might have happened if her visit to the toilet had been sincere." In *Passage to Marseilles*, Humphrey Bogart was permitted to methodically slaughter the helpless survivors of a crashed Nazi plane though the crew had done him no particular dirt. Errol Flynn, in *Objective Burma*, had his troops surround a garrison of off-duty Japs (shown eating, sleeping and relaxing) before luring them into the open on a ruse, there to slaughter them with wild cries, oceans of blood and enthusiasm unmatched until the 1964 Republican convention. This violated Hollywood's concept of the code of the American Fighting Man: the Japs, by rights, should have committed an atrocity or two before getting what they deserved, and Flynn should have been more pious in his killing.

The beginning of the Cold War caused Hollywood some blushes. As our wartime ally, Russia had been glorified in *Song of Russia*, *Days of Glory*, *Stalingrad* and *North Star*. Most of these films were hastily removed from circulation. *North Star*, however, was subjected to new editing. Russian peasants, originally shown as Nazi victims, emerged as the victims of Communist oppressors; Russian soldiers, who in the first version were depicted as mighty defenders of their homeland, were with a few artful snips of the scissors turned into aggressors. Losing all its cool in *Red Planet Mars* (which had *all* nations seeking peace except for Russia), Hollywood had no less than God preserve Liberty, Mom's apple pie and Free Enterprise at the climax, by bringing about a world-wide religious revival and by causing well-arranged disasters behind the Iron Curtain.

Though Bobby Dyer, Lucky Strike Green and even Mickey Rooney had gone to war, I stayed stuck in Jal. At a time when the world shook with history and bombs I had acne. I think it was *Confessions of a Nazi Spy* (G-man Edward G. Robinson unmasks George Sanders) that inspired me to become an undercover agent so secret it was known only to me. Secret Agent 001 hung around the pool hall, alert for any rumors of enemy troop movements, inspected the city waterworks for signs of espionage, and tried to catch Deputy Sheriff Elmer Turner contacting Berlin on his police car radio. I never fully trusted Deputy Turner after his investigation of the truckload of Italian spies I caught when they stopped for gas at Houston Wink's service station. Elmer claimed they were itinerant Mexican cotton pickers from Clovis.

To a man, Jal approved of civilian Minutemen, training under police department auspices in Connecticut and California, to meet potential Axis invaders on the beach with .22 rifles and pitchforks. We cheered when the Government herded Japanese-Americans into "detention camps" on the West Coast. We understood that Harry Wismer, broadcasting the Army-Navy football game, couldn't tell us it was raining in West Point, New York, because somebody might flash the word from Jal to Tokyo, Berlin or Rome. Our mothers rolled bandages for the Red Cross and our fathers gamely worked overtime at their desks or lathes. We ostracized the hoarder of sugar or tinned goods, and kept a suspicious eye on the Schultz and Venitti families.

Still, I felt like Crillon chastised by the French King Henry IV; "Hang yourself, brave Crillon. We fought at Arques, and you were not there." Knowing that my family had produced a real, live hero kept me going from Saturday to Saturday until I could return in triumph to Popcorn Bay. Cousin Lanvil Gilbert was pushing across France, Belgium and Germany as an infantry rifleman. I confess that I was momentarily ecstatic when news that he had been wounded at the Battle of the Bulge reached us. Had Lanvil wiped out a Nazi machine gun nest, or captured a Kraut tank company before . . . ?

"No," my mother said, reading from Aunt Clara's letter. "His socks got wet and his feet froze."

Even Hollywood was soon to disappoint me. By 1944, the Rex Theater offered so-called war musicals, although no self-respecting Home-front Commando would suffer through the first eight bars of "Don't Sit under the Apple Tree with Anyone Else but Me." James Cagney prancing through tap dances in *Yankee Doodle Dandy*, Katherine Cornell and Aline MacMahon serving Pepsi and cheese tidbits to stateside Johnnys in *Stage Door Canteen*, all the flag-waving and bugle-blowing that was *This Is the Army* (with seventeen songs by Irving Berlin)—these left Popcorn Bay dissatisfied. Nor were we mollified by Hollywood's attempts at wartime humor: Bob Hope and Eddie Bracken peeling potatoes when *Caught in the Draft*; Abbott and Costello zigging when they should have zagged in *Buck Privates*; Charles Coburn and Joel Mc-Crea suffering the hazards of wartime Washington in *The More the Merrier*. We wanted our comedy only to relieve tension just before the battle. When the paratroopers were only two minutes away from their combat-zone drop, they played the scene this way:

First Trooper: "What's the first thing you're gonna do when you get back home, Joe?"

Joe: "I'm gonna kiss my gal like she's never been kissed before!"

First Trooper: "And what's the *second* thing you're gonna do, Joe?"

Joe: "Take off my parachute!"

Spasms of tension-breaking laughter would rock Popcorn Bay. So intent did we become in our missions that only rarely were we disconcerted by technical blunders in the Actors' Guild War: scouting patrols walking in single file, so that a lone well-placed bullet would have passed through nine men marching like ducks in a row; Alan Ladd throwing a heavy hand grenade with an easy, overhand Bob Feller motion so that it carried more than a hundred yards and blew up half an advancing tank column; Errol Flynn blowing up a Japanese aircraft carrier with a single grenade, then swimming with a knife in his teeth to attack a submarine. Until James Agee would point it out years later, I would not notice that after our GI's captured a farmhouse in *A Walk in the Sun* they set about "chomping an apple, notching a rifle stock, and so on—while, so far as the camera lets you know, their wounded comrades are still writhing unattended in the dooryard." Such undetected goofs now appear frequently on my television set. It's like seeing Cecil B. DeMille putting Christ on the Cross wearing a 22-jewel Bulova wristwatch.

As our front-line troops smashed to victory, Hollywood gave us fewer blood-and-thunder pictures like *Fighting Devildogs*, *Betrayal from the East* and *Destination, Tokyo* in favor of such fluff as *Two Girls and a Sailor*, *Seven Days Ashore* and *Here Come the Waves*. Driven out of the Rex Theater in search of adventure, I boosted servicemen's morale by waving to troop trains from the Jal depot, but my father stopped this after certain spiteful rumors, probably inspired by Axis counterspies, got out about my hormones. When my mother complained because I had donated some of her favorite pots and pans to the scrap metal drive, I knew the war was coming to an end.

But there was a peace to keep, so early in 1946 I enlisted in the U.S. Army Signal Corps. In my bunk at Fort Dix, New Jersey, I was certain that Hitler was alive and hiding in Argentina. On some Pacific atoll there no doubt remained a company of fanatical Japs it would be my mission to dig out of rock with M-1 rifle, flame-thrower and tricks remembered from Popcorn Bay.

First, however, I was assigned to the Army Pictorial Center in Astoria, Long Island. Paramount once made some of its earliest smashes there. When I arrived the old barnlike studios were used to shoot army training films—"message" epics designed to show new recruits all the glory and horror of military service.

Though my seventy-eight dollar monthly salary was less than Clark Gable's, I had roles in a number of productions. Perhaps you remember me. If you saw *Nomenclature and Operation of Field Weapons*, you caught me in my first speaking role: I was the battery sergeant who yelled "Fire" to the gunners. My hand held the pointer in *Map Orientation and Characteristics of Coastal Topography.* That was my shovel you saw in *Digging of the Slit Trench,* and I don't have to tell you who fashioned the title object in *Rolling of the Horseshoe Field Pack.* In *Proper Wearing of the Military Uniform,* I was the Times Square Commando who upon delivering his best line to a bar-stool cutie ("Let me tell you about my war experiences, baby") is hauled off by a grim-jawed MP for unauthorized wearing of a fifty-mission crush hat, a sharpshooter's medal, and white socks.

But the role for which generations of fighting men will remember me is that of the Sick GI in *The American Soldier and Personal Hygiene.** In that historic film, so graphic that recruits exposed to it were later known to wear rubber gloves when shaking hands with their sisters, the camera panned to a hospital ward clearly marked by the twenty-second and fourth letters of the alphabet, respectively, then dollied in on the Sick GI.

Bashfully twisting the tail of his hospital robe, he says to a hard-eyed colonel: "But sir,—she *looked* clean!"

And that, children, is what Daddy did in the War.

1966

---

*I want it clearly understood that my stand-in was the object of the gamier closeups.

Whatever Happened to Brother Dave?

IT IS WARM AND MUGGY for North Carolina in late May, a very southern night, with flying bugs and scents of grass in the air. Young men cruising with their car windows down sound mating calls on their nightly inspections of root beer stands or What-a-Burger palaces, while on many city porches old men cherish their post-supper memories of farms they will never till again. We must escape Charlotte's shopping-center vapors and downtown exhaust clouds to savor it, though once in shaded residential sections or on semirural lanes, the grass fragrance is green, clean, and nostalgic, inspiring thoughts of forgotten alfalfa growths, of discovering Faulkner, of parking near the football field on summer nights a world ago to wrestle the price of the evening's movie and popcorn out of the sweetly moist flesh of Becky Sue or Alma Mae or Betty Lou.

Though oven temperatures prevail as the visitor drives ten miles out of Charlotte to the ordered and pastoral campus of little Davidson College, that school's football team is grimly grunting and maiming its sweaty way through the merciless tortures of spring practice. Along the rural roadways are young Huck Finns taking their country pleasures, "antique shops" with their $3.98 chenille bedspreads and old vases probably certified all the way back to 1947, Confederate flags or decals superimposed on license plates. Old country stores thrive near new red-brick ramblers with camp trailers or motorboats near at hand, and, further on, are declining shacks where poor whites or poorer blacks take the sun on rude wooden porches in the presence of ragged kids and peeling old Buicks parked in the front yards. Near midnight, en route to Charlotte's Pecan Grove Club to catch the second show, the car radio offers gut-jangling country tunes and advertisements for Chick Starter (which is not a new aphrodisiac for hippie girls, but a product to feed infant chickens) while warm-weather fliers dash themselves into eternity and gooey gobs against the windshield. They can whoop of the New South with its rapid industrialization and economic or cultural leaps all they want, but some things cannot be paved over by asphalt or changed by factory smokestacks— things rooted deeply in the southern soil, the southern soul, the southern psyche.

Welcome home. Welcome to Klan Country, as a giant billboard says.

A couple of Good Ole Boys in butch haircuts and white short-sleeved sport shirts temporarily disadvantaged by neckties are drinking from a brown bag out on the unpaved parking lot at the Pecan Grove Club, sneaking a few manly snorts in rebellion against the mixed potions their wives force on them inside, and one is volunteering probably louder than he knows that the goddamn Tar Heel football team won't never amount to a shit till they hire a big-time coach like ole Bear Bryant. The sight of a dude in a beard and an eastern-cut suit obviously too flannelly for southern latitudes is enough to bring them pause. When their eyes begin to calculate exactly where the heavy artillery should be unloaded, the visitor consults with his Confederate ancestors and offers in his best drawl, "Evenin', fellers, how y'all?" Then he slouches on by like he was moseying down to the 7–11 to buy hisself some Moon Pies and Ara-Cee Colas. This inspirational act passes him by without fisticuffs, though when the ole boys see how his hair hangs over his collar in back one says *Shee-ee-it, Hon!* and the explosive laughter sends the visitor's heart flying out in empathy toward the ghost of Thomas Wolfe.

The Pecan Grove Club is dark enough to conceal from the curious those gentlemen who might be in the company of ladies to whom they hold no clear titles. The coatless, tieless, and paunchy combination maître d'hôtel and floor bouncer, who points the path to tables by flashlight, is clearly miffed that a naked Scotch bottle should be openly flaunted rather than decently masqueraded in the obligatory brown bag. His eyes accuse the visitor of inferior breeding, inspiring one to marvel again at that limitless capacity the South has for self-deception, for honoring show over substance, for choosing illusion when reality might better serve. This is a bottle club, meaning that for a six dollar per head cover charge you sneak your own booze in as if freshly stolen and obliged to be smuggled past a convention of Methodist bishops. In exchange for such cooperative deceptions, which in no way violate or improve the law but do faithfully serve tradition, the house provides gratis setups. Beer is free on demand, delivered as regularly as one of several yawning waitresses may be provoked into action; nothing moves them quicker than the clear beacon of a green bill exposed to the uncertain light. Dinner is extra, an expenditure all except a dozen of the fifty-odd customers have avoided because they must later settle the claims of babysitters. Between musical numbers the bandleader endorses generosity by reminding customers that waitresses work strictly for tips. Out in the bar area a tough-faced little brunette complains of those SOBs at table four who expect tons of ice, Cokes, beer, and ass-pinching privileges in exchange for each four-bit gift.

Except for probably a few airline hostesses or young secretaries in miniskirts and their mildly sideburned escorts, this could be 1960 again. Women wear domed and lacquered beehive hairdos; bristling crew cuts prevail among the males. Dancing is dogged, more of duty in the couple's motions than of soul or fun. They shuffle and two-step to such vintage ballads as "Misty," "I Wish You Love," and "Poke Salad Annie," while The Frantics, who prefer to blow their music à go-go, are so obviously bored you get the impression they are all chewing gum. When The Frantics can no longer tolerate imitation Lawrence Welk or, occasionally, Johnny Cash, they up the tempo and the decibel level enough that the dance platform could not be more efficiently cleared by a black with a switchblade. And that is the signal for Brother Dave, out in the wings, to light a fresh cigarette and to prepare to spring onstage.

The Pecan Grove Club seats 550 in enthusiastic circumstances. On evenings such as this, however, owner David Rabie doubts whether Soldiers' Field has more unoccupied seats in a midnight snowstorm. Rabie is a swarthy, intense man who published poetry at age sixteen and who in the 1950s was a United Nations correspondent for an Israeli publication. Somewhere in there he came to

Charlotte to peddle oriental rugs, and somehow about eight years ago he found himself owning the Pecan Grove Club. Tonight he is full of passionate bulletins that anyone eager for the same foolish experience can buy him out for a song and a loose promise. He stands outside shortly before the second show, slapping at flying creatures and fingering a dead cigar, under a sign proclaiming the feature attraction: a comedian billed as Brother Dave Gardner. "I'm losing my ass," the reformed poet confides. "I'm paying this guy a thousand bucks a night. And look at the house."

Then why had he booked Brother Dave?

"I had him here about three years ago and made good money. He was doing more straight comedy then—not so much of this political nonsense. A year later he was deeper into the political thing and I just broke even. This time he's knocking everything— religion, the colored, even the dead Kennedys. It's a disaster. People are calling up to complain." The disaffected club owner turns his mind back from Tuesday to Friday and the special disaster of opening night: "You never saw such a house! I spent eighteen hundred dollars for promotion and then had to refund three thousand at the door when he didn't show. Kidnapped by Indians! Can you imagine that? He says he was kidnapped by the Cherokees!"

"Detained" is the word Miss Millie Gardner used when the visitor arrived at a Charlotte motel on Monday afternoon and telephoned the comic's three-room suite to inquire how the show had been going. Miss Millie, a weathered blonde who acts as her husband's booking agent, did not supply a standard response. "Well, we didn't make opening night on account of the Cherokees."

Beg your pardon?

"We were detained by some Indians. I've called the FBI."

Ah . . . yes ma'am?

"They have the full report. And I've reported it to Congressman Jonas's office."

Yes. Well. How does one go about getting, ah, detained by Indians in the America of 1970?

"We'll talk about it after the show," Miss Millie said. "I'm not sure I trust the telephone."

The first time he appeared on the "Jack Paar Show," back in 1957, Brother Dave Gardner was a minor comic who for ten years had played tired strip joints and dingy bottle clubs throughout the Bible and boll-weevil belt, working close to the horns of bullish hecklers and walleyed drunks. He had sometimes entertained Rotarians in the assault on their weekly veal cutlets, or discouraged traveling salesmen who gathered in third-rate hotels rather desperately to court fun between the exhortations of their sales managers to get out and more aggressively hawk the aluminum siding, fire insurance, or farm machinery that rode the saddles atop their small pinched lives. He had played drums on something called the "Winkie Martindale Show" in Memphis, where he first began to crack jokes, and he had a straight singing record, "White Silver Sands," that, in the long run, excited him more than it did others. He was best known in the deeper boondocks. If they wore brown shoes, white socks, clip-on bow ties, or butch haircuts, then Brother Dave likely had made them laugh at one way station or another, where laughter was no small gift. He was of and from them, the son of a Tennessee carpenter who liked to think of himself as being "in the construction industry"; he knew what it was to drop school in the tenth grade, to not make it with the quality chicks because your clothes were not the best and because you were scrawny and had never been outstanding at book reports or athletics. He knew what it was to work at dull jobs where they paid you in small coin every Friday and would not have lamented your death except as your funeral hindered commerce.

He rated no seat on the celebrity couch where Paar's favored guests grouped to smile, to crack limp jokes about Ike's golf or the hole in Adlai's shoe or the pelvis of Elvis, all the while preening and plugging their latest movies, records, new noses, or fuzzy theories. Horatio Alger was still to be believed in the America of 1957, and so when they offered Brother Dave a four-minute stand-up shot (wedged between a network station break and spiels by Hugh Downs for dog food) he nearly knocked 'em down getting into position.

Brother Dave rattled off a monologue presenting Brutus in the execution of Caesar, product of a wildly inventive brain that some later would suspect of having influenced Mort Sahl, Jonathan Winters, Bill Cosby, Lenny Bruce, Dick Gregory, Flip Wilson. The studio audience, Paar, and the folks out there in television land broke up as in corn-pone accents Caesar put the final question: *Et tu, Brute?* And Brutus, who had known trouble keeping his toga out of his bicycle spokes and who had earlier heard yon Cassius described as a "picky eater and about half smart," answered, "Naw man, I ain't even et *one*." Paar received a thousand letters and telegrams begging more. NBC-TV welcomed the unknown comic to a three-year association to include sixty-odd appearances on the Paar show alone, and RCA provided a lucrative recording contract. His first album, *Rejoice, Dear Hearts!*, sold almost as frantically as hula hoops. *Kick Thine Own Self* and seven other album successes followed, each a combination of hip, headlines, and down-home wit. He appeared in a Broadway play, banked up to thirty thousand dollars per week for campus one-nighters, and made connections with Las Vegas gambling emporiums where a hot comic smart enough to avoid house tables could depend on a weekly take-home of twenty-five thousand dollars plus free lodgings. Miss Millie, a slender blonde who married him in 1947 within six weeks of his first booking in the small St. Louis club where she bossed the hatcheck concession, knew opportunity's knock; in her role as traveling manager she efficiently guided him away from the perils of roulette wheels and chorus girls, which was not always easy, because little in Brother Dave's natural instincts rides him toward the more pious precincts when he is rolling free.

His Brutus-dirks-Caesar routine became a comedy classic, as did the bit reporting on David's slaying of "the overgrown Philadelphian," Goliath, with a smooth stone "wrapped up in blue-suede tennis-shoe tongue." Probably his best-known tale involved the high-speed deaths of two Alabama motorcyclists, Miss Baby and Mister Chuck. In that routine he appeared to put down lawmen, Dixie customs, blacks, cyclists, truckers, and casual bystanders while showing no special malice toward any. He was Andy Griffin running downhill with the brakes off, slightly zonked, and maybe plotting a practical joke to severely embarrass nice old Aunt

Bea—or maybe more than embarrass her: his routines had a way of stressing humor in death. There was about him some combination of fun and menace, one sensed, slices of the high school dropout who perhaps had read Shakespeare on his own but who still might efficiently (and not always fairly) clean your pockets at the pool hall, or deliberately direct Yankee tourists to the wrongest possible road should they be foolish enough to inquire the most direct route to Birmingham.

He increasingly became a social comic, putting the knock on JFK, on Castro, on the latest absurdity as reflected in newspaper headlines or by the careless utterances of our kings or pharaohs. If he speared Hoffa in one breath then surely in the next he would gig McClellan; if he made Democrats feel comfortable at the expense of Republicans they soon would discover ecstasy to be a two-way street. On the Paar show, after making professional liberals nervous through his near-perfect imitations of the ill-advantaged but irrepressible Roosevelt, Jabo, and Willie ("home boys," he called them), he would say in his thick winter-molasses accent that he believed in one race, the human race, and then the libs could expel their nervous do-gooder air while Paar beamed and the studio audience applauded. Yes, dear hearts, he enjoyed a merry ride, accumulating a thirty-two-room Mediterranean villa on a Hollywood hill, a luxury yacht, multiple Cadillacs, a second fine home on Biloxi's expensive sands. It was a glorious cruise, save for a little choppy water such as when he accidentally left Miss Millie behind in a West Texas motel room and didn't recall it until several days later in Louisiana, and also excepting that one major misunderstanding in 1962 when Atlanta police charged him with being in the company of an excessive number of amphetamine tablets and assorted other "uppers"—a condition inspiring Jack Paar to fresh public tears and Brother Dave Gardner to the successful investment of five thousand dollars in attorney's fees. And then, shortly after John F. Kennedy's assassination, he disappeared from the national scene.

Last winter among the snows of Cambridge, I listened again to Brother Dave's old records with a black friend, Wally Terry. We debated whether the comedian's lines sometimes bordered on racial bigotry, or whether he simply was a funny man with a rare gift for the exploitation of sensitive ethnic material, a pacesetter who so pinpointed the various insanities of our social confusions that he may have been a decade ahead of the times. Given Brother Dave's weird and conflicting pronouncements, far-out sound effects, and amazing gift for reproducing all regional accents, our repeated listenings only muddled the issue. "Whatever *happened* to Brother Dave?" Wally asked. In that instant I determined to find out.

Celebrity Services inquiries on the East and West coasts failed to locate him. He was not currently registered with any agent known to the major booking agencies. NBC and RCA disclaimed pertinent knowledge. His California home stood vacant and boarded; he had apparently left no forwarding address. Telephone operators ruined several rumors in failing to make connections in Nashville, Memphis, Biloxi, New Orleans. Then a writer friend in Charlotte, John Carr, telephoned to say that Brother Dave would be playing his city in late May.

Brother Dave appeared to "When the Saints Go Marching In," amending the original lyrics to include information that among the marching saints he expects to count Congressman L. Mendel Rivers, Spiro Agnew, Martha Mitchell, and Georgia's Lester Maddox. He was smaller than one had remembered, perhaps five and one-half feet tall, with stubby arms and a welterweight's torso. A sallow, lined face and a pompadoured crown of wiry silver hair made him look older than his forty-four years. "I'd smoke in my sleep if I had somebody to hold 'em, and I'd smoke chains if I could light 'em," he said of his nicotine habit, and taking a couple of quick drags he went to work.

"All who love America shout *Glory!* . . . Oh, dear hearts, don't you wish the other side could hear us? Wouldn't it shake up their fuzzy old heads? All this and Spiro too! *Glory!*" (*Cheers*). "Martha Mitchell, ain't she good?" (*Cheers.*) "Beloved, the old liberal commie long-haired traitor hippies"—interrupted by applause before reaching the punch line, he joined the laughter—"Yeah, them crazy cats say Brother Dave am against minority groups. No such thing, dear hearts. I'm *for* the minorities—the armed forces and po-leece. I wouldn't even mind paying taxes if it all went to them. Somebody say, 'You mean Brother Dave's for the heat?' You damn right, beloved. That ole pig, as the hippies call him, he's out there protecting society. And if you ain't a part of society, dear hearts, then what right you got to go around throwing rocks at it?

"And the military, I love 'em so much I send my shoes to Fort Bragg to get 'em shined. Somebody say, 'Yeah, but ain't it ugly for a soldier to kill?' Naw, man, that's his *gig*. You know, dear hearts, ain't nothing wrong with patriotism. By God, I *groove* on it. You can fly as high on patriotism as you can on acid. I'd love to join a patriotic outfit—I'd join the Klan, only I ain't got enough morals." (*Cheers, applause.*) "Let's all shout *Glory!* for the Israeli army." (*Uncertain applause: why cheer the Christ-killing Jews?*) "Yeah, man, that Israeli army fought them rag heads for six days and on the seventh day they rested. Dear hearts, the Israelis are fighting for state's rights just like we are." (*Boisterous cheers, now that the ideology is clear.*) "Them Jews is patient cats. It took 'em two thousand years to get their Wailing Wall back. Dear hearts, how long you think it'd take a Southern Baptist to get his *church* back?" Southern Baptists were apparently well represented, for the responsive roar sent Brother Dave into a further exploration of religious territory. This caused no break in his regular routine, simply because there is no set routine; he jumps from subject to subject, going where the laugh lines guide him, much in the manner of a presidential candidate whose basic speech is capable of alterations fitting all local conditions.

"I put one over on the Supreme Court today, beloved. Yeah, man, I sneaked off and prayed all morning! Prayer's *good*, beloved. Prayer is askin' for it and meditating is waitin' for it. Somebody says, 'Brother Dave, how come you talk so much about God in nightclubs and honky-tonks?' Dear hearts, on account of it's against the law to mention Him in school! Yeah, man, spirituality is where it's at. Course, you turn the other cheek today and some damn hippie'll take a brick and knock your jaw off.

"Dr. Billy Graham—he's all right, I dig Billy. Yeah, except he disappointed me when he got on TV and tooken up for the hippies and yippies. Said they was good cats. Billy's a Christian, you know—he thinks you *supposed* to love everybody, and I'm one of them eye-for-an-eye cats. I'm for Billy, though: he's got so many guts he prays in public. He even prays at the White House when Crafty Richard posts him some of them palace guards with their cute little Hitler hats. But Billy got on TV and said"—and here Brother Dave gave an accurate imitation of Dr. Graham in the practice of dime-store Churchill—"'I was coming out of the el-a-va-*tor* in New Ya-wuk recently, and one of those hippie fellows came along, and he *spoke* to me.' And I said, 'Hell, Billy don't you know that cheap trash will speak to anybody who'll speak to 'em?' Somebody say, 'You know good and well Dr. Graham couldn't hear him say that! Brother Dave's flipped out and is talkin' to hisself.' Yeah, beloved, ain't nothing wrong with that! Talk to yourself, dear hearts. By God, you'll enjoy the rare pleasure of listening to some-body with some damn sense."

The beehives and butch cuts were bobbing in merriment now, David Rabie's being perhaps the only grim face in the room, but then he was counting empty tables. Now Brother Dave combined spirituality and sex: "People say motels is sinful. Say, 'Motels am the devil's own doing.' Naw, dear hearts, you drive by them motels at two or three in the morning and you can hear folks digging on spirituality. Services never cease! Yeah, you can hear 'em in there saying, 'Oh, *God!* Lord *Jesus!* Ain't it *good.*' . . . You know, the Catholics got a terrible advantage over us Baptists and Methodists and Campbellites and whatnot: they can take a friend to the Holi-day Inn and bounce her off the walls for thirty-six hours and then go confess it to a priest. *We* do it and then can't tell *nobody.* . . . I ain't got nothing against sex education in the schools, dear hearts, except it makes us parents feel like we didn't do it right. . . . Can you imagine the vanity of that civil wrongs song, 'We Shall Over-come'? Now, beloved, how can any mortal do *that?*"

The good ole boys had loosened their ties, their laughter con-tained more of steel on stone, drinks flowed a big quicker from the brown bags. The bouncer, who had earlier ignored a lone heckler, moved over to encourage his silence after a flower from the bush of

Southern Womanhood called out of the darkness, "Shut up, you Yankee smartass!" Her command clued Brother Dave to his next line: "Some people say I hate Yankees. Naw, beloved, I love 'em when they come down here bringing money to invest and fleeing them damned crumbling cities and welfare lines and the demands and street barbecues of our 'New Citizens.'" (*Cheers as he pursed his lips into exaggerated thickness, then hopped around scratching himself under the arms and hoo-hoo-hooing like Cheetah in some Tarzanian rage.*) "Yankees are moving south in droves! The South's integrated now, see, and they're segregated up North and they're getting spooked about it." (*Cheers and laughter: take that, you two-faced Yankee swine.*) "The only Yankees I don't like are them that stay up yonder and grow long hair and raise liberal young'uns who dodge the draft and smoke aspirins and shoot up peanut butter."

From here he made a natural leap into dope jokes—and here he lost the crowd. Charlotte's beer addicts and whisky heads sat unmoved when Brother Dave took a deep whiff of his cigarette lighter and then pantomined euphoria. When Little Orphan Annie was nominated as the "first acidhead—you ever dig them eyes?" they made no response. "I discovered you can get high on smog, beloved. Yeah, and as soon as Washington found out you can get your head together on smog, man, they outlawed it! . . . You know, dear hearts, if them SDS cats and Weathermen and hippies and yippies and all them other crazies would smoke more and burn less, this ole world would smell sweeter and swing higher." He told a story of two hip cats in a restaurant, one saying to the other, "Let's blow this joint," and getting the response, "Naw, man, let's pass it on to the waitress." Only laughter from the band signified a familiarity with certain cultural sophistication among showfolk and hippies.

The act was now going sour before folks convinced that marijuana is pure ole dope and dope inspires you to cut up grandmaw with bread knives. Brother Dave retreated to politics: "I pulled for Barry Goldwater and he only carried five states. I pulled for George Wallace and *he* only carried five states. I believe if God was to run He'd only carry five states—and they'd all be in the South." (*Cheers: this they understood.*) "Beloved, I love the South!"

(*Cheers.*) "And I love America!" (*Cheers.*) "All who love 'em shout *Glory*! . . . Ah, that's wonderful, beloved. Don't you wish they could hear us up in Washington?" (*Cheers.*) "And you know, by God, *lately I think they do!*" (*Cheers, applause, Rebel yells.*) "Man, I don't know how to act since we finally got us a president!" (*Bull's-eye.*) "You know, the ole Yankee newspapers put the ugly mouth on those good people down in Lamar, South Carolina. Yeah, man, said they'd beat up on some New Citizens' little school-children. Naw, beloved, that ain't true! They didn't hurt them lovely children—all they did was take some chains and whip up on some old school buses." (*Loudest cheers of the night, brown bags banging on tables.*) "Course, it made the professional liberals slobber at the mouth—but we all know what a professional liberal is: somebody that's educated beyond their capacity. Like Bill Bullblight—err, Fulbright. Crafty Richard say to Senator Fulbright, 'Bill, I think we ought to go in there, by God, and bomb Hanoi and blow them damn slopeheads plumb off the damn map,' and Fulbright say, 'Oh, us doesn't dare do that, Richard, 'cause then us won't have nobody to negotiate with.' . . . Do y'all remember, dear hearts, when they awarded that Nobel Peace Prize to the late Dr. Junior on account of his efficiency in teaching our New Citizens to riot? Man, what's that Nobel cat doing giving a *peace* prize, after he done went and invented dynamite? . . . Some say that segregation is evil and integration is correct. Now, if that be the case, why do we have ladies' rooms? But we gonna get our country back one day soon." (*Cheers.*) "Yeah, beloved, them Green Berets and the po-leece and the National Guard and them other good guys has had just about enough and by God, dear hearts, they can beat you into bad health." (*Rising cheers.*)

Then he hit them with the line that caused a sudden shocked silence, a line that even many of the Good Ole Boys deepest into the mysteries of their brown bags were not braced for, and it stunned them, caused gasps, a quick dark murder of laughter. Maybe the wild grin on his face, the sheer exuberance of his delivery, were as petrifying as the line itself: "*God, wasn't that a clean hit on Dr. Junior?*"

The hard core cheered, and somebody up front shouted *Glory*! At least ten people got up and made for the exit, however. A heavy middle-aged blonde in green eyeshadow and an overflowing green pants suit descended on the visitor, who sat morosely smoking at the rear of the hall: "Are you with that idiot?" No, not really. "Well, he's gone too damned far. I love the South and I love my country, and that idiot is putting 'em down. Where's the manager?" David Rabie came with a pained look to take three minutes of perfected abuse, periodically spreading his hands in unconditional surrender. "His damn jokes are forty years old," the blonde raged. "You call this shit entertainment? Jokes about murder? I'm gonna call the *Charlotte Observer* and tell 'em what you got out here. Why did you hire that idiot?" David Rabie explained how it was to be a businessman, saying that entertainers of all creeds had played the Pecan Grove Club. He rattled off names—Brenda Lee, Maxine Brown, Roy Hamilton, LaVerne Baker, Count Basie, The Four Freshmen, Lee Dorsey—noting that "several of them are colored." When the storm blew out he turned to the visitor: "For God's sake, talk to him! Ask him to leave that offensive material out. People want to hear the old routines that made him famous, not this crap. Look at the house—count it!" The visitor did; there now remained twenty-one revelers. By the time Brother Dave ended his turn with a trap-drum recital, there were thirteen survivors.

The faithful lingered under pecan and oak trees while two black men ran to fetch their cars. A citizen in a butch haircut and a $29.95 suit straight off the rack led forward a blind man with his seeing-eye dog: "Brother Dave, this ole boy is blind and everything, but he don't beg or peddle pencils or nothin'. He's got this little newsstand down at the YMCA, and, by God, he *works*."

"Bless your heart, beloved."

"He don't set on his ass and howl for help just because he's blind," the citizen clarified.

"God bless you," Brother Dave cooed, shaking the blind man's hand. "You know, they got a rule up in Washington that if you break a sweat they'll take you off welfare."

The blind man beamed; his sponsor whooped.

"Course, a cat that sweats don't want it nohow. Don't y'all give up, you hear? We gonna get our country back someday."

He ducked into a gold Cadillac driven by his sixteen-year-old son Junior, and within ten minutes was back in the motel room where Miss Millie waited with a barking French poodle named

Mister. Mister may wear a rhinestone collar and sport sissy little ribbons atop his iron-gray head, but let a stranger approach Miss Millie even to light her cigarette and Mister has conniptions in the voice of a surly Doberman pinscher.

Miss Millie, who took her meals off trays in the room, and whom the visitor never discovered outside a gauzy green dressing gown during his six-day observation, was reading one of her seven books by H. L. Hunt. "How was the show?" Miss Millie asked.

"Nothing wrong with the show," Brother Dave said. "The goddamn house is the problem. You could of fired a .410 and not hit anybody at the second show."

"Damn those Cherokees," Miss Millie said.

Yes, *how about* those Cherokees? What had happened? It was the fifth or sixth time the visitor had put that question, receiving only vague and disjointed reports.

"We're driving along Highway 19, coming down from Tennessee," Brother Dave said, "Hell, I didn't know we was on a damned Indian reservation. Me and Miss Millie was in the lead Caddy and our son was trailing in the other one. The Cherokee patrol stopped him, man. Wouldn't let the cat go."

Why?

"They wouldn't say. But you can figure it out." When the puzzled visitor remained mute, Brother Dave added, "They're part of this third-world thing."

Beg pardon?

"Aw, man, don't you know what's happening? Who attacked a meeting of the Klan here in North Carolina two or three years ago, when the Klan cats wasn't doing nothing but burning crosses and singing hymns?"

The Cherokees?

"Damn right, beloved. They're part of this thing!"

"Dave," Miss Millie said, "the FBI asked us not to talk about this."

"Aw, he's all right," Brother Dave said with a nod in the visitor's direction. "Don't you hear that accent? He's from Texas, just like ole H. L. Hunt. Beloved, do you know Mr. Hunt?"

Only by reputation.

"Then you don't know him at all!" This from Miss Millie, suddenly and with surprising heat, her voice crackling and smoldering like a summer storm. "The left-wing press has smeared him all his life. They even tried to link him with JFK's assassination, and we all know that was ordered by Moscow."

"I got interested in Mr. Hunt's patriotic work about six years ago," Brother Dave said. "So I checked him out and he checked me out, and we got our heads together. We've become real good friends. Miss Millie and me have been his guest in that big ole house he lives in—the one patterned after George Washington's. That's the nicest, kindest, gentlest, smartest ole boy in the world. He ought to have the Congressional Medal of Honor. If America is saved, beloved, he's the one who's saved it nearly singlehanded. Here, let me show you what Ruth gave us. That's Mrs. Hunt." He produced what appeared to be a catalog advertising furniture, which Mrs. Hunt had mysteriously autographed along with sentiments speaking well of friendship and patriotism. Which seems like a minimal gift from the wife of the world's richest man or thereabouts.

Does H. L. Hunt in any way subsidize Brother Dave's work?

"Naw, man. I ain't asked him for nothing. In the first place, I don't need to: I've got bread and investments so I don't have to work, except I want to get my message across. All Mr. Hunt's got that I want is his wisdom. He's my teacher."

"You should read *Alpaca*," Miss Millie said. "It's the best novel I've ever read. There's this model constitution in there that H. L. Hunt wrote." (The "model constitution" recommends that each citizen be given a number of votes in direct ratio to his net financial worth and would preclude anyone drawing a government salary, pension, or welfare check from voting; citizens would be permitted to sell their votes to others with greater interests in good government.)

Back to the Cherokee caper: what reason had they given for detaining Junior?

"They just said he was on Indian land. When we swung around to see what the score was, they told us it was none of our damn business and to clear out. We begged, pleaded, flashed our identification—all they said was, 'Get moving.' Then they threatened us with guns."

"Dave!"

"All right, Miss Millie. They held us up about an hour or more. But it took four or five hours to get our son out of that damn mess, and that caused us to miss opening night."

And how had they ultimately freed junior?

"Dave, now, we just can't talk about this," Miss Millie instructed in schoolmarm tones.

"Them cats *had* to know who I was, dear hearts. It wasn't no accident. By God, you wait until that Bureau of Indian Affairs gets through with 'em!"

"Dave!"

The comedian invited the visitor into an adjoining room, where he offered a recording by comic David Frye. "This cat cracks me up. Only thing is, he propagandizes for the leftists. But you got to hear this one track, man." David Frye imitated Richard Nixon taking a few experimental marijuana tokes and then trying to talk hip, the humor grounded in "Nixon's" continuing to sound (even when stoned beyond the capabilities of Mount Rushmore) like the eight year old who received a black leather briefcase for Christmas and who, furthermore, was delighted with the gift. "Can't you imagine ole Crafty Richard turned on?" Brother Dave cackled.

Junior entered from the main room. "Dad, quick! J. Robert Jones is out here."

"Oh, my God!" Brother Dave pinched out a little something he and the visitor had been smoking, frantically fanning the air. "Look, beloved, would you mind waiting in here with the boy? I've got some personal business with this cat."

Junior is lanky and wiry, six feet two, with a mop of long blond hair which his mother despises and which his father disapproves of but defends on the grounds that his son would be disadvantaged in the romance department should he look exceedingly square in a hip age. In military schools for six years before withdrawing a few months ago, he is convinced that neither Harvard nor Yale teaches as much as he'll learn on the road with dad. After he had exhibited various karate chops, Junior demonstrated with flourishes the most effective methods for quickly extracting a switchblade. He was performing his third or fourth guitar solo, between lectures explaining the basic uses of girls, when Brother Dave reappeared from the main quarters: "Come on in, beloved, and meet a friend."

A small, dark-haired man wearing a sly country grin sat in an easy chair, not bothering to rise for handshakes. "This is J. Robert Jones," Brother Dave said. The visitor's mental equipment whirred and clicked: *J. Robert Jones . . . North Carolinian . . . Grand Dragon and Holy Terror of the United Klans of America . . . convicted of contempt of Congress . . . recently released from federal prison.*

Mister, the bejeweled toy watchdog, was growling and snapping another irritating concert at the visitor's heels. "Come on dog," the visitor said. "You should be adjusted to me by now."

"Maybe he don't like hippies." Though the Holy Terror smiled, his eyes seemed to calculate how much bearded beef might dress out by the pound.

"Well, I'd hoped my accent might help."

"Yeah, Bob," Brother Dave said. "He's from Texas."

"Everybody got to be from *some*where," the Holy Terror said. "Ole Lyndon's from Texas, but he never amounted to much."

"Look, beloved," Brother Dave said, laughing nervously. "Would you mind seeing me tomorrow?"

Junior escorted the visitor to his room, only a small lawn and a swimming pool away from the Gardner quarters. "You know who that was you just met?"

"No," the visitor lied.

Junior produced the Grand Dragon and Holy Terror's calling card, which was as neatly and professionally done as that of any Wall Street broker. He produced another, this one from a Klan branch located in Natchez, and bearing the red-letter legend: You are WHITE because your grandfather believed in SEGREGATION. These documents reduced Junior to helpless laughter: "Man, don't that blow your mind?"

"Have you dug those cars?" The visitor looked in the indicated direction to observe two cars parked near the Gardner quarters. He noted the silhouettes of several men. "You know who they are?" Junior asked.

The visitor guessed they might be associates of the Holy Terror.

"Yeah, man! I bet they got enough guns to waste half of North Carolina."

This was not comforting as a bedtime thought. The visitor peered through the muggy night, lamenting that he had never learned to identify automobiles beyond their color, being unable to distinguish a Ford from a Lincoln unless he discovers clues written in manufacturer's chrome.

"They'll be there when the sun comes up, man," Junior chortled. "The Klan watches after Dad everywhere he goes. And they can see *your* room as well as my old man's." Much cheered by the thought, and stabbing the air with a switchblade, he turned back to the family quarters, where sleep is always taken in shifts as added protection against midnight conspiracies.

Three or four days and nights had carelessly mingled since the visitor had been introduced to the Holy Terror. The same jokes at the club, the same laughter, had burned the mind like acid. The house had been building nightly, in size and frenzy. The first night following the appearance of the Holy Terror, Rabie counted more than three hundred; Junior had slyly intimated that the gate's quantum jump had not been merely coincidental with that visit.

Since Brother Dave performs his guard watch by night and sleeps by day, many nocturnal sessions had revealed a plethora of conspiracies. He strolled about in an old dressing gown, incessantly smoking, periodically peeking through the parted drapes to determine, one assumed, whether any amphibious assaults might be headed our way from the pool.

"Beloved," he said during one such seance, "do you know why Congress inserted 'under God' in the Pledge of Allegiance at near about the same time the Supreme Court ruled there couldn't be no prayer in the schools?"

By now the visitor did not know whether it was a plot of the Federal Reserve Board, International Jewry, charity rackets, Julian Bond, or the television networks, all of which had received their due licks. So he just said no.

"Man, to *confuse* us. To *divide* us. That's the way this thing works, see." And he would be off down the steepest ideological slopes, waving his arms and wildly scattering cigarette ashes, delivering private monologues of which the following is a typical composite: "I've always been conservative and believe in segregation for them that wants it, dear heart, and nothing not being forced on nobody. But for years, man, I trusted my government—even believed what I read in the newspapers. Then I got to thinking, 'Dammit, something's bad *wrong!*' We had the biggest bomb in the world and couldn't win no wars. And we lost China and three-fourths of Europe and Cuber and all them damn Mau Mau nations, man, and then some good Americans uncovered Alger Hiss and Harry Dexter White and them other spying Communist cats and I started seeing a pattern in it. Man, the problem *had to come from within!* And the more I looked into the thing, I decided that was only part of it: *within* was doing the mischief, but *without* was calling the signals, you dig? Like, you think the people elected Roosevelt, don't you? Naw, man, that's what the big money combines conditioned you to think. Hell, man, the *Rothschilds* put FDR in. The House of Morgan. And they started us toward one-world government. And now, beloved, we can't even control our kids. We can't even be white without having to make excuses for it, and I'm sick and tired of making excuses for being white. Old Nixon, hell he's better than what we've had, but don't you know that cat ain't his own man? *Nelson Rockefeller* put him in office. Yeah, man, set him up in a big rich New York law firm and moved him in that same fancy building ole Rocky lives in, and then went out and spent six million dollars pretending like he was running against him!"

Here Brother Dave collapsed into helpless laughter at how clever the Rockefellers, Rothschilds, Stalins, and possibly the Denver Mint had been in their conspiratorial deceptions, a thing he frequently does when revealing the larger menaces, as if to say, *Hoo, boy, didn't they put one over on humanity that time?*

"I mean, man, you can even see it in *little* things." (*Laughs.*) "Like why do our post office buildings just say 'U.S.,' dear heart, without adding 'of America'?" (*Laughs.*) "How come, beloved, the Supreme Court and the hairy kids and the damned spades all started acting up *at once?*" (*Laughs.*) "And how come JFK and

Dr. Junior rode in open convertibles or stood out on balconies where folks could get clean shots at 'em?" (*Laughs*.) "Man, don't you know them cats was following orders to be *sacrificed*?" (*Laughs*.)

Then he would sober himself as quickly as he had laughed, marching about and saying a military coup d'etat might soon be the only method left for preserving America's precious freedoms, defending the Ohio National Guard in its conduct at Kent State, enthusiastically endorsing New York hardhats in their Wall Street attacks on beards, declaring himself to be the only strict constructionist in show business and assigning even John Wayne and Bob Hope to the liberal camp. He offered a grim warning represented as being in the visitor's best interests: "Look, man, I know they wear that damn long hair and face fuzz up there in New York. But you gotta realize, beloved, the revolution is *on*. It's *here*. People are going by appearances now, dear heart, 'cause everybody's choosed up sides. I worry about my own son getting hit by a sniper because of that damn long hair. It's dangerous to walk around looking hairy, man. You could get zapped."

To Klansmen visiting the camp had been added Green Berets and their wives down from Fort Bragg, and a local lady with skinny legs and a zealot's gleam who spoke frequently of the occult, of haunted houses, of reincarnation, of séances, of a devout belief in the prophesies of Jeane Dixon and in the profits of racial segregation. There had been a young sailor with a Confederate flag stitched inside the lining of his jumper so that when he unbuttoned his sleeve and rolled it back the flag winked and blinked in all its lost glory, and the sailor in outraged young innocence had proclaimed after one midnight show that those Communists *in the Pentagon*, now, must soon be stopped. There had been private screenings of a film produced at a small college in Searcy, Arkansas (represented as having been shipped in by H. L. Hunt for Brother Dave's continuing education), which told of a conspiracy linking the Black Panthers, Ho Chi Minh, student rebels, and large segments of Congress.

One night at the Pecan Grove Club the visitor noted with shock the arrival of a party of black people. Within three minutes of Brother Dave's opening blasts he was not surprised to hear loud and disgruntled comments from their direction. Whites at neighboring tables glared and shushed. Just as the dispute approached cussing terrain David Rabie appeared, agitated about one silly millimeter short of pure panic, to say how delighted he would be to refund money. The visitor sighed in concert with the club owner when the blacks accepted. (Rabie later said, "I told them at the door, 'I don't think this is your type of show,' but they didn't get the message.")

There had been one wild adrenaline moment when two Good Old Boys in discouragingly robust health had paused at the visitor's table to sneer as Brother Dave accomplished cadenzas of abuse against long-haired traitors abroad in the land: "*Here's* one of them bastards." The visitor negotiated the best possible grip on his Scotch bottle, felt himself tense to deliver a desperate overhand smash should that necessity descend, felt some reckless ancient joy of combat surging up that he had long presumed civilized out of him, and then, fortunately for his skin and for his long years of refurbishing, a waitress came running with the bulletin, *No, no he's with Brother Dave, y'all leave him alone, now, you hear?* The ole boys laughed sheepishly and stuck out their rough workmen's hands, telling the visitor they hadn't meant nothing by it, that they was real sorry, and one had begged a private introduction after the show in behalf of his father-in-law visiting from Pine Bluff.

There had been moments, too, with Klansmen in close proximity to the visitor's bed, with intrigue heavy on the night air, when paranoia had proved contagious. The visitor debated whether to telephone friends in the East to give some clue to his associates, in the event he should be discovered in some southern creek bed wrapped in more chains than he might conveniently swim in. After rejecting the notion as melodramatic, he had surrendered to it in a midmorning relapse. Later he had informed Brother Dave of his precautions, adding (to the tune of much merriment from among Green Berets and assorted other camp followers) that should anyone offer him a guided tour of the city it would take all hands plus the goddamn dog to load him in the car.

As the weekend of the Charlotte 600 Stock Car Races approached, Good Ole Boys and their ladies flocked in from all over

Dixie. Less fun and more pure damn mischief entered Brother Dave's act: "Albert Gore is a whore." James Baldwin made the show as a "low-life, bug-eyed, queer nigger." Senator Fulbright slipped from being Bullblight to a "sissy-britches traitor." The louder the cheers the more he spewed venom, and the more venom the louder the cheers.

The cheers told the visitor something it sickened him to hear, reaffirmed something dark and crazy and ancient he had hoped, and had half believed, might be drying up in southern blood. *They didn't hurt them lovely children—all they did was take some chains and whip up on some old school buses.* Yes, the mood was as openly belligerent as before Selma Bridge, before Bull Connor's police dogs and fire hoses, before the murder of Martin Luther King. It had become unfashionable, after all that highly publicized violence had pushed Congress into a mildly militant civil rights mood, to flaunt one's prejudices. Meddling Justice Department agents, scoldings from newspapers and presidents and chamber of commerce finks motivated by the almighty dollar, had caused one to defend the Southern Way of Life only in fairly gentlemanly terms. But a new mood had come to Washington, a thing called Southern Strategy had arrived there, along with a president who received hardhats in his office on the heels of their public assaults and a vice-president whose words could be as inflammatory as any George Wallace ever uttered. Even the best people could now telephone newspaper editors to demand the crucifixion of a United States senator without losing face. *Martha Mitchell, ain't she good?* Busing of students slowed down; the Justice Department for the first time in sixteen years *opposed* integration of certain southern school districts; and when four Kent State students lay dead, our president said through a spokesman that, well, play with fire and you'll get burned. *God, wasn't that a clean hit on Dr. Junior?* Not only gas jockeys, traveling salesmen, and Klansmen were among the cheering faithful; it was no trouble to discover lawyers, schoolteachers, merchants, and physicians in the overflowing house.

So there are few surprises left in the visitor as we rejoin him yawning on the edge of his bed before dawn. The telephone rings: "Come on over, beloved. I got a little surprise for you."

Surprise! There is a black man in the room, a muscular cat with a T-shirt showing his chest to good advantage, the sleeves ripped out the better to exhibit his biceps. This dude has some hustle in him, a little jive, for earlier he has sidled up to the visitor to announce that if a man want something to love or smoke that he cannot immediately get from room service, why, then, he know where it might be got. The black man is sitting near a large color photo stuck in the edge of a mirror, and in the photo—*Surprise!*— am de Grandest Dragon and Holiest Terror ob de Newnited Klans of America, and his wife, the happy couple in colorful silk robes with tassels and decals and braids until Kingfish himself could not have conceived more ostentatious costumes for the boys down at the Mystic Knights of the Sea Lodge.

Brother Dave guides the visitor to a chair, leans over, and delivers his biggest surprise in a near whisper: "Hey, man, I been putting you on. I don't really know H. L. Hunt! What's that cat ever done for anybody? You ever hear of that rich ole thing giving a dime to charity? Naw! You know a little something else, dear heart? Brother Dave am not what you think he am. Beloved, he am a secret *liberal.* Beloved, he am believe most faithfully in the Democratic party. He am a counterspy."

Yeah, the visitor says, he am personally believe strongly in tooth fairies.

"Naw, man, I'm telling you like it is! This whole thing is an act. It's a big put-on." Brother Dave leans against a table and laughs until one thinks he might choke, enjoying what is apparently the biggest political joke since the Reichstag fire.

Junior enters from stage left, as opposed to stage right where Miss Millie is presumably in blissful slumber. He jerks his thumb toward the room he has vacated where he has been entertaining a woman companion of the visiting black dude.

"You think about it, beloved," Brother Dave instructs. "I'll be back in a little bit."

During Brother Dave's absence, Junior flashes his Klan cards for the edification of the black man: "Don't that blow your mind?" "Naw, man," the black cat says. "I done lived down here too long." The visitor dozes on the couch, only dimly aware that Junior is teaching the black man karate, that Mister is admitted to the room after scratching on a door, that the television switches from a test pattern to the early news and market reports. He is slumbering soundly when Brother Dave wakes him by wafting hot coffee under his nose. They are alone.

"You thought about what I told you, beloved?"

"It won't wash," the visitor said. "That story contradicts your entire history. I suspect you've checked me out with H. L. Hunt. If I believed in security as much as you do, I would have checked me out the minute I walked in the door."

"Why didn't you tell us you had read *Alpaca*?" Brother Dave asks in injured tones. "Not only that, beloved, but had knocked it in some damn book review."

"Dear heart, nobody asked me." There is an exchange of humorless smiles.

What had the Dallas report revealed about the visitor?

"Well, he's got all you cats computerized. I told him your name and within three minutes he gave me your middle initial—it's *L*, dear heart—and he said that you're an enemy of the people."

An enemy of the people? *Glory!*

"You didn't fool Miss Millie for a damn minute," he said.

"Or Mister." Again the humorless smiles.

"I wish you could meet H. L. Hunt, beloved. I think he might straighten you out. I mean, I don't want to talk *down* to you, man. But the trouble is that people like you are being exploited through your political ignorance."

Who is my exploiter?

"Beloved, you know that as well as I do. Oh well, as long as two cats can smoke aspirins together, man, I feel like there's always hope. Let's don't talk no more politics, 'cause we might have a fistfight or Miss Millie might sic the dog on you." (*Laughs.*)

Why had he so abruptly disappeared from the national scene? Had a boycott been enforced against his political views?

"Naw, man. I could be on national TV if I wanted to push it. But after that funny plane crash in 1966, I decided against it."

Funny plane crash?

"Yeah, I'd charted one of them executive jobs out of Biloxi for my whole family. About ten minutes before we was to take off, they said something was wrong with it and shifted us to another one. Dear heart, it didn't fly twelve miles till it fell. *Blap!* Killed the pilot, buggered up the copilot, and broke hell out of all the rest of us—Miss Millie, she still hasn't recovered. I got the message. Somebody up there don't like me. Maybe I know too much."

Such as?

The big stage grin: "I am know multitudes and reveals but small particles. I am know long division and secrets of Hinduism. . . . Beloved, let me fix you another of them nasty old Scotches and maybe we'll soon have one less fuzzy liberal with a functioning liver. And from here on, dear heart, let us speak nothing but trash and joy."

There was inconsequential chatter, Brother Dave startling his guest by saying how he digs black comedian Dick Gregory ("Dick didn't know what he was getting into when he went on that freedom ride in Mississippi, man, 'cause he's from Chicago") and Garry Moore—a Jew—who had been extremely nice to him when he first broke into television and Paul Newman ("who's politically ignorant but has the guts to act for his beliefs").

As the visitor prepared to leave, Brother Dave produced a document for his inspection. From a mobile-home outfit in Alabama, and sent to transmit certain brochures, it appeared to be a routine business letter with its half-formal, half-friendly pitch; one had seen its cousins mailed out by the thousands from congressmen to their voters, from magazines soliciting subscriptions, from countless outfits with wares to hawk. As he puzzled over its significance, Brother Dave's finger pinpointed the closing sentence: *We highly value your interest in Such-and-So Homes.*

"That means a lot to me, beloved," he said. "That shows you what they think of me in the South. They love me down here."

There was a mob scene in the Gardner quarters on the visitor's last night before he would catch a plane to the decadent East, Brother Dave in a euphoric state because an overflow house had cheered his wildest salvos. Junior ran in and out with a series of young belles, Green Berets in high spirits popped beer cans, photographers took Brother Dave's picture, and Mister almost col-

lapsed with so many strangers to intimidate. One was reminded of
getaway day when the visiting ball club has concluded a successful
road tour, has swept its last series, and now looks forward to a
long stand at home.

Not all was happiness or joy, alas. David Rabie and the comedian quarreled over their failure to reach a satisfactory financial
adjustment owing to Brother Dave's missed opening night, this
leading to more dithyrambs against the Cherokees. Then a beribboned Green Beret sergeant, skinheaded and badly wounded in
Vietnam and really quite a sincere ole boy, cursed the New Army's
coddling of recruits so that disicpline had gone to hell and you
couldn't hardly find recruits with enthusiasm for killing any more.
And, finally, it had been confided that Miss Millie had taken to her
bed with a headache rather than be in the visitor's presence once
her suspicions of his character had been verified.

Standing by the swimming pool in the warm North Carolina air,
Brother Dave touched the visitor's arm. "Look, man, if you ever get
your head about half straightened out and decide you want to
know where it's really at, politically, get in touch. I'll be your
teacher. There's not much time left, beloved, to save America."

He turned away, himself only a few hours from the road and a
dozen one-nighters in Georgia, providing Miss Millie did not carry
through her threat to cancel them because of race wars in Augusta.
At the door he pursed his lips thickly, gave the clenched fist of the
black power salute, and shouted, "Power to the people." Laughing,
dear hearts. Laughing.

1970

The Liberation of Jesse Hill Ford

THE YOUNG MAN—a Navy veteran of the Korean War, an ex-newspaper reporter and former public relations flack, a would-be novelist—came, in 1957, to the town where he would eventually kill. Though he had been reared in Nashville, less than 150 miles away, there were those in Humboldt, Tennessee, who considered him an interloper possessed of a strange life-style and vague dreamy motives, one who produced nothing the community could taste or wear or drink. It has happened to other writing men in their rural habitats: to Faulkner in Oxford, to Wolfe in Asheville, to Sinclair Lewis in Sauk Centre, to Sherwood Anderson in "Winesburg" (Clyde), Ohio.

Watching Jesse Hill Ford in his daily peregrinations to the post office, or in his apparently aimless meanderings and random jottings, Humboldtians saw him as a vagabond loafer with no visible means of support save for his schoolteacher wife, Sally. The shopkeepers, agrarians, and clerks of West Tennessee, unaccustomed to the rhythms of a writing man's life, the silent introspections indigenous to his craft, saw only that Jesse Hill Ford looked idle.

Idle he was not. Ford wrote out of the rear office of a clinic operated by his father-in-law, Dr. Charles Davis, who for more than thirty years had attended Humboldt's births, deaths, and recoveries.

He was writing from his own dark, private vision of the town itself, exposing in his short stories and novels its warts and prejudices, its greeds and xenophobia, its secret couplings and official deceptions. Not many understood that Ford loved it—as Faulkner said of the South—"not because of but despite" its crazy contortions, secret broodings, and savage eruptions.

The Liberation of Lord Byron Jones, published in 1965, outraged and shocked the town as nothing before. Not that many Humboldtians read the book (even though it became a Book-of-the-Month Club selection), for the West Tennessee village is more interested in its strawberry, cotton, and soybean crops, its feed mills and mop factories and fertilizer plants, its parties and civic clubs and duck-hunting opportunities than in the teachings or musings of literature. Word soon got around, however, that Ford's book was based upon an actual old community skeleton. In the book, as in life, a black undertaker suing his wife for divorce had the temerity to name a white policeman as her lover—and was brutally killed for it. It is the sort of sordid story people detest having told about themselves. Its main theme is that the Humboldts of this world are often cesspools of injustice, societies which honor form above substance, which deceive themselves and oppress others at great cost to their souls. Suddenly the story was in a big book for all the world to read. It was made into a movie—shot on location in Humboldt.

The book made Jesse Hill Ford about half wealthy. He established himself on the outskirts of Humboldt in a fine baronial house, Canterfield, plopped down on twenty-seven acres with a stocked pond, blooded horses, exotic dogs. But Ford's profiteering off the town's mute and buried past—as the town saw it—was another reason for rancor. So it was that more than one citizen whooped in glee or permitted a hidden smile on a moonless, frosty evening in mid-November 1970, when word began circulating through the sleepy streets: *Jesse Ford killed him a nigger out at his place tonight.* . . .

Humboldt is a town of ten thousand people (some thirty-five hundred of them black) and an undistinguished Main Street of gabled tin roofs adorned by one four-story "skyscraper." It sprawls fifty miles from the Mississippi River, dividing Tennessee from Arkansas, and is in close proximity to a corner of Kentucky; Memphis is only a ninety-minute drive away. Though freeways run near by and the same television shows reach Humboldt that benumb Los Angeles or Chicago, it remains as determinedly rural as a Clabber Girl Baking Powder sign tacked to an unpainted barn. It is one of the few remaining American places with deep roots, with a sense of continuity and family blood, and a long community memory.

But for all its Good Ole Boys, folksy habits, and country pleasures, Humboldt has problems, old problems, which it has been reluctant to solve or even to mitigate. It is, and has been, backward in its racial solutions, alternating between white paternalism and pure red-neckery. Local officials, asked to make things a bit more tolerable for blacks, have traditionally crayfished or fought in court or called for the paddy wagons. The people say "nigger" or "nigguahs" or—in attempting to pacify visiting Yankees—"nigra" or "colored folks." These terms are not unknown in Ford's own house, though he rarely is the one to use them.

Jesse Hill Ford's books have captured the absurdities of Humboldt's attempts to maintain hard-line segregation: the druggist who removed his soda fountain rather than serve blacks, the white parsons who refuse to meet with their black counterparts in the Lord's work, the arrests of blacks peacefully picketing chain stores for job opportunities, the double standards at play in the courts or even in the bedroom where white men may surreptitiously join with black women—though a special dishonor, and maybe death, awaits the couple going at it the other way around. People walk softly in Humboldt when racial fears run high.

During the filming of *Liberation*, Lloyd Adams, a Humboldt attorney with generations-old community roots, hosted a house party for members of the integrated cast and local people—both black and white. A lot of people thought that Lloyd and Bettye Rose had lost their cotton-picking minds. Among the many whites who did not attend was Jesse Hill Ford. In deciding to honor local custom he said, "There's a difference between morals and mores." It was a careful party, liquorless by plan, an orgy of pie and coffee, with a patio recitation of Shakespeare by the black leading man, Roscoe Brown, climaxing the debauchery. Even so, Humboldt police received a number of demands that the revelers be jailed.

In the fall of 1970, under federal court orders, Humboldt reluctantly integrated its schools. The transition was troublesome and hectic. Blacks lost their high school and all its traditions. All so-

cial functions—proms, plays, school dances—were quickly abandoned. Eventually all black players on the football team were dismissed when they failed to appear for a practice session as a protest against what they thought was discrimination on the part of
the white coach.

Black resentments centered on Jesse Ford's seventeen-year-old
son, Charles, captain of the football team and an all-state halfback (now a freshman starter at Furman University) who had replaced a black halfback thought spectacular the year before.
Charles Ford began receiving threatening phone calls; during the
homecoming parade downtown—on the Friday before his father
would fatally shoot a black man—some blacks threw stones at the
car in which Charles was riding.

For some time, Jesse Ford later would attest, his family had experienced a series of small desultory harassments—obscene telephone
calls, "unidentified people who'd drive up and scare us," garbage
strewn across his lawn—which accelerated when the movie version of *Liberation* played in the local theater. But with the troubled
opening of school last fall, those harassments—which presumably
had been the work of whites—assumed a curious inversion: they
began coming from blacks. And where *Liberation* had once drawn
only white ire, young blacks now charged that it castrated black
males, made sluts and parasites of black women, defamed and mis-
represented blacks in general.

Jesse Ford long has been preoccupied with violence. His writing
is replete with tales of ambush, betrayals, trickery, murder, mutila-
tions. Nor have all his thoughts on those subjects been confined to
the page. While building Canterfield, he read Truman Capote's *In
Cold Blood*—the story of a Kansas family slaughtered in their
beds—and had the home redesigned to provide clear fields of fire
in all directions. Trees were felled, leaving the house standing on
an open plain, looking a bit scraped and raw. Each family member
was assigned a window from which to defend. "Somebody might
break in here," Ford said, "but they wouldn't get out. We've got
guns and we all know our jobs." Five giant mastiffs, weighing up to
175 pounds, huge beasts with great crunching jaws—of a type
trained to hunt *lions*, now, in Africa—patrolled the Ford acres.

Signs on the approach road warned against trespassing. Heavy iron grillework protected the front door. Fort Ford.

On the night of November 16, 1970—a Monday—at approximately ten o'clock, Sally Ford heard a car circle the front driveway. It then took a sharp turn on the approach road, pulled off on the grass near a small clump of trees, and parked—facing away from the house, facing toward anyone who might try to reach the house. Sally woke her sleeping husband: "Jesse, I don't think that's Charles."

Charles was studying at the home of a girl friend. His father— later insisting that the unidentified car was in perfect ambush position—felt a premonition of fear for his son. Jesse Ford had himself twice dreamed of being pursued through his own house and shot in the head, "exploding into a dark nothingness, and then I would wake up." These thoughts flashed briefly as he pulled on a jump suit and a light jacket and loaded a deer rifle. He moved swiftly across the grass, on a blind and moonless and frosty night, toward the now-darkened car.

"I fired a warning shot in the air. Nothing happened. I mean, just *no* reaction. I went closer and banged on the car trunk with the rifle butt and yelled, 'Get out with your hands up, I've called the police!'

"The car started moving away. Just *lunged* away. I snapped the rifle up and fired—not to kill anybody, I didn't even aim the gun. But goddammit, my family had been harassed and threatened and I was damn sick and tired of it. I was *determined* to stop that car! I had to know what was happening here.

"All of a sudden the car stopped. Just stopped. The lights were still on, you know, and the motor was still running, but there wasn't a *sound* from inside. Nothing. I thought, *Oh, my God— something's wrong. Something's happened.* Then, all of a sudden, the side door flies open—*blam!*—and this girl with a little child is running like hell down the road. I thought, *My God, is this a family? What have I done?*

"I ran back up to the house and told Sally, 'Sally, I think I just shot somebody.' After a while the ambulance got here and the police came up to the house and asked me, 'Did you shoot at 'em?' I

said, 'Yes. Didn't anybody get hurt down there, did they?' And they said, 'Looks like that fella is in pretty bad shape.' And I said, 'Oh, my God! Oh, my God!' I never went back down there to the car. Never saw the fella. . . .'

Ford's random shot had killed George H. Doakes, a twenty-one-year-old black soldier from nearby Trenton who eleven days earlier had come to Humboldt to marry the mother of his infant daughter. His companion—the young woman Jesse Ford had seen bolt from the car and clatter down the road—was his sixteen-year-old second cousin, Allie V. Andrews, in the company of a four-year-old girl she was baby-sitting when Doakes picked her up, ostensibly to get a hamburger. "After the second shot," Allie Andrews remembers, "he just said, 'Ah.' I felt blood . . . his head fell on my shoulder." Doakes's body was found sprawled across the front seat, his trousers gathered loosely around his knees. He was as dead as Lord Byron Jones, the right side of his head blown away.

The next morning Jesse Hill Ford heard on his car radio that he would be charged with first-degree murder—Murder One. He seemed trapped in the most airless holes of his darker literary plumbings: a victim stepping out of his own pages.

Through the months from November to June, awaiting trial, Jesse Ford often seemed to regard the disaster as some capricious and malicious vandalism of fate against the ordered pattern of his life. He insisted that prosecuting attorneys were proceeding against him with unusual vigor just because he was who he was, or out of some vague, ill-defined conspiracy. At such moments it seemed impossible to rhyme him with his work.

As if sensing this, Ford offered explanations to the clots of friends, newsmen, and visiting journalists he almost constantly entertained—and somehow desperately seemed to need. Presiding over Canterfield with its groaning feasts and well-stocked liquor cache, he often said, "Look, I didn't want that fella dead. I wish to God he were alive now. I'd shoot off my own leg. But we've gotten tough about this whole thing because we've *had* to. I'm in a bad situation, it's a nightmare, and I've just got to get through it. And until I do, by God, I can't afford to have any human feelings." Yet sometimes the guard came down. He was given in random moments to fits of weeping. It might happen as he read aloud, played the piano, or gazed with sightless Orphan-Annie eyes across the dead winter fields toward the barns and stables. These attacks were like small repeated shatterings of some fragile inner glass.

He seemed indeed a man of many parts: a man of many conflicting truths, each of which he believed deeply in odd moments but none of which he could trust the day through.

One could see in him the two contrasting law partners [in *Liberation*]—hear, at once, the voice of young lawyer Steve Mudine, who argued passionately for an abstract, perfect justice, and likewise hear the voice of the older lawyer, Oman Hedgepath, so bent on preserving the Old South status quo that he lent himself to the protection of a murderer. Contrasting forces and ideas appeared to bang around inside Ford's head, colliding like bumper cars at a carnival, yet he seemed unaware of these repeated collisions. In one moment he might sound as crass and brassy as a bell; in another, he would weep at the sight of one of his mastiffs—bloody and groggy after a Caesarian birth—and deliver a sensitive, agonized discourse on man's fear of the dark and mysterious pits of unconsciousness.

It is not unusual for imaginative writing men—who can create their own private worlds—to sometimes lose touch with the world they and the rest of us live in, nor is it unique for men in private stress to fluctuate wildly in their emotions. Ford had a double dose: he was a writing man in private stress.

In some curious near-tribal way, Ford now appeared to draw closer to the town he had so summarily judged in his books. Even to defend it. "What I've liked about living in Humboldt," he said, "is there just isn't all that convoluted inbred literary discussion going on around you all the time. Somebody will find out I've had a novel or short story published and they'll say, 'I heard you sold an article. That's good. I sold a tractor today myself.'"

But while he may actually have entertained this whimsy, the difficulty was that he didn't deal in tractors or shingles or even hospital insurance. His was a more private enterprise, and it gave him a manner more remote, the air of someone secretly practicing witchcraft. In a local pool hall-café, the proprietor, leaning on the counter under a Double Cola sign and swatting a flyswatter against his khakis, said, over the click and nicks of cue balls, "Damn, I don't know, the man's just different. Keepin' to hisself all the time, stuff like that. He acts real funny sometimes. Only time he ever come in here, I never could figger out what it was for, but I set talking with him for it must've been two hours and he used words, you know, I didn't understand half of 'em. And I know I ain't all that ignorant." A lawyer friend recalled that in his infrequent visits to the country club Ford would "just sort of barge around real noisy and clumsy for a little while, or sit off at a table kind of stiff, and be gone again." Someone else remembered Ford's odd transports after being issued a traffic ticket for easing through a stop sign: ". . . and, sonuvabitch, for *three weeks* after that he was going around taking down license numbers of other folks he saw going through stop signs."

A local business mogul, one of those driven men who live in the big white house on the hill and devote their life's breath to the dogged accumulation of wealth and power—and who, a few weeks after the killing, would call in eighteen thousand dollars in notes Ford owed the bank—said, "He just *tries* to be peculiar. He's brought black marks on this town, writing all that trash. He hasn't even *tried* to fit in here."

Yet, in his darkest hour, the white community seemed to rally to Ford and he to it. He entertained more than formerly, plunged into beer joints and coffee shops and wrung hands on the street "almost as if running for office," one observer would say. He moved, now, with an entourage: people who had not read his books, for the most part, and some few who once had damned them. A journalist who had long admired Ford's work, and who grew close to him in adversity, alternately wondered whether Ford might be conducting a clever campaign designed to produce a friendly jury or whether—in his great and private confusion, concern, and need—he simply and quite desperately coveted the touch of humanity's hand.

Humboldt's black community originally had expected Ford to be acquitted: white jurors would see it as just another nigger killing, no cause for alarm. But in the spring a Humboldt policeman—acting on a case of mistaken identity—attempted to arrest a black man at a café near The Crossing, that place where the railroad tracks divide Uptown from Niggertown. The black man fought back, an angry crowd collected, a mini-riot ensued. For the first time, Humboldt's blacks broke windows, looted, and shouted. "It scared ole whitey to death," a young black educator later would say, grinning. "We decided maybe Jesse Ford might be convicted after all. We didn't think whitey dared let him go after that. We thought they might make a little sacrificial offering." Indeed, for the first time Humboldt officialdom began to make small surrenders: the city council was reorganized by precincts to assure the election of one black, a biracial committee magically sprouted

forth from the chamber of commerce, a young black group gained
the unaccustomed use of public buildings, the school colors of de-
funct Stegall High, which had been the black school, were resur-
rected for assimilation by Humboldt High. Little things, yes, but
more than had gone before. "What Ford's trial will prove," a local
black said, "is whether he is more unpopular than we are. I've got
to think they'll at least slap his wrists."

And, in June, Jesse Hill Ford was found not guilty of Murder
One. And not guilty of unpremeditated murder. Not guilty, even, of
involuntary manslaughter. The jury was composed of eleven whites
and a lone black.

Almost everyone has an explanation for why Jesse Ford went
free. Down at The Crossing they say, "The dude killed a nigger,"
shrugging away all mystery. In a beer joint where the jukebox
bleats hillbilly laments of unrequited love and truck-driving fools
and whisky widows, a white bartender, sucking a toothpick, says,
"That nigger boy had no business slippin' around old Jesse's place
like that. He flat couldn't-a been up to no good, and he mighta
been up to real mischief."

Others say the prosecution was awkward: while disputing
whether Ford had his place properly posted against trespass, the
prosecution introduced into evidence a photograph of George
Doakes's body that revealed quite clearly a large "posted" notice
on a nearby telephone pole. Though claiming Ford fired only one
shot, not an additional warning shot as the defense alleged, the
state somehow admitted to having found *three* spent shells from
Ford's deer rifle.

Jerry Cox is a twenty-one-year-old prelaw student at Lambuth
College in Jackson, a rising leader among local blacks, and hopes
to be Humboldt's first lawyer of his race. "Frankly," he says, "I
didn't trust either side. Probably the defense attorney and the prosecuting attorney are cousins; that's the way it works down here. But,
you know, I thought they might give Ford a suspended sentence.

"Ford had that book going against him with whites, but when it
comes to push or shove the white folks stick together. That book—

as a black man, I loved it and I hated it. Because it was true. After I read it, that old murder of Lord Byron Jones came back to me. I remember asking about it as a kid, and all the Uncle Toms said, 'Shhh, boy, don't ask no questions.' After reading it, I wanted to *get* those cats. But that book's not just about this town. It's about the whole stinking society. Not many whites would have written it, I give Ford that. I didn't get this light color in a crackerjack box, you know. Ford told it like it was. I had real mixed feelings about what I wanted to happen to that dude.

"Will his acquittal cause more trouble here? Hard to say. I think among the younger kids—teen-agers—it had a pretty big impact. One more lesson from whitey: niggers don't count, not even their lives."

Late in October, nearly a year after the shooting, a bulb-nosed little man who served on Ford's jury explained the jury's thinking. "We just didn't believe the state's witnesses," he said. "That Andrews gal, she couldn't explain what they were doing there. Said they had got lost and—well, we saw those pictures with that boy's britches down. Naw, we didn't take old Jesse's ambush theory too much to heart. Oh, I think *he* believed it but—excuse me, Jesse—it seemed a little farfetched.

"The law's clear: if Jesse believed that he or any member of his family was in imminent danger, then he had a right to shoot. We thought those threatening calls could account for the fear in him. And then, too, that little Andrews gal, she claimed to have seen Jesse right down to the color of his jacket and his hair. Well, there was just *no way*, dark as the night was and him staying out of the headlights."

"She saw me in the light when she came back with the police," Ford injected. "We proved that in court."

"Well," the juror said, "we didn't intend to let 'em railroad you, Jesse."

The conversation was taking place in Ford's kitchen around a big round table just at dusk. Outside, one could observe the roisterings of giant mastiffs. Down at the entry to Ford's property stood a half-completed stone gatehouse. It will feature iron grillework, electronic controls, and a two-way intercom connected to the main house. Sally sometimes jokes that the gatehouse represents "locking the barn door after the horse got out."

The juror, who had reddish hair and the round, comic face of a clown, leaned over and grinned. "Hell, Jesse, they couldn't have found a jury in all these woods that would have convicted you."

"No, now, I don't know," Ford said, disturbed. "I mean, Bernie, come on, they *tried*. The bastards really *did*. The state wanted to convict me real bad. We won it on merit, now. This thing has cost me thirty thousand dollars in real money and Lord knows how much in lecture fees. I lost nearly a year's work, Bernie. Hell, I went broke . . ."

Later that evening, well liquored, Ford retraced the fatal night as he had so many times before. He seems to discuss it almost compulsively, displaying an amazing patience with prying journalists. "Hell," he said in benediction, "I was protecting *my family, my home*. Why can't people understand that? Hindsight's wonderful; but it doesn't allow for the passions and adrenalines and fears of the moment.

"Let me tell you, when you're indicted by the state, facing the state's millions and its buckles and guns, and the helicopters they fly over your place taking pictures for evidence, and when you face

their battery of lawyers and investigators *and know they've got it in for you*—buddy, you'd better find out who's gonna try you, what their case is, and how you can counteract. You're on trial for your *life*, your *freedom*, your *property*. The man who fails to understand that, and to conduct his defense accordingly, he's gonna be hung for a fool.

"I don't see any betrayal of my values, or that I profaned my work, no sir! When you're up against the nitty-gritty, the name of the game is *win*. Why should I be expected to roll over and play dead for the state? The trouble these days is that people think that anything that's black is automatically beautiful. Well, they're just *people* to me—like the rest of us, hell, that's the whole point of my work—and I'm not gonna treat 'em like Brahmins.

"If the rest of this country ever succeeds in the total alienation of the white South, God help it. Who's gonna keep the store? We educate and export our best people. What if *all* of us left? This is the breadbasket of the nation down here."

He lurched to his feet and poured another drink, eyes marble-like, hard gray agates, his round face somehow flat like a pie pan. "I'm sorry as I can *be*, goddammit, but I don't thresh around at night moaning, 'God forgive me, I killed a man.' It was a . . . a tragic *accident*, but you can't linger over it forever."

There had been numerous racial incidents in Humboldt recently: a gang fight at a local drive-in, whites writing "Niggers go home," blacks stoning whites. Did Ford think his act had harmed race relations in the community?

"How could it? No race relations to speak of to begin with. It may have even helped. That sounds funny, I guess. But there's a fella here's got a pond, and some blacks had been swimming in it without permission—on his *private property* now—and when he told 'em to move on, they'd just laugh or give him lip. After I shot that fella, by God, he didn't have to tell 'em not to swim there any more. They stayed away.

"If anything has harmed race relations here it's been those snot-nosed kids fresh from law school, those HEW and Justice Department hotshots. We've got a school superintendent trying to make

integrated schools work, and all he hears is threats and intimidations from Washington. They should get off his back.

"Anybody can get on a soap box. I work quietly. Maybe once
every three years I can say to some ole boy down here, 'Do you
really believe a Negro is less than human?' and he'll study about it
and say, 'Naw, not really.' Well, that helps a little. You stay in there
with 'em, you hang on, you chip away, do what you can.

"The race thing is complicated down here. Its roots go deep in
history and blood. You won't change it overnight. Right now the
races are more hostile to each other than they've ever been. The
politicians told everybody to expect instant brotherhood, got their
expectations up, told 'em the problem was solved when a few civil
rights bills passed. Hell, we haven't even scratched the surface."

The talk switched back to the Doakes case again, became re-
petitious, and everyone began to talk a little louder, wave their
arms more, take on a whisky flush. Ford fell silent, brooding, and
suddenly said, "You can know what's happened to you, you know,
without really understanding it." Then, quite abruptly, he padded
upstairs to bed.

On a Saturday afternoon, Ford drove three visiting journalists
and a photographer on a tour of Humboldt. At the railroad tracks—
The Crossing—photographer Jim Karales was enchanted by a collection of old black men, dressed in the rags and tatters of the
country poor, sunning on long benches. He insisted on stopping,
despite a nervous reluctance on the part of the journalists, who did
not think it prudent for Ford to flaunt himself in black precincts.
"These people won't hurt you," Ford reassured. "They're good
folks, most of 'em."

Soon, however, Ford hummed and jangled with his own tensions. He drove around the block slowly, worry in his eyes. He
parked on a vacant area near the railroad tracks. "These people
don't like this," one journalist blurted. "They consider it 'looking
at the monkeys.'" Nobody said anything. There were quick, darting sippings of beer. Ford spoke softly, as if fearing that his voice
might carry: "Isn't it terrible when a man has to be afraid in his
own country?"

Karales continued to snap away, apparently oblivious to the

building tensions and the gathering crowd. Where earlier there had been only the old men sunning their bones and exchanging Saturday marketplace gossip, there now appeared young men with swagger in their steps, Afro-haired and dressed in the colorful garb of street dudes or hustlers. "Hey, man," one hard-eye ordered, "take my picture." Karales obliged. "What you cats up to, man?" another demanded. Suddenly, a young black man pulled his car alongside Ford's vehicle and silently stared into his eyes. Pure hate was there. Then he spun off, tires slinging gravel. Now blacks were pouring into the streets, eyeballing Ford's vehicle: dry, hot electricity crackled. Abruptly the black man who had departed in a spray of gravel reappeared—with three other young blacks in his car. They got out as if to approach Ford's car.

Ford called to the photographer, "Get in the car, Jim!"

Karales, true to his breed, begged, "Just one more."

Ford began shouting: "Get in the car! Get in the car! Goddammit, *get in the car or I'll leave your ass!*" Startled, Karales jumped in just as a police car, attracted by the commotion, roared up. Ford accelerated rapidly, turning back across the tracks to safely white precincts. One had seen, briefly and terribly, a flash of the panic and fear that had prompted him to snap off that fatal shot almost a year earlier. Had felt, too, something of the tensions he had been living under and realized that no man who has not been through them could judge what he might do in the same circumstance.

Ford monitored the rearview mirror. "I don't like this. There's a car following us, and I don't know who's in it. There have been threats on my life from the blacks since this thing." He quickly pulled in to a service-station lot, permitting the mystery car to go harmlessly past.

"I just don't come to town any more," Ford said. "Right after my trial, I went in a beer joint and a guy who looked like a redneck that had worked his way up to white collar jumped me: 'If it had been me, Mr. Big Shot, I'd be doing time.' I said, 'Goddammit, am I gonna have to fight some sonuvabitch every time I go out in my hometown for the rest of my life?' Well, the owner of the bar threw the guy out, but I decided right then, by God, just not to expose myself any more."

He remains in the big barred house, working until midafternoon. Then, walking in a surge and roll of mastiffs, he fishes his stocked pond, swims, perhaps rides. On weekends, usually, several Humboldt couples come in and there is a great deal of laughter (Ford's exploding without warning, crashing about like fragments of the concussion bomb he carries in his legs). There are jokes and light conversation about inconsequential things. It is pleasant enough, but to the outside observer it seems a bit feverish, sometimes forced, and maybe it is a form of therapy. "I'm happy," Ford often says on such occasions, hugging Sally or one of the children. "I'm working well now, and things are leveling out. I'm real, real happy."

After the company has gone and the family is in bed, Ford may sit staring into a cold marble unlighted fireplace, drinking, alone out there somewhere at the edge of his mind where nobody can follow, where no journalist can probe, where no one can demand that he explain—once again—that which really is unexplainable.

1971

Body Politics

I WAS LUNCHING WITH POLITICIANS in Washington recently when somebody asked—apropos of the sensationalized "sex scandals" preoccupying the media, the governed, and certainly the quaking pro pols themselves—why only Democrats had been discovered in the exercise of carnal freedoms. While I attempted to frame a response touching on the ideological, the answer came: "Well, there's no fun in getting a little piece of elephant."

Amidst the laughter, someone told of a new "campaign button" being worn by particularly well-endowed congressional secretaries: "I type 74 words per minute." There was much joshing about firing well-turned young lovelies and hiring old crones in corrective shoes. Someone repeated the joke circulating in Capitol Hill cloakrooms: "When they caught Wayne Hays and John Young, they said I couldn't sleep with my secretary. Then they caught Allan Howe and Joe Waggonner and told me I couldn't sleep with prostitutes. That leaves only my wife—and *she's* always got a headache." More yuks and chortles as everyone ordered fresh drinks.

Well, now, I fancy to enjoy a joke as much as the next man. But under the cover of giggles more appropriate to errant schoolboys convened behind the barn, our statesmen—and others—are begging serious questions having more to do with honesty and individual freedom and the workaday realities than with mere rolls in the hay or a knee-jerk morality.

We of the media, particularly, may be guilty of sins even larger than those who attempt to joke away the subject. We are springing to our microphones and typewriters to tell of hot tails—pun definitely intended—on the Potomac as though Antony and Cleopatra spent their time playing backgammon when Octavia and Ptolemy Dionysus happened not to be looking. We tell it so straight-faced you'd think our jaws were numbed by novocaine, even though our cheeks are so full of tongue we're in danger of strangling.

Politicians, including Republicans, have been running carnal fevers outside their home beds since the first hairy tribe elected a leader on about the 103rd ballot in some lightless, airless cave. So have members of the media, not to mention doctors, lawyers, plumbers, housewives, carpenters, feminists, and you name it. Even such a pious parson as Reverend Billy James Hargis, the Oklahoma pulpit pounder, had occasion a few months ago to plead that the devil made him do it. The sad thing is that poor ol' Billy James probably believes that, when all he was doing is what comes naturally.

The sex drive is among our more basic instincts, even ranking ahead of the need for Coca-Cola or peanut butter. If nature had not so willed, no species would survive. We simply would be too indifferent to procreate and would bumble around eating grass or drilling oil wells or joining the Jaycees. Sex feels so good because its primary function in nature's order is to perpetuate not only the beautiful but also the ugly, and that's why rattlesnakes and giant turtles and sand crabs and fat congressmen get that wonderful urge the same as peacocks and cuddly pussycats and beautiful blondes and handsome dudes like me.

Nature knew it must bribe us with an overwhelming instinct to make sexual music together so the earth would not remain a lifeless rock. Whether you believe that evolution brought light in its timeless and tireless work, or that God in His earliest effort said, "Let there be light," *something* brought light long before the Pedernales Electric Co-op or West Texas Utilities Company. With light came heat, without which no life might exist. In time the great hot lump of earth cooled, and the moisture in its atmosphere fell as rain, and water gathered and pooled, and the winds came and helped the water wear away the cold stone. This formed thin coatings of soil, which eventually toddled its way downhill into the water. There the sun kissed this new mixture toward the end of bringing forth original life: microscopic, tiny, jellylike floating cells. These linked together and multiplied themselves and grew the instinct to keep on doing it.

The surface waters began to get overcrowded, and just floating around like little bits of jelly became boring. So some of these cells went off and decided to become fishes and underwater plants. Then the pioneers of *those* bold groups got washed upon the shore and lay around in the sunshine and opted to turn into snakes and dinosaurs and weird-looking clumsy birds. Finally, those who got tired of living under rocks and such and who wanted to cuddle decided to turn into warm-blooded mammals. The minute *that* decision was made, it was inevitable that one day we'd have Miami Beach and massage parlors and that one day Wayne Hays could not keep his hands off Elizabeth Ray, even if it meant paying her out of tax funds.

Now, the point is that no matter what those original little cells decided to become, they fought against great odds. They had to overcome Ice Ages and Stone Ages and the big 'uns always trying to eat the little 'uns. They caught chills and fevers and everything but city buses. It rained on 'em and hailed on 'em, and things growled at 'em in the dark. They had to grow their own gills or wings or whatever. All this, now, with all manner of ugly species thrashing about making faces and otherwise threatening them. Yet, no matter how howling or hairy were the enemies in pursuit, and no matter if nature's creatures had to creep or crawl or fly away from danger, enough of each species paused to get it on sexually that just about everything but the dumbass dinosaur survived. Against such irrepressible instincts, what's a poor politician gonna do?

Things worked swimmingly well until man came along to superimpose "civilization" on nature's order. Until man decided to govern sexual conduct, a baboon or a turtle (within the confines of certain loose processes of natural selection) could pretty much kiss and cuddle who he wanted to, so long as a stronger baboon or a meaner turtle didn't object. Man, however, discovered early on that anything as good as sex needed to be rationed and made difficult or else people would have too much fun. They'd loll around in the shade, cooing and touching when they ought to be up killing whales or inventing the spinning wheel or taking Dale Carnegie courses. The kings and the pharoahs and other precinct bosses fretted that if people made love rather than war, then there would be no booty to claim and fewer excuses to levy taxes. So they

devised laws, some of which they credited to God, to get everybody out of bed and up and doing. These laws said that people
could make love only under such restricted conditions as pleased
the state. The young or unmarried would not be permitted to do it
at all, the married could do it only to each other, and *nobody*
should do it except to make babies. If a boy wanted to cuddle a
boy, or a girl wanted to cuddle a girl, they ran the risk of jail—to
say nothing of the worst possible social contaminations. If you had
some for sale, the fruit of your commerce was a trip to the pokey.
There were even laws saying that under certain conditions you
couldn't give sex away, or accept it, even in a fair swap. They finally
hit on the notion that if you showed too much imagination and
discovered especially exotic ways to do it, well, then they'd reserve
you a jail cell for that, too.

All these antilove laws haven't worked, of course. All they've
done is make people sneak around and lie and cheat and go crazy
and kill each other—or, like poor old Wayne Hays, take overdoses
of sleeping pills. It sure was simpler when we were floating around
on the water as itsy-bitsy cells and reproducing ourselves while the
sun smiled on us.

We are considering here more than sex and no less than personal
freedom. Most people do not really believe in personal freedom,
even though they think they do. While almost any American is
quick to claim it as a birthright, many fewer are willing to extend
it to others. We may give love to a child or a spouse or a neighbor,
but in the matter of their free choices we tend to become policemen
of the spirit and censors of the soul. We tell them "don't" more
than we tell them "do." It is no accident that we are so shaped and
formed: The Ten Commandments, no matter their worth, are
stated in the negative; more laws are written to prohibit people
than to set people free.

Richard Nixon once told an interviewer that people were like
children. That is the basic presumption of the state, whether its
agents label themselves liberal or conservative or lay claim to any
of the various ideological isms. The state and its agents and allied
institutions are collectively almost certain to repress, even when
attempting benign acts. Example: that welfare law which, under
the guise of assisting needy families, threatens to withhold benefits

from poor mothers and their dependent children should a non-working man live in the house. "We will allow you the freedom to eat marginally"—the state says—"but don't let me catch you doing any *loving* around here."

Our politicians are quick to proclaim that we are the freest and richest people in the history of man. That is probably true, and we are surely freer than the Russians and the Cubans and richer than the Hottentots, but before we are smitten with paroxysms of pride, we would do well to remember just how far we have to go. This free society can put you in jail for smoking the wrong substance or for spitting on the sidewalk or for thousands of other reasons. This freest government in the recorded history of man is licensed to kill you, to take your money, to lock you up, to restrict your freedom of movement and your social preferences. Now you'd think with all *that* power the state wouldn't demand the right to dictate how you may make love, and with whom, and under what conditions. But it does, old buddy. It does.

Your government will even go so far as to *entrap* you should you be overpowered by sexual instincts outside the limited permissions it has granted. Congressman Howe of Utah and Congressman Waggoner of Louisiana are far from the first men to fall prey to the state's bogus nookie salespersons. And since the slimy idea first hatched in some lilliputian official brain, prostitutes have been enticed to sell themselves—and then have been hustled off to jail by the same undercover creeps who entrapped them.

If diddling is so all-fired evil that we must discourage it through law, then why in the name of reason would the authorities attempt to *encourage* men or women to break that law? In this time of record crime are the jails so empty that clients must be solicited to fill them? Why have we become so miserable in spirit that if all the repressive laws on the books will not suffice to land our neighbor in jail, then we must get him there with trickery? These are serious questions, and they cannot be erased by giggling at jokes about "sex in Washington."

I have been waiting for one thoughtful and honest and humane man to rise in Congress and say—without pious preambles invoking the flag or claiming improbably pure institutional instincts—"Enough of this crap." No one has. No one is likely to. This is because politicians know that Americans are two-faced about sex, that although a high percentage of hanky-panky goes on among all socioeconomic groupings, the society prefers to live a lie and force others to live their sex lives as lies. So our public men are intimidated and cowed and afraid to speak out.

When poor Congressman Howe was entrapped in Utah, the press skewered him without paying the slightest attention to his constitutional rights of due process or the presumption of innocence. His political colleagues and church colleagues instantly turned into sharks. They demanded his resignation and his head. It was a panic reaction, and panic there should have been; but the panic was for all the wrong reasons and was misdirected as to source.

There should have been panic because a presumably free citizen of the Republic (no matter whether he happened to be a congressman, oilman, or mechanic) could have his freedom and rights so lightly held that the state would: (1) grubbily attempt to entrap him; (2) release to the press, before he'd had his day in court, a transcript of what he'd supposedly said; and (3) tardily admit, after the damage had been done, *that it had no transcript of actual worth but had concocted one on the basis of what its entrapping and self-serving agents claimed to have transpired*. Nixon lost the presidency for trying to hoke up tapes, but at least he *had* some. The Utah police didn't. I have not heard a politician or a churchman or *any* of Congressman Howe's critics express the slightest indignation over these police crimes—and that is what they are.

Howe's story, that he had been lured to the scene by an invitation to a party from unnamed constituents, originally sounded weaker than 3.2 beer. But if the authorities would go so far as to release a bogus transcript, then who's to say they may not have set him up? Did someone want to ruin him politically, or did the cops panic when they found they'd netted a congressman in their tawdry net—and *then* concoct their fake record to cover themselves? Either way, their guilt is the greater, for *their* crime was tracking mud across the Constitution—no matter that Congressman Howe was later convicted for trying to spend his $20 illegally.

District of Columbia police were guilty of equally shoddy practices in the case of Congressman Waggonner. First, they entrapped

him with a bogus prostitute. When they discovered they'd bagged a congressman in a town run by congressmen—rather than some poor powerless government clerk—they let him go and then covered it up until somebody tipped off the press. You'd think that after Watergate, Washington police would be the last to attempt a cover-up. Not so. Joe Waggoner could have bought the services of every streetwalker in the city and still would have done less damage to freedom and justice than did the cops.

I'm no pal of any of these particular pols, and certainly not of

Wayne Hays. I think he richly deserves his designation as "the meanest man in Congress." This, however, does not detract from his constitutional rights, nor should it make him fair game for crucifixion. Among the intimacies the press revealed was that Hays, while making it with Liz Ray, kept one eye on her bedroom digital clock. How Hays does it or at what speed is no business of yours or mine, even if you *think* we may have paid for his hurried fun from our tax monies—as Ms. Ray claims we did, and as Mr. Hays insists we did not. And even if we did, so what? Politicians have hired drones since time immemorial for reasons other than their typing speeds, most of the time to pay off political debts, and no one, not even the Washington *Post*, raises much of a stink about that. Yet such employees perform little useful work, and how is that really different from Elizabeth Ray?

The answer, of course, is not at all—though certain feminists would have you believe that the crucial difference is that the delicate Ms. Ray was exploited. No sooner had the story broken than some women writers started trumpeting their denunciations of the Washington scene under headlines such as the one in the *Village Voice*: WAYNE HAYS MUST GO. Well, maybe she was exploited, though personally I've always felt that any person—man, woman, or politician—had the option of refusing to whore.

Ms. Ray, who approached the Washington *Post* as a woman scorned (after her friend Wayne Hays advised she would be most unwelcome at his wedding reception), was suddenly so eager to attain justice that she continued to perform her debilitating special nightwork—while, with her consent, reporters skulked about to eavesdrop. When the story crashed onto the front pages, she just happened to have hot from the publishers her trashy book about Sex in Washington, and held press conferences as far away as London; within a week her book winked and blinked from stores all over America. It is a classic case of coincidence, I guess we are supposed to believe. If Ms. Ray was exploited as she claimed, then she's by now gained parity with Wayne Hays in the exploitation department. And among *her* victims, of course, are those women on Capitol Hill who've been giving us taxpayers our money's worth all along—a fact that should have been noted by the outraged women writers as they vented their wrath on Wayne Hays and his male colleagues.

Sure, they do some hanky-pankying in Washington, and the same applies to the Texas legislature. A beloved former governor, who has prayed many pious public prayers, periodically used to call a sorority house at the University of Texas to establish trysts with a lovely lady I much admire myself. And a former lieutenant governor or two notoriously got around. But all this is as true of the private sector as it is in government. Politicians—provided they finance their own romances—are no more and no less "guilty" than the rest of us.

The politician, however, is more vulnerable to the public mood. There are not enough of you out there to vote me out of my job as a free-lance writer even should I kiss a goat, but your congressman's scalp is there for the taking. Since the sex scandals exploded, a United States senator from Virginia has been accused of offering to help a female constituent in exchange for her sexual favors. The senator's name made the papers before the Washington *Post* investigated and found his accuser to be a demented lady with a troubled history of telling many improbable tales. Should someone else, however—looking to be a cover girl or the author of the next sexsational book—name almost any public figure, he'll be in hot water from his home bed to his hometown even if wholly innocent. Such people, as with the rest of us, are entitled to their full protections and rights and legal assumptions. They will not, of course, receive them because more people are less rational about sex than any other subject.

1976

The Whole World's Turned On

"When I blow I think of times and things from outa the past that gives me a image . . . A town, a chick somewhere back down the line, an old man with no name you once seen in a place you don't remember. What you hear coming from a man's horn, that's what he is."

PERHAPS YOU HAVE NOT HEARD of my singing with Louis Armstrong. Nobody reviewed us for *Downbeat* and we didn't get much of a crowd—just the two of us. This impromptu duet with Pops (also Satchmo, Louie, Dippermouth, "America's Ambassador of Good Will") took place last July in his suite at the Chalfonte, a resort hotel on the Boardwalk in Atlantic City, around five o'clock of a groggy morning.

For several hours we had been "stumbling over chairs"—Satchmo's euphemism for serious tippling—while he reminisced, smoked an endless chain of Camels, and poured with a quick hand. This mood carried him back almost sixty years to New Orleans' Storyville section where as a boy he delivered coal to the cribs of certain available ladies, lingering to monitor honky-tonk and sporting-house bands until "the lady would notice me still in her crib—me standing very silent, digging the sounds, all in a daze—and she would remind me it wasn't no proper place to daydream."

Storyville was wide open in those days. Liberty sailors, traveling drummers, cotton traders, and assorted bloods in hot pursuit of fun mingled with prostitutes, pickpockets, musicians, gamblers, street urchins, and pimps. It was located directly behind Canal Street and touching the lower end of Basin in the French Quarter, and it had everything from creep joints where wallets were removed from the unwary during sex circuses to Miss Lulu White's Mahogany Hall on Basin Street with its five posh parlors, fifteen bedrooms, and $30,000 worth of artfully placed mirrors. Miss

Lulu hired "none but the fairest and most accomplished of girls," and Jelly Roll Morton played piano for her. In 1917 the Navy Department sent in a task force to clean up the district after too many sailors turned up robbed, drugged, or dead. Preachers railed against this sinkhole, but it was the place where jazz was born and where Daniel Louis (pronounced "Louie") Armstrong, literally before he was out of short pants, learned to play a little toy slide whistle "like it was a goddamn trombone." The boy strolled behind brass bands at street parades, funeral processions, or horsedrawn bandwagons touting their appearances at local clubs. "Two bandwagons would park head-to-head," Armstrong remembers, "and blow until one band was reduced to a frazzle." The Armstrongs lived in a cement-block house on Brick Row. Armstrong's grandmother bent over a tin tub and corrugated washboard to scrub white families' clothes and his father, when he was around, attended turpentine boilers. There was a decrepit neighborhood tavern called the Funky Butt, which Armstrong remembers for its bands and its razor fights. A detective grabbed Armstrong for celebrating New Year's Eve with a "borrowed" revolver in his thirteenth year, and he was banished for eighteen months to the New Orleans Colored Waifs' Home. At nineteen he married Daisy Parker, the first of his four brides. One night she caught Louis with another doll and chastised him with a brickbat. "I ain't been no angel," Pops confessed that morning as we lounged in the Chalfonte, "but I never once set out to harm *no* cat."

Louis Armstrong's marvelous memory took me back to the night he arrived in Chicago in 1922, up on the train from New Orleans to join King Joe Oliver's Creole Jazz Band as second trumpet for $50 a week. "I was carrying my horn, a little dab of clothes, and a brown bag of trout sandwiches my mother, Mayann, had made me up. Had on long underwear beneath my wide-legged pants—in July. I am just a kid, you see, not but twenty-two years old, don't know nothing and don't even *suspect* much. When we pull into the old La Salle Street station and I see all the tall buildings I thought they was universities and that I had the wrong town. Almost got back on that rail-runner and scooted back home."

He spoke lovingly of old pals: King Oliver, Jack Teagarden, Kid Ory, Bix Beiderbecke, and a hot-licks bass drummer everyone recalls only as Black Benny. ("All dead and gone now, them swinging old cats—and I've took to reading the Bible myself.") Between dips into his on-the-rocks bourbon Armstrong hummed or scatted or sang snatches of his ancient favorites. "Hotdamn"—he would say, flashing his teeth in that grand piano grin—"you remember this one?" and out would pour *Didn't He Ramble, Gut Bucket Blues, Blueberry Hill, Heebie-Jeebies, Black and Blue.*

2.

Just how I presumed to sing with him remains unclear and possibly indefensible. Earlier, in a noisy penny arcade on the Steel Pier in Atlantic City, I had proposed to his traveling manager, Ira Mangle, that I perform on stage with Armstrong at one of his three-a-day shows. Mangle, a stoic man of generous figure, ate peanuts, staring, while I explained: I would describe both the elation and the dread of appearing with the most celebrated figure in a field wholly alien to my talents, a man who has been called "an authentic American genius" for his contributions to jazz. Paul Gallico and George Plimpton had done the same things in sports, I recalled to Mangle, boxing Jack Dempsey and Archie Moore, golfing with Bobby Jones, pitching to Mantle and Mays. Their first-person stories permitted the average sports fan to consort vicariously with champions. Out there on that stage, moving into the spotlight to join Pops in *Blues in the Night* or perhaps even *Hello Dolly*, I would represent all my peers.

Ira Mangle has been in show business almost as long as pratfalls. He is neither easily rattled nor easily amused. When my special plea was done Mangle gazed into my face, chewing all the while. When the peanuts ran out he smiled and walked away.

Now, days later, sitting at a table holding the wreckage of our midnight snack (sardines in oil, Vienna sausages, Chinese food, soda crackers, pickles, beer) Pops and I somehow cut into *That's My Desire.* My uncertain baritone mingled with the famous voice that has been likened to a "cement mixer . . . rough waters . . . iron filings . . . a gearbox full of peanut butter . . . oil on sandpaper . . . a horn wailing through gravel and fog."

Once—when I came in on the break behind him at precisely the right point—Pops gave me some skin. He reached out his dark old hand just as he does on-stage when Joe Muranyi has ripped off an especially meritorious stretch on clarinet, and I turned my hand, palm up, as I had seen Muranyi do. Leaning across sardine tins and cracker wrappers Pops lightly brushed my open palm in a half-slap, the jive set's seal of approval, the jazz equivalent of the Congressional Medal of Honor. And there was good whiskey waiting in the jug.

We had already siphoned off generous rations, waving our arms a bit much, gently boasting and exaggerating. "Hey, Pops," my host said (it is his all-purpose salutation, as well as what friends call him, and saves everybody memorizing a lot of troublesome names), "this is the way I get my kicks. Having a little taste . . . talking over the olden times in Storyville and Chicago . . . remembering all the crazy sounds that always seemed to be exploding around you and inside you. *Everything* made music back then: banana men, ragpickers, them pretty painted streetwalkers all singing out their wares—oh, *yeah*! Everything rocking and bobbing and jousting and jumping." He grinned that huge, open grin again. "Ya know, Pops," he said, "my manager, Joe Glaser—Papa Joe, bless his ole heart he's *my* man, we been together since we was pups, why to hear us talk on the phone you'd think we was a couple of fairies: I say, 'I love you, Pops,' and he say, 'I love *you*, Pops'—well, anyhow, Joe and Ira and all them people don't like for me to talk about the olden days. All the prosty-*toots* and the fine gage and the badass racketeers. But hell, Man, I got to tell it like it was! I can't go around changing *history*!"

(Often one gets the feeling that Pops prefers those "olden days" to the frantic existence that has become his life. He once told writer Richard Meryman, "I never did want to be no big star. . . . All this traveling around the world, meeting wonderful people, being high on the horse, all *grandioso*—it's nice—but I didn't suggest it. I would say it was all wished on me. Seems like I was more content, more relaxed, growing up in New Orleans. And the money I made then—I lived off it. We were poor and everything like that, but music was all around you. Music kept you rolling.")

Though two weeks earlier Louis Armstrong wouldn't have known me from any other face in the multitudes, we had reached a stage of easy friendship—all thanks to him. For though I have known three Presidents and two wives, I sat down to face Armstrong that first night in Washington with a head full of wind and dishwater. There seemed nothing I was able to ask or say, not even banal comments about Washington's dreadful humidity, for on the couch beside me sat a living legend, a talent so long famous and admired that I considered him of another age and so was struck dumb in his presence—as if I had come upon Moses taking a Sunday stroll in the Gaza Strip or had encountered Thomas Jefferson at a Democratic National Convention.

Downstairs, I knew, Shriners offered hotel bellboys five-dollar bribes for Louis Armstrong's room number. No telephone calls were put through to him from the Shoreham front desk unless you knew a special secret. In Armstrong's suite (a palace of curved glass, rich draperies, soft carpets, and pillows of psychedelic hues) he sat wrapped in a faded robe. A white towel around his neck soaked up juices from the last of the evening's two one-hour shows, while Pops accepted photographs of himself from a thick stack presided over by his hovering valet, Bob Sherman. On each he scrawled "Hello, Louis Armstrong" in a round, uneven hand. Ira Mangle asked his star if he would like a drink, a snack, another pen, a crisp handkerchief. Mopping his brow, Louis declined with grunts and headshakes. "You go ahead," he said as I sat there tongue-tied and witless. "Ask me anything you want. Won't cramp my writing style. Just doing the bit for a few of my fans." Out of the silence Ira Mangle suggested that Armstrong discuss a recent TV tape cut with Herb Alpert and the Tijuana Brass: perhaps Armstrong would compare the two generations of music and judge the younger man's artistry. "Oh, yeah," Armstrong said. "He blows pretty, all right. Nice young cat." Mangle then prompted him to say something of his popularity with he public, his friendships in show business, the world figures who have toasted him. "Everybody's been real nice," Pops said.

Mangle's helpless shrug left me on my own. Finally I said, "Well, I seem to have come down with a bad case of buck fever. Can't think of a damn thing. Maybe I'd better run along and return another night." Quickly Armstrong cast aside his pen. A look of pain passed his face. "Aw, naw!" he said. "It ain't like that! We'll just loaf and chew the fat and have a little taste of bourbon and if we feel like stumbling over chairs—well, hell, we all over twenty-one! Ira, get my man a little taste." Then he launched into a story, and the generous act got me functioning again.

The men who handle Armstrong thought we got a little too chummy. Valet Bob Sherman, a dapper middleweight with a heavy-weight's torso and a Sonny Liston scowl when one is needed, nailed me backstage at the Steel Pier. "You'd better cut on out tonight after about an hour," he said. "Otherwise, you're gonna wear Pops out. He needs rest." Later, when I tried to leave at a decent hour, Pops protested. "Man, I'm just starting to *roll*. Won't be hitting the sheets for some-odd hours on. Here"—he splashed liquid into my glass—"relax and have another little taste." Waiting in the wings for his introduction one matinee, mopping his face and carrying that golden trumpet, he waved me over: "Where'd you go last night, Pops? Had to stumble over chairs all by myself. Ira and them people keep you away from me?" Well, yes, I admitted. "Aw, they ought not to do *that*!" Armstrong said, "They *know* Pops is still gonna be unwinding when first light comes. Don't pay them people no mind."

Armstrong's associates can hardly be blamed for their vigilance: he is a most valuable commercial property. Last spring a two-month recuperation from pneumonia cost more than $150,000 in bookings. His sixty-seven years, his respiratory ailments, and his grinding travel schedule—Ireland, England, Denmark, France, Spain, Tunisia, New England, the Midwest, the West Coast and two major TV bookings in August and September alone—cause concern for his health.

He is not the world's most docile patient. He walked around with bronchial pneumonia for two weeks last spring before anyone knew it. His trombonist, Tyree Glenn, was one of his first hospital visitors; Pops coaxed him into rehearsing a duet he wanted to put in the show. Nurses managed to clear the room only after a one-hour concert. The Washington booking was the first to follow his illness. Yet he stayed up all one night reveling with me, another with old music-world cronies (Duke Ellington and Clark Terry turned up at the Shoreham on July 4th to lead the midnight-show crowd in singing *Happy Birthday* to him), and on his night off he dropped by Carter Barron Amphitheatre to catch Ella Fitzgerald's performance—and ended up doing several numbers with her. Pops played two shows of his own each night and one two-hour benefit for wounded Vietnam veterans at Walter Reed Hospital.

A week later in Atlantic City he stunted and cheered at a night-club until dawn, and the following night railed—in vain—when he learned that Ira Mangle had wired a second club expressing regrets that Pops would not catch the late show as promised. "Damnit!" he complained. "All them cats over there live and *breathe* Louis Armstrong. They *love* Pops! If I go back on my word to them people it's like—why hell, it's like the United States Marines losing a goddamn *war*!"

3.

Armstrong has a zealot's faith in certain old remedies. He is quick to offer his medical opinions: "Man, a heart attack is nothing but so much *gas* accumulated and bubbled over." Armstrong on cancer: "Nowadays it has come in fashion to die of it. What they call cancer is merely the bodily poisons fermented because people is so full of fevers beating and working in the blood." Germs: "I always carry my mouthpiece in my hip pocket—never pitch it around where germs can crawl over it and into its parts." To rid himself of possible heart disease, crawling germs, or malignant tissues, Armstrong recommends the removal of "bodily impurities." For this he relies on a laxative called Swiss Kriss. It is his old reliable among an assortment of wonder-working products that seems to enhance his unusual vigor. One dawn he gave me three Swiss Kriss sample packets. The following night, as we blitzed another midnight snack of sardines and supporting embellishments, Pops asked, "You take your Swiss Kriss yet?"

"Ah . . . well; not yet."

"Get my man some Swiss Kriss," Armstrong instructed Bob Sherman. "Be just the thing to clear him all up. Flush out the bodily impurities." Sherman didn't move a step. He dipped into his pocket and produced a thin packet of olive-drab substance.

"Lay in on your tongue," Armstrong said. "Take it dry, then send some beer chasing after it. Beer all gone? Well, bourbon do it too." I turned the thin packet in my hands to stall for time. "Active ingredients"—I read aloud—"dried leaves of senna. Also contains licorice root, fennel, anise, and caraway seed. Dandelion, peppermint, papaya, strawberry and peach leaves. Juniper berries—"

"Oh yeah," Pops broke in. "Got all *manner* of elements in there. Lay it on your tongue."

"—Juniper berries, centaury, lemon verbena, cyani flowers, and parsley for their flavoring and carminative principles."

"Here's your chaser, Pops." Armstrong nudged the bourbon glass over while I frantically searched for something more to read. Bob Sherman celebrated my discomfort with a grin as Armstrong, hooting and exhorting like an evangelistic witch doctor, urged the treatment on.

I know not what Swiss Kriss tastes like on the tongue of Louis Armstrong. In my mouth it registered flavors of creosote and licorice with slight overtones of Brown Mule chewing tobacco. It neither improves bourbon nor bourbon it. Just as the main body of surprise had passed my host reproved me:

"Looka here, Pops! You left half of it in the bag!" He poked the dose under my nose. "Don't never do nothing halfway," Pops said, "else you find yourself dropping more than can be picked up."

"Take off your shirt" he ordered, suddenly.

"Beg your pardon?"

"Gonna teach you another little trick. Now this"—he grabbed a brownish bottle from a nearby table—"is called 'Heet.' H-e-e-t. Swab myself down with it when I come off stage all sopping wet. Cools me down and dries me out and steadies the skin. . . . You ain't got that shirt off, Pops." Armstrong circled me like Indians attacking a wagon train, crying a sales pitch as he daubed my chest, ribs, back. "Don't that cool you like rain?" he said. "Ain't that a goddamn groove?"

"Now you take a man's eyes," he said, ominously. "You ever have any trouble with your eyes?"

"No . . . not really . . ."

"*Must* have trouble, else you wouldn't be wearing them eyeglasses! This little remedy gonna pull all the bloodshot qualities right outa your eyeballs." He brandished a new bottle. "Witch hazel. Now, I take these"—he was ripping into a package and extracting two gauze pads—"and I dab a little on there, like this, swoggling it all around. Now I put them babies on your eyelids and it won't be thirty seconds until you feel it cooling up all the way back inside your *cranium*!" He marched about, rattling on, while I sat in darkness, feeling like a man who has stumbled into Mayo Clinic by mistake. "Take them pads off in another three minutes and you can feel heat on the underside like you had fried an egg there! So, quite *nat-ur-ally*—you gonna see clearer and sweeter and cooler than you ever did see before."

"You use all sorts of nostrums, don't you?" I said.

"Use whatever *helps*. You know, it wasn't long ago I believed in all kinds of old-timey remedies like the voodoo people. Yeah! Various dusts and herbs and junk like that." He laughed to think on days when he had been so medically unschooled. "Now I just use things do me some good, ya dig? And it works, Pops. Do you know

I am the only one left from the olden days in Storyville still blowing? Oh yeah, lotta cats lost their chops. Lips split and god*damn* the blood spurt like you had cut a hog and the poor cats can't blow no more. Now, I got this lip salve I'm gonna expose you to. Keeps my chops ready so I don't go in there and blow cold and crack a lip like I did in Memphis so bad I lost a chunk of meat."

Armstrong snatched the pads away and leaned forward with his face almost against mine, pulling his upper lip outward and upward, trying ineffectually to talk under the handicap. I leaned in, much in the manner of a man judging a horse's teeth for age, and saw in the middle of that talented lip a sizable flesh-crater. "My poor damn chops would be tender as a baby's bottom," Pops said. "Oh, *no way* to tell you how them chops could throb." He poked a small orange tin at me. "I order this salve from Germany by the caseload. Bought so much the cat that boils it up named it after me. See, it says 'Louis Armstrong Lip Salve.' You write something nice about that cat for Pops, ya hear? Aw yeah, he's *fine*!" He reached for my pen: "I'll write it down so's you don't forget."

He selected a cocktail napkin and printed in large, undisciplined letters: ANZACZ CREME MADE IN MANNHEIM GERMANY. He turned the napkin over and printed BY FRANZ SCHURITS. "That cat saved my lip," he said. "Reason his salve's so good it draws all the tiredness out. So—quite naturally—your chops rest easy. You oughta try some . . . only you don't blow so it wouldn't benefit you." He daubed his own lips with the wonder potion. "Oh, *yeah*! I got this other little tidbit here! I see you got weight problems—now no offense, Pops, 'cause most of us go around bloating ourselves up with various poisons which—quite naturally—causes some heavy stomping on the scales. All the sweets and sugars a person eats just goes right down there and hangs over your belt and *looks up at you*! Fat is made outta sugar more than anything else—you know that? Yeah! Why, a year ago I weigh two hundred and some pounds and now I'm shed off to a hundred and sixty-some and feel retooled. Between my Swiss Kriss and this Sweet'N Low—it ain't like real suger, you can eat a ton of this—I got no more weight imbalances which throws the body off center. Here"—he again sprang across the room to produce yet another packet—"it goes groovy on grapefruit. You want to try it? I got plenty grapefruit."

When I demurred, Pops looked somehow betrayed. "Well," he said, "you come on back tomorrow night. I'll lay it on you then, Pops."

"Quite naturally," I said.

4.

Louis Armstrong is sophisticate and primitive, genius and a man-child. He is wise in the ways of the street and gullibly innocent in the ways of men and nations. After four marriages, reform school, international fame and personal wealth, there is still a fetching simplicity about him. (Of his friend Moïse Tshombé, kidnapped and facing a return to the Congo, he says, "I pray each night they won't kill him. When I played Africa in '59 that cat was *so* nice to me. Kept me in his big palace and all . . . fed me good . . . stayed up all night gassing. I had this little tape recorder that cost me several big bills and Tshombé dug it so much I laid it on him. They ain't gonna kill a sweet cat like that, are they? So maybe he hung out with the wrong cats—that any reason to *kill* a man?")

The on-stage Louis Armstrong is all smiles and sunshine, almost too much the "happy darky" of white folklore. When he has finished *Hello Dolly* in a spasm of body shaking, jowl flapping, and gutteral ranges, and has the joint rocking with applause, he sops at his ebony, streaming face with his white handkerchief and rasps, "Looka here, my Man Tan's coming off!" Maybe his white audiences break up, but they no longer laugh at such lines in the black ghetto. One soon learns that this "happy" image is not all stagecraft; privately Pops is often full of laughter, mugging, instant music, irrepressible enthusiasms, and vast stores of colorful misinformation.

He is not all Old King Cole merry old soul, however; his waters run much deeper. I have seen Pops swearing backstage between numbers, his face wrinkled and thoughtful and sad only seconds before he burst back on stage, chest out, strutting, all teeth and cutting the fool. He can be proud, shrewd, moody, dignified—and vengeful. "I got a simple rule about everybody," he warned me one evening. "If you don't treat me right—shame on you!" * Cross him or wound his pride and he never forgets. My innocent mention of a noted jazz critic sets off a predawn tirade: "I told that bastard, 'You telling me how to blow my goddamn horn and you can't even blow your goddamn nose.'" When he was young and green somebody gave him fifty dollars for a tune he had written called *Get Off Katie's Head*. "I didn't know nothing about papers and business, and so I let go all control of it." Pops did not share in the money it made under another title. He has never performed the tune in public and never will. Of his father, Pops said, "I was touring Europe when he died. Didn't go to his funeral and didn't send nothing. Why should I? He never had no time for me or Mayann."

He is big on personal loyalty. "Frank Sinatra—now there's a man carries a lot of water for his friends. A most accommodating gentleman—if he digs you. My wife, Lucille, she's another one that when she's with you she's with you one thousand percent.** And my mother, why she would work with you—laugh, cry, or juice with you. Only tears I ever shed was when I saw 'em lower her into that ground."

He is generally a relaxed man, able to take a quick nap in strange rooms or on buses. "I don't like nothing to fret me," Pops said. "You healthier and happier when you hang loose. Business I don't know nothing about and don't want to. It must have killed more men than war. Joe Glaser books me, pays my taxes and bills, invests me a few bundles. Gives me my little leftover dab to spend. And that's the way I want it. Don't want to *worry* all time about that crap! I don't even know where I go when I leave this pier until today I overhear Ira say something about Ireland and France and

---

* Armstrong despises a couple of comedians who use their audiences or associates as targets in their acts. "Ain't nothing funny about putting another man down," he judges.

** Lucille holds the record as Mrs. Armstrong. They have been married twenty-five years, and live in Queens—on Long Island.

such places. I go wherever they book me and lead me." (Both Armstrong and Joe Glaser are wealthy men. Armstrong commands top money—$20,000 to $25,000—for guest shots on television. He accepts eight to ten such jobs each year.)

Nothing worries Louis Armstrong for long. "Mama taught me," he says, "that anything you can't get—the hell with it!" This philosophy may be at the root of Armstrong's rumored differences with militants of the Black Power generation. Nobody has flatly called him Uncle Tom but there have been inferences. Julius Hobson, a Washington ghetto leader, said during Armstrong's Shoreham appearance last July, "He's a good, happy black boy. He hasn't played to a black audience in ten years. I'm glad I saw him though, but I wouldn't come here if I had to pay. He's an interesting example of the black man's psychology but if he took this band"—two whites, three Negroes, a Fillipino—"down on U street it would start a riot." Armstrong, who remembers that not long ago everyone cheered him for having an integrated band, is genuinely puzzled by such comments.

He was not eager to talk civil rights. When I first mentioned the subject, as he dried out between shows in the dingy dressing room at Atlantic City, Pops suddenly began to snore. The next time he merely said, "There is good cats and bad cats of all hues. I used to tell Jack Teagarden—he was white and from Texas just like you—'I'm a spade and you an ofay. We got the same soul—so let's blow.'"

One morning, however, he approached the racial topic on his own. "When I was coming along, a black man had hell. On the road he couldn't find no decent place to eat, sleep, or use the toilet—service-station cats see a bus of colored bandsmen drive up and they would sprint to lock their restroom doors. White places wouldn't let you in and the black places all run-down and funky because there wasn't any money behind 'em. We Negro entertainers back then tried to stay in private homes—where at least we wouldn't have to fight bedbugs for sleep and cockroaches for breakfast.

"Why, do you know I played ninety-nine *million* hotels I couldn't stay at? And if I had friends blowing at some all-white nightclub or hotel I couldn't get in to see 'em—or them to see me. One time in

Dallas, Texas, some ofay stops me as I enter this hotel where I'm blowing the show—me in a goddamn *tuxedo*, now!—and tells me I got to come round to the back door. As time went on and I made a reputation I had it put in my contracts that I wouldn't *play* no place I couldn't *stay*. I was the first Negro in the business to crack them big white hotels—Oh, yeah! I pioneered, Pops! Nobody much remembers that these days.

"Years ago I was playing the little town of Lubbock, Texas, when this white cat grabs me at the end of the show—he's full of whiskey and trouble. He pokes on my chest and says, 'I don't like *niggers*!' These two cats with me was gonna practice their Thanksgiving carving on that dude. But I say, 'No, let the man talk. *Why* don't you like us, Pops?' And would you believe that cat couldn't *tell* us? So he apologizes—crying and carrying on. Said he was just juiced and full of deep personal sorrows—something was snapping at his insides, you see—and then he commenced bragging on my music. Yeah! And dig this: that fella and his whole family come to be my friends! When I'd go back through Lubbock, Texas, for many many years they would make old Satchmo welcome and treat him like a king.

"Quite naturally, it didn't always test out that pleasurable. I knew some cats was blowing one-nighters in little sawmill stops down in Mississippi, and one time these white boys—who had been dancing all night to them colored cats' sounds—chased 'em out on the highway and whipped 'em with chains and cut their poor asses with *knives*! Called it 'nigger knocking.' No reason—except they was so goddamn miserable they had to mess everybody else up, ya dig? *Peckerwoods*! Oh, this world's mothered some mean sons! But they try such stunts on the young Negroes we got coming along now—well, *then* the trouble starts. Young cats, they ain't setting around these days saying 'Yessuh' or 'Nawsuh.' Which I ain't knocking; everybody got to be his own man, Pops. No man oughta be treated like dirt.

"If you didn't have a white captain to back you in the old days—to put his hand on your shoulder—you was just a damn sad nigger. If a Negro had the proper white man to reach the law and say, 'What the hell you mean locking up MY nigger?' then—quite naturally—the law would walk him free. Get in that jail *without* your white boss, and yonder comes the chain gang! Oh, danger was dancing all around you back then.

"Up north wasn't much to brag on in many ways. Not only people put your color down but you had mobsters. One night this big, bad-ass hood crashes my dressing room in Chicago and instructs me that I will open in such-and-such a club in New York the next night. I tell him I got this Chicago engagement and don't plan no traveling. And I turn my back on him to show I'm so *cool*. Then I hear this sound: SNAP! CLICK! I turn around and he has pulled this vast revolver on me and cocked it. *Jesus*, it look like a cannon and sound like death! So I look down that steel and say, 'Weeellllll, maybe I *do* open in New York tomorrow.' That night I got every Chicago tough me or my pals knew—and it must have been eighteen hundred of 'em—to flock around and pass the word I wasn't to be messed with. And I didn't go to New York. Very very shortly, however, I cut on out of town and went on tour down South. And the mob didn't mess with me again. They never wanted me dead, wanted me blowing so they could rake in my bread.

"You was running a very large risk to buck them mobsters and all the sharpies. They controlled everything. Cross 'em just so far and—BLIP! Your throat's cut or you're swimming in cement with lumps on your head. You needed a white man to get along. So one day in 1931 I went to Papa Joe Glaser and told him I was tired of being cheated and set upon by scamps and told how my head was jumping from all of that business mess—Lil, one of my wives, had sweet-talked me into going out on my own to front some bands and it was driving me *crazy*—and I told him, 'Pops, I need you. Come be my manager. *Please*! Take care all my business and take care of me. Just lemme blow my gig.' And goddamn that sweet man did it! Sold his nightclub in Chicago where I had worked and started handling Pops.

"Sometimes Joe Glaser says I'm nuts. Says it wasn't as bad as I recall it. But then Papa Joe didn't have to go through it. He was white. Not that I think white people is any naturally meaner than colored. Naw, the white man's just had the upper hand so long— and can't many people handle being top cat.

"Passing all them laws to open everything up—fine, okay, lovely! But it ain't gonna change everybody's hearts. You know, I been reading the Bible this last little bit and them Biblical people had wars and riots and poverty and bad-asses among 'em just like *we* got. Nothing new happening!

"It's much the same they talk about making marijuana legal. They think they're gonna do that and say, 'Everything's cool now, babies, it's all right and set square.' But how about them poor bastards *already* been busted for holding a little gage and have done their lonesome fifteen and thirty and fifty years? My God, you can't *never* make it all right with them! Many years ago I quit messing around with that stuff.* Got tired looking over my shoulder and waiting for that long arm to reach out and somebody say, 'Come here, Boy. Twenty years in the cage!' BLOOEY! Naw, they can't undo all the years of damage by passing a few laws." After a moment's brooding he said, "That's why I don't take much part in all this fandangoing you hear about today. All I want to do is blow my gig."

Louis Armstrong's first professional gig—as a substitute cornet player in a Storyville honky-tonk—brought him fifteen cents. He was fifteen years old. "But I sang for money long before I played for it," he says. "When I was around twelve we formed this quartet—me, Little Mack, Georgie Gray, and Big Nose Sidney. We'd sing on the streets and in taverns—pass the hat; might make six-bits, a dollar. Good money. After hours all them prostitutes would be juicing, having a little fun, and they would offer us big tips to entertain 'em. Carried their bankrolls in the tops of their stockings. Some would hold us on their laps and we would sniff the pretty scents and powders they wore."

Though he had taught himself to play the little toy slide whistle and a homemade guitar, Armstrong really familiarized himself with musical instruments in the New Orleans Waifs' Home. He began with the tambourine, then the snare drum, then ran through the alto horn, bugle, and cornet. Soon he was the leader of the Waifs' Band, playing picnics and street parades. Old-time drummer Zutty Singleton, a kid then himself, was so astounded at hear-

*In truth, Armstrong smoked grass until he died in the early 1970s; fearful of being busted, however, he had friends carry it for him and smoked only among those he trusted.

ing Armstrong's horn that he moved closer to see if the boy was actually playing those fabulous notes. On his release from the home, Armstrong took one-night jobs filling in with bands until a few months later he landed a regular job at Henry Matranga's in Storyville. "I wasn't making no great sums so I kept on delivering coal, unloading banana boats, selling newspapers—though there never was any doubts I would follow music at that point. Had to work for extra bread, you see. For when I am sixteen I start hanging out with the pretty chicks and need operating money."

King Joe Oliver took Louis Armstrong under his wing. "He was the best," Pops says. "Laid a new horn on me when mine was so beat I didn't know what sounds might come of it. Advised me . . . took me home for red beans and rice feasts. Taught me about blowing trumpet, too. Lotta claims been made that Bunk Johnson put me wise to trumpet—Bunk hisself helped that story along. No such thing. Joe Oliver was the man."

When King Oliver left Kid Ory's brass band to go it alone, seventeen-year-old Louis Armstrong took his chair. In the eighteen months he played with Kid Ory at Pete Lala's, Armstrong's reputation grew. He was with the Tuxedo Brass Band in 1922, when King Oliver called him to Chicago—then the center of jazz as New Orleans once had been. In 1924–25 Armstrong was with the Fletcher Henderson band but quit because "The cats was goofing and boozing—not blowing. I was always deadly serious about my music." From Henderson he joined Lil Hardin's group (she was his second wife) and also worked in Erskine Tate's pit orchestra at the Vendome Theatre in Chicago. Then he went to work at the Sunset Club for Joe Glaser—who immediately billed him as "The World's Greatest Trumpet Player." This title had been generally conceded to Joe Oliver—and King Joe was playing at a rival club nearby. It came down to a head-on contest between the two great trumpeters. "I felt real bad when I took most of Joe Oliver's crowds away," Armstrong says now. "Wasn't much I could do about it, though. I went to Joe and asked him was there anything I could do for him. 'Just keep on blowing,' he told me. Bless him." *

---

* Years later, when Joe Oliver was on the financial skids, Armstrong several times helped him.

5.

Armstrong first played New York in 1929, fronting the old Carroll Dickerson band at Connie's Inn in Harlem. He arrived there with four carloads of sidemen, ten dollars, and after two car wrecks en route. "Blew four shows a day," he remembers. "Wild stuff. Knocked myself out—blowing crazy and carrying on. Going in with cold chops. Wonder I got a dime's worth of chops left." In mid-1932 Armstrong made his first swing through Europe—and Europe flipped. By 1935 few disputed that Louis Armstrong was the king of jazz.

Though with the advent of television and smash hits like *Hello Dolly*** Armstrong became more popular than ever, jazz purists say that he is no longer inventive, that he is too commercial, too much the clown. A decade ago Raymond Horricks wrote that his trumpet playing "in recent years . . . has declined as a creative force on account of the contact with unsympathetic supporting musicians and of Louis' own increased exploits dressed in the cap and bells of a court jester." Even a dust jacket plugging a record Armstrong made with Ella Fitzgerald carries this curious advertisement: "Unfortunately, of late, Louis has confined himself almost exclusively to remaking the blues of an earlier age and pedestrian popular songs so that each impression was but a fainter and dimmer carbon of the original talent."

He is impatient with this criticism. "Aw, I am paid to *entertain* the people. If they want me to come on all strutty and cutting up— if that makes 'em happy, why not? For many years I blew my brains out. Hitting notes so high they hurt a dog's ears, driving like crazy, screaming it. And everybody got this image I was some kind of a wild man. Joe Glaser told me, 'Play and sing pretty. Give the people a show.' So now I do *Dolly* how many times? Six jillion? How ever many you want to say. Do it every show. And you got to admit, Pops, it gets the biggest hand of any number I do.

"There's room for all kinds of music. I dig it all: country, jazz, pop, swing, blues, ragtime. And this rock 'n' roll the young people

** "The best-selling record of all time"—Ira Mangle.

believe is a new sound—babies, it comes right outa the old spir-
ituals and soul and country music and jazz. Like I have said, 'Old
soup warmed over.'

"Each man has his own music bubbling up inside him and—
quite naturally—different ones will let it out in various ways.
When I blow I think of times and things from outa the past that
gives me a image of the tune. Like moving pictures passing in front
of my eyes. A town, a chick somewhere back down the line, an old
man with no name you seen once in a place you don't remember—
any of 'em can trigger that image. Or a certain blue feeling or a
happy one. What you hear coming from a man's horn—that's what
he is! And man can be many different things."

Pops is right: if the critics have soured, the people have not.
"Can't even go to a baseball game," he said one night. "Went to
one Dodgers-White Sox World Series game and cats was climbing
all over my box seat. Some of the players asked what in hell was all
that commotion up in the stands. Sometimes them big crowds can
spook you. Get to pressing you and grabbing your clothes. You get
a funny feeling they might trample on you. Especially in Europe. I
draw a hundred thousand people over there blowing outdoors.
And they go crazy."

Each afternoon and evening a limousine with Pops and Bob
Sherman in the back seat made its way slowly along the Boardwalk; police and firemen walked ahead to clear the massed crowd.
"Hey! That's Louis Armstrong!" someone would shout, starting a
stampede of old women, small children, bald-headed men. ("Hey,
Louie, looka me!" "Satchmo—over here!") They clawed at the car,
knocked on windows, snapped cameras in his face, tried to poke
their hands inside for handshakes. Pops smiled and waved in return, seldom missing anyone, though he might be chattering away
about Storyville.

Through the entire Atlantic City engagement a wizened, aged
little man in hand-me-down clothes haunted the backstage area.
After each show Pops courteously received him in his dressing
room. "You really got your chops tonight, Pops," the old man
would invariably say. Armstrong would beam: "Aw, thank you,
Pops. How you been?" After a few moments the old fellow would
go away content. I later learned that he is known to Armstrong's

entourage as The Clipping Man. "He lives in Philadelphia," I was told, "and anytime he sees Pops' name in the paper he clips it and mails it to him. If Pops plays within a hundred miles of Philadelphia he makes the scene and hangs around for his two or three private moments after each show." The Clipping Man was around so much that for days, seeing him standing patiently in the wings or sitting on a bench backstage, silent and pensive, I had presumed him to be a stagehand. One night he encountered me in the alcove outside Armstrong's dressing room. "You know Pops long?" he asked. No, only a few days. "I been good friends with him for thirty years," The Clipping Man said.

6.

One night near the end of Pops' ten-day Atlantic City run we dallied in his dressing room long past midnight, having a little taste, while on videotape heavyweight contender Joe Frazier repeated his brutal knockout of George Chuvalo. Freshly toweled by Bob Sherman, wearing a faded robe and a handkerchief tied around his head so that he resembled Aunt Jemima, Pops bounced around the cramped room, grunting and grimacing as gloves thudded against flesh, sucking in air and occasionally throwing an uppercut of his own.

After he dressed we walked along the Steel Pier, dark now except for a few dim lights on the outer walkway. The noisy crowds had been dispersed and the gates locked; a few sleepy night watchmen prowled the shooting galleries, fun-house rides, and endless rows of concession stands. Strolling the walkway, we could hear the ocean boiling beneath us. Pops peered up at a tall tower from which a young blonde on horseback plunges into a giant tank of water three times each day. He shook his head. "Ain't that a hell of a way to make a living? And them cats in there fighting on the box—beating each other crazy for the almighty dollar. Pops, some people got a hell of a hard row to hoe."

We paused at the end of the pier jutting into the Atlantic; Pops lit a cigarette and leaned on a restraining fence to smoke. For long moments he looked up at the full moon, and watched the surf come and go. The glow from his cigarette faintly illuminated the dark old face in repose and I thought of some ancient tribal chieftain musing by his campfire, majestic and mystical. There was only the rush of water, gently roaring and boasting at the shore.

"Listen to it, Pops," he said in his low, chesty rumble. "Whole world's turned on. Don't you dig its pretty sounds?"

1967

About the Author

BORN IN PUTNAM, TEXAS on January 1, 1929, Larry L. King grew up on Texas farms and in Texas oilfields. He began his writing career for newspapers in Hobbs, New Mexico, and Midland and Odessa. King has won the Stanley Walker Journalism Award and a television "Emmy" for documentaries; he has been nominated for a National Book Award and a Broadway "Tony." He has served as Ferris Professor of Journalism and Political Science at Princeton and has been a Nieman Fellow at Harvard and a Fellow of Communications at Duke University. A member of The Texas Institute of Letters, P.E.N. International, The Authors' Guild, Actor's Equity, and The Screenwriters' Guild, he lives in Washington, D.C. with his wife-agent-lawyer, Barbara S. Blaine of Corpus Christi, and their two children: Lindsay, 5, and Blaine, 3.

About Edwin Shrake

EDWIN (BUD) SHRAKE'S SEVEN NOVELS include *Blessed McGill* and *Strange Peaches*. His screenplays include *Kid Blue* and *The Songwriter*. A former newsman in Dallas and Fort Worth, Shrake has been a contributing editor for *Sports Illustrated*; his work has appeared in *Harper's* and many other periodicals. Shrake, a graduate of TCU, now lives in Austin.

About Paul Rigby

DAILY CARTOONS BY PAUL RIGBY have appeared in newspapers in Australia, Europe, the Far East and the United States. A native of Australia, Rigby studied at schools of art in that country and Europe and has illustrated books on travel, sport and politics. His cartoons, paintings and murals have been exhibited on several continents, and his assignments have included tours to the USSR, China, Vietnam, New Guinea, Europe and the United States. He was named Cartoonist of the Year in Australia five times, has twice won both the New York Award for Graphic Arts (1980 and 1984) and the Page One Award (1982 and 1984). He is now cartoonist for the New York *Daily News*.